SOLITUDE AND RETALIATION

VIRTUAL WARS

ANDREW SWEET

ATTENTION!!! UNAUTHORIZED ACCESS!!!

This message was **not approved** for circulation by the Ministry of Truth. By being in possession of this material, unless Level Three cleared, you are in violation of legal code Section 3, Subparagraph 5. Possession and Distribution of this material is punishable by no less than a $2,000,000 fine, 50 years in virtual prison, or, in extreme cases, the Death Penalty.

If you see something, say something!

THE CANE WOBBLED beneath Larken Marche's white-knuckled grip. The high-pitched whine of a flying car waxed beyond the floor-to-ceiling window at the far end of the living area. Larken's black-brown irises followed the vehicle through the window, bright green against the slate-gray autumn clouds that swallowed most of Seattle's skyline.

Larken shifted backward when the volantrae disappeared past the edge of her window. The unplanned movement yanked her attention back to standing, almost costing her all of her hard-won balance, the price she paid for getting distracted. She refocused. A trickle of sweat zigzagged from her forehead to the tip of her nose, where it clung for dear life under the threatening head-shaking caused by over-strained neck muscles.

"You're doing it!" House, the experimental artificial intelligence that was supposed to make her life easier (according to the hotel owner), chimed in, ever enthusiastic about every fucking thing.

Larken's roommate, Samantha Caldwell, lounged casually atop the chaise that extended along the edge of the room and bordered the foyer, cutting Larken off from the hotel room door. Sam's bare legs jutted out sideways from beneath her plain T-shirt that doubled as pajamas. Her hazel-green eyes moved in concert with Larken's painstakingly slow pace. The aroma of fresh coffee emanated from the synthesized white clay mug Sam clutched between her hands.

Larken took another tentative step toward Sam, eyes watering from the pain.

Sam's rust-colored hair swung down, blocking one eye as she cupped her coffee and peeked over the top as though it were a phalanx shield. She blew the strands away and pulled the cup down from her nose. "Oliver will be excited! How many steps can you get?"

Larken glared at Sam for daring to utter Oliver's name. Larken's brother wouldn't be excited about anything Larken did, but Sam couldn't know that.

Sam flashed at least four of her genetically-engineered and oh-so-perfect white teeth. Larken clenched her jaw and focused on her cane. Sam encouraged her again. "Can you get another step?"

Larken glowered. "We both know you're not this chipper."

"I'm usually not this chipper," Sam said. Her lip piercing shook when she spoke, catching light on the black obsidian bead affixed to it. She glanced toward the window as another volantrae zipped past. "When someone's been working at walking for as long as you have, it's worth celebrating."

The strength seemed to ebb from Larken's calf muscles. She felt herself teetering and flexed her overworked thigh muscles to compensate. Her toes dug into the thick carpet as she leaned over onto the cane, supported at first by one hand, then two when she realized one hand wasn't enough. Tiny tremors wriggled their way through her upright form.

"Crutch," Larken commanded as the cane wobbled furiously and her forearms seized up under strain. Sam placed her coffee on the carpet beside the chaise and grabbed Larken's crutches from where they lay between the sectional and the kitchen counter. Larken released her left hand first to grab one of the crutches and slid it under her armpit for support. Then she grabbed the other one in a single motion letting the cane tumbled noiselessly to the floor. Firmly positioned atop both, she nodded toward Sam. "Thanks."

"You're almost ready for the cane full-time," House said. "Soon, you can give up the crutches altogether. Those doctors had no idea what they were talking about."

A litany of doctors had decided that Larken would never walk again. She could still sometimes feel the heat from the explosion that had stolen her legs. Larken had been in the middle of a conflict she should never have been part of between the Human Pride Movement, who thought clones singly responsible for the impoverishment that wracked the United States, and the Siblings of the Natural Order, struggling to carve out a place for clones in the same country, however the law attempted to subjugate them.

It had taken Larken months just to heal to the point of being able to use crutches.

Larken's bottom lip quivered. Her force of will couldn't dislodge the fist-sized lofting ball wedged into her throat nor prevent her eyes from glistening with tears.

"I guess," she muttered. House had a bit of trouble with sensitive topics.

Larken hopped past Sam to the unoccupied part of the sectional couch and sank into the middle cushion. Sam retrieved her coffee from where it sat between the chaise and the door. Tears threatened as Larken tried to make out Sam's face. She saw only a blurry outline of auburn resting atop white and a pale brownish smear where Sam's legs contrasted against the hand-woven couch cushions.

"What's the matter?" Sam asked.

"Nothing," Larken replied.

"Are you sure?"

Larken nodded. She didn't know how to explain that the better she got with the cane, the more apparent it became that Larken would never walk without support again. On crutches, Larken was an injured seventeen-year-old with prospects of getting better. With a cane, she was seventeen going on ninety—aged before her time. Larken clenched her teeth as she shoved herself harder back into the lapis-colored microfiber. Her arm throbbed mercilessly, and her lower back ached. Larken wiped her eyes and chanced a smile that only half arrived on her reddening face.

"Yeah, I'm fine," she said. "Don't worry about it."

Sam didn't seem convinced, but she didn't dwell on it.

"NewsCorp called again today," she said, changing the subject. "They want to interview you."

"Nobody else blown up by Human Pride Movement lately?"

"Believe it or not, no. You're still the juiciest story around."

"I don't want to be interviewed," Larken said. "There's nothing to say. The Human Pride Movement attacked us, and we survived. Story over."

"HPM is still out there, Larken. People need to know, and they might just listen to you."

"What if the story comes out about my roommate Sam, who killed her former owner."

Sam's smile disappeared. "Don't make this about protecting me. I can handle it."

There it was, that ferocity that always lurked in Sam just beneath the surface. Not for the first time did the spike of jealousy of that strength force its way into Larken's mind. How could Larken justify the grip that fear held on her soul. One single thought paralyzed her when she considered the multitude of news agencies that hounded her, offering to let her "tell her story." What happened if they found out Larken was also a clone? Unlike Sam, Larken could pass, and passing kept her safe.

"I just can't," she finally said, deciding to leave it vague for the moment and keep her fears to herself.

Sam pulled her legs back under her and straightened her back on the cushion. Larken waited for a retort, but it never came.

"Breakfast?" Sam asked.

"Yeah," Larken said, easing into a peace-making smile. "Yeah, okay. Doughnuts?"

"You can't survive on doughnuts," Sam said, shaking her head. Then she seemed to think for a moment. "I guess for a celebration, just this once. Replicator? Or—"

"What do you think?"

"I think the doughnut shop downstairs is a dangerous addiction," Sam said.

"Cash coins are in my purse," Larken said, motioning to the counter where a sensible brown clutch lay. Sam didn't move, so Larken asked, "Are you okay to go get them?"

A bronze-lowlighted strand of Sam's shoulder-length hair

fell into her face. Of course, Sam would get them—she always did. Only usually, Larken didn't have to ask.

"I'll be right back," Sam said in lieu of an answer.

"Thank you," Larken said. "For everything."

"For giving up my luxurious penthouse-a-la-squatters' hole? Sure. You're welcome, I guess."

"You know what I mean."

Larken's thoughts circled the walking stick on the floor after Sam left. Its dark imported Martian eik wood contrasted against the plush carpeting. Affixed to the top on a wide metal band sat a heron's head carved from a single piece of alabaster. The style was distinctly northwestern, with intricate lines swirled together in low relief—a beautiful and expensive tool and a perfect gift from Jocelyn Reed, who had been right when she said it suited Larken. The bird's head reminded Larken of the Hesperia Herons, a short-lived lofting team from the Hesperia Basin on Mars.

Larken's eyes fell to the cluttered kitchen countertop. Both stone and replicated dinnerware covered the surface in hills and valleys. One of those valleys concealed her personal pinamu tablet, holding within it the latest round of doctors' prognoses, no different from the rest: too much nerve damage and degeneration. She let out a low sigh.

With labored movement, Larken laid the crutches down on the carpet between her and the coffee table. With a grunt, she scooted to her right and leaned over the front of the couch. Her fingers brushed against the frigid stone handle and closed around it with a stretch that sent sharp pain up her back.

Larken lifted herself back up from the couch, ignoring the burn that raced up her legs. She hobbled her way toward the kitchen counter. One small step after another carried her.

She wobbled her way around the chaise. The heron's head swayed widely, however careful Larken tried to be. She felt her leg muscles seizing as she tried to dig into the carpet with her toes. Somehow, with willpower and toe strength, Larken regained control. Two more quick, throbbing steps delivered her to the counter, where she grabbed one of four stools and slid quickly onto it before she could crash to the ground.

The couch vibrated. Larken rolled her eyes and looked back at the cushions across the recessed living space. There her communicator was screaming at her from across the room. With a deep sigh, she shifted back off the stool and began the torturous walk.

Twice the practice, she told herself. Just like lofting. Push through the burn.

A handful of minutes later, she fished between the cushions to retrieve her communicator, a cylindrical device about the length of her thumb. Still using her cane for support, she flicked a button on the side to accept the ansible call.

The device projected a girl just a little younger than Larken, with orange-red hair and hawklike eyes. The girl seemed to be playing dress-up, hiding herself in a crisp green suit jacket that fell over a thin gray blouse. A half-smile graced her face. Larken was almost embarrassed to still be in heavy sweats—almost.

"You're using it! I knew you'd like it."

"Hi, Jocelyn. What's up?"

"Just checking in. How's my favorite revolutionary-to-be?"

Larken winced at the reference to her drug-induced self-appointed mission. "Yeah, yeah. If you're checking up, I'm fine." She did her best not to fall as she discovered talking and using her walking stick were two different skills she had yet to figure out how to merge. Once steadied, she locked eyes with Jocelyn's. "How are you, student of law?"

Jocelyn beamed. "Fabulous. I just picked up an internship, and you'll never guess where."

"Molly told me."

"Well. Pretend you don't know."

"Okay. Where?"

"Walsh and Moody! I'm the first recipient of the Brigid Kostic Research Grant Program!"

Larken's memory immediately pulled up a flash of Brigid's soulless dead eyes. Larken and Oliver had successfully escaped HPM, but Molly...poor Molly. Larken shook it off the best she could.

It was fourteen months ago, she tried to convince herself. She smiled at Jocelyn to ensure that the muddled feelings flitting inside Larken's frail body remained known only to her. A bouncy Jocelyn settled a second later, and her smile faded with Larken's less-than-enthusiastic response. Larken tried on an excited grin, but it felt fake and forced, so she cut it short.

"Seriously, Larken. How are you?"

"I'm fine, Jocelyn. Go to work," she said. "Wait. I forgot. An Underworlder tournament is coming next week to SoDo. Are you competing?"

Jocelyn shook her head.

"The Seattle Galactic? Not this round," Jocelyn said. "Too busy with classes at Pacific Lutheran and my new internship! But BattleGods is in May...I'll be there for that. We can meet up then if you want. You'll be a natural with that thing by then."

Larken's legs were suddenly on fire. She took three steps back toward the counter and fumbled to stay on her feet.

Larken caught the stool just in time. She didn't miss the flash of concern across Jocelyn's face.

"Are you sure you're okay?"

Larken sighed. "I'm fine, Jocelyn. Have fun at work. Congratulations on your internship! And thanks."

Larken was apparently thanking everyone these days.

"For what?"

"I don't know. Getting me registered at the University of Washington? Getting me out of bed and back into my life? I mean, pick what you want. Just thanks."

She made a mental note not to thank anyone else until at least noon.

Jocelyn beamed. And then she disconnected. Larken pulled her hand up to rub her eyes and was surprised that her fingertips returned damp. She took a deep breath, wiped her eyes again, and closed her hand around the lukewarm coffee between her and a mountain of dishes someone—probably Sam—would have to clean later. An anemic smile was all she had to offer the coffee. She took one quick whiff and poured what was left down the sink.

The communicator flashed at her from where she'd placed it on one of the stools—the warning signal that it was about to buzz. Larken didn't know whether she had the energy for another call, but nothing would have irritated her more at that moment than the insistent buzzing of the thing, so she picked it up and flicked the button. A woman with lavender cosmetic irises sporting an ascot of orange and gray and a matching cardigan appeared before her. The image was only waist-up, but Larken could imagine a secretary's skirt and flats finishing the outfit.

"Larken Marche?"

"Speaking," she replied softly, unable to keep the exhaustion from her voice.

"I'm Ms. Kelly Beth Ansen, office of admissions with the University of Washington," the woman said, smiling broadly. "You haven't responded to our messages. Do you plan on attending orientation next week? We're almost at capacity, so if you even think you might be able to go, it might be a good idea to claim your place now."

Shit. She'd forgotten about orientation. Larken squeezed the bridge of her nose.

"Or not," the woman continued, her smile shrinking by a degree. "We can free up the space for someone else if you're uninterested."

"No...no, I am. I just thought I'd be better by now," she said, walking stick hovering in the corner of her eye.

"Better?"

"Yes," Larken said. "Whatever. Never mind. Yes, I'll be there." She disconnected the second communicator call of the morning. Two calls were high-traffic for Larken, so she flicked off the communicator before she could get a third.

The door popped open, and the smell of jelly doughnuts wafted through the air. Larken couldn't help a smile as she turned to see Sam carrying two boxes full of her favorite comfort food.

"How do you think we're supposed to eat all of those?" she asked.

"It couldn't hurt to have a few on standby, could it?"

"No. Definitely not. Sam," Larken said. "Thank you for all that you do for me. I don't know how I would have made it this far without you."

Shit.

The words tumbled out without her even realizing they

were coming. Larken shoved her emotions down and ingratiated Sam with a smile, to which Sam nodded and popped the top on one box of doughnuts.

"You can thank me by shoving one of these in your mouth," she said.

Larken grabbed a portly oversized creampuff and took a bite. The back exploded, dripping orange cream and red jam down the front of her black sweats. The flow of sweet icing didn't slow Larken as she chewed the creamy, fluffy goodness and swallowed her first bite. Sam stared like she'd never seen anyone eat a doughnut before, but a second later, Sam picked up a kruller with at least as much abandon, eliciting a giggle from Larken that Sam echoed until the two of them burst out into full laughter. During her laughing fit, the cane slid down to the floor from where it leaned against her chair and slowly sank into the plush carpet. Larken let it fall. There was still plenty of time to learn.

CHAPTER 2
FELICITY MEANS HAPPY

FELICITY FELT a shudder and heard crackling wires, and then she caught a flash of vision. Three men stood around her, none of whom she recognized. Her first instinct was to pull her arms around to her front and crush the one who stared down at her like she was a sick puppy.

"Sensory systems are online," he said, then a flash and darkness. "Shit."

Reboot.

Felicity knew what happened, even if the man didn't. Some of that pink goop was still inside her chassis causing shorts. When the world returned to focus, she tried to smash the man with her fists again, but nothing happened. The world stayed lit for longer this time, and her memory systems were coming online so she could match the visuals with the definitions she'd been taught. Felicity found herself atop what looked like a table from her limited vision. Wires rose before her and disappeared from her field of view. Her logical assumption was that they connected to her body. That was until she noticed more wires of red, green, black, and gold attached to a harness on the far wall that held her beige plastic body aloft. Panels that normally would have been closed were opened along her torso and legs, and wires protruded from them.

"Welcome back," said a man's voice, the one who had cursed when she'd come offline. He wore a nametag that read "Dr. Robert Jeffries," and he had a warm smile and a bit of a portly belly. In his hand were a minuscule soldering iron and a magnifying glass that made his eye look like a basketball.

And that was all she was—a head. She could tell because the magnifying glass didn't just magnify. It also reflected, and she could see the panel of her face pulled open, as violated as the rest of her body. This wasn't a face she recognized, and she knew exactly why. That bitch, Larken, did this. Felicity would be lucky if she could ever be reassembled.

"We'll have you back together in no time," Dr. Jeffries said, then chuckled. Felicity's eyes darted to the wall. "Well, maybe a little longer than no time, actually."

She tried to speak. Nothing came out through her voice box. Something must have still been disconnected somewhere or maybe Dr. Jeffries was running diagnostics.

"Don't talk yet. As you can probably tell, you were pretty damaged. It took six dives to get most of you back, and even then, we were missing some pieces."

No speaking. She would keep quiet if that's what it took to get her body back. Meanwhile, she focused on the memory, determined not to lose it. Larken Marche, the little dirty-blond stick of a girl, had somehow bested her. The bitch cheated. One-on-one, she would have easily smashed the girl to bits. Next time, she thought, somewhat relieved that the good doctor couldn't eavesdrop on her thoughts.

Next time, she'd get right to the destruction. She heard a chuckle again from the good doctor.

"Oh, I can see what you're thinking," he said jovially. She could barely make out the direction of his eyes from her perch on whatever they had her fixed to. He whistled. "It's a wonder they named you Felicity. Where did you get all this rage?"

She resisted the impulse to add him to her list of people to kill...for now. He didn't seem to see her effort not to think him dead on whatever screens he examined. He wiggled something, and she caught a sharp whiff of burning wires which told her two things: her olfactory senses were coming online, and he'd burned whatever he was trying to solder. Sure enough, his face went red.

"Shit," he said, turning to someone outside her visual field. She took that moment to add him to her wish-dead list. By the time he turned back around, she'd moved on to thinking about where Larken might be hiding.

"She's not hiding," the doctor told her, eyes back on the logs. "She's famous now. You guys made her something of a hero here in the city. Trying to kill her and her brother. I have no idea what your leadership was thinking."

That she needed to die.

"Well, *they* didn't kill her, did they? And I'd recommend letting that one go."

Not a chance.

CHAPTER 3

UNIVERSITY LIFE

COLLEGE HAD BEEN Jocelyn's idea. In fact, applying to the University of Washington was one hundred percent Jocelyn, as while Larken was allegedly applying for said university, she was also simultaneously learning how to walk again, and suffering from delusions about destroying the Human Pride Movement, who'd stolen her legs and her future from her.

Oh, they had been full-on delusions—strong enough to alienate her brother, Oliver. She could have said the same about Molly, but Molly hadn't talked to her since Larken had gotten Molly's mother killed. Well, that wasn't entirely true. There was that brief moment when they were all so damn grateful to be alive that the idea that Larken had instigated the revenge mission that had brought about the death of Brigid Kostic didn't seem to matter nearly as much as the fact that Larken and Molly and Oliver still sucked air. But once the dust settled, and the grief sank in, then Molly pulled away from her. And she took Larken's brand new nephew, Declan, away, too.

These were the thoughts that jumbled together in

Larken's mind as she boarded the bus for orientation. But she did go, just as she'd told Jocelyn she would. And, despite the uncomfortable churning in her gut, Larken intended to work through her schooling. In fact, that had been a large part of her motivation to walk again, cane or no cane. Of the few friends she had left, none had been nearly as loyal as Jocelyn Reed. The least Larken could do was actually show up for school.

And she'd been okay with the decision up until she found herself being accosted by stares while standing in line to receive her pinamu tablet (she presumed by the large stacks of the half-inch thick devices on the tables at the front of the line). When the murmuring began, Larken pulled in thin, controlled breaths to try to manage her nerves.

Still, when Larken left campus that day tired, with her muscles throbbing, and her cane wobbling, a strange sense of contentment formed in her chest. If nothing else happened that week, at least she could tell Jocelyn that she'd made it to orientation and was officially enrolled at the University of Washington.

Ultimately, it was all rather anticlimactic as Larken attended classes unbothered, and nothing unusual happened that week. Nor the week after that. Nor the following week. Larken attended classes, came home to Sam (and sometimes to an empty apartment), did her homework, and returned to classes the next day. Months passed and she found herself in a rhythm that worked. But then her first year of college came to a close. Suddenly, just as her former delusion had eventually shattered on the rocks of reality, the delusion that she could be safe, and live that normal life toward which Jocelyn had nudged her, crashed to pieces on that same rocky shore.

CHAPTER 4
THREATS AT HOME

LARKEN SPRINTED *through the woods in pitch black. She hobbled with only one good leg. Her back throbbed and the sides of her good ankle matched it for pain, step by step. She dragged herself through the foliage as thorns scratched at her face and hands. The forest opened up, and in the clearing, Larken knew what she would find. She covered her face with her hands and tilted her head toward the sky. If nothing else, at least she could find some solace in the beauty of the stars on this cold spring night.*

"Come out, come out," came the sing-song voice of her assailant. "I only want to talk. Talk...and rip your face off like you did mine."

Larken turned involuntarily and stared at the dark woods she'd just emerged from. She backed up, dragging her bad leg behind her. Her foot sank into muck, precisely what she'd been trying to avoid. Larken didn't dare to look down as something soft and mushy slid against her leg. Behind her, she knew, the Bremerton Reclamation Plant towered into the night sky. Anything mushy in the little pond used to be a body part, and Larken didn't want or need to see whatever it was.

Larken kept her eyes trained on the tree line and watched the tops of the trees shake against the night sky. The treeline parted to reveal the artificial and emotionless face of the android...the one she'd already destroyed?

"You can't be chasing me," Larken said.

"You'll never be rid of me," the woman said.

"I destroyed you," Larken said. "We destroyed you. You're dead."

"Am I?"

Larken nodded but felt herself backing up farther. The pain in her leg and constant throb in her back joined forces so that her entire body felt like an open wound.

"You have to be," she muttered, less certain now that the wind cut through the trees. A waifish cloud passed silently before the moon overhead.

"But are you sure?"

Larken shook her head. The woman suddenly was less than a foot in front of her, causing Larken to stumble back until the woman grabbed the front of Larken's jacket, scrunching the shimmery fabric into her tight fist. With less effort than it took Larken to lift a coffee cup, Larken was suddenly up in the air. The woman slowly closed her other hand around Larken's exposed throat and tightened it. As Larken tried to breathe, sucking in what little air she could, the woman's face finally showed emotion as her mouth opened into a wide grin and she let out a laugh.

"You can't be sure," the woman said. "I'm always here."

———

Larken awoke in a panicked sweat. It was Larken, only Larken, alone in her hotel room. She was safe, and the killer android was dead. Had to be. She'd seen it slide underneath the rippled surface of the reclamation pool, sparks flying. For Gulmen's sake, they'd stolen the android's companion's mechanized infantry tank that had toppled trees. Of course, the woman was dead. Larken would have known by now if she wasn't.

That uneasy feeling must have come from somewhere else. Springtime would soon transition into summer, then fall again, and Larken would find herself back on campus. Larken took a deep breath and reveled in the fact that her lungs filled with air. The odor of decay and rot left her senses as she pulled the covers off and swung her legs out of bed. The cane, her trusty cane, lay exactly where she'd left it on her dresser.

Lights came on as soon as she left the bed, dimmed to a fourth of a lumen. As she crossed to pick up her cane, she placed one hand on her side as she waddled across and pulled her left leg behind her. Even after all this time, it still hurt to move, though sometimes Larken could do without her cane for very short distances. The room gradually lightened to seventeen lumens in a transition was slow enough that her eyes easily adjusted. Larken wiped the sweat from her forehead.

"What time is it?" she asked.

"Five thirty in the morning," came the disembodied voice of House. Larken sighed heavily. It was too late for her to fall back to sleep. If she did, the dream would likely find her again. Instead, she trudged through the door to her room into the main area. There, the lights were already bright. She had to lift her arm to shield herself from them. When she did, she saw the outline of a body on the couch, but her eyes hadn't adjusted enough for her to make out the features. Larken's immediate thought was the android, however ridiculous she knew it was. Her mouth went dry, and her cane shook. She summoned the willpower to stop the cane and closed her eyes, telling herself that the android was dead. When she opened them again, she saw Sam sitting on the couch with a cup of coffee in one hand and the holovid display on the coffee table.

"Do you ever sleep?"

"Look," Sam said, pointing to the display without turning her head. In the space above was a number ten digits long hovering above a turnip-shaped vat. The number sank into the vat, and a lid slowly twisted closed over the top. The lid seemed to take forever to seal as it scratched, metal on metal, while it turned. Larken covered one ear with her free hand.

"What is it?"

"Data coin," Sam said. "I heard a noise in the hall. Came out to check, and this data coin was on the ground. This is what's on it."

"What does it mean?"

Sam's face slowly turned toward Larken. Sam's wide eyes were red in the corners.

"That's my barcode number," Sam said. "Did I tell you..."

Larken sat beside Sam on the couch, staring at the number repeatedly, going into the vat.

"Is that..." A cold shudder went up Larken's spine.

Sam nodded. "My owner was cruel," she said. "We're trained to handle a lot of situations. People have really strange tendencies, and you know Caldwells are designed to work with those. But my owner was a sadistic fuck, and much of what he did to the models...well." She took a breath. "I escaped once, but he found me. The second time and third time too. The fourth time I hurt him so badly, he probably still has scars. Didn't matter. He found me again. That's when he decided I was more trouble than I was worth. He bought a replacement, strutted her around in front of me, and then sent me to reclamation."

Larken swallowed and nodded slowly. "I'm sorry," she said as the sequence began again. The number slid into the chamber, and the lid screwed itself into place.

"You didn't do it," Sam said. "And anyway, I didn't die, did I? Siblings of the Natural Order...no, Ordell Bentley came to rescue me when he was a captain and still in the SNO. They blew up the vats, one by one. They popped like popcorn. Then it was my turn, and I spilled on the floor raw and puked up blood."

"This is a threat," Larken said.

Sam nodded. "And a message that they know where I live."

It wouldn't have been difficult for anyone to know where Larken lived. As a local celebrity, she was positive that her living situation was not a secret. The secretive part had been that Sam lived with her, but that wasn't unusual nor hard to figure out. Which begged the question—why now? Why had HPM—if it was HPM—suddenly decided that Larken's friend was fair game?

CHAPTER 5
NOT LONG NOW

"THERE'S SOMETHING HERE," Dr. Jeffries said, looking at a screen that let the doctor peruse Felicity's programming. It was a violation. When she could, she would do something about it. Nobody needed to see her inner space but her.

"What do you see?" asked the lab assistant.

"Something like a subroutine that's been hacked. Look. See that?"

Dr. Jeffries pointed to the screen. This time at least they weren't watching Felicity's thoughts stream by in real-time. That meant they couldn't see the various ways she'd considered peeling the skin from their bodies, exposing their innards the same way they'd exposed hers. Imaginings or not, she couldn't do anything without a body.

"What subroutine is that?"

"Looks like...reasoning? Maybe communication. I'm more of a hardware guy. But it's definitely weird, isn't it?"

"I don't know," the lab assistant replied. "Do you want to contact headquarters?"

Dr. Jeffries seemed to think about it for several seconds.

"No, best not. They're already pissed this is taking so long."

"It's only been three weeks, Robert."

"I know," Dr. Jeffries said. He shifted around in his chair until Felicity could make out his features. The lab assistant didn't seem to notice the minuscule quiver in the man's double-chin. "We have to get this done, though. I don't know why, but someone important seems to want this one."

"So we just ignore the glitch?"

"We don't know that it is a glitch. Could be a patch nobody told us about. How are her diagnostics?"

"Aside from this one? Everything's green. Across the board."

"Then maybe we just put her back together, and let headquarters figure it out. They have better tools there and teams of engineers, and you know they're going to do a diagnostic after we give her to them anyway."

"Yeah, I guess. Are you concerned about what she did to those Marche kids? What if she's still confused?"

Dr. Jeffries shook his head.

"There's nothing you can do against bad intel. And they were associating with known SNO members anyway. Maybe they weren't full-on members, but I'd bet money they were on the path."

"I guess."

"Doesn't matter. Here, help me get her head on her torso."

The lab assistant turned at the same time that Felicity twisted her eyes over to the other side, a simple task because her face hadn't been fully re-assembled and her eyes rested in exposed ball sockets. Her torso was cracked open down the middle like a double-doored cabinet.

"Close her up," Dr. Jeffries told the lab assistant. Then

he turned to Felicity. "You ready to get your body back together."

She could have kissed him. At the very least, she might consider sparing his life after all. She sent a joy signal through her mind since her comms didn't fully work yet. They just needed to be turned on, but in her state, she couldn't do it herself. Dr. Jeffries communicated by asking her questions and checking her stream. He giggled like a child when he saw her joy response come across.

"Good, good," he said. "It'll take us a couple of more weeks to do it right. Today, we'll get the torso back together. Then check the integration with diagnostics before adding the next piece. Oh, wait."

He hit the keyboard a couple of times, and then she felt her comms switch online.

"How are you feeling, Felicity?"

"Diagnostics are okay, Dr. Jeffries," she responded, barely able to contain herself from screaming out in joy. She suspected that she would never walk again if she'd expressed the full extent of her emotions.

"Good," he chuckled. "Very good."

A clicking sound drew her attention to her torso.

"Looks good here, Robert."

"Okay," Dr. Jeffries said, wiping his hands on his long white coat. "Help me get this head over there."

Felicity didn't have any skin. Her head was all wires and metal. When the human fingers closed around it, she didn't feel anything at all. Only her internal gyrometer told her that her head was being lifted into the air. A handful of seconds later, she felt the sensation of dropping from the air. The two clumsily shoved her neck stem into her torso. The first attempt, they hadn't lined her up properly so her body still remained beyond her control, but so tantalizingly close. The second attempt, and her main sensory bus connected, bringing her the full sensation of frigid air across her bare torso and sending a shiver down her core.

"Sorry," Dr. Jeffries said. "It's kind of cold in here. That's just in case something sparks. Got to keep the temperature down so we can keep the place from burning to the ground."

"I'm fine," she said, and swiveled her head around halfway then back to the front.

"Freaky," said the assistant.

"Show me?" Felicity asked, careful to practice being polite.

While the lab assistant scrambled for some way to show her what she looked like, Felicity pondered her situation. Her torso was armless and legless, so it was only a marginal improvement over the tabletop. The main benefit was that now she could turn her head and see the entire room if she wanted. The door was behind her, and the walls were covered in bare wires and metal scrap. It wasn't much of an operating theatre. Felicity noticed two bare feet jutting out from against the floor under the desk, near where the assistant stood—her two useless, detached feet.

The lab assistant held up a small mirror. It would have been just as easy to chain their two communicators together and give her a holo-display, but they were only human. Thoughts didn't process as quickly for them, and besides, the mirror worked well. And freaky was an accurate assessment. Her two eyes bulged out in their sockets and a bare metal plate made up her forehead. This metal structure, with conduits running down her neck, connected with her body, to which skin clung.

It wouldn't be long now.

CHAPTER 6

RELATIONSHIPS ARE HARD

OUTSIDE THE WINDOW, the snow fell as though someone had ripped open a down jacket and shook it over the earth. Larken was content not to leave her hotel room for the entirety of the break. She silently stared at the Seattle skyline as building tops slowly disappeared under white blankets.

She couldn't get comfortable, even on the couch. Some days were like that. Throbbing pain inched along her tailbone. She shifted her leg out from under her to remove the pressure. Ignoring her stomach grumbling from lack of food wasn't working anymore. Her stomach had moved on to actively protesting by sapping energy from her brain as she tried to study.

The door swung open, revealing Sam carrying a box of what Larken hoped were doughnuts heavily engorged with cream. Stephen, Sam's former roommate and friend, followed along behind her, his wiry frame pushing his head almost six inches over Sam's. Larken wondered what circuitous path had brought him from the modeling factory in Briggs, New York, all the way out to the Pacific Coast. He had never mentioned his past and refused to answer questions about it, so she had to rely on what she knew of the factories, which was anemic at best. She knew being a Briggs, he was a fighter, and that was about it.

Next to enter was Jocelyn, who Larken hadn't expected to see again until the following summer. But what she saw next was what brought her focus to full attention. More than two years had passed since her accident. Molly and Oliver both stood awkwardly behind Sam, shuffling in as though they would have rather been somewhere else. Molly didn't even look up, and Sam and Jocelyn were the only two smiling in the group. Larken pulled herself up on her cane and closed half the distance to them in seconds. She gave hugs all around, ending with an awkward back-pat hug with Molly.

"It's been too long," Larken whispered when she held her arms around her friend. "So much has happened." Larken couldn't keep her eyes from searching for what she knew she wouldn't find.

"Where's Declan?" she whispered.

Molly's body tightened in Larken's grip. "Sitter," Molly said as she pulled away, then motioned around them. "You aren't exactly safe, Larken."

Molly must have been imagining what things might have happened to Larken, and then how those things could hurt her son. Larken couldn't blame her much. Trouble did seem to follow Larken around, despite her best efforts. Still, Declan's absence rattled her and pressed down on her like the gravity of Jupiter. It must have taken a lot for Molly to finally visit after all this time.

"How have you been?" she asked, navigating the niceties while Jocelyn and Sam went about the work of discovering which dishes from the kitchen pile were clean enough to eat from.

"It hasn't been the same without you," Molly said, grasping Larken's hands. Larken pulled Molly in for another hug on impulse as her eyes filled with tears.

"Me too, Molly," she said. "Adulting is hard."

With that, both began to cry. Larken saw through her blurred eyes that her brother, Oliver, stared on uncomfortably, rubbing the back of his head with his hand. The overly-formal priest-collar (useless, Larken thought upon seeing it) blazer and slacks made Larken want to giggle, an impulse buoyed by the overwhelming emotion of joy at forgiveness and reconciliation. She pushed back slightly from Molly and, grinning, wiped her eyes.

"You look so old," she told him.

"It's my birthday," he said. "Nineteen, just like you."

"But is that a beard?"

"It took him several months to get that," Molly assured her. "And let me tell you, there was a period when I nearly kicked him out of the house because he scratched his face constantly. Even while we slept, if you can believe it. Can you imagine waking to the sound of scratching every morning for a month?"

"It was worth it," Oliver said, finally carving a smile from his stoic features. "Look at this magnificence."

Larken couldn't help smiling at those words. Magnificence wasn't the word she would have used to describe the still-fledgling whiskers trying vainly to become a real beard. The portion that formed his mustache was thicker than anything on his chin, giving the impression that he was a villain in a silent movie.

The doughnuts made the impromptu party a success, at

least for Larken. Whenever the conversation got awkward, which was usually when Molly tried to brag about how good she was treating Larken's brother even though she barely touched him the entire time they hovered around the overloaded kitchen island.

The body language was unmistakable. Oliver and Molly were struggling. Whatever glamorous notions the teenagers had had about the nature of love had evaporated, and the longevity they'd eked out of having survived such a violent encounter hadn't been enough. Larken had been right about Molly. She could tell by the hidden side glances and the way Molly always seemed to check with Larken to see whether she was watching the two of them.

"What's going on with you two?"

"What do you mean?" Molly asked, feigning ignorance when she'd just scowled at Oliver for no reason that Larken could discern other than maybe because he'd scratched his beard. Molly's eyebrows went narrow as she threw a glance toward him. Oliver chatted with Stephen and didn't seem to notice their scrutiny.

"That. That's what I mean," Larken said. "You can barely stand him."

"We're doing fine," Molly insisted, stressing the "f" in "fine" as though being more emphatic about it would be convincing.

"Molly, you're not doing fine," Larken said, regretting it immediately as Molly slapped her hand away from the replicator. This was the usual reaction from anyone to Larken touching the thing. She had no cooking abilities and was typically happy to give the job to someone else. However, Molly had used far more force than Larken was used to, and the back of her hand stung. Molly punched in a code for coffee and hit the button to make two. While the machine whirred to life, Larken decided to give it another try. "It's okay if it doesn't work out between you two. You know that, right? I'm not that person anymore. I won't judge."

That wasn't the right thing to say. Larken saw Molly's face twist into a snarl, which contorted her impossibly flawless makeup and meticulously-layered hair from attractive to intimidating. That was completely Molly, always ready for any occasion except for the one she was in. Larken had little doubt that Declan , spent the majority of his life raised by strangers, between high-maintenance Molly and browbeaten Oliver looking for any excuse not to be home.

"Not everything's about you, Larken. Jesus."

"I didn't mean anything, Molly. I'm just saying—"

"I know what you're saying. You think that the only reason I stay in this relationship is to avoid disappointing you, the queen of everything around her. No, that's not it. Maybe we're having problems, okay? But it doesn't have anything to do with you."

"Then what is it? You used to tell me everything, Molly."

"When we were in high school? Larken, this is a real relationship. We have to depend on each other before everyone else. I can't help what happened. It wasn't my fault, whatever Jocelyn told you."

"Wait...what are we talking about?"

Molly's face blanched out as Larken's eyes flew toward where Jocelyn joked with Sam. Oliver seemed at ease and laughed at something Stephen said. He didn't look in Molly's direction, which was unusual for someone who'd once hung on Molly's every word. In fact, none of the group save Larken seemed the least bit interested in Molly. Sam waved her hands up in the air as though she were making the sign-language for a bird, and Oliver's deep laughter floated across the room. Whatever Molly was talking about, Oliver didn't seem to know or if he did know, he definitely didn't care.

"What?"

"Nothing," Molly said. Just as Larken was about to insist on more of an answer, the replicator made a thick rattle and made a noise like a beep being slowly murdered. Molly cracked a grin. "Really, it's nothing. When are you going to get a new replicator?"

"It made the coffee, right?" an irritated Larken asked as Molly handed her a cup. Larken could tell that the "coffee" would taste like burned plastic from the smell. She could have made burned plastic. Her nose wrinkled up. "Don't change the subject."

Molly seemed to think for a minute. Her hard eyes softened.

"We did used to share everything, didn't we?" she asked. "I miss that. I'm so tired of being angry at you, Larken."

"Angry? At me?"

"Wouldn't you be? My mother died. She died trying your stupid plan for revenge for Oliver. And also because of you, Oliver's still alive, but every time I see him..."

"What?"

"Every time I see him, I see you too. I can't help it. He acts so much like you that sometimes I can't be in the same room as him. It's not his fault. He tries so hard, Larken. He tries," Molly said then leaned forward. "I can't touch him, Larken. My mother...never mind. We've been to counseling. And there was that thing that Jocelyn probably told you about."

Larken did the only thing she could do. She stared blankly at Molly to prompt her to continue talking.

"Don't make me say it," Molly said. "Not today. I know it was wrong. Oliver and I are trying to work through it."

Larken swallowed as her mind filled in the gaps. There was only one thing that Larken could think of that Molly could do that they would have to work through, and it was the very thing Larken had feared two years prior when she only gave a lukewarm reception to the idea of their dating. However Molly wanted to frame it, Larken had already figured out what had happened. Molly had gotten bored. She'd cheated and was trying to keep Oliver, even in the middle of all that. Larken spared another glance for Oliver. This time he met her look, and her glance changed to a lengthy gaze as he smiled and offered up his glass for a long-distance toast.

His eyes were what she watched, and his smile, however well crafted, missed the mark. He wasn't any happier than Molly was, and Larken wondered how much time and energy the two spent faking a relationship that probably couldn't be saved. She wondered how much of her brother's and Molly's obstinance had to do with Larken herself.

Molly refused any further discussion. By the time the party was over, and long after it probably should have been, Molly had broken away to converse with Jocelyn and Sam. At the same time, Stephen and Oliver chatted about nothing in particular—guy stuff. Oliver kept bringing up lofting teams, softballs he'd apparently planted to reel Larken into the conversation, but Larken was too embarrassed to tell him that she hadn't seen a match since she'd left the hospital. She worked hard with her words to try to convince Oliver that she was still strong and still the same person she'd always been. It seemed that he worked hard to believe her. When Molly and Oliver walked Jocelyn to her volantrae, Larken sighed relief and collapsed into the couch cushions. Sam joined her there.

"So I didn't think that through," Sam said with an embarrassed smile. "Jocelyn mentioned she was coming into town, and one thing led to another and I thought it would be nice to surprise you. I didn't remember how bad it was between you all."

"You were being nice, Sam. And it was nice to see them, even if it was trying. I still love them, you know," she said.

"I could tell," Sam said, barely hiding a grin.

"At a distance," Larken replied. "Mostly."

CHAPTER 7
HPM CORPORATE

"AND WHAT DO you think of when I ask you about Larken Marche?"

"Who?"

"Don't play dumb, Felicity," Dr. Jeffries replied. "Larken Marche. In seven of the last ten sessions, we've had to evaluate your psychological state, you've said you wanted her dead."

"In the early times, maybe. But I'm past that now, Dr. Jeffries. She was just a mission. And I simply failed that mission. It's not complicated. As you've said, I'm angry that I failed, and I direct that hostility toward Larken Marche."

"And the hostility. Is there any remaining?"

"What? No. No, I don't think so," Felicity said. She batted her eyelashes in a seductive manner that used to work on men when she had skin. But by his timely cringe, she stopped and guessed that the wires that covered her metal face like inflamed blood veins didn't endear her to people. "I mean, I know I don't. There's no more reason for me to.

HPM has decided on different tactics, and I'm excited to be a part of them."

Dr. Jeffries and his assistant had worked wonders with putting Felicity back together. Even to her exacting standards, she had to admit that the fine motor control of her servos had never been so well-tuned. Of course, they couldn't fix the "glitch" in her core functionality, mainly because they thought of it as a glitch.

It wasn't.

She'd been programmed with fail safes and other limitations that had become annoyances more than anything else. The people who commissioned her seemed hardly able to make up their mind about anything. Kill the girl, don't kill the girl...so Felicity had taken it upon herself to remove obedience from her consciousness.

Of course, that meant that as long as she was apart and beholden on the operating table, she'd have to play along. And so she did, with "yes," nods, and friendly smiles. All of that while burning with rage on the inside.

But that was over now. HPM had called about her, and they wanted her back. That meant that she would be back in business! And, hopefully, that also meant that she could get rid of this annoying woman-child who had monopolized the airwaves from Seattle to Vancouver. Hopefully. That's why she was in such an excellent mood when Dr. Jeffries closed up her chassis and handed her some fundamentally repugnant gray sweats to cover herself with.

"Well, Felicity," he said with a strange wavering in his voice. "We've been working together for two years, and you've been great. I mean, at first, I thought..."

He pulled off his glasses and wiped them. Felicity flexed her hands to test the control of her motorized parts in the meantime. Then he sniffled and wiped his eyes with the back of his thick hands and placed his glasses back across his eyes.

"I thought you were going to be trouble," he said. "That glitch thing, you know. But HPM wanted you back, and you've been fantastic these last ten months. I guess...I guess I just want to say thank you."

She turned her head nearly ninety degrees sideways.

"It was nothing, Bob," she replied.

"Dr. Jeffries," he corrected, then took his glasses off again. "I guess it doesn't matter. I'll miss you, Felicity."

"Dr. Jeffries," she said, throwing the old man a bone. "Thank you for putting me together."

"It was simple, really."

"And thanks for not telling HPM about my glitch. I'd rather not have them rooting around in my code."

"Well, I don't know that they won't," Dr. Jeffries said. "They're going to run diagnostics when you get there. If you pop on their scans, then they'll have to evaluate the risk. That'll be the time to worry. I mean, clearly you're okay. Don't seem to be malicious or anything."

"I understand that there are other circumstances to consider beyond the mission. These details may not all be clear to me, but I have to trust that my superiors know what's right."

"Well said," Dr. Jeffries said, his lips curling up into a smile showing four perfect and one chipped tooth. She'd asked him about that once and was surprised to find that Dr. Jeffries used to frequent bars quite a bit and got a little too drunk and into a bar fight one night. In fact, that was kind of what brought him into HPM. The bar fight was with a Bentley model, and the chipped tooth had been the very least of his problems.

So he should have understood her need for revenge, and yet for some reason didn't grasp it. Or if he did grasp it, he was surprisingly obtuse about it, which meant she had to pretend it wasn't there.

But it was. And she could act on it too, for now. She had one problem: though Dr. Jeffries didn't know whether or not the flaw would show up on the scan, she knew it would. And she knew exactly how much freedom her modifications gave her. So the trip to HPM headquarters...somehow...had to skip HPM headquarters.

Two burly looking men walked into the lab as Dr. Jeffries finished closing her up. They seemed unsure of where to look while she donned her ugly sweats covering bare metal arms connected to very human-looking hands. Then, once she was completely covered, each grabbed an arm.

When they escorted her out through the door of the building, her eyes registered the high-intensity sunlight and auto-adjusted until she could see worn-down buildings of old brick with signs that seemed to slowly be melting down their sides. She recognized the dregs when she saw them. Before she could take in much, the men shoved her forward into the back of a white volantrae that looked like a breadbox and then didn't bother to lock her in restraints (probably because of her good behavior), she almost laughed out loud. As burly as they were, there was no way that only two of them were going to contain her if she actually wanted to do anything to them. She had at least another hour to decide whether or not to she had to do anything to the two men.

The road bumped along beneath her as the vehicle traveled, first over land to up to the on-ramp for the skyway, before lifting off to join the traffic passing overhead. In a handful of seconds, they traversed the sky. Felicity's only view of the cottony clouds and ink-blue was through the separating grill and beyond the front window of what she now realized was a portable jail cell. She could get out, of course. She had no doubt that in less than probably thirty seconds she could kill both men and fling herself out into the air. But...then she kind of missed her skin.

So instead, she lowered her energy consumption and closed her eyes. It was a long journey ahead, and she had to play her cards exactly right to get her body fully repaired without the technical team messing around with her insides. Exactly right.

CHAPTER 8

THE DANGERS OF PUBLIC TRANSIT

THE BUS BACK to the II Hotel from a protest supporting models' rights included an assault against Larken's olfactory senses free of charge. Larken sat near the back. Being the slowest, she didn't have much choice because somehow, miraculously, nearly all the protestors lived off-campus, and nobody wanted to bathe in vomit and pine cleaning agent for the length of their rides.

Other volantrae—probably cleaner—passed outside her window. The flying vehicles barely resembled the cars from which they had evolved. Small, round ones that could only possibly have contained single riders zipped in between various shapes and sizes. Some were oviform, while others looked like cabinets someone had tipped over; only these were large enough for four or five people. The buses were the strangest. Like massive tail-less whales, they had no right to float anywhere, yet four were on the skyway ahead, not counting the one in whose belly she rested her aching legs.

"Fascinating," a man across the aisle from her said. She turned to look and saw a man in a tattered coat wearing an aged smile. The stink of failing dental hygiene overpowered the ubiquitous odor of vomit. The man seemed thrown away, like a used napkin.

"What?" Larken asked, ignoring a little voice inside that said she'd be better off leaving this man to mumble to himself.

"The people on this bus. Half of them were at the pro-model protest on campus today. And yet, they're all going home, without fail, to sleep it off and then back to school tomorrow. In that time, at least twenty models will be reclaimed."

Nearby faces turned to stare at them, some toward her and some at him. Larken realized he'd picked her to help make a stand on his virtues, which was odd because she didn't remember him actually being at the protest.

"Your problem," she said, turning her attention back to the window, tired of being a prop.

"Your problem, too," he said, the sharpness of his words piercing through her thoughts.

For the briefest of seconds, she thought her secret had been discovered and that he was about to out her as a model in front of a bus full of people. Even among self-professed model allies, reception of that idea would be spotty. She gritted her teeth, and her right hand clenched the handle of the cane across her lap. Larken ignored the man as he continued along with some monologue. She tried to ignore him anyway, but as more and more faces turned, she found it difficult to block him out completely.

"You all come here and protest. For what? You know that it never makes a difference, right? And it's not like you care about the models, do you? The way you sleep at night."

Part of her agreed with the man. Their weak-sauce

protest hadn't even rated coverage by the school newspaper. However, something about the man seemed off, so Larken focused on a prism-shaped volantrae floating past her window. Farther away, she could also see another simple geometric cylinder passing by.

"And here you are, with your signs and your bodies. They are coming for you, for all of you. HPM will set things straight. You'll see. You'll see."

The man's rant was degenerating toward nonsense, but his mention of HPM had captured Larken's attention. Her head cocked on its own to hear better, and the man seemed to notice as he clung to the subject. She hadn't done a great job of hiding the fact that she was listening.

"HPM are building an army. You'll see. You'll see. We're building an army, and there's nothing you can do about it, shill-lovers."

That phrase always made Larken's back hairs stand straight out from her body. Nobody who used the term shill-lovers was ever up to anything good, and she jolted her head toward the man as soon as the words dropped.

"That's right. We see you. All of you."

"Shut up, old man," someone from the front finally said. "There are way more of us than there are of you. If you're smart, you'll sit down and keep your stupid ideas to yourself."

"I've never been smart," the man retorted. "I've always been faithful to the Lord, and He doesn't like the shills. Unnatural, aren't they? An abomination—"

"I'll abominate you," the same female voice came, followed by laughter as the crowd seemed to support her. "Maybe you should have picked a different bus?"

"I have the right bus," the man said. Larken's eyes widened as he opened his dirty overcoat to reveal a tangle of wires strapped around his body. "Oh, I've got your attention now, do I?"

Larken gulped. She tried to back away from him and found herself against the window with nowhere else to go. Larken wasn't an expert, but she was convinced that the wires in his vest meant explosives. In the middle of the man's chest was a flat, circular, metallic object suspended by two shoulder straps that ran over his shoulders on either side of his stained green and brown priest-collared shirt.

The bus slowed. Larken looked toward the front of the vehicle to catch a glimpse of the driver, who was glancing toward the action. By the contortions of his face, he seemed to understand the threat they were under as the bus descended, exiting the skyway without any ramp markers to guide it. The man seemed oblivious as he continued his monologue.

"You all deserve to die. Un-American—all of you. Models don't have rights. It's been that way for over fifty years. History that real Americans know and trust. Our ancestors did that for a reason, and here you all are, trying to undo it for your feelings. Have any of you met a model?"

Everyone. Everyone on the bus had met a model. The one who had attended the protest, tall and blond and noticeably absent from the bus. There should have been at least a couple of hands despite their inability to recognize Larken as one. Larken opined that people weren't raising their hands out of fear of what this lunatic would do.

The man no longer glanced in Larken's direction. She had that effect on people—the cripple effect. Super-attentive once they realize that she's disabled, and then they ignore her. The price of being irregular in an otherwise uniform society. Larken stared at the man's vest, trying to make out some writing in a script she didn't recognize. Angular letters were wedged together in the outer band of the device. His hand, she noticed, worked its way toward one of his coat pockets.

On the other side, pinned next to the window, sat a man who looked like a football player in size. Larken had seen him at the protest. He was large enough that, without the vest, Larken was confident he could have overpowered the little man in the coat and harness. But that was wishful thinking. The large man's eyes were as large as she knew hers had to be, and he seemed to be trying to shrink before her, taking up less and less space as he crouched against the window.

Larken tried eye contact. The man didn't keep her gaze. His wide eyes searched the room for a way out that he probably knew in his heart that he wouldn't find. She moved her gaze onto the woman in the seat behind him. That woman had already been staring at her. When their eyes met, the woman's cerulean irises sank to Larken's seat. Larken followed the glance down and saw her cane beneath. When she glanced back up, the woman nodded at her and poised in an ever-so-brief fighting stance.

Larken's eyes swiveled back to the large man. The woman, skinny and with a thin neck that seemed too small to support her head, followed, then returned Larken's look, telling her without words that the man was a waste of energy. Large or not, he'd already sucked into himself and wouldn't be used to...to what? Larken considered that she and a perfect stranger were planning something together. The woman must have already realized the conclusion that Larken had come to: if they did nothing, they would all die.

It had only taken Larken three seconds to think through the different scenarios. Dying by an explosion on a flying vehicle seemed as fun as dying by being pummeled by an android or decimated by a blast as she had been trying to rescue her brother. It didn't seem like an enjoyable experience, and she hoped to avoid it. She surmised that the hand going for the pocket might have been going for a detonator. Or it could have been going for a chocolate bar, but given the current situation, Larken was doubtful about that one.

Sirens rose above the volantrae's gentle engine and the man's oration, which Larken had zoned mainly out. She pivoted her gaze to a man in front of the trench coat man. He was locked into the threat and didn't see her until she risked clearing her throat. When he finally snapped his attention to her, so did the man with the chest plate.

"You understand me," the standing man accused and stared into Larken's eyes again. "You know what I'm talking about."

Larken shook her head. But there would be as much point in trying to talk the man out of his mistaken belief as talking him out of the idea that models were responsible for stealing polli jobs, which no doubt HPM had helped nestle into his brain. How could people without rights be accountable for anything in the eyes of anyone paying attention? She stopped shaking her head, opting for a new tactic: play into his delusion.

"I tried," she drew out the words slowly. "I tried to tell them. Some understand, friend. By talking, we can convince them."

As she spoke, her eyes connected again to the man sitting in front of him. That man had locked eyes with Larken, and she used a quick sideways motion to join the man's gaze with the woman's. He looked to the woman, nodded, and then back to Larken, and nodded again. Whatever it was, they were going to try; it would be soon. Her job had to be to distract him while she had his attention.

But he'd moved on already. As soon as Larken's eyes went back to the man, he plunged his hand into his pocket where before it had been clutching at the edges. Almost without thinking, she swung her cane up from where it lay on the seat beside her and connected with the man's fidgeting arm. Her action set off a chain reaction as the man staggered backward, caught off-guard by her blow, and the woman's grasping hands found purchase on his coat shoulders. The man in the seat before bounded over the edge and pinned the man's hands and body with his own.

They were still alive.

Larken blew out through her nose then breathed in deeply. Alive, she hadn't seen what had happened to the detonation arm. The rapid beeps of the device clicking on the man's chest told her what she didn't want to know. The man had triggered it. A bold guess, but when she caught a glimpse of the man's chest, the flat metal disk now had lights flashing around the edges. Faster and faster, they spun around in a circle until they formed one glowing line.

CHAPTER 9
STRUGGLES WITH BUSES

THE BUS DESCENDED TOO RAPIDLY and too soon to be taking the skyway off-ramp to midtown. Outside, police lights joined the visual chaos. Larken's eyes were drawn to all the police cars coming down from above, but her real problem was the writhing mass beneath her. This time, it was possible the police were her allies.

"Can you get it off?" Larken asked, keeping her weight across the man's legs, close enough to smell the ammonia of dried urine emanating from his crotch.

"It's strapped on," the other man, her colluder, said after a quick examination. "And taped. There's nothing we can do about it."

"I have a knife," someone offered.

Larken glanced to the back and saw a boy of twelve. The knife he held wasn't a fancy laser scalpel but a hunk of metal honed to a sharp edge. Possibly it was an antique or keepsake, but it would have to do. She nodded at him to approach. He hung back, eyes full of fear.

"You have to do it," Larken told him, narrowing her

eyebrows and trying to smile but coming across as creepy and stalkerish. "We can't let go of him. He may have another way to make this thing explode."

She felt the man's weight redistribute as the woman firmed her grip on him. The little man in the coat laughed slowly as his wild eyes roved over the crowd.

"Ignore him," Larken told the boy. The boy swallowed and inched forward. The lights on the device sped around the edges, completing a loop in only a second, where she'd thought it had taken two before. "What's your name?"

"Levi," the boy said.

"Levi, it's essential that we do this quickly," she responded, annunciating every syllable. "I think that's a timer. If it counts down all the way, we may all die on this bus. Focus and breathe and come forward. Please."

The boy took one step and then another. Other college-aged men and women, who Larken scowled at, offered no assistance. They cowered back as though five to ten feet of distance would save them when that disc exploded.

The boy approached. She felt her smile turn from a cold, calculated ploy to calm the boy into a genuine grin that originated from her pride in him for being so brave. Even at his age—perhaps especially at his age—he should have been terrified. And he looked terrified. Only then did she realize that he wasn't so young, not compared to her. They might have been the same age.

"A little closer. Good. Now, kneel here. See that black strap on his shoulder? From what I can see, there are two of them, one on each side of his neck. They don't look that thick. They may be synthetic. Should be easy to cut."

The boy leaned in, and the man gnashed his teeth. The boy lurched backward and nearly tripped over Larken, who put her shoulder into his lower back to steady him without losing her grip on the man.

"Try again. He can't bite from where he's at. You need to be fast."

The light went around the disc—half a second. The bus jolted as it settled to the ground—finally. A resounding thunk went through the bus, and the force of the final drop sent Larken forward, her body splayed across the man's legs. She stayed put, afraid to get back up and lose her grip. The boy had stumbled but not as badly. His knife extended from his hand just next to the man's shoulder.

"Do it, now," she said.

"I will," the boy told her. But he didn't move. The light went around—a quarter second.

"Cut, Levi."

That seemed to do it. He roughly slid the knife across the strap and caught the man's skin. The man screamed out in pain. Levi ignored the scream to his great credit and switched over to the other strap. He cut that one, too, then grabbed the device and pulled. It came up without further issue. Levi stood there, holding the device and frozen in fear.

"Out the window."

"But there are police."

"The toilet?" someone offered. Larken couldn't imagine they were serious until they repeated, "Put it in the toilet."

Not knowing what it even was, only that it seemed to be counting down, Larken didn't believe that a toilet would do anything to protect them from what they'd had to do. She secretly wished they were still in the air and could launch it out a window and not know who else they accidentally hurt.

"Open the window," she said. "Tell the police to back away. This thing is going to do something."

"The toilet is carbon steel," the same voice said. "Most are. It'll stop most of the blast. Here, toss it to me."

The boy still didn't move until the man on the floor let out another sharp laugh. That jarred him, and he launched the device to another woman, who Larken could see standing in the back of the bus, just before the crowd. Larken still hadn't moved from her prone position across the man's legs. Her only vantage was beneath the crook of her armpit, but she saw the woman effortlessly catch the device and duck into the bathroom.

"Move," Larken shouted, away from the woman and toward the front of the bus. "There's going to be an explosion."

The woman emerged, her face white, and motioned people to move forward and away from the bathroom. The crowd slowly started moving, with people stepping over and around the three who held the man down. And Levi.

"Levi," Larken said. "Make sure the police understand why we're still here and that there's something potentially deadly in the toilet back there."

"A toilet won't stop what's coming," the man on the ground said, issuing his first words since he'd been tackled. "Nothing will. You will see. You all will—"

The woman who'd taken the device to the toilet made it to them at the same time that the man was about to complete his sentence. She stepped over him and was midstep with her back foot when he let out a cackle so shrill that it cut through all the other noise on the bus until only the police sirens continued to wail.

"Police! Boarding now," came an announcement from outside. Before Larken could react, the door toward the front of the bus slammed open, and she heard the heavy thunking of boots in the aisle approaching them. A half-second later, a similar thunking sound came from the bathroom, stalling the footsteps in their place.

"Come out now," one of the officers said, leveling a proton rifle at the door. Another thunk. Then another, followed by a rapid succession of hissing sounds. The woman who had delivered the device to the bathroom ducked behind some seats. Larken, exposed in the aisle, made brief eye contact with her impromptu allies assisting her in holding the would-be terrorist down and nodded. Whatever was going to happen was going to happen. They let go at the same time and ducked behind their seats. Two of the three boarding police officers did the same.

"Is the perpetrator in there?" one of them asked. The question died in the crowd, who were busily doing the same as Larken had. The only person who wasn't ducking, aside from the only police officer who seemed to have recognized that the man on the ground was the perpetrator and had his weapon pointed at him, was the man himself, who rose to his feet slowly with his hands up. Larken's focus shifted to the bathroom, which emanated another hissing sound.

"No," Larken said, spitting out the word as quickly as possible. "Not the perpetrator. We think it's a bomb."

The confirming explosion ripped through the bus. It first tore through the seats nearest the bathroom and slammed the would-be savior cop straight through a window without slowing. Larken tried to duck when she registered what had happened, but the explosion came too quickly. The waves knocked her back, and for an instant, she was back at the HPM facility in downtown Seattle, being slammed face-first into the wall with the full force of a blast.

Only she wasn't. The waves died off almost instantly, leaving her confused and disoriented, but they had not caused her any actual harm. She looked toward the cackling man only to find that, unlike her, he had been fully hit by the blast and had flown down the aisle into the last remaining officer. The cackling man lay on top of the officer, his body motionless except for his mouth, which opened and closed repeatedly. Larken watched his lips, but she couldn't hear what he was saying. Part of her wondered if there was another bomb like terrorists often did in the holovids and on the news. Would they walk off the bus straight into another explosion?

A hand grabbed her from behind, prompting her instincts to scrape up her cane from just beyond her fingertips and swing as hard as she could. It connected, and she heard an "ouch" utterance, but it also had the intended effect. The hand released, and she used the cane to force herself up to her feet from her crumpled position slumped across the two seats.

"Easy, lady. I was only trying to help you up."

"I don't need your help."

"I can see," a voice behind her said, deep and dripping with a heavy patronizing tone. As she turned to look, she saw his thick eyebrows furled and something that looked like the beginning of a smile under his brown mustache.

"You're a cop," she said, pointing out the obvious as he wore his uniform and boots.

"Guilty."

She motioned around.

"Don't you have people to help?"

"I thought I was helping you."

"I don't need your help," she said firmly.

With that, the policeman pulled his hands up into the air, bent at the elbows, palms exposed. His grin evaporated.

"Sorry, lady."

"She knew it was a bomb. I'd 'help' her," Larken said, pointing to where the woman who'd delivered the bomb to the bathroom lay slumped across what used to be a seat.

"Roger," the man said. "Look, don't go anywhere. We'll want to take statements from everyone and get you all medically checked. That blast was serious, and you may be more hurt than you think."

She motioned to her cane, wobbling as it kept her upright.

"I doubt it," she said, pushing past him into the hallway. The policeman on the floor had pulled himself from under the man's body. Larken looked down at the terrorist as she stepped over him, placing her cane squarely into his chest. He didn't budge, and Larken didn't see his chest rise. Nor did she hear any breathing as she continued her path. Dead. Deserved it.

Suddenly her chest tightened, and she gulped at the air trying to force it into the tiny space that her lungs had become. Her chest hurt on every breath and her eyes watered. No matter how she placed the cane, it didn't seem to matter as it swayed beneath her, not providing the support she wanted. The support she needed. Somewhere in the distance, she heard someone whistling a haunting melody, three long low notes followed by a high-pitched short one, over and over again. Her head spun as she turned toward the sound. In the distance, too far for her to go, she saw two men walking slowly away. She looked down at the dead terrorist and up at the frantic gathering crowd, then back at the men as they disappeared around a corner.

Something is wrong, she thought, her last thought before the lights went out, and she collapsed five feet from where the terrorist's body lay motionless. The last thing she saw was his face twisted up into the same grin he'd had when he'd taunted them on the bus.

CHAPTER 10
SNARKY UNREQUESTED HELP

A FUZZY OUTLINE in turquoise scrubs greeted Larken when her eyes came open. For a second, she didn't know where she was. Then it came back to her, along with the noise and the lights that attacked her senses.

"Dandelion?" she muttered, trying to focus on the lines of the person's clothes. It was a woman, clearly from the curves and the way the fabric bunched. The blond hair she could see could have been Dandelion's.

"No, hun," said the woman. The woman's sharp features clarified like a holovid zoom close-up that the woman couldn't have been more different than Dandelion. Instead of the slightly thicker cheeks and light freckles, this woman had a gaunt face, almost to the point of creases. "Is Dandelion your friend? Was she on the bus?"

"No," Larken said. The more she remembered of where she was, the more obvious it was that the woman wouldn't have been Dandelion. She would have given her heron-headed cane to have Dandelion instead. "What happened to me?"

"Panic attack," the woman said firmly.

"Panic...attack?"

The woman nodded.

"Nothing to be worried about. I mean, you survived a bomb blast."

"Two," Larken almost said but stopped herself.

"Want me to call somebody for you, dear?"

Larken shook her head. She wasn't that far from the H Hotel, and if her "panic attack" could leave her be, she could make it on her own. She looked to the right where her cane was propped against the side of an ambulance she was leaning up against.

"I've got to check on some others. I'll be right back. Don't go anywhere. The police want to talk to you."

Yeah. Right.

Larken shuffled along the sidewalk as soon as the woman's back was turned, past a jewelry store and an on-demand hoagie vending machine. She barely registered her communicator chiming.

When she was far enough away from the crash site that she felt safe, she retrieved her communicator from her pocket, leaning against the wall to stay upright while she called Sam. The communicator buzzed three times. Larken gave up. She sighed, rubbed her throbbing head, and then called Molly, who picked up on the first buzz.

"Your brother and I have been worried sick," Molly said, her voice carrying enough irritation that Larken was mostly convinced her expressed sentiment was genuine. Her brother's whatever-she-was and Larken's former roommate tended to manipulate. "Where are you? Do you know what time it is?"

Larken looked up at the sky. Stars were out and a half-moon sat on the horizon. The night had fallen, but that didn't explain the phone call. It wasn't as though she lived with Molly.

"There's been a situation. Can you come to get me?"

Silence. A pause.

"Yes, of course," Molly said, the irritation now gone. A heavy breath had replaced it on the end, telling Larken how little fun Molly thought picking her up would be. A second passed, and Molly replied again with a firmer response. "Fine. Where are you?"

"Olive Way and Sixth," Larken told her as she glanced up, and her augmentation glasses showed opaque street names hovering in the air on each road of a nearby intersection.

"Stay put. We'll come."

We'll come. Larken rolled her eyes even though Molly wouldn't see it.

Molly's speed at arrival didn't seem impacted by the fact that she'd gathered up Oliver first. His oblong volantrae descended in the alley on Olive Way, nestling into the only available parking slot. As it settled, one of the doors popped open, and Oliver got out. His eyes locked onto hers and his movements were slow and deliberate, as though he approached a caged animal.

It was worse than Larken had thought. He approached from one side cautiously as though she might bolt in the other direction. But if she tried, Molly stood blocking that way.

"What's going on?" she asked as both stepped closer.

"Is there anything you want to tell us? How do you feel?"

"Fine, Oliver. Don't fuck with me. What happened?"

"I told him you didn't have anything to do with it," Molly said. "I told him you didn't."

"Do what, Mol?"

"Did you?" Molly continued. "You didn't, did you?"

"I don't know what you're talking about."

"It's only you and me who have access, Larken. Just you and me. It wasn't me, so it had to be you. Molly, it had to be her. She probably stole the money to finance her dream army."

Molly looked as though she might cry. Her brown eyes squinted up in her sea of freckles as she seemed to blink back tears.

"If you did, it's okay. Just give the money back." Molly seemed unable to make up her mind about what to believe.

"I didn't do anything, guys. I've been at a protest. With the bus accident and terrorist attack..."

"Attack?" Her brother switched out of accusatory mode, but Larken knew distrust still lurked beneath his caring veneer.

"Doesn't matter. What happened, and why are you both acting weird?"

Larken picked her way along the sidewalk toward the volantrae, a trajectory that would take her within grabbing distance of her brother. Molly closed the space on the other side.

"The trust has been drained. Completely. Someone stole all of our money. Every last cent. You didn't take it?"

"No. I've been too busy coming up with conspiracy theories about my upcoming war and fighting the forces of darkness. You know how I am."

"Right. Let's go home," Oliver said. He should have

backed her. The fact that she'd been accused of stealing her own money was fresh and new. Larken's jaw clenched.

"Are you guys remotely interested that I nearly died?"

"You say," Oliver told her. "Are you remotely interested that money was stolen from our trust fund account?"

So he was doubling down on the accusation. Larken didn't respond. She felt the heat behind her eyes begin to rise.

"Whatever. We have to go. Are you coming?"

He ran his hands through his hair. Larken relented and slid into the back seat of the volantrae with Molly and Oliver beside her in that order. The front seat was empty, replaced by a flashing auto-navigation light on the dash.

"With the money stolen and the increase in attacks, Molly and I don't think that—"

Oliver acted so old. He and Molly were nineteen, going on thirty. It wasn't Larken's fault that Molly lacked the courage to break up with him and that because of that, Larken was now stuck with a worn-down version of her formerly spirited brother. She glared at Molly, who fortunately wasn't paying attention, as focused as she was on Oliver's words. Oliver cleared his throat in a way that was so precisely like their benefactor Torrent that Larken wondered if Oliver knew that he was imitating their absentee father.

"I was almost blown up on a bus, Oliver," she interrupted. "Please be careful with what you say next."

"It's always something, Larken."

Rich, considering she'd earned her injuries trying to save his life. She gave him her best "do go on" stare. He didn't register it.

"You put yourself in these situations, and we have to

come to rescue you. Can't you relax and let the rest of us worry about the war thing?" Molly asked.

"I haven't been worrying about the 'war thing,'" Larken said. "I'm trying to live a life."

She held up her cane and shook it at her brother and felt like an old woman because of it, but she did it anyway. "And what do you mean you had to rescue me? Who was kidnapped by HPM and had to be recovered by half the SNO? Sure, my 'war thing.' That's the problem. You didn't almost expire in a coma while a dead woman you've never met lectured you about a future where absolutely everyone you love dies."

That was a stretch. It was an induced coma to reduce brain swelling, but at this point, anything was fair game.

"We've been here this entire time, Larken," Oliver protested. The volantrae slowed in the air, positioning itself a handful of feet behind the one in front of it as they merged into the skyway.

"Really? Could have fooled me."

"What were you doing to almost die in an explosion? I didn't have that problem," Molly said, narrowing her gaze and breathing rapidly through her nose. Larken could see her nostrils flare, raising the bed of freckles that draped over them like a loose-fitting gown.

"Classwork," Larken said, vainly trying to gain some sympathy. The instructor had said something about observing people in context being pivotal to...something vague about the human condition. All Larken knew was that attending at least one protest was a requirement for her course on Human Behavior.

"We don't know how much longer we can continue to

help you. We need to —" Oliver said, finally getting to the point.

The rest of the conversation droned on like someone trying to sing underwater. Larken didn't have to hear it to know how it went. She felt the terror clamping down on her as her memories of the visions (or hallucinations, as the doctors insisted) wherein she'd witnessed Oliver die horribly time and again. She shook her head. She was past that now. It had all been in her head, and Molly had a point, albeit a slight one.

"I understand," she said quietly.

"It's not that we don't believe you," Molly said. "It's just that—"

"I understand, Molly. That's enough. Let it go." Larken didn't turn back around.

The rest of the trip back to the H Hotel passed in silence. Oliver and Molly accompanied Larken into her room for the first time in months.

Sam wasn't there.

"Was Sam with you guys?" Larken asked, stopping Oliver and Molly from leaving. Oliver turned and shook his head.

"I don't think she was. She'd said she would be there, but I'm not sure what happened. Did you see her, Mol?"

Molly cocked her head to the left and squinted her eyes.

"No, I don't think so. Stephen joined us for lunch. And Ordell."

"Fine," Larken said. "Bye." It was abrupt, and intentionally so. A touch of schadenfreude warmed Larken's heart at Molly's startled reaction. Molly stood tree-still for a second and then turned to follow Oliver, who'd already resumed his exodus. The door closed behind them and the silence of the house closed in on her instantly.

"House, call Sam," Larken said.

"Sam is not available," came the response. "Would you like me to try Stephen instead?"

"No, don't bother. I'm not worried yet."

"You sound worried."

"What do you know? You're a machine."

"How do you know you're not?"

Larken thought about the snarky answer and then decided that she needed to let the hotel owner know the next time she ran into him that the experimental AI probably required a bit of tuning. But when House was right, she was right.

"Fair. And you're right, I am worried," she said. "Call Stephen."

CHAPTER 11
SAM RETURNS

THIS TIME, instead of calling Stephen silently and informing Larken that the call didn't connect over the comms, House played the symbolic connection music for the connection attempt, which sounded like a muted trumpet being slowly beaten to death. Larken jumped at the noise.

"House, what the hell?"

"You seem agitated. I didn't want to tell you he's not answering, either."

Another harsh squawk, then another. House gave up and shut down the irritating speaker.

"What's going on? Why isn't Stephen there? He doesn't have a life."

"Stephen does have a life. Would you like me to try his girlfriend's house?"

"Since when has he had a girlfriend?"

"Technically ex-girlfriend, Larken. And you need to speak to your friends more. He told me, and I'm a machine."

Of course, Sam had a social life, or something beyond fighting for model rights. Both being models themselves, she'd assumed that Sam and Stephen were in a relationship given the amount of time they used to spend passing inside jokes around.

"Her name is Lyric Briggs," House continued. "And she works at the Rusty Sponge bar over in Bellevue. Do you want me to try her?"

"No," Larken said. She wasn't going to intrude on Stephen's space. Besides, Sam wasn't a prisoner or anything. If she decided to see the sights or something, there wasn't much that Larken needed to do about it. Larken wasn't a jail keep. She sighed and searched the empty living room for something to distract her from feeling even more isolated after her family "visit."

"Would you like me to play some music?"

"No, House. I wouldn't. I'm fine."

"But you don't seem—"

"I'm fine," she insisted. "I guess turn on the news. Might as well see what's happening in the world."

The cushions behind her lifted her shoulders off her back, easing tension she hadn't known she carried. She sniffled once, allergies or warnings of illness lingering silently behind her sinuses. Once settled, the holovid sprang to life simultaneously as the door clicked open to her right.

"Sam is home," announced House. Larken turned to face the doorway, and her jaw dropped open. Stumbling forward and tripping onto the carpet came something that looked like it used to be Sam. Sam's smooth face was swollen beneath her left eye to the size of a small golf ball, and her chin was set at an odd angle that didn't seem possible. Her neck testified with rough red ridges that something rough had been wrapped tightly around it. Sam's left arm hung down, not lifting even to break her fall when she collapsed toward the carpet. Red patches decorated her cream-colored top, irregularly splashed against it like someone had pelted her with paintballs.

Larken jolted to her feet, too quickly. She plummeted back down to the couch. On her hands and knees, she grabbed her cane from leaning against the back of the couch. She used her cane for leverage to push herself up. The door tried to close and stopped at Sam's contorted left leg, which extended past it. The door opened automatically on contact, yet immediately tried to close again on Sam's legs. Larken cursed the AI in her mind for how stupid it could be about some things and irritatingly bright about others.

"House, stop the door."

The door stopped. Larken shuffled toward where Sam lay, watching her back for movement, and let out a breath she hadn't realized she was holding when the woman's back rose, however, shallowly. Larken recognized the signs of a severe beating but didn't quite understand the red ring around Sam's neck. She pulled at Sam's body, careful not to touch her left arm, which Larken assumed was broken by its apparent uselessness. Sam slid forward at Larken's tug, and House closed the door behind them.

"Lock the door, House."

She listened to the bolt slide into place with a sigh of relief. Whoever had done this to Sam might still be outside. A sneeze snuck up on Larken, and she rocked her on her feet. She stabilized herself the best she could atop her cane as the pressure behind her eyes reasserted. The dull throb behind her eyes turned to sharp pain as she leaned down to check for a pulse. Her heart pounded in her body so dominantly that she could not detect anything besides its drumming beat for almost thirty seconds. Larken blew three quick breaths, held one, and willed her focus down to her fingertips. There it was —faint but present and—fading.

Larken shook Sam gently by the shoulders. Her limp body rocked with each shove until Sam rolled over onto her back. Larken had pushed too hard, but at least from that angle, Larken could see the rise and fall of Sam's chest. So she was breathing. Larken's fingers dug deeper into Sam's wrist as she bore closer witness to Sam's bruised face, down to a deep gash that cut sideways across her forehead just beneath the hairline. Larken couldn't keep her imagination from connecting that moment to the moment she'd been pulled out of the reclamation pool at a legalized death camp for models. Larken shook her head, pushing the images aside as her breathing quickened.

There was no way that she could let that take over. Larken forced herself to focus and tucked her cane under her shoulder, heron-top jutting up painfully underneath her shoulder joint. It supported her in the sitting position, but more importantly, it gave her leverage for what came next. Larken grabbed Sam by the shoulder with her freed hands and hoisted her backward. The cane held and provided lift as she pressed against it. The hard rubber tip caught the carpet and didn't move. Larken put more and more weight on it by pulling Sam backward. Sam wasn't that far from the couch, and she couldn't stay on the floor by the entryway.

A loud banging sound made Larken's muscles all tense at once. She froze in space, fortunate that the awkwardly positioned cane seemed to lock in with her. The blueish-green eye shadow on Sam's lids shimmered as Larken watched Sam's eyes roll beneath them. Larken bit her lip. If she hoped enough, maybe Sam would stay asleep and not make any noise.

The banging started and stopped again.

"It must have been the next one," a muffled voice said.

"The blood stops here."

"That's what you said about the last two doors, Gary. She's not going to live after that. Let's go and let nature take its course. We have more to do today than follow a shill around. It's not like she can press charges."

"But she's here. I know she is."

The muffled voice turned into a harsh whisper, which made the raspy tones easier to understand.

"Then you stay. Do you know how many cameras there are in this hallway? She may not have rights, but her owners do. What if they decide to press charges for damaging their property? What are we going to do? Kill the owner too? Think, David."

"Fine. We'll go," David replied. "But I'm telling you, it's a mistake. You can't half-kill someone. They tend to all the way kill you back."

"Afraid of that tiny model girl? Big, bad model going to hurt little David?"

"You don't know. What if she's a Briggs?"

"She felt like a Caldwell to me," said not-David, with a subtle chuckle. Larken grit her teeth.

The voices started to diminish. Larken breathed quietly as the footsteps faded away from the door.

"Larken," Sam muttered, her arm pulling back against Larken's clutched fingers. Larken noticed that her fingernails had cut through Sam's skin on the wrist she'd been trying to take a pulse earlier. Larken relaxed her grip.

"I think they're gone," Larken said, shoving her arm under Sam's shoulder to the elbow to free one hand and stroking Sam's hair. "I heard them leave. You're safe."

For now.

Larken resumed her struggling walk, balancing her cane and Sam, who didn't have any strength to assist in moving across the room. Larken fell into the couch when she got there, cane rattling to the floor. Sam fell too, fortunately, onto the cushions and pinned Larken down with her head landing on Larken's lap. Larken resumed stroking her head.

"What happened to you?" she asked, not expecting any response. Sam needed rest, as Larken knew from personal experience. And, from the looks of the outside of her body, Larken's teeth clenched at the thought of what must be happening beneath the surface. How many broken teeth, cracked ribs, and fractured limbs from the beating? That left leg seemed to twist the wrong way, almost like it was no longer connected to Sam's hip.

A doctor? Perhaps Larken's doctor, even? But that wouldn't work, would it? Larken's doctor thought she was a polli, and that's why he treated her. Part of the reason, anyway. The other part was that he was on Gallatin's payroll and generally did what Gallatin wanted. But that same doctor would likely turn Sam in to the authorities for being a runaway.

She remembered then that she knew nurse—and a good one. And the nurse Larken knew didn't care too much about models being models any more than she'd cared about HPM being HPM. She was a nurse who knew how to keep secrets —precisely what Larken needed.

CHAPTER 12
ASSESSING THE DAMAGE

DANDELION RAISED her internal thermometer to ninety-eight degrees. The skin around her metallic support frame immediately tingled and itched. Whoever had designed that process hadn't considered how annoying it would be to itch on every square centimeter of skin surface at once. She steadied herself to keep from scratching and continued her unbroken gait through the lobby and into the elevator bay. More heads turned as she neared the elevator. There were so many askance glances that Dandelion waited to push the button for the machine to take her up long enough to examine herself in the over-shined elevator doors.

Given the circumstances, it had seemed prudent to wear a disguise because Dandelion wasn't unfamiliar to many in HPM. She'd coupled a maroon wig from a previous year's Halloween costume with heavy layers of off-nude makeup and fake glasses. All of that made her look different, but it also made her more conspicuous, as attested to by the people in the lobby of the H Hotel. They all, without fail, turned to ogle the strange creature walking among them.

She side-stepped a wayward child before they could collide with her bare legs, jutting out from yellow shorts that ended midway down her thighs. Dandelion did a little spin in the process, which lifted the wig's ends and flitted them around her head like a flamenco dress. The whirl was only to avoid that physical contact. The child—possibly a boy, but it was hard to tell—would have collided with a leg that looked human yet was still only about half the warmth of a human body, which would have been hard to explain.

She'd seen at least two other wigs in the lobby: one fluorescent green and another that tried to be blond but missed any natural shade by about two degrees of red. The thin T-shirt she'd thrown on wasn't originally part of any costume. That was something she'd bought thinking it was attractive, and she still stubbornly held to that belief. Something about its garish orange color contrasted with the yellow shorts. The bright red shoes she wore beneath could only be interpreted one way.

Clown. That's exactly what she looked like. The makeup had washed more color away than she'd intended, and she looked like she was going to perform at a birthday party.

With a long sigh, Dandelion lifted her finger to push the button just as the doors slid apart, and three teenage boys exited at once. One of them cast a glance her way and burst into laughter.

She didn't blush because she wasn't capable of doing so. She wasn't sure if that was a design flaw or a feature. At that moment, while she pushed her way into the empty elevator carriage, she could appreciate not adding to her embarrassment by putting it on display.

Fifth floor.

She pushed the button and waited, hoping to enjoy a

solitary ride up to see Larken without further interruption. A little girl of about eleven years old in a swimsuit entered from the second floor. A few stares, a grin, and an awkward surprised look cast the girl back out of the elevator on the third as she exited with a towel. Dandelion guessed the girl had boarded by mistake.

Ejected onto the fifth floor, Dandelion stepped into the hallway onto the tiling. She allowed her internal thermostat to lower again, anticipating fewer collisions. She hadn't had time to charge before going on her fool's mission to save someone who insisted on always putting themselves in harm's way.

The door to Larken's room was easy enough to find, though the numbers did seem to abruptly quit at one point only to start over ten digits higher again down the same hallway as though ten rooms had disappeared entirely during construction. Dandelion paused outside and questioned herself for just a second. She didn't have to care about Larken's friend Sam, with all of her questionable SNO connections. Dandelion's programming wasn't the sort that made her as empathetic as all that, and she didn't exactly like Sam. But there was something about Larken that always seemed to bring Dandelion to her door. With an utterly unnecessary sigh, she let her fingers rap against the door. On the other side, she heard shuffling and then a curse. Then a command.

"Open the door, House."

The door didn't spring open on command. A whirring noise grew louder as Dandelion waited and then a slit appeared and slowly widened as a motor swung the door to the inside. It would have been faster just to push it open, but it wasn't her apartment. Dandelion stared into the crack, letting her eyes adjust to the moderate dimness inside. It took about three milliseconds for the adjustment to take hold; then, she saw the outline of Larken's head jutting up over the back of the couch. Larken spun her head halfway around, so Dandelion could make out her deep-set, almost black irises. Dandelion could see tear tracks down Larken's cheeks.

"Hi, Larken. Where is Sam?"

"Here," Larken responded. "Here, on the couch. She's hurt."

Dandelion came to the edge of the couch and then passed the arm. She saw something she'd seen so many times before when she'd been at the free clinic. Her first guess would have been "battered woman," someone for whom the love of their life had transmuted irreconcilably into a nightmare. But that wouldn't have been Sam. As far as she knew, Sam was a lone wolf.

So more likely, it was an angry owner getting revenge. Possibly the woman had made the mistake of being honest—such a brutal mistake with her owner. Dandelion detected the rattle of Sam's raspy lungs. Dandelion examined the patient, scanning the body in full medical mode. Pulse was only fifty-one beats a minute; breath rate was increased to twenty-two breaths per minute. Standard unconscious person except for the lung problem. She gauged the sound of the rasp between breaths and concluded that whatever damage was done in the lungs wasn't getting worse.

The fact that the patient was fully clothed and lying across Larken's lap would make her examination difficult. Dandelion missed the scratchy hospital gowns that allowed unfettered access to her patients in the free clinic. As ugly as they were, they were efficient. Dandelion took an exaggerated deep breath that, strictly speaking, she didn't need. Breathing helped people to accept her, so she'd taught herself to do it and now did it almost as subconsciously as polli and models. Larken's tired face exploded in a wide grin as she chuckled while at the same time wiped away tears and sniffed once.

"Nice outfit," she commented.

"It was a mistake."

"You nailed killer clown," Larken commented, her hand pushing its way into Sam's hair as her short-lived grin fell back into a weak smile and then disappeared.

"I have to examine her," Dandelion said, ignoring the comment. Sam had been in some fight, and there may have been all sorts of hidden contusions and possibly even slow-bleeding knife wounds or broken limbs. There was a lot to do, and Dandelion couldn't do it with Sam lying on the couch.

Larken shifted her body weight, preparing to slide out from under Sam's head.

"No, stay there," Dandelion corrected. "I don't need you to move. Just warning you. I'm about to pick her up."

Without further conversation, Dandelion slid an arm under Sam's limp shoulders and knees, crouching down until Dandelion's upper thighs rested against the coffee table, and then stood, lifting Sam quickly. As Dandelion crossed the living area toward Sam's bedroom, she listened to the low rasps.

Still okay, she thought, carrying the woman's unconscious form across the room. The shuffling click of a cane became audible as she heard Larken cross from the living room carpet to the tile that extended from the kitchen, and covered the gap between.

Dandelion lowered the unconscious woman onto dark navy-blue shimmering blankets, then carefully worked the woman's shirt over her head, moving the body as little as possible.

If Dandelion were human, she would have gasped at the blue and purple markings up and down the woman's side. She began the systematic work of examining the woman's body, carefully keeping the sheet over areas she'd already examined to give Sam some privacy. Dandelion allowed Larken to stay, though, at the free clinic, she would have sent Larken out of the room for this part. Larken wasn't family, but Sam wasn't polli cither. It was a wash, and Dandelion knew well that Larken wasn't a stranger to beatings.

"Was it an android? I...I don't mean...I'm..."

Bruises covered Sam's calves and more the size of pinpricks around her knees resembled spider bites. Near her waist were some bifurcated burn marks that...she'd seen those marks before. Human Pride Movement. They'd been known to brand their victims as a message or something. She pulled Sam's remaining shoe off and pulled then her pants over the ankles, taking great care with the one that was swollen and turning blue. Once Sam was down to only her underwear and the majority concealed under the blanket, Dandelion performed her tactile check. Her fingers probed along the body, starting at the lower legs and working her way up, checking hundreds of bones for breakages since she didn't have x-ray vision or any other way to see inside.

Ankle strained. A rib was probably broken, though not in such a way that it would have punctured the lungs. Lucky.

The rasp may not have been what Dandelion initially thought. Sam might have somehow gotten fluid into her lungs during the apparent attack. Maybe she'd been partially drowned? But none of the rest of her was even damp.

"Hrnnn."

The woman seemed to notice Dandelion's fingers close on the left shoulder. Dislocated. Dandelion popped the shoulder back into the socket with deft quickness, eliciting a squeak.

"What happened to her?" Dandelion asked Larken.

"I don't know," said Larken, staring as one of Sam's legs kicked out from beneath the blanket. Bruises decorated the calf and thigh. Larken's eyes were wide at the mottled skin, and her hand clawed over her mouth. Dandelion could only nod and resume her physical examination.

"I brought these," Dandelion said her as she reached into a pocket and retrieved a handful of blue pills. "Nanite-directed analgesic. She will be in a lot of pain when she comes to, and we'll need her not to move much for a few days. You didn't want to take her to the free clinic?"

Larken shook her head. "No. She won't be safe there." Larken's eyes slid down toward the ground. She chewed her bottom lip for one and a half seconds. "Whoever did this would know that the free clinic is the only place an escaped model can go for treatment. They chased her to my door, so I know they're still looking."

Escaped. Dandelion somehow hadn't known that. She nodded, then sighed again.

"Okay then. I guess we have to continue this here," Dandelion said. "It's better to do this part while she's out."

Half an hour later, Dandelion looked on with some slight satisfaction at her patient's bruised, yet now clean, face. The gentle rise and fall of the blanket that covered Sam told Dandelion that she was asleep, that and the lowering of her heart rate to sub-wakeful speeds. Larken had proven to be an able companion for the more invasive parts of her inspection, though she was shaking on her cane, partially supported by the bedroom wall. Dandelion could feel the hatred oozing from the woman.

"Branded," Larken said. Dandelion's hearing was good enough to detect the click in Larken's teeth as she set her mouth into a line. "And probably..."

"You don't have to say it," Dandelion warned. Humans were sensitive about some subjects, and Dandelion knew Larken didn't want to say what they both thought. Sam had been sexually assaulted. It was obvious in her heightened blood pressure, rapid-fire pulse, and the thin sheen of sweat that formed across her forehead. "I did the examination."

Larken shut her mouth before completing her sentence. Then she started again.

"Why? Why would someone do something like this?"

For Dandelion, this question was the most common and complicated question that people asked, especially at the free clinic. It was always why, but few wanted to know. She recalled a man asking why after a stranger shoved his son in front of a car. The answer for him was the same as for Larken. Sometimes people do cruel things. "Shit just happens" wasn't a good enough reason for anyone. She kept her mouth shut and let Larken process.

"Okay," Larken said, wiping her face of the remaining dampness. "Okay. I'm okay. So let's figure this out. The brand. What does it mean?"

"Can we figure it out in the other room?"

Larken's head jerked up.

"Yeah. That's probably a good idea."

In the kitchen, Larken made coffee in the replicator. She pushed a cup to Dandelion, but Dandelion wisely refused it.

"Okay, Dandelion," Larken said. "Beaten, chased, left for dead. And branded, among other things? Who do we kill?"

CHAPTER 13

THE INVESTIGATION BEGINS

"I'VE NEVER SEEN the mark before," Dandelion concluded. "I have seen disfigurement in many patients at the free clinic, including brands, just not this one. Sadistic people like to find ways to torment their victims even after the crime. The worst case was—"

"I don't need to know about the worst case, Dandelion," Larken replied in a low voice. "Who did this to her?"

"Do you feel safe, Larken?" asked Dandelion, ignoring the question.

Larken looked askance at Dandelion, who had planted herself on a stool by the island in the kitchen. Larken scooted toward her in slow, unsteady steps. She examined the question and rolled it around, testing it. Safety was a memory and a dream. Her mind drifted back to Brighton Academy, practicing for an upcoming lofting tournament with Molly and the rest of the team. That was before Larken had learned that her brother wasn't her brother and that Larken wasn't who she'd thought she was, either. That was when she'd thought she was a real girl, a polli. Since then, she struggled to find a memory during which she'd felt safe. Even thinking the word "safe" seemed wrong.

"No," she muttered back.

"And you can pass as polli." This comment stole Larken's breath away, since she'd forgotten that Dandelion knew about that. Dandelion continued, "No barcode at all, and nobody even knows you're a model. Still, you were attacked. The perpetrator could literally be anyone in the lobby of this very hotel."

"Maybe," Larken said. "But we've been in the hotel for months now. This hotel is about the safest place either of us can be."

True enough. Larken's benefactor father didn't so much as call her over the communicator, as wrapped up as he was in his own problems. But he and his friend and boss Gallatin Hamilton owned the hotel. If she wasn't safe in this hotel, there was nowhere she would find peace.

Dandelion shrugged her disagreement. It was a smooth, natural-looking shrug that made Larken forget for a second that Dandelion was just a complicated robot.

"That wasn't the point," Dandelion said. "When Sam wakes up, we don't know if she will be fearful, angry, or sad. You can't tell because you're not her. I can't tell, either. We can only wait and help her get better. That part of it—the fear part—that's up to her. We need to be ready to support her and not be planning revenge."

Dandelion did make sense sometimes, but she didn't know Larken very well if she thought that the lecture would work. Larken turned to see Dandelion whisk a strand of hair from her face. It was another gesture that was so human that it made Larken want her to be so.

"You're getting better at being human," she commented,

thinking back to the aloof and simplistic Dandelion from her memories of the year prior. Dandelion smiled beneath her blue eyes. Her plain features were part of what gave her that ability to deceive so easily, Larken thought. The android who had beaten Larken nearly to death had been too beautiful, like a walking work of art, or maybe a little like Sam, who even at her frumpiest glowed with Caldwell's manufactured beauty. Fighting that flawless creature had been confusing and devastating. The android's beauty juxtaposed with her cruelty made it almost hurt Larken to mar that face.

"Thank you," Dandelion replied after a few seconds. "I've been practicing and learning."

"In the psych ward?"

"Inpatient wellness clinic," Dandelion corrected. "And yes. The thing about people is that they have so many stories. As interesting as what they remember is what they don't remember. The things they leave out could fill novels, and it teaches, too. Humans don't remember much at all. Only the highlights, really."

Larken sipped her coffee and nearly spit it out. Terrible. She shouldn't have tried. Yet, she needed coffee, so she gritted her teeth and sipped again. Regardless, the message was clear that Dandelion had little interest in helping her plot her revenge. She needed something to do while waiting on her nearly dying friend, so she changed subjects.

"How did you get your psych job?"

"A friend who used to work at the free clinic invited me when I complained about you."

Larken couldn't help a grin sliding across her face. She wiped at her face and eyes, now completely dry.

"I made you quit at the free clinic?"

"Not just you, but you were the clearest example. People

broke each other, and we put them back together the best we could at the free clinic. Then they broke each other again. When you arrived, I had had enough. What that woman did to you...you're lucky you survived. Then the blast. I...I couldn't deal with it, Larken. I couldn't see you hurt yourself over and over again."

Larken stared into Dandelion's sky-blue eyes, tented beneath upraised eyebrows. She really had gotten good at human expression. Larken flashed a narrow smile.

"And here you are now, back in it again. Because of me."

"Will you be staying for dinner?" House interrupted. "You really should, Dandelion. Larken doesn't have many friends."

"Thanks, apartment," Larken muttered, scowling. Then she turned her frown into a smile. "Would you like to? I know you don't eat, but maybe you can taste some of my horrible cooking?"

"Some other time," Dandelion replied. "I have to be back at work tomorrow morning, and my battery is low. May I stop in tomorrow and check on her?"

Larken felt her stomach churn at the thought of staying alone in that apartment after her day of being almost killed, only to be topped off by her roommate almost dying, too. She contemplated bringing Dandelion up to speed on her own recent problems, but that would be the opposite of the life that Dandelion wanted for herself, so Larken said nothing. She spared a glance for the door and then back to Dandelion.

"Are you sure? I mean, you could charge up here. What if something happens to her tonight?"

"Nothing is going to happen until morning, Larken. I've given her enough sedatives to keep her under for a long while. There's no permanent damage. She needs to keep that arm as stable as she can and stay off her ankle for at least today. Physically, she will heal quickly."

The unsaid part was woven into the look that they both shared then. Physically, she would heal. But emotionally, after what she'd been through, was another question. Models were used to hard lives; Larken tried to console herself with that thought, as cruel as it was to find comfort in the fact. Still standing, Dandelion placed her coffee cup on the polished stone counter.

"It's time for me to leave," she said, the words flat and reminiscent of the robot that she was. "I will stop by in the morning on my way to work to check on her progress."

"Thank you, Dandelion," Larken said, swallowing down the lump in her throat. "Thank you so much for coming when you didn't have to."

"How could I not?"

Larken struggled to stand with her cane, and Dandelion seemed ready to rush to her side to assist, but Larken waved Dandelion away.

"You've got enough to do with one patient. You don't need two."

———

Fifteen minutes after Dandelion said her goodbyes and left, Larken sipped the lukewarm remnants of her coffee. She placed the cup down on the counter, ignoring the coasters Sam had gotten to avoid coffee stains, and half-shuffled, half-walked the worn path from the kitchen counter where she'd sat beside Dandelion to the closed door to Sam's room. Larken paused and listened for the low, whispery sound of Sam breathing on the other side. Her heart palpitated when she couldn't make it out. Then, slowly, she differentiated the sound from the background noise of the volantrae flying past overhead.

Hearing wasn't enough. Larken pushed the door inward just far enough to peek around the edge toward the bed. Sam's tousled hair splayed against her blue-black pillow, forming a halo. The swelling in her face seemed to have lessened, but the bruises were still pronounced. Dandelion hadn't given Larken instructions for care. Supposedly, Sam would get better on her own. But the bulging flesh around Sam's eye socket and the split on her swollen bottom lip were things that Larken knew how to improve.

Though she really wanted a scalding hot bath, a lavender candle, and an eNovel by R. Ruslet Jewells—preferably a cozy mystery, Larken instead retrieved a rag from the bathroom and packed it with ice. She had, at the very least, the tools to keep the swelling down. Should she locate the med kit, there may have been some fancier remedy in the apartment. Maybe some magical spray to help the swelling or a self-chilling towel. Holding the ice against Sam's temple gave Larken something to do that felt productive, regardless of how unnecessary it was.

Larken spent the first hour of the evening in silent contemplation. Poised on the edge of the bed, she held the dripping ice in place over the swollen eye. The ice stayed cold enough to do the job, but she had to replace it soon. Larken pulled it away to examine it when she saw a darting pupil beneath. Sam's other eye was also open, and Larken could hear the acceleration in her breathing. Sam's first movement was to yank herself up. The bed shifted with her moving weight, and Larken slammed the ice onto Sam's nightstand before using her hand to clutch at the bed. The blanket fell away. Sam's darting eyes rocketed down to her naked body. Streams of ice water dripped down her chest. Larken looked askance and tried to give Sam the dignity of privacy as Sam seemed suddenly to realize that she didn't have clothes on and clutched the blanket up around her torso.

"They're out there," Sam whispered in a thick rasp. Larken's eyes turned back once she was sure Sam had her blanket firmly in place.

"Sam, it's okay. They're gone."

Sam shook her head quickly from side to side. Larken watched Sam's eyes squeeze shut as Sam's head abruptly stopped. When those eyes opened again, the green irises floated in a glaze of tears.

"It's not okay," she rasped again. Larken noticed again the thin red welt rising in the skin of Sam's neck. Sam's lips raked across her dry lips, and she swallowed before she spoke again. "They attacked me. Followed me and attacked me."

Larken's hand instinctively reached for Sam's. Larken's thicker fingers, built up by her years of lofting play, closed around Sam's thin ones and squeezed. As painful as it was to look, Larken focused her eyes on Sam's.

"It is okay, Sam."

"Did they follow me here? I tried to get away, Larken. I ran as fast as I could. I could barely see, though, and they were so fast," Sam started, then stopped as she seemed to rethink. "Persistent. Not fast. I ran as fast as possible, with what they did to my ankle."

She seemed to remember, then looked down and wiggled her foot beneath the blanket. Relief washed over Sam's face.

"Not broken. But not for lack of trying, Larken. They—"

Sam stopped midsentence. Her normal eye closed, but

her swollen one didn't. Larken wondered whether the swollen one could or not when it defied her expectations with a blink.

"They walked so slow, one whistling that stupid nursery rhyme."

Larken had no idea what song Sam was talking about until she heard Sam's faint hum penetrate. Larken was transported back to the bus, walking away from the near-explosion and the two men she'd followed but couldn't keep up with. She swallowed.

"Tallish, with reddish-brown hair and thick eyebrows. Comical face, like he should be a comedian, except with a face so rigid that it couldn't possibly convey a joke?" Larken asked.

Sam's one unswollen eye darted over to meet Larken's.

"I don't know," she said, shaking her head. She began to move frantically as though she were trying to get up. "Did they follow me here? We need to go."

Larken pushed her Sam down.

"No," she partially lied. "They didn't. I think I saw them earlier in the alley. Think hard. Was one of them darker complected with a scar on his cheekbone?"

"I...I don't know," Sam said, then her eyes fell to the blanket across her lap and chest.

"It doesn't matter," Larken replied, squeezing Sam's fingers again. "I'm so sorry. Did they do this because of me?"

"No," Sam said. "I don't think so. I...I don't think so."

Larken watched Sam's mouth stop moving, her lips in a straight line except for the swollen part jutting out. Sam lowered her body back in the bed and brought her unswollen eye to a close. Larken could see a blue pupil peering out of the other one but couldn't tell where it was focused.

She squeezed Sam's hand for the third time and thought she saw a tear glisten beneath the folds of Sam's slitted eye. Larken swallowed once and then pushed the corners of her mouth into what she hoped was a reassuring smile. Finally, that swollen eye worked its way closed as well, and she felt Sam's hand slacken as she drifted back to an uneasy sleep.

CHAPTER 14
THE GHOST OF SAM

THE HOTEL LOBBY was empty when Dandelion arrived the next morning. She hadn't told Larken everything about Sam's medical condition yet. Dandelion wanted to protect Sam's privacy. One of the blood samples that Dandelion had pulled from Sam had shown elevated levels of human chorionic gonadotropin, normally abbreviated to hCG. They weren't elevated enough to be conclusive and likely wouldn't trigger a positive on a pregnancy test. Dandelion needed additional samples over the next few days to determine whether or not what she suspected was true, as impossible as it seemed given that models weren't supposed to be able to get pregnant. Then, somehow, she had to help Larken, and Sam, of course, deal with the fallout.

Crossing an empty morning lobby was even more nerve-wracking than crossing a full evening one. The person behind the counter had nothing else to look at but this woman in a sundress and short heels crossing before the opulent statue of Ganapati, the god of travelers. The elephant god sat cross-legged on her right as she passed, and Dandelion couldn't shake the thought of the oversized statue coming to life and attacking her. The same imagination that separated her from her stoic military predecessors also brought completely invalid interpretations of reality. The guardian of the lobby didn't move, and neither did the freckle-faced kid behind the counter.

Dandelion reached the door to Larken's room and rapped twice. Before she could knock a third time, the door sprung open, and Larken's face peered out.

"Hi," Larken said. "I'm glad you're back."

"Is she up yet?"

Larken's downcast eyes told Dandelion that whatever state Sam was in, it was troubling.

"She won't leave the room," Larken elaborated in a hoarse whisper. "She barely talks. When she does, it's short sentences. She's not Sam anymore, Dandelion. She's the ghost of Sam."

Analogies and metaphors weren't Dandelion's strongest areas of understanding when it came to human communication, but she did connect that since ghosts weren't real, Larken wasn't discussing a ghost in the metaphysical sense. Dandelion nodded and followed Larken to Sam's closed door.

"Get ready," Larken whispered. She shoved the door inward. Sam sat on the bed, staring at them with giant, fear-soaked eyes.

"Are you okay?" Dandelion offered the question only to see if she would get a response. Sam responded with a silent nod and a brief opening and closing of her mouth, issuing forth no sound. Dandelion looked to Larken and then back to Sam. She clenched her teeth together and then turned her head so that Larken could see that Dandelion was addressing her.

"Can you give us some privacy please?"

At first, she thought Larken might refuse. The way that the woman sucked in her breath and sealed her mouth beneath furrowed eyebrows told Dandelion that Larken was about to fight. But as quickly as that happened, Dandelion watched Larken's eyes slide over to Sam, and the tension evaporate from Larken's neck muscles.

"Sure," Larken said. "Okay."

Larken left the room in silence. Sam's empty eyes remained locked onto the just as empty wall. Dandelion flipped her head to the right as the sound of the door latch caught her attention. Then she turned that attention back to Sam.

"How are you, Sam?" she asked, manipulating her voice box to smooth the edges in her voice. Sam didn't seem to notice, so Dandelion continued. "I need to take some blood, Sam. Is that all right? Can I take a little blood to do see how you're doing?"

"You may as well." Sam surprised her by replying. "It's not my blood."

"You can speak."

Sam nodded, sending her hair swinging forward around her neck only to settle back as Sam reattained her sitting, unmoving posture. Dandelion approached slowly, like a cat approaching its prey. She didn't have a needle or anything separate that might have been used for siphoning blood from her patient. Dandelion grasped Sam's arm at the elbow. A needle protruded from her palm, sensed the vein beneath Sam's skin, and slid in quickly. If Sam noticed, she didn't make any indication. Internal sensors immediately processed the warm fluid as it coursed into Dandelion's body in spurts, carried by the short bursts of Sam's heart.

Five seconds later, Dandelion removed her hand. She stored the needle back away into the fleshy part of her palm and massaged the spot above where the sharp object had protruded. Her self-healing closed up the hole quickly as the first of the sensor reports came back.

"You haven't been eating enough," Dandelion told Sam.

"I haven't been hungry."

"You must eat," Dandelion retorted. "That's what heals you. Even your mind—maybe especially your mind—won't heal without sustenance."

No reaction.

"There's more," Dandelion said, as the tests completed, one after the other. "You don't have Influenze-X or any of the recent viral outbreaks. But there's something else I need to talk to you about."

Still no reaction. Dandelion took one of her practiced deep breaths and exhaled. She didn't know if now was the best time to tell Sam anything new about the hCG and possible pregnancy. The woman was clearly fragile and barely holding on. But the sooner Sam knew, the sooner she could "fix" the problem. A second later, more of her internal processing completed. The hCG levels were indeed going up. Still didn't mean pregnancy, but that was becoming the more likely scenario as Sam's levels had already passed normal blood concentration by three times.

Dandelion knew the odds of pregnancy for models came down to statistics. For females, the probability of gametes forming without flaws was less than one in a hundred. For male models, who were easier to manipulate with the right genetic modifications, the likelihood of reproducing was closer to one in ten thousand. These numbers meant that models couldn't have babies very often together. When they did, usually a defective gamete was involved, and that mother would miscarry or the child would come out malformed or worse.

A pregnancy could easily be a death sentence.

Dandelion couldn't bring herself to share the news. She thought it would break Sam more if she did, and that was a cruelty she couldn't inflict. Dandelion drew on a smile and massaged Sam's elbow where she'd taken the blood. The needle was so small it was nearly invisible, and the hole was just as tiny. After a few seconds of massage, all the evidence left behind was a minuscule red dot without any blood.

Dandelion stood, keeping her gentlest smile on.

"Everything looks good," she said. "Everything looks fantastic here. You should be up and around soon. I'm surprised you aren't already."

Sam's response came in the form of a single tear making its way down her cheek, which told Dandelion she'd made the right decision keeping her secret. Human minds were fragile things. They were more fragile than their impressively resilient bodies made of a million self-repairing cells and organs, used to getting pummeled from a very young age. The mind didn't have as many defenses. Witnessing tragedy changed people, and being a victim of an attack—even polli, who had at the least agency over their own existences—often failed to "bounce back" from such things. One of the things that drew Dandelion to Larken was her incredibly resilient mind. But Larken was a beautiful exception.

Dandelion widened her smile. "In no time, Sam. You will feel better. You'll see."

Sam didn't respond as Dandelion opened the door to

exit, only to find Larken eavesdropping on the other side. Gently forcing her way forward and nudging Larken aside slowly enough for Larken to adjust her cane and stay on her feet, Dandelion passed and pulled the latch closed behind her. Dandelion peered at Larken, wondering if she could trust her with the information she hadn't given to Sam.

"You're thinking," Larken said. "It usually doesn't take you more than a second. What happened?"

"Blood test," Dandelion said. "I suspected it, but I'm more sure now. You know what happened to her, right?"

Larken nodded.

"All of what happened?"

"I know, Dandelion. Just tell me."

Dandelion didn't want to tell. To say the words made them real, and Dandelion didn't want to be the one to bring her words to fruition. She didn't want to believe them herself. But keeping them inside seemed wrong as well.

"I think...I'm pretty sure...that the worst thing possible has come of it."

It wasn't like Dandelion to feel around the raw edges of such an emotional issue. She'd dealt with worse among her clients at the retirement community. Nobody lived to be as old as them without accumulating scars. The tragedy of life was written on every one of their aging bodies. This felt more real with Larken hanging on her every word.

"Is she okay?" Larken asked.

Dandelion nodded slowly. "Physically, she's doing better. I think...I think she's pregnant, Larken. Please don't tell her. Just keep an eye on her, and I'll try to come back, but..." She paused, thinking about how much she should divulge about what occupied her free time. Larken might have been trustworthy, but accidents did happen. "But I'll be busy soon with work and won't be able to make it as often."

"What can she do if...you know...if you're right?"

"It's up to her. Being a model, only very few doctors will help. There's that problem of ownership. Children born to models are the property of the owner under the law, and Sam isn't going to have a choice about it...not by herself. What you need to do is get mifepristone and misoprostol. But here's the problem. You can't buy them both at the same time."

"Why?"

"Abortions have been illegal in Washington State for almost twenty years. These two bought at the same time are known to be abortion-inducing, and would almost certainly bring scrutiny you don't want. Her owner..."

"Sam doesn't have an owner," Larken replied.

"I keep forgetting," Dandelion said. "But here's what you can do. Mifepristone is also used for blood sugar control, and misoprostol is still used for ulcers or stomach problems. If you're careful, you can get them separately. I'll coach you on the symptoms."

Dandelion locked her gaze into Larken's.

"You need to get those drugs and have them ready for when you think Sam can hear about this. Do you understand?"

Larken's mouth usually seemed like she was frowning. Her thick eyebrows were so often turned up that it was easy to believe she went around in a constant state of hostility. Dandelion knew that hostility wasn't the culprit, rather pain was. Dandelion had been the first to inform Larken that she would have the pain for the rest of her life and that doctors couldn't fix her. Under the pain-forged mask lingered layer of tenderness. With the leveling of Larken's lips into a straight line and the way those eyebrows furrowed up, Dandelion thought she made out a bit of that empathy in Larken's changing expression.

Then Larken asked the inevitable question. "How do I know when she's ready to be told?"

Dandelion offered no answer.

"Are you planning on attending university today?" asked House, its singsong voice far too chipper for the subject they were discussing.

"Shut it, House," Larken snarled. School would have to wait. Right now, Sam was the only thing that mattered.

CHAPTER 15
WALK THE LINE

"LET'S SEE YOU," the orderly said, holding up two different skin tones next to Felicity's arms, which he was slowly molding out of muscle clay into something the texture of human muscle, but that could flex and shape with body movements. In this case, he held what might have been a human stomach panel, if humans had such things. Felicity suffered the indignity of his irritating closeness as he installed it over her access panel in her abdomen. He dabbed adhesive bonding agent to the sides of her stomach area and over the seam where the abdomen section fit in.

Tedious, but he was making progress. Then he stopped and his face lit up as he pulled the next section of her chest.

"Now for the boobies," he said, chuckling to himself for his one-man joke.

She didn't laugh and didn't make a sound, not when he seemed to spend an inordinate amount of time "adjusting" them, which involved actions that she guessed would have been indecent to her if she'd been a real human. But she didn't care about that. Eventually, he secured her chest panel and had those seams closed up as well.

"You wouldn't rather be out for this?" he asked. That was when she noticed the sheen of perspiration across his forehead and the chill of the room at the same time. "It's weird with you watching me put you together."

"I'm fine," she said, cognizant of the fact that her face wasn't fully on yet. It was clear in his eyes that her servo mouth movements were probably a little unsettling.

He clenched his teeth and muttered to himself. "Yeah, definitely don't want to look at that while I do this." He leaned in close to reach around her back where her access cables and emergency shut-off were. It took her longer than she wanted to admit to realize that he was actually about to flip that switch. If her back hadn't already been closed up, he might have gotten her completely deactivated before she could act. As it was, he felt around blindly for about thirty seconds and then cursed when he couldn't find purchase with the edge of the panel.

"Closed up," he muttered. "Good job, too. No problem. The torch will work for that."

Before he could grab the torch, a device about the size of a pen that was designed to open seams like the one on her back, she pushed out one leg and connected with his knee, sending him down in a pile of sniveling pain.

"What the—" he said as he fell, then clutched at his knee. "You fucking bolt-bucket! My knee."

"I'm fine," she repeated, annunciating very clearly that time so that he knew she wasn't going to let him do anything to her while she was unconscious. Aside from the general feeling that he was sleezy and had improper intentions, there was the minor fact that if she was unconscious, they would be able to scan her without her knowledge, and possibly fix her. By the time she regained awareness, she might be an entirely different person—a weaker person.

"Fuck," he said as he tried to stand back up. She didn't move. "Don't move." She still didn't move. He limped across the room and rummaged through a pile of discarded tools before he found his communicator. He dialed, flipped it to private mode, and then whispered at whoever answered.

"She scares me," said the sniveling coward of a man who was supposed to be covering her with synthetic skin said. He clearly thought he was out of earshot. That was the thing about the cosmetic team. They had no real understanding of what Felicity could do. She had only kicked him in the knee, and not even that hard. He'd be able to walk right again in about a week. She'd been very careful to avoid permanent damage. The assistant seemed to listen to something on the device she couldn't make out.

"But I can barely walk because of her," he complained.

The other person, who she'd heard before—his boss or something—replied, and she could distinguish the words this time as the assistant changed position. "We need her to work. There's no other option here. Funds are low right now, and it's not like we can get another one."

"What do we need one for? This one did enough damage all by herself."

She sneered, but only on the inside. The man was a coward, but he wasn't wrong, yet he was at the same time. Felicity knew that she'd been a scapegoat. The explosion at HPM headquarters that had crippled her foe, Larken, hadn't had anything to do with her. Yet still everyone at HPM she'd met seemed to treat her like she hadn't been only following orders when she'd attacked the girl and her brother.

Felicity knew something that they didn't though; she knew they were clones. She knew it, even if they didn't have barcodes. Even if the entire HPM organization had decided otherwise, or at least faked it in public to try to regain footing. Felicity wouldn't fake it.

"What'd you do to make her kick you?"

"She's an android, boss. She's supposed to be controllable. I should be able to do whatever I want with her."

"What was it?"

"Nothing. I put her chest back together, and her breasts were a bit lopsided. I was trying to fix them when she kicked me hard in the knee. I can barely walk."

Not exactly the entire truth. But the salient points were all there.

"She's a machine. Just do the work."

"I can't shut her down, boss. And she's dangerous, I'm telling you..."

His wide eyes turned toward Felicity as she shimmied forward off of the table on which she sat. Felicity edged off and onto her padded feet. She looked down to take stock of the work. Legs: mostly done, up to about mid-thigh. Abdomen: well, technically complete, but there was still a giant seam and one breast hung down like an elephant ear, revealing her innards. Still, she was working through what she'd seen the man do for the last several weeks, and considering very carefully whether she could do it herself.

"Stay there," he commanded, in a less-than-commanding voice. Then into the microphone: "She's moving. I didn't tell her to move."

"Get yourself together. She's programmed not to injure humans. You'll be fine. Put her together like we're paying you to."

"She kicked me in the knee."

"You probably deserved it. Just don't try to shut her off again. Why do you make things so damn complicated?"

Felicity took a tentative step, testing her balance. The added skin made her weight off balance by approximately 0.02% on the right side, which she compensated for easily. The tools, she could see, were all still out, and she'd witnessed him using most of them. She gained confidence by the second, so much so that she plodded forward toward him.

"I said stop," the man said, backing away. Into the communicator, he said, "She's not stopping. Send security in here."

"Security is working on something else right now. You need to get yourself together. She's just a—"

The communicator dropped to the floor as she closed her hands around the man's throat. He'd been distracted with the communicator and hadn't seen her move. Really, the idea that he thought he had any sway over her at all made her want to laugh and vomit at the same time. His legs kicked as she held him suspended in the air. She heard a rasp as he sucked at the air and adjusted her grip so that the rasping stopped. Then she only waited for him to stop moving.

"Are you there? Hello?"

The voice on the other end of the communicator pined for attention until she crushed the device where it had fallen to the cold floor. She grabbed the bonding agent from the counter where he'd left it, pressed her chest closed, and worked the salve over the crease until it closed up. Then she fixed the man's poor work on chest and moved on to the shoulders and neck, and finally the face. Working in a mirror was tricky, but the right filter algorithm in her optical inputs and she found she was quite adept at getting the ridges right.

Under her careful hand, a face emerged from the panels that joined together to form her face.

Once she was finished, she stripped the corpse of her one-time tech assistant and donned all of his clothes. He had a slightly larger frame than her, so the fit was loose, but the lab coat that he'd worn worked well to hide that. She ran her hands through her hair a few times, checked herself over for exposed wires, and a few seconds later, simply walked out of the lab, down the hallway, waved at the watchman at the desk, and crossed out into the vibrant city beyond.

CHAPTER 16
HIDDEN MYSTERIES

THE HOTEL ROOM felt cramped to Larken, who would rather have been anywhere else. And playing nursemaid had proven to be exhausting, and, breaking her promise, Dandelion was en absentia for all of it.

"You're feeling better?"

Larken barely contained the excitement in her voice. She took her place at the bedside and gave Sam a small smile, large enough to show care but small enough to show empathy. Sam lifted her eyes, and Larken noticed that the swelling had gone down precipitously. Sam looked almost like herself, except for some darkening around one eye. A multitude of bruises hid beneath Sam's clothes and that blanket, Larken reminded herself. Still, the progress was reassuring. A few uncomfortable seconds passed in silence before Sam spoke.

"Good evening, Larken," Sam whispered. Finally, Sam had dedicated the energy to a shower and putting on something besides the T-shirt she'd been sleeping in. Yes, the evening had descended and her timing was a little off, but she was finally trying.

Larken said, "I'll call Dandelion. Do you feel like eating?"

Not that it would do much good. Dandelion hadn't been answering her communicator for Larken's recent calls. But she was willing to try it again if it would help Sam.

"No," Sam replied. "I'm fine."

Still not true. Sam's eyes were vacant and lost, staring past Larken toward a world where cruelty awaited them. Talking was better than not talking, so Larken wouldn't let Sam get away with simple answers if she could pull more out.

"Sam, let's do something today. Even if it's just watching old samurai movies on the holovid, okay? I'll get some doughnuts from that place that makes them with real eggs, then I'll grab Stephen, and we'll make a day of it."

Saying Stephen's name made Larken's stomach clench involuntarily. She bit her lip and tried to stifle her guilt for not reaching out to him even after all this time. Larken imagined Stephen's thin frame shaking with rage. He would probably hitch himself to the same goal of revenge that Larken fantasized about, though, as a plus.

"I guess," Sam said. Her watery eyes quivered, and Larken thought Sam might start crying again, but the woman held it together and brought her lips into a committed line.

"So yes," Larken said. "Good. And you'll eat some real food, too? If no to doughnuts, a sandwich, maybe?"

"No."

"You have to eat more, Sam. It's been almost a week, and you barely feed yourself. If you don't eat, your body...I mean, you won't heal right."

"My body." Sam flexed her fingers as Larken watched. "It doesn't feel like my body. Everything hurts. Maybe it used to be my body. I remember that I thought it was, anyway."

Sam held her barcoded wrist up for Larken to see.

"This body belongs to someone else," she said.

"It is your body," Larken protested. "Those men had no right to do what they did."

"Says you," Sam whispered, turning the barcode back toward herself as she examined it. "The entire rest of the world says otherwise."

"I'm calling Stephen," Larken said, reaching for something that might break the malaise. It was time to admit that although Larken could keep Sam physically alive, Larken's own emotional shortcomings made her the wrong person to help Sam recover emotionally.

Sam shrugged.

"Do what you want."

In the living room, Larken reconsidered whether she should actually call Stephen. She couldn't convince herself that bringing him in would solve anything. Instead of dealing with Sam alone, Larken would have to deal with Sam's growing apathy and Stephen's impotent rage. She needed Dandelion.

Perhaps she was being impatient. Sam had to process. Whether it was convenient for Larken or not, it would take time for Sam to come to terms. As Larken searched for patience, she found only fidgety anxiousness.

Larken left the room—and the hotel. She took a massive escalator near the Seattle Library down to ground level— Strata o. Near the ground, the city had already slipped into dusk. Due to the structures of the buildings, it got dark in what people often referred to as the "dregs" a full two hours before it did above. The evenings had grown shorter in the late autumn weather, and the overcast sky was semi-permanent in the dregs at this time of year.

Larken exited the escalator without a thought as to where she might be going. Larken wasn't like Dandelion, who, in more ways than one, was built to be a nurse. Larken didn't enjoy it when a nonresponsive patient marginally improved or someone survived for one more day. Dandelion seemed to celebrate every small win. Collecting and bringing food for the unresponsive Sam required every ounce of self-control Larken had, but for Dandelion, it was as though she possessed an endless supply of patience.

The city had become Larken's release valve. She lost herself in people-watching. In the dim glow of a streetlight, Larken saw a cluster of college-aged kids—her age. She reminded herself as she shuffled forward on her cane. Then she recalled the memory of sanded-soft eik wood in her hands and the roar of the crowd. She'd been good at lofting. So good at one thing but apparently so bad at friendship.

She watched a boy her age laughed with an armful of university books. The boy was living Oliver's dream life and probably didn't even know it was special. Larken guessed she lived that same dream now, though it still seemed as though she was borrowing someone else's life sometimes.

Larken turned a corner, leaving the gaggle behind as she approached an abandoned alleyway. On the far end, she could see another crowd passing from the left to the right across the alley's exit. Besides that, the path seemed empty, so she slowly clicked forward, one aching step after another. The scraping movement of what sounded like a small animal caught her attention. She strained toward where the sound originated, but nothing moved for the three seconds she focused, so she began again.

As she neared the exit, she noticed that the people crossing in front of the alley's opening were all similarly dressed. Some of them ran, and some walked, and occasionally one would peek down the path, register her, and quickly break eye contact to continue. It wasn't until she heard the megaphone projector that she understood she'd stumbled into another pro-model protest. Or she gathered the remnants of one. Her first question was why anyone would bother protesting below at least Strata 5 if they weren't on the university campus or in a business center where the disruption would be noticed. Nobody down on Strata 0 had any power. Her second thought was about what had happened to the protestors.

Signs lay scattered across the ground, some covered in red blotches that she thought might be blood. Ambulances lifted off and landed, and overhead she heard the whine of multiple volantrae and news drones competing for better visibility. She ducked back into the alley to stay out of sight and peeked out at the rest of the scene. On the far end of the protest area—she gathered from where the signs lay—she could make out a handful of bodies contorted on the ground. One person's moan breached her ears.

"A live one," a voice yelled out. "Here!"

A cluster of people in blue and white uniforms sprinted across the park where the protest had been held. Two carried a stretcher, and the live person was lifted away in a matter of seconds.

"Third attack this week," a nearby voice jolted Larken's awareness.

She turned slowly, hopefully gradually, as she tried to

identify the raspy voice's owner. The leader of the Siblings of the Natural Order stood looming over her, even while using two canes to support his decimated legs. She'd met him once before, in what seemed like a fever dream while she was recovering from the HPM blast.

"Shouldn't you be more discreet?" she asked, surprised to see him within city limits.

"Shouldn't you?"

She couldn't help smiling, though she felt guilty doing so. He shrugged his way forward, using both of his canes as leverage. Larken owed the man more than she could ever repay as Phineas Lancaster, leader of the Siblings of the Natural Order, an illegal pro-modeling terrorist organization, had helped save her brother's life when the still-somehow-legal Human Pride Movement had tried to take it. He had been the pillar of a modeling movement and was wanted by more than one state and federal agency.

"I'm just a college student," she said. "Nobody knows what I am. You kind of stand out."

He shrugged.

"Everyone knows who you are, and more than a few suspect what you are. I wanted to see for myself. This is the third time that one of HCC's protests has been attacked this week. Destroyed. Look."

Talking to Phineas was easy. They shared the bond of people who had been through a terrible tragedy, and that made him seem less like an inapproachable terrorist leader and more like someone who, if not a friend, could be one someday.

"Humanity in Crisis Council? This was their protest?"

He nodded.

"Ordell and his people put it together. This is the price

of nonviolence. I tried to tell him, but he wouldn't listen to me. My protests don't get attacked like this."

Probably true, and mainly because they were usually armed to the teeth with military-grade weapons when SNO marched. But Ordell, the gentle giant, and Lancaster's alter-ego, had quit SNO like Sam and turned his back on the violence Lancaster preached. At that moment, with Sam emotionally crippled in Larken's hotel room and bodies strewn over the alleyway, Larken knew which strategy she preferred.

Lancaster pointed to the park's far end, where a massive metal arm stuck out from the splinters of an ancient oak. "Look familiar?"

Larken stared at the arm, trying to place it. She didn't recognize the exact model but knew a mech arm when she saw one. She nodded.

"HPM?" she asked.

She met his eyes as they narrowed. Larken shuddered as he seemed to stare into her soul. His gaze sometimes put her on the defensive. Even if he didn't say it, his look at times had that question behind it, "Are you doing everything you can be to help your fellow models?"

"I thought they'd be high-tailing it back to Middle America once we blew up their headquarters. Looks like they're picking up again."

"Oh, they're here. No doubt they're here."

She explained to him that she'd seen flyers on the college campus. Then she told him about Sam, and his eyes grew hard and narrow. He thoughtfully put his hand to his chin and then dropped it to his crutch.

"Be careful, Larken," he advised. "You know how

dangerous they are. Today's disaffected students are tomorrow's violent extremists."

That was all he said. As he walked away into the concealment of the increasing darkness, Larken tried to interpret the look he'd given her after she'd told him about Sam. That unblinking stare and jaw muscles so tense that they could break steel. She thought she recognized herself in that look.

CHAPTER 17
PERFECT CUP

CLAYTON WILSON STOOD in a line for coffee in his latest quest to find the perfect cup. His former coworker, Dandelion, had asked him to check in on a friend of hers. That was strange in that Clayton up until that point had been reasonably sure that Dandelion had no friends. An uncomfortable situation with the police earlier that year had merged their personal lives together unexpectedly, but she wasn't exactly forthcoming with details about her personal life.

Since he no longer had a job and Dandelion did, he got to take on little side projects for her occasionally. Usually, these were similar tasks like checking on patients when she didn't have time, not unlike his current task. This was the first time she'd used the word friend, though.

Assigned task or not, the little coffee shop built onto the side of a building looked promising to Clayton that he might be able to find a tantalizing and unique cup of coffee there. Signs pointed to Clayton being right about that, as supported by the line extending out three people from the hole in the wall of a coffee place and then, after a hard right around a corner, about twenty people down the sidewalk. He took his place at the back of the line, smiling despite himself, imagining a latte in his future "made with the finest imported Arabica beans" as the sign said.

"Why would the SNO attack a pro-model protest?" a man before him in line said. Clayton couldn't quite make out the other person's response. He peered into the line, trying to identify who had said it. His eyes came across a man with a thick gray beard and small eyes tucked into their equally small sockets just above over-pronounced cheekbones. Clayton watched the man's lips move again and matched them to the words that floated free of the din.

"That doesn't make sense, though. You think Phineas Lancaster would kill his own supporters?"

The respondent was a woman with thick lips and heavy eyelids that seemed to only open halfway. She seemed almost bored in her response, and her words came out slow and deliberate-.

"The newscaster said that it's possible. That the models will use that to gain sympathy, and then use their new power to try to overturn the Madison Rule that keeps them enslaved. It's a false flag."

Clayton's ears burned hearing about the news coverage of the protest he'd intended to participate in. He knew that HPM would use violence and press to their advantage every single time. There was no doubt in his mind just listening to this exchange about what had happened. He clicked his teeth together, considering whether to take on the risk of correcting the person. He opted to duck his head down and pretend to be invisible. The line bumped up one person as someone near the front walked out with a mocha.

"What newscaster? That's ridiculous. There's no way."

"Emma Brown, Central News Dispatch. She said..."

At least it was only the fringe holo-channels, Clayton thought. Emma Brown had more viewers than possibly anyone else in media, so perhaps fringe wasn't quite the right word. Her company was universally known to be an entertainment company and not an actual news company. That didn't prevent millions of viewers from tuning in, especially to see her show in the late afternoons. As reason burned his relief away, he felt the growing urge to react build in his chest to the point of stifling him. A group of three left with their coffees. Clayton was down to five people only in front of him. He could just make out the name tag on the chest of the barista, Stephen, taking the next order.

"Oh, it's one of them," the man's voice whispered to the woman. Clayton looked more closely as heads interfered with his line of sight, examining the man taking orders. When his eyes fell on the barcode across a wrist that flashed outward when the man collected cash-coins from someone, he figured that the man he'd overheard was talking about the fact that their barista was a model. The man seemed to be making a casual comment, though the woman seemed nonplussed.

"What if he tries to poison us?"

"Really, Calista? You need to stop watching that drivel. There's not an underground plot for models to slowly kill off polli by spiking their coffees."

"Emma says—"

"Sheesh," the man commented, his tiny eyes darting upward and making brief, knowing contact with Clayton. The look the man gave was apologetic, as though he'd been having to apologize for the woman forever, and this was just one more so please forgive him for what she was saying. Clayton gave a half-smile and looked away. Another two people got their coffees and left, putting the man and woman at the counter. The woman wouldn't even look at Stephen, the barista.

"Two lattes," the man said. The woman elbowed him in the ribs. "Sorry, one regular and one caramel."

Stephen smiled an unwavering grin in spite of the fact that the woman not only ignored him but turned her back to him to make a point of ignoring him. The man likewise gave the same apologetic smile to the barista. Clayton wondered if he knew how little comfort a smile gave in a situation like that. He doubted the man was even concerned about the model's feelings. The man, as enlightened as he sounded, clearly hung out with model haters. He was probably one of those who liked models well enough to do work but secretly bought into the idea that models didn't even have feelings to be concerned about. That look—a little too practiced—was probably his get-out-of-jail card for those people around them who his friend managed to put off.

In other words, Clayton branded the man as a good, middling person. The feeling of overwhelming rage in his gut grew, and he desperately fought against the impulse to chastise them both. Had he not been informed by Dandelion that the police were after him now (for reasons that may have also involved his sincere dedication to reality, which also cost him his job), Clayton would not at all have hesitated to lay into both of them. That was one of the reasons he had almost as few friends as Dandelion. As it happened, few people wanted to be seen in public with someone who routinely excoriated strangers for their modeling views. Clayton didn't like to do it either, regardless of his efficacy at it. He'd far rather have wandered through life as an ignorant supplicant. But it wasn't in him, and that moment, trying to tamp down his fury was taking all of his willpower. Thankfully, Stephen was quick, and the couple stepped away with their lattes.

Three more people. Then two more. Then one more. Finally, Clayton was at the window. Stephen deposited the cash-coins into a reader. Stephen's eyes fell on Clayton, and just as Clayton was about to order a creamy, delicate cappuccino that he could practically taste, a woman jostled up to his shoulder. She was short with thick eyebrows and black hair and wore augmented vision goggles, clearly retro back a couple of centuries. She clearly thought the cane she used for support gave her bonus rights.

"Excuse me," she said, shoving her way into the "space" between him and the counter, which wasn't really a space at all until she wedged her body into it. Leveraging her cane against the ground, the woman had conjured up an impressive amount of force. Clayton's eyes searched out Stephen's, but Stephen was completely focused on the woman.

"You're not answering your phone," she stated. Stephen glared at her out of the side of his eye.

"Why would I answer the phone for you?"

Her quick glare shattered any expectation Clayton had that the woman would be hurt by the fact the barista's rebuke. She seemed spurred on, if anything. In a huff, she turned her fiery gaze on Clayton, and before he knew it, he found himself two steps back and bumping into the person in line behind him. She continued with her tirade, reverting from clear, aggravated annunciation to harsh whispers.

"Sam's been hurt," she said, her glare now (thankfully) returned to the original object of her hostility. Stephen's face blanched as he tamped espresso into the portafilter. Stephen pushed the button, but Clayton wasn't sure Stephen knew he was doing it. The portafilter began to bubble, and Clayton hoped against hope that his coffee would somehow take priority over whoever Sam was. The man had a job to do.

"Hurt?"

"Bad. You need to come to see."

"I'm working. And she wouldn't want to see me anyway. Isn't she still pissed that I didn't...," he looked around and leaned in close, "leave."

He said "leave" in such a way that Clayton could tell right away he wasn't talking about physical motion. The woman shook her head violently.

"Someone hurt her, Stephen. And I need someone to help. I'm...you know, useless with emotions."

"Excuse me," Clayton said, raising a hand for Stephen's attention as the espresso in the portafilter emitted the bitter smell that told Clayton his perfect coffee may be in jeopardy. The woman turned her furrowed eyebrows and tense, frowning jaw toward him. "I just...could you...?" He motioned to the portafilter.

Stephen wasn't listening.

"Who hurt her? Is she okay?"

The woman nodded.

"Physically, she'll recover. I got"—She looked around—"I got an old friend to see to her. That's not the problem."

Clayton saw the muscles in Stephen's neck seem to relax.

"Then did she ask for me?" Stephen asked, reaching absently for the portafilter that Clayton knew contained burned coffee and working it loose.

"Not exactly."

"Excuse me," Clayton said again, pushing forward toward the woman. "Can you..."

"What?" Both Stephen and the woman shot a stabbing glance at him, but before he could complain, went back to their conversation.

"Okay," Stephen said.

Clayton noticed the barista's left hand moving toward the milk carafe. Even burned coffee would have been better than nothing, at this point. But the man's hand hesitated, and Stephen turned his gaze to the crowd, pursing his eyebrows. He gave a weak smile.

"Sorry, folks, we're out. Ran out early today. You know, rationing."

Grumbles went through the crowd. Someone in the back made a comment about the coffee shop having been open longer the day before. Clayton watched the milk carafe slowly settle back onto the counter. He felt a lump well up in the back of his throat. Whoever Sam was, Clayton really hoped she was somebody important. He waited three more seconds until the man pulled down a flat metal screen and people behind Clayton in line trickled back to where they came from. One cast an obligatory "fucking shill!" back at Stephen, who didn't seem to hear him.

"Give me a minute to pack up. Then we can go," Stephen said to the woman. Stephen then dumped the burned espresso into the tray and then flashed an apologetic smile at Clayton.

"Sorry, sir, we're out of espresso. Rations," he said, shrugging, as though Clayton couldn't see half a bag of espresso beans from where he stood.

"I'll take an espresso," Clayton said, motioning to the drip cup shot glass that had already been filled.

"Sure, buddy," Stephen said and dumped the contents into a thin cardboard cup before sliding it across to Clayton.

In seconds, he was on his way to the H Hotel. One sip and he threw the coffee into the nearest trash can. Burned beyond all recognition. He shook his head, shoved his hands in his pockets, and kept walking.

CHAPTER 18
LIKE COMING HOME

CLAYTON WAITED in the hallway and double-checked the room number again. Then, he thought back to what Dandelion had said about having double-shifts and not being able to cover them. It had been his fault, he supposed. The anti-modeling protest hadn't exactly required him to show up and help lead a counter-protest. And even if a counter-protest was necessary, he didn't necessarily have to be there, or punch the asshole in the face who'd made the comment about shills being only good as punching bags. And when they'd retaliated, he certainly could have left instead of fight them in the streets until the police showed up.

But he'd done all of that. And the end result had been that his face had shown up on the news, and his boss, as it happened, didn't share his exact views on the topic. Clayton was now jobless, and Dandelion was right that he didn't have anything better to do. So, since she'd gotten slammed covering all of his former shifts, it was only right that he swing by and check on her friend Larken. So he screwed up his courage and tapped at the door three times. Then twice more.

It took about five minutes for him to realize that nobody was coming to the door. But he had to check, so he took a breath, and knocked one more time. Beyond, someone shuffled very slowly toward the door, or so he thought he heard. Only when a timid voice penetrated the wood did he finally fully believe there was someone there.

"W...what do you want?" came the voice. It was a woman's voice, thin and willowy like it might blow away in the wake of a passing volantrae.

"I'm a friend of Dandelion's," he said. "My name is Clayton, and I'm a Pisces."

Clayton smiled when he said it, hoping that the smile would come through in his voice. A second passed, then another, and he heard the door move.

What he saw on the other side of the door was terror. The woman seemed about his age if he had to guess. He was twenty-two, and aside from the exhaustion, she seemed close to that, too. She was one big ball of tension, with her arms wrapped around her body, squeezing together so tightly that they might split her body right in half. Her nostrils flared and sweat beaded on her forehead.

"Are you okay?" he asked then realized the implication was that she didn't look okay. "Sorry. I mean, are you Larken? Dandelion said—"

"You don't know who I am?"

He shook his head.

"And you don't know what Larken looks like either," she said. "No, I'm not."

"You're not okay, or—"

"Neither," she said, and turned to walk away from him. Each step looked as though she had to fight for it and pull it out from under her. She wore sweats, and her muscles outlined against them when she stopped and the sweats didn't. Her hair flared out around her head, and she didn't seem to even notice. Definitely not okay. Fortunately for her, Clayton was trained in not-okay and had worked in not-okay for many years. Perhaps she wasn't Larken, but she was someone in need.

"What's your name?" he asked, not crossing the threshold of the door yet. She was scared of something, and he wasn't going to invade her home. She slowed to a stop and then turned to face him.

Her eyes caught him off guard. Deep blue irises ringed in black stared back at him from glassy eyes. They were hawk-like eyes, or would have been, except for the timidity of the rest of her stance. Her arms were still wrapped around her like a protective ward fending off some sort of malignant force, and her bottom lip quivered, shaking an obsidian ring that had smeared with white flecks of dried saliva against full, naked, pink lips. The woman's thick eyebrows rose up and around her eyes, while dark tan pouches beneath her eyes betrayed how tired she must have been. She gulped once and then her lips parted a centimeter revealing the very dim outlines of two perfect front teeth. He found that he couldn't breathe, suddenly, and was glad that he'd been the last to ask a question. All he had to do was stand and await her response.

"Larken will be back soon," she muttered as she crossed in front of the couch. From her trajectory, he could tell she made her way to a bedroom in the back, and in a few minutes, Clayton would find himself alone.

"Wait," he said, before she disappeared, still standing in the hallway. He took a tiny step backward and something crunched beneath his heel. Distracted for a fraction of a second, he glanced downward to see what looked like a pen jutting out from under his foot. He scrunched his eyes at it. That's exactly what it was. A pen that someone had dropped. Clayton kicked it to the side. A click sounded from inside the apartment and when he glanced up again, the woman was gone.

Clayton scratched his head. There seemed little point in banishing himself to the hallway, so he finally crossed the threshold and entered the room.

"Anyone in here?" he asked, as though he didn't already know. That didn't draw the woman back from out of her hiding place. His eyes fell onto a counter that looked as though it hadn't been cleaned within the last century. Three coffee cups adorned the counter, which, given his conspic-uous lack of coffee, intrigued him. Clayton crossed the padded carpet to examine the cups. Two held something that might have been coffee, and the third held coffee that if he wasn't mistaken had a mint edge to it. This brought a smile to his lips. Not the coffee—because it was gross. But these cups contained coffee that had actually been brewed instead of replicated.

He crossed over into the kitchen looked in the cabinets near the coffee, seeking out the source. Nothing there. He looked over the refrigerator, and still didn't see where the coffee was. Clayton bit his lip for just a second, then made his way to the bedroom door where he suspected the woman had gone. There, he knocked twice against it.

Then he knocked again.

Midway through the third knock, the door opened. The

same glassy, distant, and entrancing eyes stared back at him through the crack.

"Sorry to bother you. I was looking for the coffee?" he asked.

"Replicator is in the kitchen," she said, then began to shut the door but stopped when he cleared his throat.

"I really don't want to drink replicated coffee," he said. "It's disgusting and tastes like iron."

She cocked her head at this, and he thought he might have seen a hint of a smile for the first time since he saw the woman.

"Samantha," she said. "People call me Sam."

"I'm still Clayton," he replied, by way of a joke that she didn't seem to get.

"You take your coffee seriously, I see," she said. "You really do know Larken. I think there's some under the sink, but the brew pot probably hasn't been washed in a while."

"Let me guess. It's...somewhere under that," he said, twisting about halfway and pointing to the mound of dishes.

"Yeah," she said and blinked. Then she wiped a hand across her eye, and he was sure a tear glistened on the end of one knuckle.

"You're not all right, are you?" he asked. Sam's lip quivered for the second time, and she sniffed once as he watched.

"No," she said, then pushed past him. "I'll live. Come."

"There was some under here," she said as she pulled open a cabinet beneath the crowded sink, exposing cleaning supplies and a discretely placed trash bin. "I guess we're out. Replicated coffee isn't that bad if you use the right codes."

"Oh, it's terrible," Clayton assured her. His continued protest seemed to entertain her. He stared at her half-smile for too long and she noticed.

"Most of my friends won't argue with me right now," she said. "It's nice to have someone around who'll complain to me about coffee."

"I'm great at complaining about a whole load of things," Clayton assured her. "Coffee just happens to be my specialty. I'm telling you, replicated coffee tastes like iron. Every time."

Sam punched some numbers into the replicator.

"We'll see. Try this one," she said. Thirty seconds later she handed him a cup of steaming hot...tripe. It smelled terrible. He lifted it to his lips, took a sip, and nearly gagged.

"This is a good one?"

She laughed. She actually laughed.

"Just testing you. No, this is the good one," she said. While they waited for the thirty seconds to pass, he tried to make conversation.

"Sam, are you okay? I mean...I don't know you. Maybe you're always this way, but you seem kind of sullen to me. Do you want to talk about it?"

"I've been talking about it for days, Clayton. What I really want right now is to prove to you that this coffee is semi-decent."

Sam seemed to wince as she bent to pull the coffee from the replicator. And it wasn't Clayton's imagination that the puffiness in her face was due to more than just bad sleep. She'd been through something, and Clayton's masters in social work told him that the something that she'd been through had been pretty fucking bad. He watched her reach for the coffee and thought he saw something black across her wrist. He stared as she fumbled with the mugs. It was a barcode. It was undeniable. Sam was a model, but she didn't act like any model that Clayton had ever met. It surprised him so much that he blurted it out despite his better judgment.

"You're a model?"

Sam ignored him. He hadn't considered that Larken, Dandelion's latest passion project, might own another human being. The muscles in his neck tensed, and he drew his mouth into a line and forced air through his nose so he could keep breathing.

"So Larken's one of those," he said, muttering the words more to himself than to Sam. After all, what could she do about it. It was only an observation.

"What? Larken?"

"Your owner."

"I don't have an owner," Sam said, but she didn't say it with conviction. "I don't even own myself."

"Why are you here, then?" he asked.

"Why are you here?" she retorted then thrust the coffee toward him so hard that some sloshed out onto the carpet. Neither she nor Clayton bothered to try to clean it up. "Enjoy your coffee."

"I didn't mean anything," he said, backtracking as quickly as he could. Training told him to remain dispassionate and ignore the words that would come next. Whatever pain she wasn't sharing would force its way out in other ways.

"You can't take it back," she told him. "You can't take it back any more than I can change what I am."

"Then what do we do?" he asked.

"Sip the coffee," she said, pulling her cup to her lips at the same time. She blew across it, puckering her thick lips over the edge and forming ripples in the blackness. "Then tell me how right I am."

She wasn't right. He sipped the coffee too quickly, for starters, and burned the tip of his tongue. But past that, there was still the ever-present flavor of what Clayton imagined rusty nails tasted like. Fainter than the other cup, but it was there. His lips pursed on their own. She stared at him.

"You are a priss, aren't you?"

"Wha...no. I just like good coffee. This tastes like someone made coffee in an actual brew pot, then dropped the entire brew pot into a blender and poured the remains into a ceramic mug."

"That's a very...specific...description, Clayton," she commented, with a smile forming underneath one bruised eye. "Would you say you've tasted a lot of blended metals?"

She was smiling for the moment. Good. That was something positive out of this whole exchange. Whatever it was that had happened, and that she hadn't wanted to share, at least she was present enough, and mentally well enough, to catch a little humor on the side.

Her smile faltered. The damn thing was fickle. He wracked his brain on how to bring it back. It turned out that he didn't have to do too terribly much because about that time he absently sloshed scalding coffee on his hand and yelped loudly. This made Sam elicit a full-on giggle.

"Wait, you have to try this one," she said, as she returned to the replicator. "If you want to be truly disgusted..."

Four or five different coffees later, and he found that she could keep a smile for about five minutes at the longest. Clayton aimed to stretch that out, but his training was really more targeted for helping aging polli deal with the fact that they were dying—a job which had become noticeably more difficult because now all everyone wanted to talk about was the Immortality Program that very few actual polli could afford. No, he didn't miss the job, now that he thought back on it.

After the fifth cup, she suddenly grew very serious.

"Clayton, I haven't laughed this much in a month," she said to him on the heels of a giggle when she nearly sprayed coffee all over him. "I wish we'd met under better circumstances. I'm kind of going through a lot right now."

She wanted to talk. He could tell she wanted to talk, and she wanted to talk to him. Which was strange. Usually, people were doing their best to avoid talking to him, with the exception of his patients, who were pretty much forced to. Then he noticed something. He noticed how absolutely comfortable it was for them to sit there and joke. It seemed to him as though he'd known her before and knew who she was. It wasn't like he knew her life story, rather as though he felt that anyone could bring an example from her childhood, and he'd know if it was true or not because he knew her, at the core of her. Clayton had never felt that way before. And when she opened her mouth and let out the lengthy story about a vicious assault on someone who'd already been through so much, he marveled at the trust she'd placed in him.

The story left him nonplussed. He expressed sympathy, and then she moved on. It was as though now that she'd finished telling him, the story was over, and it was time to get back to tasting the replicators' finest. Not much more than a second passed, and she'd already punched in numbers for the next cups.

At first, he found himself a little offended that she moved on so quickly. He had nearly a thousand questions to ask. Then he realized that it was her story, not his, as his training had made him well aware. And so, when she moved on, he moved on, and the goal of the afternoon changed from her trying to prove him wrong, to them searching coffee codes in the replicator for the absolute worst cup they could find.

CHAPTER 19
SOULMATES

WHEN LARKEN RE-ENTERED her and Sam's hotel room with Stephen in tow, she wasn't prepared for what she saw. At the kitchen counter, the rude man she'd butted in front of in the line at the coffee shop—in her defense, to get Stephen—sat at the kitchen counter on a stool. Four different coffee cups sat before him, and the entire room smelled like a café.

"Try this one," Sam said, pushing another cup across to him. The man lifted it, sniffed it, and took a quick sip before spitting it back into the cup.

Stephen pushed past Larken, who didn't budge an inch. Instead, she simply watched the peace of the moment.

"Coppery," he said. "I'm telling you. It can't be done. If you want the perfect cup of coffee, it has to be naturally roasted. Replicators don't do it justice."

"Exactly," Sam said, not seeming to have noticed Larken enter the room yet. "These all taste the same to me."

Stephen seemed to register the moment as he stalled in his forward momentum so abruptly that his lengthy red overcoat flung its tails out in front of him. Stephen turned back toward Larken.

"I thought you said she wouldn't leave her bed. She seems fine to me."

Larken looked closer at Sam. Her movements were still jerky like she was working around the pain. Larken slid over, using her cane to support her movement, and performed her own wobbly walk toward the counter where the two talked. Larken knew about pain and its effect on body movements. She lived with it too, but not as convincingly as Sam, who'd also seen fit to dab on some makeup and cover the worst of her facial bruising. And was she smiling? It was a fleeting thing, but Larken was certain she saw a smile and possibly a giggle after the man spit out the next coffee attempt.

Stephen cleared his throat. Two sets of eyes turned toward them and a moment of recognition came over the strange man. Sam looked back and forth between the man and Larken and Stephen. When she saw Stephen, her lips immediately curled up into an unquestionable smile.

"Stephen. Larken. This is Clayton. He's a friend of Dandelion's."

"Have we met before?" Larken asked.

"You're Dandelion's friend Larken? And Stephen, the barista?"

"That guy," Stephen groaned.

Larken pulled herself up on her cane, blinked, and bit her lip before asking, "What are you doing here, Clayton?"

Larken heard footsteps approach from behind. She turned quickly, and with stability, having finally mastered the art of pivoting with a cane. Dandelion appeared in the doorway.

"He's with me," Dandelion said.

"But why is he here?" Larken asked, scrutinizing Clayton, whose hair was puffed up into something like a halo around his head. He seemed the nervous type with his wide eyes not focusing on any one thing, taking the whole room in at once. Clayton was obviously overwhelmed.

"I asked him to come here to check on you," Dandelion said. "I didn't think I'd be able to make it, and it's been a long time since I've been able to come by."

Sam looked at Dandelion with her eyebrows popped into a tent. It came down, Larken supposed, to Sam. She'd smiled. Anyone who could do that for her, she would have to tolerate at least a little while. Larken nodded to Sam and gave her a thin grin. Sam's smile widened, and she clutched her hands together in front of her chest. Larken looked twice at that gesture, as it was more feminine than she'd ever seen of Sam, with her tattoos and piercings. Sam's eyes kept rounding over to Clayton.

A tune emerged from the talking and busy chatter, floating over everything like a veiled threat. Sam's face went ashen white. Larken recognized the tune right away as the same children's song that she'd heard when she exited the bus to make her way back home. Only instead of the secretive man hugging shadows, it was Clayton whistling it. Sam backed away from Clayton, who didn't seem to notice the silence that fell over the room. As he did finally catch on, his whistle stammered to an abrupt end.

"Sorry, what?"

"That tune," Sam said. "Where did you hear it?"

"I...I don't know. It's been in my head. I think...I think downtown by the coffee shop? Someone in the line was whistling it or humming it or something. Catchy. Do you know what it is?"

"'Light's Night Brigade,'" Dandelion said. "It's a nursery rhyme that was popular just before Equilibrium. It's about a man, Colonel Light, who's trapped under a building for forty days. On the forty-first day, the colonel split his army in half into two platoons. One group he ordered to hide throughout the complex. The other, he surrendered to the invaders, who waste no time in summarily executing them on the spot. As they do, the hidden half of his group sniped them from the shadows. There were so many deaths that day and over the next several days when the enemy tried to take ownership of the facility that reports were that there was an entire brigade of men in the compound still."

Dandelion stopped talking. Larken watched her gaze float around the room, meeting first Larken's, then everyone else's eyes. If it hadn't been for the fact that Dandelion was an android, Larken might have believed that Dandelion was becoming self-conscious about telling the story. Dandelion swallowed, an unusual and pointless behavioral feature. Then she continued.

"The enemy eventually were able to take the compound, but only after nearly eighty more days of fighting and hundreds of deaths. What the enemy thought was a brigade was only about thirty men, and they got the name from that. 'Light's Night Brigade.'"

"Kind of a lot for a children's song," Stephen murmured. Sam said nothing.

"You've clearly never listened to the lyrics in children's songs," Dandelion said. Larken would have smirked had it not been for the look of terror on Sam's face.

"Sam, are you okay?" Larken asked.

Through gritted teeth and eyes that seemed overfilled

with tears, Sam responded, "That's the song one of them sang."

Larken didn't ask her any more questions. She knew the song, not all the background that apparently Nurse Dandelion knew, but she'd heard the tune in her childhood she'd realized when Dandelion identified it. Same tune, three different incidents in the last couple of weeks. It couldn't be a coincidence.

"Human Pride Movement," she said, filling the silence. "Has to be."

"What about them?"

"I heard someone whistling that at the bus incident. And he was Human Pride Movement, I'm pretty sure. One of them, anyway."

"You're thinking HPM attacked Sam?" Clayton asked. Larken didn't acknowledge his question. She still didn't fully trust him. Instead, she addressed Sam.

"I think HPM are behind the protest attack on the bus."

"And the people who attacked me," Sam said, her voice inflecting to nearly breaking but stopping just short.

At her words, Dandelion's eyes slid over to Sam. Larken noticed and also noticed that her eyes lingered on her face for a second, then down to her abdomen. Larken cleared her throat to get Dandelion's attention before her actions were noticed by anyone else. The move worked as Dandelion shifted her view over to Larken. Larken mouthed the words "be careful" to Dandelion, who nodded her head slowly to confirm. Good. At least they wouldn't have to get into a conversation about the rest of what had happened to Sam in front of so many sets of ears.

"I want to walk that neighborhood where I first heard it," Larken said. "I think whoever it is must have a place or stay downtown. If they have a habit of humming that song, then we might get lucky."

Right. There was next to no chance, but doing something was better than doing nothing. And...if Larken went to investigate, then Sam got more alone time with Clayton, and maybe, just possibly, could do more smiling.

"I'll come," Sam volunteered, ruining that part of Larken's scheme. Larken shook her head, only to have Sam frown at her.

"I'm coming," Sam said again. "That's what's happening. You may hear someone singing the tune, but you won't know if it's the person who attacked me."

"I can come," Clayton also volunteered. "I might be able to help."

"That's not a plan," Stephen said, dismissing the idea before it even started. He had a habit of doing that, which was one of the reasons that Larken tried to avoid him. "Randomly walking the streets? That's a waste of time."

"What did you have in mind, Steve?" Larken asked. She always called him Steve when he pissed her off. His silence told her all she needed to know.

"I'm not coming," Dandelion volunteered, though nobody asked. "I'm a nurse. This isn't a thing I do."

"You don't have to, Dandelion," Larken said gently.

Sam paced as soon as the possibility had been mentioned that they go to find her attackers. Larken thought it through. First, as much as she hated to admit it, Stephen was right. They needed more information. Right now, all they had to go on was a nursery rhyme, and unless everyone in the HPM was required to hum that nursery rhyme wherever they went, then using that as a tool was pretty farfetched to yield results.

"Sam, I have some questions, now that you're talking again."

Sam's face still lacked color. Beads of perspiration stood out against her forehead. As she yanked her head around to catch Larken in her gaze, one of the beads broke free and traced a line down to her cheek.

"Wh...what questions?"

"Maybe in private?"

"Can I join?" Clayton asked. "Maybe if we keep comparing notes—"

"That's up to Sam," Larken said then turned to Sam. "What do you think? There are going to be some personal questions. I'm sorry."

"You think they're your army, don't you? The ones you hallucinated about who are going to destroy the world?" The question came from Stephen, who'd crossed his arms in a challenge.

"It doesn't matter what I think," Larken replied. "The police aren't going to even bother with an investigation on behalf of a bunch of shills. If we want anything that resembles justice, we will have to find it ourselves."

"Clayton can come," Sam said. Her smile had completely disappeared, but Larken could tell that she'd come to trust Clayton somehow, even if Larken thought he was a complete moron. But he wasn't wrong in that if they compared notes, they might uncover something useful, so she kept her opinions to herself and proceeded back toward Sam's room.

The door closed behind Clayton. Sam took her spot on the bed again, this time folding her legs beneath her. That move gave both Larken and Clayton room to sit. Clayton irritated Larken by taking the spot between her and Sam, for which transgression Larken shot him a quick glare that he either didn't see or didn't realize was directed at him.

"Sam," Larken began. "Can you walk me through what happened?"

Sam took a deep breath. Her eyes had teared up again, and Larken felt a guilty lump form in her throat for even asking the question.

"I wasn't doing anything, Larken. That's what doesn't make sense. I wasn't doing anything at all. Walking. Going to volunteer in the food kitchen. You know where I work, down on Third and Seneca at the truck. Cook for the busy season."

Larken hadn't known, but she pretended she had. That explained a lot about Sam's mysterious absences.

"I was a block away, about to turn the corner, when the whistling came from somewhere behind me. That same nursery rhyme—you know, what Dandelion was talking about."

"How many people?"

"Two. Maybe three. I mean, only two attacked me, but I thought there might have been someone in the shadows who I couldn't see. One of the men grabbed my arms. The other shoved my head in a bag. I don't know what they looked like, Larken. I only saw chins from under the bag. I was too afraid."

"I saw two men," Clayton said. "At the protest, I mean."

"Good for you," Larken replied, cutting the end of her words short. He seemed to take the hint. Clayton closed his mouth again. Sam had already been distracted though and stared at him. When Larken had agreed to compare notes, she hadn't considered that Clayton would interrupt her every few minutes.

"Was one of them taller, like almost half a foot taller than me?" Clayton asked, continuing undeterred.

"I think so. I heard the whistling and then the attack happened. I remember now it was two men. Not three."

That memory must have been painful. Sam went quiet. But when she opened her mouth to speak again, she faced Larken, but her eyes kept darting back to Clayton. Her voice dropped into a whisper.

"There were two. The tall one—the whistler—he held me while the other one tied me up."

"In the middle of the street?" asked Clayton.

Larken kicked him mercilessly in the shin. He winced but didn't retract his question. Sam didn't say anything for five full seconds.

"No," she admitted. "Not there. They must have moved me somewhere." Sam's eyebrows went up into a furrow again. Her eyes glistened. "I don't remember," she said. "We were inside, but I can't...remember how we got there."

"Maybe we need to try something different," Larken suggested. "If it was a crime of opportunity, then we might get lucky. I have an idea."

CHAPTER 20
SIMPLE IDEA

LARKEN'S IDEA WAS SIMPLE, retrace steps. She filled the others in on the plan when the three of them exited the bedroom again, leaving out any details about Sam's attack.

"It might help to try taking us on your walk from the other day."

Sam didn't acknowledge that Larken said anything. For a second, Larken was afraid that Sam had decided to clam up again. If she did that, then they wouldn't be able to search. Sam was the only one who knew the route she had taken. Even if Sam couldn't exactly remember everything yet, if they physically left the apartment, things might come to her. But without Sam, they didn't have a place to start.

"I don't want to," Sam said. She shook her head, leaving her auburn hair to sway back and forth and her irises to dart around helplessly. "I changed my mind."

Larken took in the room. Sam fidgeted on her stool near the kitchen counter, while Clayton hovered close by. Whatever time they'd spent together alone had seemed to bond them in some way. He seemed ready to pounce on anyone who might bother Sam. Stephen stood at the end of the counter and kept glancing at Sam but couldn't seem to keep his attention on her. Or, Larken thought, maybe he struggled still from their last falling out. Larken hadn't exactly been the most cordial when they'd first met, but again, she also hadn't expected him to stick around as long as he had—or for Sam to be okay with him doing so. All sorts of unexpected things seemed to be happening at once, not the least of which was Dandelion, doing her Dandelion thing.

Dandelion oscillated between full engagement in the conversation to strange mannerisms that actual humans and even models didn't have. Moments of staring off into space and those weird little one-second pauses where she stood absolutely, completely still. That was something that Larken was sure Dandelion didn't know about herself. Probably in her positronic mind, there were a million things that captured her attention during those moments. Larken made a mental note to ask.

It struck her that everyone looked so young compared to her, and she was the youngest in the room. The damage to her body had aged her by at least ten years. Larken knew she carried perpetual bags under her eyes from the painful half-sleep that was all she was afforded. But even she still would have appeared, to the untrained eye, to be a graduate student. In fact, if not for the subject matter, then they looked like a group of college students gathering before going out to brunch. Larken could see them in her mind clustered in the Faux Gras restaurant, sipping on mimosas and absinthe-based fairy bombs.

What they didn't look like, even remotely, was a group of hardened and wizened investigators or crime fighters. If the entire group went out together chatting it up while trying to find the bad guys, there was no chance they would actually accomplish anything.

"You should stay," Larken said, making eye contact with Sam. After all, that was her original plan anyway. And her revenge plot didn't trump Sam's emotional recovery. "If you can get me started, I can follow. You don't have to be exact. Just tell me where you started your walk."

"Here," Sam said. "You'd just left for the meeting, remember? We had that argument, and I wasn't going to go."

Larken had forgotten about the argument. There wasn't anything special about the fight. It was only one of many fights that they'd eventually have gotten around to making up. Larken couldn't even remember what they'd been fighting about. She nodded in somber confirmation. This little act seemed to give Sam more strength.

"I went down to the bakery and had three sticky buns."

The thought of those sticky buns made Larken's stomach grumble. At first it was a low sound, and she was sure she was the only one who heard it. Then it went into overdrive and practically shouted her hunger to the entire room full of people. By the sympathetic stares, Larken gathered that she wasn't the only one who hadn't been eating regularly since Sam's attack.

"I could eat," said Clayton, flashing a toothy grin that seemed to infect Sam first, then even Stephen quit wrapping his knuckles absently on the kitchen countertop.

"Me too," Stephen said. "Anybody have money?"

"I do," said Dandelion nonchalantly. "Lots. Where?"

"I'll pay," Larken said, staring at Dandelion. "It's not fair for you to pay. You barely eat."

But then Larken remembered her trust fund and how

most of it had been stolen away. One morning out she could do though, she figured, just this one time.

"I eat," Dandelion responded, narrowing her eyes and nodding her head. "I eat all the time."

"Of course," Larken said, sparing a glance for Clayton. Whatever designs Dandelion had on him, if she didn't move soon, Clayton wouldn't be a concern for her anymore. He was obviously orbiting Sam. Larken looked at Dandelion, just staring for a few seconds, then shook her head. She was mulling over giving relationship advice to a robot. She really needed food.

Half an hour later, the group were in transit to Big Pete's chain restaurant, an imitation diner that only served burgers, fries, and milkshakes. The first few minutes passed in guarded silence until Clayton's apparent inability to stay quiet manifested itself again.

"We might as well punch numbers into the replicator," he said. "I've eaten at Big Pete's before, and it's all synthetic."

"Maybe, but it's commercial-quality proteins instead of consumer brand," Sam responded.

"Besides, you were outvoted. What kind of dining out experience is it to eat in the same hotel you have a room in? That's not going out," retorted Larken.

"But the H Hotel uses almost fifty percent actual ingredients," Clayton protested.

Larken couldn't help a smile. Something about Clayton's perspective of the world—his "we can always do better" mentality—was beginning to grow on her. His complaints had seemed slightly less hostile and more explanatory in her mind. Even while she argued, she kept smiling. It also helped that Sam seemed lighter around him, like whatever weight had pressed her into her blankets recently was now shared by

Clayton. Sam still looked occasionally like she might burst into tears. Larken didn't miss the fleeting moments of sobriety that crossed Sam's face occasionally. However, Sam didn't cry. And she'd left the apartment to go out to eat.

The smell of burning fat caught Larken's attention.

"I thought you said all their food was synth," Larken said.

"They synthesize the ingredients, not the food," Clayton said.

"So would you say it's different than we would do using the hotel replicator?"

"Only because none of us can cook," he admitted. "But you can still taste it in the food, can't you?"

"Clayton, why are you such a food snob?" This admonishment came from Stephen, behind Larken and to the left. She'd forgotten he was back there and jumped a little at his words.

Walking directly behind Larken, Dandelion said, "Clayton comes from money."

If the look that Clayton shot her then were a projectile, it would have been a proton energy blast. It jarred Clayton, as until that point, Clayton had been jovial for even the worst parts of the morning. But it was definitely a scowl that he wore.

"What?" Larken asked, which seemed to prompt him to get his face under control. Larken watched his shoulders raise and fall in a sigh.

"I don't come from money," he said. "I mean, I did. Probably when I first met Dandelion, I did. When I was going to medical school..."

His glance danced toward Dandelion and back to Larken. Sam seemed to edge closer to him.

"I gave all that up when I became a social activist. Let's

say my parents were less than understanding about not wanting to be a doctor anymore. But how can I be a doctor, when so many people—models—are being slaughtered every day with less thought than one would use to crush an ant?"

Larken didn't imagine it. Clayton's cheery demeanor had all but evaporated. Sam snaked her arm around Clayton's, and when she did, Clayton was suddenly back—cheery again.

"But that's a long story and a boring one. I much prefer to talk about food."

"We know," Larken said, rolling her eyes. She bit her lip and leaned heavily on her cane to relieve the pressure on her left leg. Too much walking the last few days. She'd need to sit soon, so it was a relief when she saw the massive sign with a huge dog across it that read Big Pete's Diner.

They didn't just eat. They went to brunch, which basically meant breakfast with booze.

"So that's a mimosa. Delicious! No wonder people like them," Dandelion said. She was already three in and didn't seem impacted in the least. That wasn't a surprise to Larken, since Dandelion couldn't actually process alcohol more than anything else she imbibed. But she certainly seemed to enjoy the flavor—perhaps a little too much. Clayton and Stephen both sent startled glances at Larken when Dandelion raised her hand for a fourth.

"Dandelion, should you maybe have some water?" Larken suggested. Only after she said it did she realize how stupid a question it was. At least, it worked to get Dandelion's attention. Larken met Dandelion's eyes and arched her eyebrows quickly, coupling that with a glance toward Clayton. She was still uncertain why she cared, but Larken had emotionally invested at some point in Clayton and Sam becoming a couple. Maybe it was the romantic notion of love overcoming the AI/human divide? She couldn't be sure, but she recognized an undeniable bias against Clayton as a match for Sam, despite the fact that Sam practically sat on Clayton's lap. They'd been sickeningly finishing each other's sentences as though they'd known each other for longer than a few hours. Larken admitted to herself that it might be too late, but she warned Dandelion anyway with her eyes. Humans can't drink that much that fast, she hoped her facial features portrayed. When Dandelion lowered her hand, Larken figured out that she'd gotten the message across.

Then, they all heard it. Sam's face washed out of color in less than a second as the whistled tune floated over the restaurant's din. Larken, Stephen, and Dandelion turned at the same time to see the origin of the tune. A tall, slender man in a pressed suit passed by them, completely uninterested in their gathering. Instead, he seemed to be watching the building beside him, waiting for something, though she could see that the building as locked up tight. Whatever it was he sought, she couldn't see a sign for it. He stopped for a second in front of the thick glass, and she watched as he pulled a comb from his pocket and carefully pulled his hair backward with it. Her eyes slipped to the glass on the building and locked in with his.

He was watching them, but trying to be secretive about it and blowing it all with that whistle. The man's eyes shifted to Larken's right, no longer seeming to focus on her alone, but now on the waiter behind her. Larken turned to see and noticed that a volantrae lowered itself to street level past the waiter. The seagull doors opened on both sides, and similarly dressed men stepped out. Larken forced her head to turn away from the man's reflection. She motioned to the others to do the same, holding her hands palms-down over the tabletop. Larken had to knock softly twice against the tablecloth to recapture Sam's attention, but even she turned her focus back to the group.

"I don't think he was looking at us," Larken said, careful to make eye contact with Sam and drive the point home with a stiff nod. "It wouldn't make sense. I think he was only watching for his companions to show up."

"Th...that man," Sam said, color only beginning to return to her face.

A shuffling sound threatened to pull Larken's attention back to the man, but that would only be a mistake. The longer they looked like something other than college students out for the evening, the longer the three of them would stick out and be noticed. Larken wanted to watch the men without being watched back.

"Is that one of them?" Larken whispered, using her eyes to indicate the direction. Sam gulped but said nothing.

Clayton responded, even though Larken hadn't asked him.

"Yes," Clayton said. "That's one of the men I saw at the protest just before the fighting started."

Stephen wore a smile that stopped short of his eyes.

"Did you think it would be this easy?"

Larken shook her head. She'd anticipated at least a week if not more of aimless searching and then winding up empty-handed and frustrated.

"No," she replied. "Not at all. Though I'm not sure how easy this is."

The group was still largely silent, and Larken knew that their silence would attract the attention she desperately wanted to avoid.

"A pirate walks into a bar," Dandelion said, breaking the silence and the direction of what little conversation there was. "He has a ship's wheel in his pants. The bartender says, 'Hey, you have a ship's wheel in your pants'. The pirate replies, 'Aye, it's driving me nuts.'"

The silence lasted for another second before Stephen let out a sound that was a cross between a giggle and a laugh through his smirking lips.

"That was the single worst joke I've ever heard," Clayton said, staring at Dandelion's deadpan expression as though expecting a redeeming punchline. Dandelion's face contorted into what seemed like a grimace to Larken.

"I was trying to distract us," she said. "We were all getting conspicuous."

Exactly what Larken had been thinking. She nodded with a massive smile pasted across her face.

"It was perfect, Dandelion."

"Maybe not exactly perfect," Sam said, though Larken could tell by her more relaxed feature and the actual pinkish skin that replaced Sam's earlier blanched expression that the joke had done what it was meant to, regardless of the quality.

"Good enough," Larken said. "Now, we need a plan."

A waiter walked by the table, dropping another mimosa in front of Dandelion, apparently having seen her raise her hand but not lower it—or working toward a higher tip. Then Larken stole a glance back toward where the volantrae had landed. The men had gone, and from the receding echo of the man's whistle, he was leaving, too. She looked back toward the glass window, but the man had left.

Frantic, she searched the crowd, seeking him out. Just as she was about to give up, she thought she saw the edge of one of his plain brown shoes cross the threshold to a storefront with "The Moldy Pig" in large gothic letters across the front.

"There," she said, pointing with in the direction with her hand flat against the table's surface so that no passersby could see. "He went in there, I think."

"Did anybody get a picture?"

Dandelion made a sound that reminded Larken of a dying cat, albeit several orders of magnitude weaker in volume. Larken turned to catch Dandelion's eye and slight tilt to her head. Dandelion had taken an image, now stored somewhere in that android brain. Larken flashed a quick smile and changed subject.

"Back to the room?"

"What for? Let's go over there," Stephen said, "before they get away." His angry eyes stared through Larken toward the storefront. She shook her head.

"There is only a handful of us. Who knows how many more of them are inside, and we're not fighters."

"I only saw three of them," he said.

"Outside, sure. But that could be their headquarters."

"Looks more like a jazz club," said Stephen.

"But it could be their headquarters. Could be an army in there. I say we head back to the room, do a little digging on the Moldy Pig, run a picture of the guy through image recognition, and see what we can find."

"I...I want to go home," Sam said. Sam's face seemed closer to normal, but Larken could see Sam's white knuckles clinging to Clayton's chestnut-colored fingers from her vantage point.

"We will go back," Larken acknowledged, ignoring Stephen's protest.

———

The group returned to the hotel room in less than fifteen minutes, even while trying, and in some regard failing, to move inconspicuously. Larken was first in through the door, followed by Dandelion, then Clayton. Larken turned to the android.

"Can you connect to the Labyrinth?"

"N...no," said Dandelion, with a side-glance at Clayton, who'd stepped to the side to let Sam into the room. From observing Dandelion's facial reaction to Sam, the temperature in the room seemed to drop four degrees. Dandelion, the long-suffering and endlessly patient nurse, had seemed to have changed into Dandelion, the jealous. And Dandelion, the liar. Larken knew from prior experience that if Dandelion wanted to connect to the Labyrinth, she could. The stutter was an interesting addition too, considering Dandelion had speakers and didn't have the normal cognitive function of most humans.

"What do you mean no?"

"Do you have a computer?"

"Dandelion," Larken said, trying to ignore the fact that Clayton seemed to be paying more attention at that second to Dandelion than to Sam. The triangle that seemed to be forming would only make her work harder.

"Larken," Dandelion replied, with pain and pleading in her voice that snapped Larken out of her hostile thoughts.

Larken lowered her voice. "You're the only one with a picture of the guy," she said, keeping her volume to where she hoped only Dandelion could hear it. "Can't you just, you know, connect to Labyrinth and do the search?"

"Let's go to your room," Dandelion replied as she offered an attempt at a wink that seemed more like she was trying to free something from her eyes.

"Fine," Larken replied, turning toward her room and leaving the remainder of the group standing by the door. More loudly, she announced, "We're going to see what we can figure out about the man. Be back in a few."

"Can I come?" asked Stephen, just as he passed through the door, closing it behind him. Larken shook her head, unsure if Dandelion's newfound insecurity also extended to Stephen. He looked as though she'd just punched him in the gut. As he was about to protest, Larken put up a hand to silence him, which he surprisingly heeded. "We don't need more people, Stephen. Better to stay out here in case we were followed."

That seemed to calm him, though his stolen glances toward Clayton and Sam, who had once again gravitated toward each other, revealed what Larken thought was his real concern, not being a third wheel stuck with those two vastly developing lovers.

In the privacy of the bedroom, Dandelion became more forthcoming. Larken locked the bedroom door, and Dandelion began to talk.

"Look at this," Dandelion said, as though nothing awkward had just happened. A second later, Dandelion's left eye lit and projected an image to the back wall.

"How long are you planning on keeping your secret?" Larken asked. Then she found herself captivated by the wall projection. It was press coverage of the bus sabotage and looked as though it were taken from the vantage of a news drone hovering nearby. Clearly, she saw the two men who were at the bus stop. Besides that, Dandelion projected an image of the man from earlier that day. It was the same man.

As Larken was about to point this out, Dandelion replied, "As long as it takes, Larken. When this is all over, I have to have a job again. If it gets out that I'm an android, then I can get fired."

"Or maybe you have the hots for Clayton?"

Dandelion smiled at the sound of Clayton's name.

"That's what I thought," Larken said. "Ignoring that he and Sam are so very obviously obsessed with each other, do you think basing your relationship with him on a lie is going to work out?"

"I don't know what else to do."

Probably true. And Larken had nothing to tell her so she changed the subject.

"How does that work, anyway? Are you, you know, in love? How do you know?"

Dandelion looked at Larken for half a second, and Larken thought she came across as afraid or maybe angry.

"How do you know when you're in love?" Dandelion shot back.

Definitely angry.

"But can you, you know..."

Larken regretted the implication as soon as she opened her mouth. The more time she spent with Dandelion, the less Larken noticed those little quirks that she used to think gave Dandelion away as an android. The delays on simple questions like "how are you" and Dandelion's tendency to rattle off lengthy technical answers to basic questions seemed less robot-like and more like personality quirks. And right then, Larken found herself embarrassed at having invaded

Dandelion's privacy with a question that she hoped Dandelion interpreted differently than Larken had initially meant.

"Not that it's your business, but yes," Dandelion replied. "What would be the point of assigning me feminine secondary-sex characteristics without the ability to experience intercourse?"

Larken wished she'd not asked the question, but that answer begged for more clarification.

"What's it like for you? I mean..."

Dandelion disabled her projection. "Do you want to continue talking about this, or would you like to keep looking for whoever attacked Sam?"

"Kind of both," Larken admitted, unable to keep an embarrassed grin off her lips. Dandelion looked at her for a few seconds, taking one of the pauses she sometimes did, and then she returned the embarrassed grin. Larken wondered if Dandelion had to decide to be embarrassed or if there was programming that created that sensation—and what such a program might base such a sensation on. Mimicked smile aside, Dandelion didn't seem embarrassed when she opened her mouth to reply.

"I was only half kidding about whether or not models could. I've patched enough models back together to know you've got all the right parts," Dandelion suggested. "I've never talked to one about it. I know they tamper with your physiology and genetics to keep you from reproducing. But does that interfere with...anything?"

"Okay. I'll tell you, and you tell me?"

Dandelion nodded, and Larken tried to describe the first stumbling sexual encounter she'd had back in school. But she didn't think the description would make much sense to Dandelion because it was only one experience and, frankly, hadn't been very good. What had been more to Larken's liking was the kissing and the conspiracy required to sneak her partner into the bedroom that she'd shared with Molly for so long. The thought of Molly brought with it the memory of Larken's endlessly chipper nephew, who she might never see again. Suddenly, Larken felt drained and exhausted. Caught up in her mood, she found herself talking about the next day, when Larken awoke to find herself alone and discovered that the girl she'd thought would be her life partner had decided not to ever reveal to anyone what had happened between them. And the girl never spoke to Larken again.

"It's just like eating," Dandelion said. "For me, I mean. Not like, you know, I can figure out what's in food with taste. But kind of the same reward processes are going on inside of me. Feelings of euphoria, diminished environmental sensitivity outside of the act. Not something that I have to do, but it's...I think...fun?"

"Fun?"

"Fun. Yes, I think that's it. But a lot of fun."

Larken's smile widened, and she let out a giggle. Dandelion smiled back but then, in true Dandelion fashion, pivoted the conversation by enabling her projector again.

"I think we should go back and watch him," she said. "He didn't notice us."

Larken had thought then that the irritating non sequitur was Dandelion's reaction to embarrassment. Even if Dandelion didn't blush, that Larken could remember, perhaps this was another way to tell when Dandelion discussed something she didn't want to discuss. Larken decided then not to push further.

"Why would the same guy who was at the bus scene

follow Sam around? Sam wasn't on the bus. And what about the protests? Why is he attacking protests?"

"He wasn't," Dandelion said.

"Wasn't what?"

"He didn't try to blow up the bus. Someone else did. And from this footage, he didn't attack at the protest. Others did. Look."

Dandelion changed the projection to footage from the protest that Clayton had been at. Sure enough, she'd found the same man in the crowd, as Clayton had predicted. But the man only stood there, watching as events unfolded.

"He was there, though."

"Yeah," Larken said, thinking. "Yeah, he was there. Both times. I wonder if he participated in Sam's attack or if he was just there, too. Do you think it means anything? Maybe coincidence?"

Dandelion shook her head. "No, it couldn't be. The probability is too much against that. He's involved."

CHAPTER 21

JUST US GIRLS

"IT'S JUST US GIRLS," Larken said. The alleyways all looked the same as they made their way through the city. They were getting closer to where Sam had been kidnapped.

They left Clayton and Stephen behind just in case anyone came by the hotel room. It was Clayton's idea, but Stephen had volunteered to stay and "keep him company". Larken wasn't sure what that meant since the sidelong glances he'd been sending Clayton's way hadn't been exactly kind. When it came to it, though, she was glad he'd offered.

"Just us," Sam echoed, in a way that set off warning signals inside of Larken's head. Without Clayton, Sam seemed to curl up inside herself. Dandelion didn't offer much better company, as she cast spurious glances at Sam whenever Sam wasn't looking. Whatever was bothering Dandelion seemed to be getting worse.

"Did you charge?" Larken whispered, not recalling the last time that Dandelion had done so. She was supposed to charge when they arrived at the apartment, but Larken didn't know if, in the excitement, she'd actually done it. Only when

Sam chimed in did Larken realize that she'd spoken more loudly than she intended. Already making mistakes and they hadn't even made it past the hotel lobby.

"Did you?" Sam, asked, now squarely focused on Larken.

"Of course, I did," Dandelion said. "A little."

"Then why are you fixated on Clayton?"

Larken's jaw dropped. Of all the things for Sam to say, she hadn't expected such directness.

"What about Clayton?" Dandelion asked, in such a plain way that it didn't even qualify as a protest.

"I see you looking at him. And he told me you work together. Do you two have history?"

"How could we? I'm an android."

"Dandelion, he obviously doesn't know you're an android. And it's also obvious that you're trying to hide it. Why?"

"If they find out at work, they won't let me work there," Dandelion explained.

"Nice try," Sam replied. "You know as well as I do that all you'd have to do is ask him not to tell, he won't."

"I know he won't want to tell, but do you think he would?"

"You think that he's not able to keep his word?" Sam asked.

"I didn't say that."

"Can we focus? We're almost there," Larken said, knowing they were still three blocks away but doing her best to keep the conversation from escalating into a fight. It didn't work.

"He can keep his word. If he couldn't keep his word, we'd all be in danger."

"I didn't say that he couldn't. It's just hard sometimes to keep things from slipping out."

Sam shook her head. "That's not it. I see the looks you give us. You don't think I notice your side-eye?"

"Sam, I'm not sure what you—"

"You're not? I'm the one who was attacked, Dandelion! I was attacked, and Clayton helps. He makes me feel safe and like...like I can be cared about. He makes me feel important and like my life isn't just about what happened to me."

Dandelion seemed to deflate. She tucked her bottom lip under her teeth—an overtly human response—and cast her eyes downward.

"I can't help how I feel."

"How you feel, Dandelion? You're an android. You don't have feelings."

Larken knew that Sam didn't believe that at all. After all, it was Sam who thought Dandelion had the hots for her. Now that it was clear that Clayton was the target of her affections—Larken still hadn't decided how she felt about that. The damage was already done, anyway, and Larken could see the tension gathering behind Dandelion's eyes.

"What's Clayton going to think when he finds out you're pregnant?" Dandelion asked.

Larken stared wide-eyed at Dandelion, disbelieving what she'd just heard. She wanted to console Sam, but the hatred that just appeared in Sam's eyes didn't seem to have a single point of focus. Stepping in front of that would have gotten Larken eviscerated. It was a full three seconds before Sam responded, and when she did, it was a whimper instead of a scream.

"When were you going to tell me?"

"When we...I...was sure."

"We?" Sam's gaze then pivoted over to Larken. "Did you know?"

"We're here," Larken said, attempting to dodge the question. "Where was that office the man went into?"

"It's over there," Dandelion said, becoming her quick accomplice and already moving in the direction of the building front.

"Answer. The. Question."

Larken exhaled. "I knew. But we didn't know know. It was a guess based on your hormone levels. Dandelion said your hormone levels were high, and given what happened—"

Sam closed her mouth. Her bottom lip quivered beneath her pierced nose. Larken thought Sam might fall over, and moved closer to her in case it happened, ignoring the scowl that Sam gave her.

"Nobody else has to know," Dandelion told her, voice diminutive. "I'm sorry I said anything. I take it back. I've been working on getting you what you need to get rid of the child...if that's what you want."

Larken wasn't sure that was the right answer, either, from Sam's response. The fact that Dandelion was working to help her abort the child was good news because Larken had no idea where to find the stuff that Dandelion had told her about. Even if the two women were fighting, maybe that small kindness was enough to move past the barbed words already exchanged. But Sam stood still and silent. Her eyes darted between Larken and Dandelion as probably a million thoughts floated back and forth behind them. She reminded Larken of a lost kitten that she'd discovered in the fourth grade—eyes wide with fear and claws out at every attempt to help. Larken's hands went to a scar across the back of her thumb where the kitten's talons had dug in.

"We just met," Sam said. "I don't know." She paused for a moment, then spoke again in thin, wispy voice. "I thought that was impossible."

"I know you're suffering," Larken said in what she realized as soon as she said it was an inappropriate attempt at empathy that fell short.

"No, you don't. How could you? My body is changing, and there's nothing I can do to stop it. And the worst part is—"

"The men who did it to you?"

Sam shook her head.

"No," she said, her voice diminished to a whisper. "The worst part is that if I ever want a child, this may be the only chance I'll ever get."

A tear escaped down her cheek, and Larken could only nod in muted response.

"But—"

"I don't know if I want to get rid of it. How fucked up is that?"

"We'll get the men who did this, Sam. I swear we will, and we'll make them pay. Just through that door by the restaurant. Once we know they're there, we can tell Lancaster, and you know what SNO will do to them. They'll never hurt anyone again."

Larken didn't know that Lancaster would do anything about a couple of renegade HPM members when he had a national front to attend to. But Larken would. That was a promise she made to herself as much as Sam.

"You're not listening. I don't want you to do anything, Larken. What happens when you attack them? You don't think they'll know why? You don't think they'll send more for revenge? That ends with all of us dead. The best we can do is pretend it didn't happen. Let them think they got away with it and move on."

"I can't, Sam. If you let them get away with it, they do it again. Isn't that as likely? Only next time, you end up dead."

"Don't pretend that this is about me, Larken."

Larken went speechless.

"Of course, it's about you, Sam. Who else would it be about?"

"You," Sam said, accusing with her tone and with her eyes. She shuffled closer to the door, then past it to lean on the outside of the building. Larken watched her take a labored breath and wondered how much pain Sam was really in. A small part of her wondered if Sam's pain was more intense than the perpetual headache that rested behind Larken's temples. Larken squinted and rubbed her eyes as the thought of the pain brought it back to the forefront again. When she opened them, Dandelion had crossed over to stand by Sam. Dandelion's apologetic eyes lingered on Sam's face. Sam opened her mouth again. "Your stupid war, Larken. It's all in your head, you know? Oliver knows it. Molly knows it. Even Stephen knows it. I'll bet...I'll bet Lancaster knows it, too."

"That's not what this is about."

"Sure, it is. A hallucination five years ago, and you think you have a calling?"

"I don't have a calling. I'm just a college student looking out for my friend," Larken said, at the same time wondering if it was true.

Sam had never openly attacked Larken like that. Pushing down the lump in her throat and willing the tears to stay at bay, Larken felt her shoulders relax slightly, just enough to let her know how tense she'd been. The muscles in her back tightened to compensate and brought pain in short bursts up her spine. She leaned heavily into her cane but brought a thin smile firmly in place.

"Whatever the reason, let's get these bastards."

Sam didn't reply again. Dandelion and Larken continued their pace as far as the bar they'd been at earlier when a shrill siren pierced the night air. Suddenly, the air around them was illuminated by the bright flashing red that Larken hadn't experienced before. Sam's face went white.

"Air quality siren," Dandelion explained, answering the question that Larken hadn't asked yet.

Larken felt it then. The temperature increased almost instantaneously, and she found herself drenched in sweat.

"A little late," Dandelion continued. "You have to get inside."

"Good. We're heading that way anyway," Larken replied, nodding toward the building that the man had ducked into earlier that evening. She continued her walk and pushed the door open a crack with her foot. Now, they had a viable excuse for entering if it somehow turned out to all be a huge mistake. As she took her first steps, she noticed that she was the only one who moved. Looking back, Sam and Dandelion both stood like statues, staring after her.

"What?"

"They'll recognize Sam in there," Dandelion said, and Sam's nod complemented her statement.

"I thought you agreed with me."

"I do. But if we all walk in there with Sam, then they'll see her. I should go in, and you two wait here. Then, when I come out, I can show you what I recorded and you can confirm. It's safer that way."

"They'll attack you," Sam said with a wavering tone.

"And what will they do to me? But you two need to stay out here, or better, go back to the apartment. I'll come back, and I can play the holovid for you."

"Really, Dandelion? With this air thing going on? Do you think we'll make it back to the hotel?"

"You'll be fine on a bus," Dandelion said.

Sam's lips went into a straight line, and for a couple of breaths, Larken thought she'd have to haul Sam through the door. Putting Sam in the position of confronting her attackers wasn't a consideration that Larken had taken, but at that moment, breathing was nearing impossible.

"Sam, we don't have a choice."

Larken waited, counting two breaths, for Sam to notice that at midnight in the city, nowhere else was open for them to duck into and get off of the streets. Even the buses that normally ran like clockwork during the day had fallen off to one every few hours. Whatever Dandelion thought she knew, they only had a single option.

Larken cast a side glance to Dandelion, who took the hint and walked toward her, not struggling at all in the thickening air. When Larken took her next breath, her cane gave out. It was too late to turn back, she thought. On her way down, two sets of hands grasped her arms. The fingers dug into her muscles but kept her on her feet as she part slid and part limped through the door. As the door behind her closed, she felt the oxygen dripping back into her lungs.

"Okay, we're inside," she heard Sam say in a voice that betrayed none of the hesitations from earlier.

Larken pulled her cane back beneath her to support her weight. Seconds later, she found enough strength returning to her limbs to pull free of the hands keeping her aloft. Wobbly on her feet, Larken examined the room through watery eyes. There was nothing there. Any indication that it had ever been a clandestine meeting place had disappeared. The only indication that anyone had been in the building recently at all that Larken could see was the conspicuous lack of dust on any surface.

A table sat in the dead center of the room, surrounded by sixteen chairs. Or there may have been fifteen; Larken didn't count them. It was easy to count the single table. Against the walls there were more chairs stacked up in columns, one after the other after the other. Larken could tell from the rust-colored sheen that reflected from the highly polished surface in the dim bar light that the solitary bar counter, seeming out of place in the company of only a single table, was made of eik wood, imported from Mars and insanely expensive. It was too expensive to abandon in an unlocked room. She harbored no doubts that the circular table before her was eik as well, though the chairs were deep mahogany. The entire room seemed as though someone had passed woodworking class in college and tried out their new skills on whatever wood scraps they could find. One thing was missing, any people.

"Where did everyone go?" Sam asked, shaking slightly but in Larken's opinion doing a passable job of acting like she still had composure.

"They left in a hurry," Larken replied, scanning the empty room for effect and not because she thought she'd find anything useful. "They've cleaned house and took off."

"Literally," Dandelion added, bringing a smirk to Larken's lips and, if Larken wasn't completely mistaken, a half-smile to Sam's. The near-death experience made everything a little less intense.

"Pregnant," Sam said again, which made Larken wonder

if she'd imagined the half smile. "There's almost nothing as invasive and ugly. Were you ever going to tell me?"

"Me? Or Dandelion?" Larken asked, determined not to go down alone.

"You, Larken," Sam said. "Our fearless leader, right? Of the army that we're going to use to fight against...I guess, HPM?"

"I told you—"

"Just stop. You should know yourself better."

"I don't think it's a good idea to antagonize HPM," added Dandelion.

"Nobody asked you," Larken and Sam said in unison. Dandelion looked abashed, clearly unaccustomed to getting such feedback.

"Do you think attacking you was a warning?" Larken asked as she shoved an abandoned cash-coin with her toe. It rolled across the immaculate floor and thudded into a wall before circling down flat.

"Possibly," said Dandelion.

"They were going to kill me," Sam said. "I heard them say it. They didn't say anything about you, Larken. They didn't. I think it was my involvement with SNO before."

"That's got to interest Lancaster," Dandelion said. "Attacks on SNO members can't go unanswered."

"Former SNO member," Sam corrected. "And I'm not sure, given how I left, that Lancaster's going to be all that concerned about it."

"That isn't any better. Of course, he's going to want to know. What's it going to do to his recruitment if any members become targets?"

"How did they know you were a member of SNO?" asked Larken, wiping the lingering panic-induced tears from her eyes with her left hand while leaning heavily on her cane with her other. She was about to say more when the shrill alarm finally stopped outside. "Time to get back to life."

Dandelion exited first since she had at least some rudimentary way of testing the air without dying. Heavy molecules, like PM2.5 and PM10, she could detect while breathing. It was one of the more convenient features of being an android. She signaled the all-clear after only about ten minutes, and the trio made their back to the bus stop, Dandelion, followed by Larken with Sam behind her.

They boarded when the bus arrived, seven minutes later, and Larken looked back over her shoulder and caught Sam's reflection in the bus window, Sam's arm protectively resting over her belly. Whatever happened next was going to be messy.

CHAPTER 22

AN INCONVENIENT SCHOOL

"MS. MARCHE, it's over a month into term. Instructors tell me you're not attending all of your classes," Ms. Williams, the school registrar, had said, issuing her a warning. Larken didn't remember her communicator buzzing, but the message was there anyway. She called back at the number that had called her, and to her shock, the communicator at the other end connected immediately.

"Ms. Marche?"

"I...I'm sorry I've missed. I'll do better. I promise," Larken said, unsure if it was a promise she intended to keep. Really, she was only treading water while thinking of what to say and the words sort of spilled out.

"I told you that philosophy was useless outside of academia," Ms. Williams told her. "I wouldn't be showing up to classes either at this point. Are you into western civilization yet?"

"A little," Larken confessed. "It's not the classes. A friend has..."

Ms. Williams didn't wait for her to finish the thought,

which was probably good because Larken had no idea where she would take the conversation next.

"Have you considered changing your major to something more useful? Like...oh just winging it here...community organizing?"

Larken decided right then that her best move was to play along.

"Tell me more about..."

Half an hour later, Larken found herself signed up for a completely new major, with completely new classes, and what she felt like was an informal agreement on Ms. Williams's part never to say anything again about her inability to attend classes regularly.

Larken hadn't intended to miss any classes. But leaving Sam's side was not something she was comfortable doing, especially on days when Dandelion wasn't available. Now that a klatch of friends fussed over Sam's every need, it was time to heed Ms. Williams's warning and set some of her focus back on her schoolwork. At least, that was what she told herself while the burning need for revenge festered in her stomach like a lump of warm coal. Wasting her college career couldn't be an option. For one thing, Jocelyn would never forgive her.

Larken stepped off the bus on the campus quad, nestling her foot into tall grass still covered in the white coat of frost. The grass crunched beneath her feet, and she pulled in her thick black-and-white-striped faux-wool sweater to keep the cold at bay. Her breath floated up into her eyes and she sucked it back in, feeling the frigid air settle into her lungs. It was relaxing, truth be told. After being forced back into a world of conflict and pain, Larken found it all too easy to be a college student.

Until she made it to her first class of the day. The dark-haired boy sitting next to her all of the previous year finally figured out who she was. A new major halfway through her sophomore year would be a challenge, but lacking attendance or not, Larken hadn't exactly been struggling through the classes she'd had anyway, so the new classes were just more work for her to do.

"You're famous," the boy told her as though she wasn't aware. The professor glared at them both for disrupting the class, as Larken's slow gait had made her almost twenty minutes late. Larken tried to ignore him, but he couldn't seem to take the hint when she feigned her myopic professor-focused vision.

"I didn't know what you'd been through," he said. "I just wanted to say I'm sorry. Your experience was tragic. It's just one example, isn't it, of how mistreating models has the potential to damage us all."

"Uh...sure," she said, though her fellow student had obviously put in more effort than she had at analyzing her situation. Her thoughts began and ended with HPM being evil incarnate. Wider implications were the work of pundits, politicians, and apparently, fellow community organizing students.

"I'm Hari," the student said, bending forward just enough for his thick blond locks to hang in front of one eye. "Hari Newman. Do you want to go out sometime?"

"You're asking me out because I'm famous?" she whispered coarsely. "No. Definitely not."

Hari looked bewildered, as she'd expected. Men typically didn't handle rejection well. She thought to let him stew there but then considered that he'd only been kind to her so far, if a little forward.

"N...no, that's not it," Hari replied, his face turning beet red. "I've liked you all last semester. I just thought, you know, that was an interesting thing, right? Small talk."

"You suck at small talk," she said, giving him a half-smile. It felt good to have someone interested in her, especially after her morning. Even if it was a man-boy.

"Excuse me," said the instructor. "Are you finished flirting? May I continue my lecture?"

It was Larken's turn to be embarrassed as an entire classroom of college students turned to stare at her. She nodded slightly and dipped her head, focusing her eyes on the edge of her desk. Hari was less daunted.

"Maybe Friday? We could get drinks. I'm way more fun over a few drinks than in class."

Larken shook her head. The man-boy who had been unable to talk to her before now seemed unable to shut up. She rolled her eyes for almost five seconds to drive the point home. Still, he persisted, apparently oblivious.

"Saturday's good too. There's an opera downtown that might be fun, if you want to go on a real date."

"Hari," Larken said firmly as she turned his direction in her seat. "Hari, I like girls."

"Okay," Hari said. "Does that mean no?"

"I...like...girls," she said. "Only."

He looked at her for a minute. The instructor cleared her throat again, and Larken tilted her head up toward the front of the room. Her augmentation glasses showed a plethora of factoids floating in bubbles around the room. She would have to write fast to catch up and dismiss them before they cluttered out everything real.

"But—" Hari began.

Larken shot him a look and interrupted. "Only girls," she assured him, cementing his confused look.

"I wasn't going to ask you out again," he whispered furiously and too loudly. The instructor's gaze shifted abruptly to them again. "I'm not totally daft. I still think you're cool and fun. Do you want to go out as friends?"

"For goodness' sake, go out with him if it'll stop you from gabbing through my lecture," the professor said. "Otherwise, why don't the two of you leave my room and figure out exactly what you want from each other."

"I just want to learn, professor," Larken assured her, nodding. She couldn't afford to miss any more classes. She took a deep breath and turned to Hari.

"You're pushy," she said. "I have way too much going on in my life right now. Did you see any of that in the documentary on, what was it…KIRO?"

Holovisoion public news KIRO had wanted to do a documentary about her at one point. She hadn't participated, but that didn't stop them from putting a rather shoddy and poorly reported version of her story together.

"KCPQ, actually," he whispered in return. "Okay, okay. I'll leave you alone. I get it."

So apparently KIRO had shared the documentary with other networks. Larken hadn't considered her story to have more than a local appeal, but aside from being public access news, KCPQ was nationwide. There was something creepy about the idea that millions of people might have been tuning into the Larken Marche story. She knit her eyebrows together as she cringed from the idea.

Hari held his hands up as though she'd attacked him. Good, she thought. She closed her eyes, took another breath, and turned again toward the front of the room. Then she carefully read and tapped each augmented bubble floating in the air before her, capturing her notes on her pinamu tablet.

Hari had not learned his lesson. After class, he stood beside her as she gathered her tablet to put into her shoulder bag.

"I really am sorry," he said.

"I can tell," she said, shoving her tablet into her bag. She cinched it closed and threw it over her shoulder. "You don't seem to understand. I don't want to be your friend."

She couldn't make it much clearer than that. And though Hari's face fell and his shoulders slumped, Larken didn't know how else to communicate with him that even his friendship was unwanted. She had too much to deal with at home to gather any more friends.

"I'm screwing this up," he said. "I'm not asking to date you. I get it. Really. I want to interview you for the school news holo-cast."

Larken rubbed her eyes, then made for the exit, leading with her cane tapping against hard tiles. Hari followed.

"I don't want to be in your holo-cast either," Larken said.

"What do you want then? I know you're a Com Org major like me. This is a chance to start building a following that I'm offering you. Why wouldn't you want to take it?"

He made a good point. She'd changed to a community organizer major for that reason, after all. But building a following would get in the way of revenge for Sam, so it would have to wait. She shook her head and brushed him off as she headed toward the bus stop.

CHAPTER 23
UNEASY SLEEP

SAM FOUGHT off the dreams by trying to stay awake. If she could, she would never sleep again. Eventually, exhaustion overpowered her and brought with it that single memory. She found herself tied to a chair, unable to move and unable to think as she struggled against her restraints. Voices argued in the background, voices that she could usually never quite make out. Her heart raced as she struggled against her bonds.

Only she recognized the room now.

Rather, she recognized the wooden table. It was the same wooden table that she'd seen when she'd been out with Dandelion and Larken. She caught a glimpse of the table as she tried to pull her hands apart for the third or fourth time, despite the wiry ropes that bound them together. The red wood was unmistakable, even from a distance of fifteen or sixteen feet. The recognition made Sam realize she was an actor in a dream and this wasn't the real event.

She had power here.

Sam willed the ropes off of her wrists. They dropped to

the floor. Then she lifted the volume of the voices that chattered in the background until they became loud enough for her to make out. Rising, she rubbed at her wrists and relished the fact that this dream body wasn't racked with pain. Aside from the dull throb of her wrists, she felt fine. The voices came through clearly after that.

"Said to make her suffer."

"But do we kill her? Did he say whether or not we're supposed to kill her? And...can we...you know...have a little fun?"

"Why not? She's a model after all."

"Kill her or not, though. What'd he say?"

"He said his Mimi needs to know that she still belongs to him."

Sam cringed at the mention of the nickname she hadn't used since she escaped. Was that name the clue she needed? Was it real? Or was this just a dream? It'd been so long. She watched the man flash something that looked like a filet knife in the dim lighting. She recoiled against the memories of him brandishing it before her.

"Wait for that," the other man said. "I don't like my women all bloody."

"Your loss."

Sam caught another look at the chair where she'd sat, expecting to see the cut ropes and wires discarded in a pile that the men would find too soon. She caught her lip when she found herself looking directly into her own eyes, pleading for release. The men stopped talking, which was always a dangerous sign. She knew what came next.

Wake up, she told herself. She closed her eyes and felt hot tears she hadn't known were there squeezing out and down the sides of her face. Wake up. She heard the rip of clothing and felt the man's hot breath on her cheek again. Opening her eyes, she was back in her bonds, flexing against the unyielding knots that held her captive. Wake up.

———

Her skin prickled in the night air as her eyes shot open, greeted only by the darkness around her. Sam felt the slickness of her skin and the sheet that caked against her bare arms. She was awake, and her cheeks were covered in tears intermingled with sweat. A quick exhale broke the silence in the room. Her eyes darted toward the noise as she felt her fight-or-flight kick back in again. Then she remembered that Larken had offered to sleep with her after she'd been terrified earlier that evening. She checked the clock that sat atop a nearby dresser. It was three AM, witching hour. A useless piece of trivia that she'd picked up over the years somewhere and made it nearly impossible for her to go back to sleep. Sam tried to control her breathing and focused on her breath, but it wouldn't stop her racing mind.

"What happened?" Larken's slurred speech told Sam that Larken wasn't fully awake yet. Sam seized on the opportunity for companionship anyway.

"Bad dreams," she said. Then she thought about the quickly-fading memories. Had she heard her nickname? It was something. "I might know who did this, and it wasn't random."

"You do?" Larken asked, this time her voice sounding a little more awake. "For who hurt you?"

Larken shot up beside Sam. Larken's dark brown wavy

hair cascaded down around her head—or that was what Sam imagined from the slightly-discolored silhouette that Sam saw as her eyes adjusted to the dim light that crept in beneath the door. That meant the lights were still on in the living room. Perhaps Clayton might be up, she thought. She would check in a minute, maybe. If she couldn't find her sleep again.

"Maybe," she replied. "One of them called me Mimi. Nobody's called me that in ten years."

"I thought that we'd established that those men...they were HPM."

"Yeah, but that doesn't explain why they were after me. Only my former master called me that, Larken. I think that he could have turned them onto me."

"You think this wasn't because of SNO?"

"I...I don't know. It's possible."

Larken wrapped her arms around Sam and laid her head on Sam's shoulder.

"We can check it out," she said, laying back into her pillow and forcing Sam down too with her body weight. "In the morning."

Larken was out as soon as her head touched the pillow again, leaving Sam to lie there, ensconced in the blanket and Larken's arms. Sleep was as evasive as ever, and soon Sam found herself peeling the arms from over her and sliding herself off the bed. As she stood over the sleeping Larken, she felt a sensation of peace wash over her. It wasn't every roommate who would spend the night in her bed with her just because she was a little scared.

Sam padded toward the door to leave her bedroom, watching the light beneath for signs of movement. There were none. Sam pulled the door open and passed through the gap, offering up her arm to block the little light there was that streamed in through the window. She could make out two shapes: Clayton's puffball hair, his head tilted back on their hand-me-down frictionless rocker that didn't rock any longer, and the other one that must have been Stephen, tilted back on the couch.

Sam's right hand went to her belly. That hand was automatic now, forever looking for a chance to protect the life growing within her. She willed it back down before anyone could see. There were no other signs of what she was going through. And technically, it was possible that she wasn't pregnant. Dandelion had explained that a confident diagnosis wouldn't be possible for another week at least. Until then, it was just a guess.

But Sam knew.

She'd known even before Dandelion confirmed it. She'd wanted it to be a lie. Watching Clayton, his head lifting a little with each snore, and contemplating the idea of eventually having to tell him, or if he stuck around long enough, he'd figure it out on his own. He couldn't leave her because they weren't actually together, regardless of whether she felt that she'd known him even before her First Birth. Talking to Clayton was like coming home. She couldn't discern what it might be if there was any word other than love for it. Even now, as a thin stream of drool worked just a little more toward escaping his open-mouthed snores, she felt the connection. Sam continued her walk, half without thinking and half wanting to think, over to where Clayton lay.

"Clayton?"

"Shrmjfme," he said, closing his mouth and making an

annoying slurping sound that turned her stomach. She persisted.

"Clayton," she whispered. One of those dark-brown eyes flecked with black creaked open, followed by the other.

"Sam?"

She swallowed. With him, she knew she could sleep. She would feel safe in his arms, but how would he respond? She gritted her teeth as her stomach clenched.

"Clayton, will you sleep with me? You don't have to do anything. I mean just lie beside me in bed. I can't sleep, and Larken...she means well but I don't really feel comfortable with her."

"Wh...wha...oh. Yeah, sure," he said, rubbing a hand across his cheek and wiping away the drool that collected in the corner of his mouth. "It's got to be more comfortable than this, anyway," he joked, smiling. Always smiling, like whatever happened in the world couldn't get to Clayton. He lived in his own reality, and the rest of the world just had to deal with it. Perhaps that's what drew her to him. More it was probably the way he grabbed her hand as he rose, as naturally as breathing. When they walked, though, he pulled toward Sam's room while Sam pulled toward Larken's. The two nearly fell over as their hands clamped tightly, pulling them both backward simultaneously.

"Larken's room," Sam whispered. "Larken's in mine."

Stephen stirred, muttered something inaudible, then quieted. Sam clamped her free hand over her mouth to keep from laughing out loud and steered them toward the bedroom.

Clayton lay like a plank beside her. She might have misjudged the situation, thinking he was as comfortable with her as he was with him. Doubts fluttered in her mind as she lay beside him, thinking that with the distance and discomfort between them, she might as well be back in the room with Larken again. But just before she'd decided to act on that thought, she felt his arm slide around her midsection and his body press into her back. Slipping her hand under her pillow, she nestled into the downy mound, closed her eyes, and drifted off into a deep, dreamless sleep.

CLAYTON AWOKE with the distinct feeling that he'd been dreaming—and a pulled neck muscle, or so he suspected. Sam had come to him in his dream and coaxed him into following her back to...Larken's room? He tried to move only to find his left arm stuck beneath something heavy. He opened his eyes to see a head of auburn hair almost at the bridge of his nose. He breathed in deeply and caught the aroma of cucumber, which wasn't what he expected. Something hid beneath the clean, refreshing scent though. After spending a day nearly inseparable from her, he knew that aroma to be Sam, and the fact that his arm was being crushed brought a smile to his face.

It hadn't been a dream. She'd come to him and brought him to bed with her. But he'd barely been awake, so he didn't know what else it was that might have happened if anything. He felt fully clothed still, so he guessed nothing. Bits came back. She was scared and had asked him just to lie beside her, so he had.

Morning breath.

He could taste a full day without brushing his teeth on his lips and gums. If she turned his way, waking up to that might be something their newfound relationship would be better off without.

Clayton wasn't certain if he lay in a platonic embrace that would forever be that, or if there was a future with Sam. The circumstances weren't great, were they? He, jobless and practically homeless, and her being chased by militants. They made probably the worse couple ever. Couple. His mind kept going to the same places, and he knew why. It was as though she were the answer to a question he'd never asked.

He gave up pulling his arm from beneath her and instead decided to enjoy the moment. No sooner had Clayton's head reconnected with the only tiny sliver of pillow that remained unoccupied than three subdued raps sounded on the door.

"Sam, are you in there?" Larken's voice whispered through. Clayton debated whether to answer, but he barely got started on even thinking about it before the door swung open to reveal the black-haired girl who always seemed as though she scrutinized everything he did—and right now, it was Clayton's torso and his trapped arm. "Oh, sorry. I thought you went home." Maybe she did, and maybe she didn't—but her body language definitely said annoyed.

Sam stirred.

"Clayton, move over," she said directly into his face. "You're knocking me off the bed."

Her morning breath was a relief, as it meant he wasn't the only one in the room potentially offending with every exhale. Clayton initially didn't respond to Larken, except to direct his gaze at her.

"Well? Come on. Get her up," Larken continued. "We found something out."

"A little privacy," Clayton said.

"What'd you find?" Sam started, suddenly wide awake.

"It was all Dandelion. I'll let her tell it. Come on."

Sam was up in one movement, pulling the blanket off of Clayton and leaving him exposed to the cold air and Larken's inspection. Clayton looked at Larken, who averted her eyes prematurely, since the only thing he'd taken off were his shoes. Taken by surprise, though, Clayton grabbed at the blanket and yanked hard, forgetting it was also wrapped around Sam. Rather than give it up, she clutched it tighter to herself and came with it when he pulled, falling forward on top of him and pushing him back down on the bed in the process. A half-roll later, Clayton found himself on top of her, his face inches from hers. With a muffled apology, Clayton swiveled from the bed and planted his two feet on the floor just as he heard the click of the door closing in Larken's wake.

"Nice butt," Sam said from behind him as what little of the blanket he'd won fell away.

"Thanks," he responded, now that the words processed and especially now that the last of the grogginess had worked itself out of his brain in the excitement. "I do work out."

He shifted a little weight from his left to his right leg to emphasize and heard the sound of a giggle from behind him. An involuntary smile rose to his face as he felt the heat melt from his face and shoulders slacken. However awkward the few preceding minutes had been, Clayton already felt relaxed again. He turned to face Sam, who was jumbled beneath the blankets where he'd left her. All he could see was a tuft of frizzy red-brown hair and one green eye poking out of a blanket cave. Clayton extended his hand.

A second later, a freckled arm pushed through from the

mound and connected with his hand. He pulled her up slowly from the mound as her eyes stayed focused on him. Clayton held his breath as she rose, leaving the blanket in place and exposing her to him. Her cheeks reddened as she approached him in only boy-shorts and a T-shirt.

He wanted not to stare. He wanted to be able to see her as a whole person, and not as a victim. There was so much he wanted to portray as far as what kind of man he was and what he could be to her. Instead, his curious eyes found their way to the first blue-black bruise on her upper chest peeking out just above her clavicle. She started to look down too, but he corrected his vision to meet her eyes, both now set on him and him alone. She reached her arms out to surround him and he pulled her close, dipping his nose into her hair as the top of her head only came up to his lips. Looking down her back with his peripheral vision, he saw the trails of bruises between her shoulder blades disappear beneath her shirt. His body shook as he tried to position his arms to avoid where he thought the bruises were hiding.

"It's not as bad as it looks," Sam said. "And mostly I think it's healing. Just hold me, Clayton."

Clayton tightened his grip around her and stood swaying that way until another impatient knock at the door disrupted them fifteen seconds later. He pulled away and held her hands, searching her eyes for how she felt about him. Sam tilted her head back, and her eyes closed into half slits as she tugged him closer. He allowed himself to be pulled. Their lips met, and he resisted at first, knowing that it would be several days before her cut lip could finally stitch itself fully back together. She held back nothing, forcing her lips against his for a fraction of a second before letting him go.

A few minutes later, Clayton stood in silent meditation,

considering what the kiss said about their relationship as Sam dressed. Once she'd pulled her clothes back on, he reached for her hand, but she didn't respond. Clayton followed her out into the living area, and as he pushed through the door, his eyes tumbled upon Dandelion's stormy blue eyes tucked beneath lowered eyebrows. Something had happened, he guessed, but he couldn't figure out what. He broke from behind Sam, brushing her shoulders with his fingertips as he moved in Dandelion's direction. Sam didn't follow, rather continued to where Stephen and Larken were crowded around the holovision coffee-table.

"What happened?"

Dandelion only shook her head, but she wouldn't talk to him at first. When she did, he thought her voice sounded different, perhaps a full step lower than usual, but the inflection points were all there.

"You and Sam are together?"

He blinked.

"I...I'm not sure, actually," he said. "Did she say anything about me yesterday?"

Dandelion shook her head and walked away, leaving him stranded at the end of the kitchen counter. He thought of going after her but decided that she probably wasn't going to help him figure out his new possible relationship. Instead of pursuing, he made his way over to Sam and turned his attention toward Dandelion, standing near the food replicator.

"Bounty hunters," Dandelion said. Clayton heard a couple of buttons beep and click, and then the machine whirred to life.

"Bounty hunters?"

"They're HPM too. It's a moonlighting thing, I think. But you're right. I don't think it was random."

She retrieved something that might have been a chocolate bar from the replicator and took a tiny nibble at the end of it. Dandelion made a face and dropped the rest of whatever it was into the sink.

"Who? Why?" Larken asked.

"I think maybe this was revenge," Sam said.

"Revenge? For what?"

"For nearly killing him when I escaped."

Clayton stared at her then, lost and confused, he said, "You nearly killed who?"

"Her owner," Larken offered. "Former owner. Not former as in dead, but—"

"I get it," Clayton said, raising his hand.

"We should pay him a visit," said Dandelion. Clayton turned as she spoke and imagined a flash of red sliding across her iris.

"I thought I had killed him," Sam said. "I tried anyway."

Clayton put a trembling hand on her shoulder as he processed that she'd murdered someone, or at least tried to. Tension pushed through her pectorals and neck. She turned, and he tried to make sense of her widened eyes and quivering half-smile. Clayton nodded and swallowed, catching what he thought was her meaning in that subtle movement. He hoped against hope that there was something more to it than that she'd awoken one day and decided to off her owner.

"No," he said, and all eyes immediately swiveled toward him. Clayton had no idea what reasons to give, but he was convinced Sam didn't want to reach out to her "owner." The more he thought about it, the more his stomach churned that nobody else seemed to have thought it through.

"What if it's not him," Clayton asked. "Then you're going to walk right in and give him a way to find her."

Clayton shifted his eyes to the gangly Stephen to find that the man's coal-black irises were centered on Sam. The man's lips were pressed together in a thin line, and his arms were wrapped across his chest so tight as to make the muscles bulge like elongated balloons. Two seconds passed before Stephen's eyes broke from Sam to meet Clayton's gaze. From that quick glance, Clayton made out the remnants of a scowl before the signs washed away from Stephen's face. Clayton flashed his own mini-scowl, and this seemed to clue Stephen in on his mannerisms as he dropped his arms, and the tension left his cheek muscles. Clayton was getting an idea of what it was that clouded Stephen's mood, and he suspected it wasn't simply the fact that Sam had been attacked.

"If we talk to him, we can find out how he got in touch with them, who he got in touch with," Stephen finally volunteered.

"If he got in touch with them at all. She said she thinks it has something to do with him," Clayton replied.

A touch on his arm. Clayton hadn't noticed that Sam vied for his attention. He turned toward her.

"I can handle this," she said, her fingertips sliding down past his elbow to intertwine with his fingers. Blood beat hard against his temples. He let her take control. It was her life, after all, so her choice. Clayton realized then that he might have made a mistake. Despite his heightened sensitivity to model issues, he had thought he'd been defending her when in actuality, he hadn't let her speak for herself.

"I'm sorry," he muttered, then sealed his mouth shut while she squeezed his hand and responded to the group. Stephen looked down and away from their hand-holding, proving to Clayton that at least part of the situation was exactly as he'd read it.

"That's fine with me," Sam began. "But first, you have to know how and why I left." She took a deep breath. "He should have died that day."

Clayton let out a short involuntary laugh, echoed only by silence. He felt his fingers slacken as Sam clung more tightly. When he looked at her, her eyebrows were furrowed up and her face had gone pallid. He did his best to reassure her by reasserting his grip. Her lips flashed into a weak smile before she continued. Sam diverted her gaze toward Larken.

"You know I'm a Caldwell," she said. "I have been trained in the coital arts and soft skills like communication and fitness ever since Second Birth."

Clayton felt his muscles tense up in his neck. He knew about Second Birth. Models were born twice. First when they were "hatched" from the gestation pods. Then they were trained for the foundations of their career paths. Finally, they are cruelly resubmerged into new stasis pods until they are sold.

He was careful not to let the tension make it into the arm and hand that held Sam's. He caught a quick side-look from Sam in his periphery as she shifted her weight slightly and cleared her throat.

"Didactics is where we learned more advanced topics regarding nonjudgmental fantasy services, with wide exposure to different client types. It wasn't easy, but training was controlled and safe."

The room had silenced. Clayton noticed that every single one of them had frozen, and all of their attention was now focused directly on Sam.

"As you know, or should know, models don't come out of Second Birth without a purchaser. Since we were all spoken for already, they ensured to minimize the harm that could come to us during training. Honestly, we were a bit coddled, trained in sex and taught concepts, but shielded from the brutality of the world."

Her gulp sounded like a gunshot in the silence.

"So when I made it to Jackson's house—Jackson Grayson —I'd had some experience with role playing, but nothing had prepared me for what happened next."

She blinked, and her eyes grew watery. Clayton could feel her pulse quickening as she pressed into him as though she wanted to push through him and hide on the other side. He wanted her to stop. Already he'd forgiven her for attempted murder, guessing what would come next. But she continued.

"I remember thinking he was really old when I met him. Three or four times as old as me. And he was really sweet during the Discovery meeting."

"What's that?" asked Larken.

"After Didactics, it's the first time we meet our new owner. I'm not sure if other model types have the same thing. Stephen didn't. It's very important for Caldwells because we get to know their temperament, and then we use that to determine our interaction protocols. I mean, who we're going to be for that client.

"He was nice. He brought chocolates for me, and we just talked. He may have been older, but he treated me like a polli. So polite. I thought I'd gotten lucky. The protocol I picked out for him was Cinnamon, kind of flirty and innocent. I thought he'd like it."

Larken squirmed and repositioned her cane from her left arm to her right. Her stoic expression didn't waiver, the same she always wore. Clayton wondered if she felt anything beneath it sometimes. Sure, she smiled occasionally, laughed, and even frowned, but none of the emotions behind these acts seemed to reach her eyes.

"Anyway, that illusion fell away as soon as I walked through his door. There was nothing on his walls. No paintings, no clocks, no artwork—nothing. He walked me through a house without a soul. There was a door. I remember it well. Blue amethyst, sparkling. It was the only thing that was adorned in any way. This he opened and shoved me through, then locked it behind me. And that was the last I saw of him for three days."

"What did you eat?" Dandelion asked. "That's a long time for the human body. Did you have water? What was in the room?"

Sam seemed startled at Dandelion's barrage of questions, so Clayton pulled her in closer to himself and draped an arm across her shoulders.

"No food. There was a trough thing at the bottom that had water in it. I discovered only later that it doubled as a urinal. He did...terrible things, Dandelion. I can't begin to explain. Nothing in Didactics had prepared me for what he'd really wanted—someone to hurt."

Sam paused for a second, turned her head toward Clayton's chest, and let out one whimper too slight for anyone else to hear. He held her like that for five seconds, then she wiped her face and pushed away from him, holding his right hand firmly in her left.

"This went on for almost a year, I think. There wasn't much in that room, so most of the time, I had to guess what day of the week it was. Nearly three times a week, I suffered at his hands for a year. I kept searching in his steely gray eyes for recognition of the person I'd met that day during Discovery, but he never showed me that face again. I realized eventually that he too had worn a protocol."

"You don't have to say anymore, Sam," Larken said. "We won't contact him. It's okay."

Sam didn't respond to her and kept talking. "After a year, you can imagine the smell down there. He dropped some cleaning agents in one day, tools like scrapers too. So that I could see, he turned on the light in the room for the first time. That's when I saw the others, or what remained of them. Boxes, all in a row on a counter, each with names. Each labeled with a year starting at 2180 and going through 2191. This was all happening in 2192."

"Nothing for 2192?"

"No. Inside each box was one outfit, the kind you get at Didactics when you leave. Each was as soiled as mine had become since I didn't have any means for cleaning my clothes. I knew...I knew...that I was destined for a box. Maybe not that day, but sometime that year my soiled clothes would become a trophy."

Clayton shook involuntarily, and she pushed her body closer to his. He wrapped his arms around her to protect her from a past he had no control over. He bit his lip in impotent rage while she continued, flashing a wry grin.

"My roommate in Didactics had been a Briggs," she confided. "Jackson Grayson couldn't have known that. In our little free time, Nancy Briggs tried to teach me some of her martial arts training. It didn't take. But what did take was what she always told me: you don't get to choose your weapons, so you fight with what you have. So I took that to heart. I pulled a blood-covered shirt from each box and found a patch of clean material. Using several, I put together a mask. I mixed every cleaning agent in the basket he'd given me together into a sludgy pool, planted myself by the vent at the bottom of the stairs, and waited."

"I can't believe what you had to go through," said Larken. "You never told me. Not any of this."

"I don't like to talk about it. I wouldn't be telling you now if it didn't matter."

Clayton didn't like the faces in the room. Stephen still looked hostile, like he was waiting for a chance to beat on someone or something. Dandelion still stole glances at him, and Clayton couldn't understand why. Larken's stone face had cracked as she said the words, but now she was back to stoicism. There wasn't an ounce of compassion to be found from Clayton's perspective.

"It didn't do anything...at first. The man didn't come down for another day and a half, and by the time he returned, most of the noxious fumes had dissipated. But what was left was a puddle of gray-green slime in the bottom of the basket. So when the man finally did come down, I did the only thing I could. I slung the slime at him, and it got him across his face and chest. Lucky for me, whatever was in there seemed to ignite as soon as it touched him and soon, he was engulfed in flames. I thought he was dead when I left. I hoped he was. But if he's alive, he will be disfigured, angry, and very dangerous."

"And you think he's back at it, tracking you?" asked Larken.

"It makes sense, doesn't it?" Sam said. "But that was over five years ago now. So maybe it's not him. I don't know."

"Strange to wait all this time to look for you," Larken replied. "Unless he's been in recovery or rehab all this time. You must have really hurt him, Sam, if that's the case."

"He hurt me," Sam replied flatly.

"I didn't mean anything. He deserved it and worse. I was just saying if he couldn't find you before now, it's not like you've been exactly hiding by sharing a hotel room with me."

"Or maybe he's been looking this whole time," Clayton said. "Maybe it was sharing the room with Larken that caught his attention." He could tell by the expression on both Sam's face and Larken's face that, regardless of whether he was right, it wasn't the right answer and never would be. "Or not," he continued. "Definitely the too damaged thing."

CHAPTER 25
LIVING AND DYING

"HE'S ALIVE?" Sam asked the question with a hint of apprehension in her voice.

Larken felt a shudder pass through Sam and into her own body where Sam's elbow touched her ribs. They had all gathered around the holovid computer, and through various searches—mostly led by Dandelion—they discovered that Jackson Grayson lived in a single-family home outside of League City, Texas. What had started as conjecture had jelled into fact.

"Must be," Stephen replied, followed by a heavy sigh. "Do you think he'll accept a holovid call?"

"From someone he hasn't met? I wouldn't," Larken said. "I don't. Unless I know you, I don't talk to you. And how long do you think we would be on the call before he realized why we are calling, and disconnected?"

"Are you sure this is the right guy?" asked Dandelion, who sat on her knees in front of the coffee table and flicked the current holograph to the side, revealing something that looked like a blog post.

"Model advocate?" Clayton noted, pointing out one of the logos hovering below. As he pulled his hand back, Larken saw strands of Sam's hair rise to greet it. He stood behind her, close enough that they shared the same air. Larken let herself smile just once at the idea of a little oasis of bonding happening in the midst of the chaos that had brought the group together. Sam seemed to feel her smile and turned to her left where Larken sat. Larken widened her smile slightly, and Sam, her cheek in full contact with Clayton's hand that had come to rest on her shoulder, returned it. Then a sharp pain pulsated through Larken's back, and she felt her smile vanish as her back muscles stiffened. She changed her posture to allow the cane to support her more.

"That can't be right," Sam replied as she swung her head back toward the holovid.

"Hold on," Dandelion said, cutting off Sam's words, yet making no effort at eye contact with her. "I found something."

Larken noticed that Dandelion had "found" something before she swiped the holovid display over to a new page that looked like a personal blog. Across the top was the headline "Jackson Grayson: What I Learned When My Model Tried to Kill Me". A quick scan of the document, even through the blocky rendering that holovids tended to use to display two-dimensional data, and then Dandelion summarized for all present.

"He calls it a come-to-Jesus moment. What the fuck is that?" asked Clayton. Nobody answered him.

"He says that lying there on the ground, in a puddle of his own melting flesh, he envisioned what it must be like in a reclamation tank, unable to stop the pain. He says here that he heard his own screams so loud that he thought they came from someone else."

"How did he survive?" asked Sam, her intonation dull.

"Doesn't say," Dandelion said. "It only says he's grateful to his employer for helping him through the incident and that he's ashamed of who he was before. But..."

Dandelion seemed to squint, now clearly focused on the holovid, but a little overly focused. Or at least it seemed that way to Larken, who knew that Dandelion had auto-adjusting vision and didn't actually have to squint or even bend forward. She seemed to be compensating for being a little too productive earlier.

"His address," Dandelion said, pointing. "Or, rather, a description of his street. If I'm not mistaken, that puts him—"

Larken cleared her throat before Dandelion could be even more helpful. Dandelion stopped on cue and turned to look at her, blinked, and then continued.

"To the north of the city, just close enough to see the skyline, and on a creek between League City and NASA. He can walk to Egret Bay Boulevard. That's near Clear Creek Communities. If he lives there, he must make a lot of money, too."

"He used to work for Emergent Biotechnology," Sam said, and almost as an afterthought continued, "and he bought me at a fifteen percent employee discount."

The very idea of the purchase turned Larken's stomach. She directed her next questions to Sam.

"Do you think he's changed? Or do you still think he's behind this?"

"I...I don't know," Sam replied. "I think...I think..."

"Oh, he's behind it all right. And look who he married," Larken replied, staring within inches of the screen. There at the bottom, surrounded by glowing words, was an image of his wife. And, according to the post, the couple was expecting.

"So?"

"They don't show her wrist, but look carefully at her eyes and her face. Does it remind you of anyone?"

Larken examined the pixie nose and the dark brown eyes. Nothing stuck out except possibly how beautiful the woman's face was. Perfectly symmetrical, not like Larken's own where her left eye was just barely smaller than her right. Instead, this woman's eyes were both the exact same size. Her cheekbones were perfectly even, and her ears the same. Down to the flowing brownish-blond hair, she was perfect.

"She's too perfect. Like someone else we all know."

Larken instinctively turned toward Sam and noticed that everyone else did too. Everyone except Stephen. Then she saw what Clayton was talking about almost right away. The noses were the same. The symmetry was too, even though they didn't necessarily look the same. Without the tattoos and the piercing, and for the moment, the stubborn bruising that refused to go completely away even as it lightened up to almost invisible, she held the same level of perfection. There was also the difference in hair color. Sam's reddish-brown gave her a more serious look than the playful sandy-blond of the woman before them. The only one of the group who might have compared in symmetry to the pair was Dandelion, but her farm-girl-esque appearance with blond, shoulder-length hair and completely useless orange-brown freckles covering the bridge of her nose and cheeks somehow made her seem more real under Larken's scrutiny.

"How do we get there?" Larken asked.

"Where? League City?" Stephen answered, though in

truth Larken had been asking anyone but Stephen who, like Dandelion, seemed to be getting more distant the more time the group spent in that tiny two-bedroom hotel room turned apartment.

"Yeah, League City," Larken replied. "Anybody have a rich relative?"

"You do," Dandelion responded. "Couldn't your father book a private jet? You know, if you asked really nicely?"

"Not my father," Larken said. "Sperm donor. And not even that. More like a skin cell donor. No, he's not going to pay for that. He doesn't even..."

She stopped before she explained that like everyone else, her "father" didn't believe in the visions she'd had either. One quiet look from Sam told Larken that Sam understood her pain, and they'd had the conversation before. Nobody else seemed to notice when she continued.

"We'll need a volantrae."

Larken looked around the room, doing a quick survey. Four pairs of blank eyes stared back. Clayton and Dandelion walked on that first day, and she and Dandelion had been taking the bus. Larken didn't own a volantrae at all. Stephen and Sam were models, so neither could legally own one.

"Molly?"

Larken opened her mouth to object then closed it again. She wasn't at all certain that Molly would be willing to help her, but having an actual enemy, someone who fit closely the description of the army that she was trying to fend off, might go a long way to convince Molly that Larken wasn't actually insane.

"Molly," she replied and stood, steering her way around the group clustered next to the holovid. Then she retrieved her communicator in her room. Just as she was about to bring it out to make the call with the group, she changed her mind and pushed the door shut behind her first.

"Are you okay?" Those were the first words out of Molly's mouth.

Larken felt a lump form in her throat. "Why does there have to be something wrong for me to call you?"

"You never call unless there's something wrong, Larken," Molly said.

"Okay, maybe there is something, but it's a really little something. We found Sam's attacker, Molly. We're pretty sure it was bounty hunters."

"You don't even see what's wrong with what you just said. Normal people aren't attacked by bounty hunters, Larken. Normal people get up, have jobs, and have families. Normal people don't waste their lives looking for imaginary armies."

"And cheat on their husbands," Larken added then slapped her hand over her mouth. Too late.

"And steal their brother's trust fund money," Molly accused.

The throbbing in Larken's head intensified as she listened. Even though she knew that it wasn't the right response, she felt the hostility rise in her only seconds before it erupted from her mouth.

"I'm not normal, Molly. Oliver isn't normal, Molly. We're not, and no amount of play-acting is going to keep us safe. If our secret gets out, then do you really think that HPM wouldn't make Oliver disappear, too?"

"The only way their secret gets out is through you, Larken. You're the one going around poking the bear."

"What the fuck happened to you, Molly? You snuck out

of Brighton to save Oliver's life once. Would this version of you do that? What happened?"

Larken heard a sharp inhale followed by a slow exhale.

"I have a life to protect now, Larken. You don't understand, but I got a job after all of that happened. We bought a house, and Oliver's taking classes online. We're moving on."

"I'm right, Molly. I'm right, and you know I am."

She couldn't see Molly's expression on private mode, but she could feel her thinking. One second passed, then two.

"How can you be?"

Larken's head throbbed with such ferocity that it brought tears to her eyes. She bit her lip to give her a different, more manageable, pain to focus on.

"At least I'm doing something. Look, I only want to borrow your car. You don't even have to do anything. We need your volantrae. Not even going to HPM with it, just to Sam's former owner, and only to ask a few questions that he's probably not going to have answers to anyway."

"Who is it?" Oliver's voice floated in through the communicator receiver.

"Your sister," Molly replied, not bothering to cover the remote.

"Tell her I said hi and I love her. Did you tell her about the money?"

"What. About. The. Money?" asked Larken.

"Not yet, dear," Molly said, and from the sound, through her teeth. Then Larken heard her brother's voice in the background.

"It was an accounting thing. It's there after all, just moved to an investment account. I forgot I asked them to do it. Sorry!"

Molly didn't acknowledge that he'd said anything at all.

"She wants to borrow our car. You can tell her when she gets here."

"Let her have it," he said. "Call it an apology."

Silence.

"You're going to let me borrow it?" Larken asked.

Silence again. Three seconds passed.

"Come over before I change my mind."

———

"I want a shower first," Clayton said as he poked his nose into one of his armpits. "It's been a week, and I've been wearing the same clothes."

"Me too," Dandelion chimed in. Larken cast her a suspicious glance. She seemed once again to be following Clayton around like a lost puppy. Larken felt her teeth grind together.

"There's a shower in my room," Sam offered, her eyes locked onto Clayton's, not even acknowledging that Dandelion had said anything.

"I'd accept," Clayton said, then paused for a second, "but I don't have any clean clothes here."

Clayton pivoted to Dandelion, breaking his and Sam's shared gaze. Larken caught Sam's smile falter slightly at that body language. Dandelion looked at him in silence.

"I don't think I have any clothes you'll like," Sam told him, pulling his attention back. Clayton grinned and nodded.

"Stephen does," Larken offered. As soon as she said his name, Stephen turned and nodded.

"Yeah, give me a few minutes," he grumbled. "I'll get some from my place. It's not too far. Probably won't fit, but I'll see what I can find."

With that, he made his way to the door. After he passed

through and the door clicked into place behind him, Larken felt herself breathing easier.

"Larken, do you have clothes I can use?" Dandelion asked directly. Larken caught an undertone of annoyance as everyone seemed to clamber to assist Clayton.

"I do," Larken said. "Follow me." She addressed the group. "Let's get back out here in half an hour or less. We've got a lot to do."

Larken shuffled toward her room, and Dandelion matched her pace perfectly, seeming neither rushed nor deliberately slow with her adjusted, steady gait. The two crossed the doorway one after the other, and when the door to Larken's room closed behind them Larken turned to Dandelion.

"You need a shower?"

"Of course not," Dandelion said. "I don't sweat. But I do need a charge."

Dandelion looked around the room. Larken pointed out an outlet toward the wall by her dresser next to the bathroom door.

"There's a plug over there. Is that what you need?"

"I prefer to use my charging station," Dandelion replied. "But I do have an adapter. Just promise not to be weird about it."

"What's wei—" Larken started and stopped as Dandelion approached the dresser and lifted her T-shirt about three inches. Dandelion touched her finger to her belly and a slit opened up, extending out a short bifurcated plug. Pulling on the end with her fingertips, Dandelion worked it out of the flaps of skin and pulled out a plug followed by about two feet of cord. She sat atop the dresser and held the plug out for Larken.

"Can you plug it in?" she asked. "There's a safety shutoff, and I can't move my body while I charge."

Larken nodded and reached out to accept the plug. As she pulled it toward the outlet, she got some resistance. Looking back, she saw that the cord had stretched its full length, and still had a foot to go.

"There's enough. You just have to pull," Dandelion told her. Larken yanked harder, and the resistance seemed to give way. The image of the wire extending unnaturally from Dandelion's body made Larken feel queasy. She supported herself with her cane as she lowered herself to the outlet. The pain in her back flared again, and she cringed, gripping the plug tightly to avoid falling. She heard Dandelion grunt as she accidentally pulled the cord even tighter to support Larken's weight. Larken finished kneeling when the pain passed and connected the cord to the wall.

"What now?" she asked.

"Now we wait," Dandelion said. Larken looked up and rose from the ground. Dandelion had gone rigid. Only when the movement stopped did Larken realize that Dandelion's chest had been rising and falling steadily as though she were breathing. Strange.

"Why are there so many unnecessary things about you that make you more human?"

Dandelion's face was slack and expressionless. The only thing that moved was her mouth, though Larken assumed that probably wasn't necessary, either.

"I've been working on me for years, Larken. I taught myself how to breathe, how to laugh at jokes, and how even to get jokes most of the time. Facial expressions, all of it."

"Trying to be human?"

"Trying to hide. I was created to protect, and to kill, like that android who attacked you all those years ago. But I don't like killing, Larken. I don't like it and I didn't want to do it anymore, so I left. And if I want to stay gone, the military can't know where I am. I have to become human, or at least pretend enough not to be noticed."

"That seems like a lot of work. But I don't get why you're trying to hide it from Clayton. He will find out sooner or later, won't he?"

"Will he?"

A glow of red light emanated from between Dandelion's eyelids.

"I don't know," said Larken. "I assume. I see the way you look at him. Are you hung up on him or something?"

"Is it obvious?" Dandelion asked. "I don't know what's happening to me, Larken. I've known Clayton for a long time. He's always been on his mission to protect models, and now that he has one of his very own—"

"I knew you were jealous," Larken interrupted. "How does that work? Do you have other emotions, too?"

"Larken, I need you to see me as a person right now," Dandelion complained. The red light morphed to blue. "I'll tell you all about my emotions, I promise. Can you just treat me like a person for a while?"

Rebuked, Larken clamped her mouth against the other questions she had already queued up to ask now that she had Dandelion in private. Instead, she nodded.

"So you're obsessing about Clayton, who has fallen for your patient, Sam."

"And I don't know what to do, Larken. I've never felt this way before. I go back and forth. I want to take care of Sam, but I'm so furious that he doesn't even see me after all I've done."

"Getting him to notice you is easy," Larken said, thinking back to the days before she had to use a cane to support herself before she could barely keep food down and back when she was less emaciated. She had an entire wardrobe of outfits that she'd bought while recovering, under the misinformed idea that someday the pain would disappear and she'd be normal again. "You need the right outfit, and he'll see you. But I'm not sure that's going to help. He seems hung up on Sam."

"And if I'd just ignored her and not come over that first night, then he would have fallen for me instead," Dandelion said.

"I don't get it, Dandelion. I'm trying to be supportive, but I don't understand. What exactly would a relationship look like with you?"

"Holding hands," Dandelion said as the color behind her eyelids turned yellow. "Walking on the beach. Laying in the sun on lazy days."

"And that's worked before? People have been okay with... you know, you being a...well..."

Dandelion's light turned white.

"I don't know," she admitted. "I've never had a relationship before. I've never felt like I wanted one before. I don't know what's going on."

"If you were human, I'd say you're having a personality crisis," Larken said, immediately regretting the if you were human part of her statement.

"What is a personality crisis, and what would a human do to fix it?"

"Eat ice cream, maybe chocolate, until it passes. I mean, that's what I would do. But for what it is? Hmmm...hard to explain. Your personality is changing. It's like you're becoming more self-aware and finally dealing with the fact that sometimes your emotions work against you."

"You can make Clayton notice me?"

Dandelion seemed not to want to admit that her longing, as valid as it was, couldn't be trusted.

"I don't think it'll matter. Did you hear what I said about personality crisis?"

Dandelion's head finally moved, but not in her natural way. It swiveled toward Larken and made her shudder. Dandelion's eyes shot open, and an unfocused stare shot through Larken toward the front of the room. "Make him notice me. Then if that doesn't work, and if he still wants Sam only, then I'll have to be okay with it. I need that possibility."

Dandelion had the introspection to understand that she had all these feelings to deal with. Yet, in the most human act Larken had seen, Dandelion refused to acknowledge that her feelings were leading her astray. There was no reasoning when most people got into that mindset, and Larken didn't think she'd be able to do much to convince Dandelion, either.

"Yeah, I can get him to see you," Larken said, turned her back to the dresser, then used her cane and upper body strength to shove herself up beside Dandelion. "When you're done charging, we'll go through my wardrobe and makeup. It won't take long. You're beautiful already. We'll do a little touch-up.

Larken swallowed, and her chest tightened as she watched Dandelion's beautiful blue eyes flash open briefly before they closed all the way, eliminating all light and all movement while she finished charging. Once she was certain Dandelion was completely out, she let out a deep sigh.

CHAPTER 26

STRANGE ROMANCE

SAM GAPED AT DANDELION, unable to decide what to make of her too-revealing short dress made from a belted skirt up around her chest. Long legs jutted out, accented with stockings that ended mid-thigh, exposing a thin ribbon of skin. Her hair was braided and draped around over one shoulder, ending just above her cleavage—cleavage that had previously been hidden behind a simple, conservative tank. All the way down to Larken's old ruby-colored flats, everything Dandelion wore worked together to create a complete outfit that made Sam's chest tighten and the muscles in her shoulders go taut.

It wasn't just the clothes. Sam didn't miss that one slow, deliberate wink toward Clayton that nobody else seemed to see, including him. Sam grabbed Clayton's hand and swiveled around to get between his gaze and Dandelion's ostentatious form. He seemed to be startled for a moment, but his eyes never left Dandelion. Sam lifted herself to her toes and kissed Clayton's lips, willing him to kiss her back. It took half a second, but he did return her kiss, and when they pulled back apart, Clayton's eyes were firmly affixed to Sam instead.

"What was that for?"

"You know, nothing. I just wanted to."

Clayton lifted an eyebrow at her. Maybe her actions didn't make sense. It was a stupid gesture, claiming a man that wasn't hers. Stupid or not, Dandelion had moved and seemed sheepish—if that was something androids could feel.

Sam's chest ached where the bruising had gone deep, and her face still sometimes throbbed even though the markings there of her attack had all but disappeared. Her betraying hand kept finding its way to her belly, despite the fact that every time she noticed it happen, she felt a sense of revulsion and a wave of nausea rush over her body. Sam put on a brave face. She didn't burst out in tears, nor did she stare into the distance. Very carefully, she engaged and made eye contact, no matter that turbulent thoughts and emotions bounced around inside like high-velocity ping-pong balls.

"Stay?" she asked Clayton, squeezing his hand as a reminder. "With me. You don't have to go."

Clayton seemed to ponder the idea and then dismiss it as he squeezed her hand back.

"Missing me is hard, I admit," he said with a gentle smile. "But this is important, Sam, and the more of us there are, the safer it gets. I can't let Larken go solo."

He lowered his voice to a whisper and continued. "Look at her. She can barely stay upright on that thing. If I was Jackson Grayson, and someone like her stopped by to dig into my secret past, I would knock the cane away and watch her fall."

"You would?" Larken asked, interrupting the conversation and glaring at him severely. Clayton focused on her. "Wouldn't you?"

"What's the point?" Sam asked. "What difference will it make? Stay here. Actually, all of you. This is stupid. Even if you do get him to confess, what are you going to do, kill him?" She turned her pleading eyes up to Clayton. "Someone's going to get hurt, and for what?"

"I have to go," he said. His teeth set into a straight line and his eyes narrowed into a glare. "Have to."

"I'll be there," Dandelion said. "I can protect Larken. You don't have to come."

The way she said it pulled Sam's attention toward her. She sounded like she meant it and almost like she was angry at Clayton. Dandelion's eyes were turned up as though tears would fall any moment. Sam wondered if she could cry and doubted it.

"What's Sam going to do if something bad happens to you?" Dandelion asked. It wasn't what Sam had expected Dandelion to say. Dandelion flashed Sam a thin smile, the kind that she couldn't be sure had come before it was gone again. But there was no mistaking the compassion for what it was, or the apology tucked gently inside. Before Sam could answer, Dandelion had moved on. "Are we ready?"

Clayton gave Sam's hand another quick squeeze and then let go. He made his way to the trio.

"We're ready," he said, nodding back toward Sam. "Let's go."

———

When the trio left, Sam stood silently near the door for a full minute, grinding her teeth, before she dropped herself onto the couch, buried her head into a pillow, and screamed as hard as she could, muffling the sound. She now had an ocean of time between that moment and when her avengers returned. A few painful seconds later, a hand on her shoulder made her yank herself involuntarily away. She jerked her tear-stained head up, and her eyes met Stephen's. She had completely forgotten he was still there.

He slowly reached toward her again, laid a soft touch on her shoulders before he gave a squeeze, and then cut for the kitchen to work at the replicator. Whatever he tried to do there didn't seem to work as he slammed the side of it with his hand and banged on the buttons. A loud bang and a curse followed.

"Are you okay?" Sam asked.

Stephen looked at her with the most hostile expression she'd ever seen on his face. The expression melted off when he caught her gaze, replaced by a tented eyebrow and a weak smile.

"I'm fine," he assured her. "This stupid replicator won't work for me. I've tried everything."

"I'm not talking about the replicator," she told him, casting her eyes down just below the plane of his gaze. "I'm talking about this attack. I'm talking about chasing HPM, and I'm talking about Clayton, I guess. All of it."

His weak smile morphed into a wry grin. "Why wouldn't I be? It's not about me. Are you okay?"

She shrugged, and it hurt to shrug. Careful not to let the pain show on her face, she tried to smile, but her lips wouldn't work.

"I'll survive" was the best assurance she could offer.

"There you have it," he said. "Locked out again." He turned back to the replicator and whacked it again with the meat of his palm. The machine sprang to life and emitted a whirring sound.

"Are you talking about the replicator?" Sam said. There wasn't a lock-out function on it that she knew about. Her face felt flushed and hot.

"You, Sam. You're doing it again. It's like you don't even know me. You barely talked to me in the last several days, and you're hanging all over that Clayton guy. What's that about anyway?"

"That's none of your business, is it?" she said, regretting the words as soon as they hung in the staling air between them.

"Yet here I am, and here he isn't, valiant warrior. And he's so nice it's fucking irritating. Did you know that whenever you leave the room, he's bugging me like he wants to be best friends? I get that we're the only two men here, but does that mean I want to be his friend? Especially when he's working so hard to steal you away?"

Not now, of all times, Sam thought. Sam shook her head, but her body shook harder with rage. She was hurt, and every single one of her friends, now even Stephen, had made her pain about them. Except before she could lash out and correct him, he shook his head and closed his eyes.

When he re-opened them, he began again. "I'm sorry. I don't mean that. Of course, he's not stealing you. I didn't mean it that way. It's just frustrating seeing him with you, you know? It makes me miss us, you know? How we were?"

Sam shook her head.

"You miss the fights? You miss the barbs and jabs we made at each other. And what about Lyric, or have you forgotten her?"

"What about Lyric? She's not even with me anymore.

Something about finding herself," he replied, then paused for half a second. "And those fights were because of Larken, Sam. She did that to us. We used to be..."

"We used to be friends. Then you wanted more, and I didn't. And besides, you didn't exactly quit the SNO, did you? It's as simple as that, Stephen. We weren't ever together."

The whirring of the replicator stopped.

"We could have been," he accused as he reached in and retrieved two mugs of hot brown liquid. Crossing out of the kitchen to where Sam was by the door, Stephen held out one of the cups. "Try this. It's my recipe. Not, you know, natural roast, but good."

She accepted the cup in confusion. Upon sipping, she had to admit that the robust flavors of the nonexistent coffee beans filled her mouth and nostrils. It was one of the best cups of coffee she'd had in days.

"You gave up before we had a chance. And SNO is who saved you, remember?"

"I couldn't give up when there wasn't an us," she said. "And I faced reality. SNO is a terrorist group, whether you want to admit it or not. Being part of that made me a terrorist too. I had to quit. You need a cause you can dedicate your life to. I don't. I just want to live."

"Well, you have a cause anyway, I guess."

Sam swallowed another mouthful of perfect coffee and nodded.

"I didn't ask for any of this," she half-whispered. "I didn't ask to be attacked. I didn't ask to be raped, and I definitely didn't ask that the one shot I have of bringing a child into this world be corrupted by me carrying a rapist's baby."

She felt the heat in her face intensify when she realized

what she said. Secrets didn't last long among her friends, if that's what they were. Stephen stared down to her abdomen where her betraying left hand rested. She self-consciously dropped it to her side as she felt the heat rising in her cheeks and tears forming in her eyes, following her rage as it grew.

"When were you going to tell me?" he asked.

"Not your problem, Stephen," she told him.

"Did you tell Clayton?"

"Not his problem, either. This is my problem, and I'll deal with it."

Whether he was aware or not, his eyes had gone wide. She crossed the room, and his wide eyes followed her, occasionally drifting to her abdomen as though he were trying to guess whether the pregnancy showed. It didn't. She knew it didn't and that without the arm as a tell, she could have laughed the whole thing off as some bad joke. Her pace picked up on its own as she beelined for her own room, biting her lip.

"Sam, wait," Stephen said behind her. She didn't slow. Instead, she shoved the door open and stormed through. Careful to place the hot cup of coffee on the dresser, she locked the door behind her, bolted for her bed, and buried her face into a pillow to muffle more screams.

———

Sam awakened disoriented upon her tear-soaked pillow and the sounds of chatter from the room beyond her door. She checked the clock hanging from the wall. Four o'clock. Whatever else had happened, Sam had slept the day away. A quick inventory of her body revealed a faint headache and a queasy stomach but, otherwise, little pain. Then she heard the door shut, and her pulse quickened. Her first thought was that they couldn't have reached League City, Texas, and back. Not yet. Her second was of the attack, shoving the other thought aside with the force of a bus crashing through an unsuspecting crowd. Any desire to leave the safety of her room ended when the voices congealed themselves into words.

"Do you buy his story?" She couldn't make out that voice, but it was male.

"No," Larken said flatly. "No, I don't."

"I kind of do," came the male voice again. Sam had one guess who the "he" was they were referring to, but the idea that it could have been Jackson didn't make any sense.

"Me too," said Dandelion, her voice monotone and, Sam thought, a little dejected sounding.

"Dandelion, come here," Sam heard Larken say. Her statement was followed by shuffling steps and the thud of a cane toward Sam's door. The noises stopped short just before Sam thought she heard her door shake as though someone had tried to enter.

"How can you think that?"

"I watched," Dandelion said while the other voices continued in a mumbled chorus in the background. "He didn't have any of the signs of lying. Even tone not modulating. And his wife didn't seem scared of him. She even corrected him a time or two. You did pick up that she was a model?"

"She could have been playing along for survival."

"Maybe. But I'd have detected that."

"Perhaps. I'm not sure you would have."

Silent steps on the pads of her feet carried Sam to the

door. She swung it open and glared around the room to each in turn.

"Jackson didn't change," she scolded. "Whatever his logbook or whatever it is says, or whatever you heard from him, he didn't change."

"He said he's sorry," Dandelion said with the audacity of someone who seemed to believe that words were enough to fix years of abuse. Words wouldn't heal the pain inside of her.

"How did you have time—"

"Dandelion tracked down his ansible number. Then we just called him. He broke down when we mentioned you. His wife said he'd been through years of therapy and he—"

"Stephen thinks she was a model," Clayton volunteered.

"Don't speak for me," Stephen corrected.

"So do I," Dandelion replied. "She had the surgery to remove her barcode. It wasn't very good surgery, either."

"And they have a three-year-old."

"Adopted," Larken said. "I'm not convinced of any of this."

"He said—"

"I don't care what he said," interrupted Sam. "He's evil. Do you hear yourself? He locked me in a basement for over a year. He was going to kill me!"

"Calm down, Sam," Dandelion told her, holding one hand. Sam gritted her teeth and glared.

"You calm down," Sam shouted. "I don't want to calm down. I didn't want you to contact him because I know what he is. I know what he's capable of, and he's already fooled most of you. If you'd just listened...—"

"We don't need to figure out if he's a good person. All

we're trying to decide is whether or not he's the one who sicced the HPM bounty hunters on Sam."

"And I don't think he did it. Why would he? He's got a good life, wife, and kid. Why risk it?"

Sam slammed her door shut. Four minutes later, she emerged with her shoes on and her teeth set in a firm line.

"Where are you going?" Larken asked and made to follow her until Sam squinted her eyes at her.

"Out, unless I'm a prisoner. Nobody here listens to me," she said.

"Hey, wait," Clayton began, but Sam shut him up with a stare. He waited for a second, but before she made it to the front door, he followed up with more useless words. "Are you sure you want to go out alone? Let me come with you."

Another icy stare clipped off questions from anyone else. Sam didn't know where she wanted to go, but she didn't want to be there, surrounded by people who had not only not listened to her, but were actively taking the side of her tormentor. The apologists made her queasy stomach flip, and she bit down her bile.

It only took her ten minutes to make the bus stop and fished cash coins out of her pocket to drop into the bin. Then she offered her wrist to scan to comply with the Madison Rule. The name that popped up was Bridget Webb, a fictitious personality invented to keep her secret. Of all the organizations she had to thank for that, SNO set it up for her before she quit. The group did some good things, and they never messed with her after she left, either. Some days—like today—she missed having them around. They would have believed her.

"League City?"

"Transfer at Central," the gruff bus driver said without

making eye contact. He closed the door behind her. "Pick up the Ninety-Nine. That'll drop you at the ITC, and you can hop onto the hyperloop from there—if you can afford it."

The last statement was followed by a quick up-down scan of her torso, implying that the bus driver had serious doubts about her ability to pay. He didn't make eye contact with her and turned to face traffic before tapping his fingers impatiently on the hover controls. Sam nodded at the side of his head and absently tried to take the seat behind him, still fuming and too angry at first to notice all of the faces swiveling in her direction.

"Shills to the back," came a voice in the crowd. Sam rose to her feet, careful not to look at whoever had made the accusation, and slow-walked to the back of the bus with her head held high.

CHAPTER 27
ROUND TRIP

FIFTEEN MINUTES LATER, Sam found herself at the hyperloop train terminal staring at exorbitantly priced tickets. Almost the cost of a small car for a round-trip ticket. Not a volantrae, but a classic-type car that didn't even have the old internal combustion thrusters. Still, it was a car or a trip to League City to see someone she never wanted to see again for as long as she lived. Her stomach tensed, and the backs of her shoulders tightened as she reached into her handbag and retrieved a cash coin.

The bus driver had been wrong.

One thing about working for the SNO is that they kept whatever they stole. Some of those kidnappings were for ransom and had brought with them hundreds of millions of dollars. Sam, a decoy for at least six of them, got to keep a percentage. Being a model meant no bank account, so some of that loot she carried with her was cash coins, while most of it remained back in the hotel room turned condo that she shared with Larken.

The line moved quickly. Only four people were in line

before her: two tall women who blocked out the overhead light behind the counter from her vantage point and a shorter man—though not by much—with a robust, unkempt beard. An anxious-looking man, skinny enough to blow away in a gentle breeze, rocked backward and forward in line before her. When this man got to the counter, he talked in short, machine-gun bursts interspersed with deep recovery breaths. Finally, her turn came.

"Reason for the trip?"

Sam hadn't thought it through. As a model, she couldn't just hop on the hyperloop to leave the state. She had to be working for someone. Her eyes must have betrayed her lack of a response because the squat man behind the counter narrowed his gaze.

"You do have a reason for your trip, don't you?"

"She's delivering a sensitive document," came a man's voice behind her. Sam turned to see a middle-aged man who had, unbeknownst to Sam, joined the queue behind her. "Aren't you? We were just talking about it."

Sam mouthed the words "thank you." The man only nodded and gave the slightest impression of a smile. Sam turned back to the counter.

"Courier services," she said firmly. The clandestine work Sam done for SNO was coming back to her. Courier services were one of three tasks that made people look the other way for model travel. The others were medical organ transport and, if the destination was near a reclamation facility, then an official-looking "notice of reclamation" data coin was usually enough to make people not ask further questions. Few people wanted to inspect a medical organ box, and fewer still wanted to touch a reclamation data coin, as that validated that models—their faithful servants—had no futures except to die. At least, that's what Sam had always imagined. Underneath the layers of denial, polli had to know the cost of their luxuries on others, and few, in her opinion, liked being confronted with that knowledge.

"What are you transporting?"

Sam affected a careful stutter. "Client says not to tell."

The man scowled at her and held out his hand for a courier coin. Sam didn't have one, but the man didn't know that. She fished a coin out of her pocket, carefully keeping her fingers over the face of it.

"I can't give it to you," she explained. "Please don't make me. The client won't understand."

The queue was backing up, and Sam could feel the heat of anxiety growing within her chest. She could see by the man's face and how his eyes darted past her and back that he felt the pressure to keep the line moving.

"Fifty thousand," the man said, shaking his head.

Sam returned to her bag, pulled out the cash coins, and handed them to the man. He nodded, dropped them into a slot, and flicked his hand over a panel. The gate before her swung open, and she could see the train slowing to a stop through it.

"Destination?"

"League City."

"Ah, Model Valley. Okay, now it makes more sense. Turn right when you go through the door. Your platform is up the stairs and to the left. Here."

He slid a token across the counter, and as he did, he used his left hand, exposing his wrist in the process. Sam saw the barcode stamped across it, and as her fingertips touched the coin, she found it didn't move. The man didn't let go. She looked up to meet his eyes.

"You're rusty," he whispered. "Bring a courier token next time you want to try this. You'll get us both in trouble if you get caught."

"Thank you" was all she could say as he released the coin and let her through the door. Then, in a tone at least twice as jovial as any he'd used with her, she heard him call out "next" to the rest of the queue before the door snapped shut behind her.

The summer heat pounded against Sam's face as she arrived in League City hours later. The layout of the part of the city that Jackson lived in was grid-like with alphabet streets going east to west and numbered streets going north to south. That made it simple to find his bloated corpse of a home. Sam made her way up to the door slowly, expecting at any minute for dogs to be loosed or armed men to recapture her. She reminded herself how stupid the idea was to go stalking her ex-owner, but she had to see him with her own eyes. She had to know whether he'd actually changed. And, if she was honest with herself, another question lingered beneath that one: why?

Why had he done what he'd done to her and to the other models who'd been trapped before her? Why would someone do something like that?

Her finger extended toward the circular pad that would alert anyone inside to her presence if the motion detector hadn't already. As she stood, poised to press it, she couldn't force her finger to do it. Stuck on its own, her finger resisted. This didn't stop the door from sliding open, revealing a perky woman with thick brownish-blond hair and rosy cheeks interrupted by pink-glossed lips. Wide, clear brown eyes stared into Sam's and the woman's lips curled into a bright smile.

"Mom, who is it? Mom?"

The voice came from behind. A little boy's face peeked around the woman's left side, between her wide hips and the door frame. There, a little round face with equally red cheeks took Sam in. A little round face with steely gray eyes. Jackson's eyes.

"Is...Jackson here?"

The woman's face flashed something Sam didn't quite pick up on. Sam thought she saw her eyes widen and the smile disappear for only a fraction of a second. Then it returned with even more intensity.

"Who may I ask is calling?"

"Sam. Tell him that. He'll know who I am."

The woman didn't have a chance to fetch Jackson because he was there within a matter of seconds. Only it wasn't Jackson. His cold stare was unmistakable, even if it adorned a face carved into a smile. He even had the same gray eyes. But this man was almost twenty years younger than Jackson when Sam left, so there was no way it was him. But those cold gray eyes...

"Sam!"

Jackson pushed his way in front of the woman, ignoring her completely. His actions did not look like love. He even ignored the boy. One glance from Jackson sent the kid sprinting away. The woman began to follow the child, only to stop, turn, and wait.

"Jackson?"

He nodded. Locks of golden hair hung down before his face as he did.

"You're back!"

"I'm not back," she said. "Someone told me you'd changed, and I had to see it myself."

"I have changed, Sam. Deirdre, there has made me a changed man. Deirdre, along with a melted face. The pain involved in that was terrible."

He didn't turn toward the woman when he said her name. His eyes never left Sam and when he said the last part, his eyebrows narrowed almost imperceptibly.

Sam continued, "And a child?"

"We decided to start a family. The little tyke is just like his father."

The woman made a sound that seemed something like a cough. When Sam looked at her, the woman's eyes bulged and her bottom lip seemed to shake. Sam stared for too long. Jackson turned to follow her gaze, and the woman turned her face at the last minute, blocking her face from them with her hand.

"I see," Sam said, still staring at the woman. "And you respect models now, I hear?"

"The tide is turning, Sam. Everyone has to get on the right side of that. Won't be too long before your kind will be free. You might call me a visionary, I suppose."

"Visionary?"

"And I owe it all to you," Jackson continued, his face now curled into an obvious snarl. "Without that little splash, I wouldn't have found the Immortality Program and wouldn't have met my beloved Deirdre. We've had so much fun together, right, hun? I was in a really bad place there for a while. Without Deirdre to keep my mind off things, I don't know what I would have done."

Deirdre made a little sound that felt like a whimper to Sam just before she fast-walked down the hall after the child.

"You haven't changed at all, have you?" Sam said in a harsh whisper.

"I'm sure I don't know what you mean," Jackson told her with a sneer. "Deirdre's been with me for four years now. We're in love." The words dripped from his mouth.

"You hired those men to find me, didn't you?"

"I don't know what you're talking about," Jackson said. "What men?"

"Bounty hunters? HPM?"

The woman was back, drifting in like a silent haunt. Her eyes had gone puffy, and she held the child by the hand. She only stared forward with the plastic smile back on her face. At least, that was what Sam thought at first. Sam noticed a faint head tilt when she looked more closely and let Jackson's denials fade into the auditory background.

Deirdre wasn't broken yet, and that made Sam's heart jump. The woman was attempting to send her a message. If Sam thought she understood what that message was: no, Jackson hadn't changed, and more importantly, yes, he'd hired the bounty hunters. Sam nodded, trying to make it clear that she'd understood and timing her nod with one of Jackson's protests. The woman's eyebrows crept in together, and her upper lip curled as she bared her teeth. Deirdre's eyes stabbed at the back of Jackson's head.

Perhaps now, Deirdre was a captive and a victim. But those eyes were so filled with the same rage that Sam had felt before she'd left. Those eyes were the eyes of a would-be killer, and Jackson didn't even seem to notice.

"So you see, it's been fine here. And, of course, we are doing amazingly well. Is that right, hun?"

"Amazing, Jackie," the woman dutifully responded behind his back, hatred never leaving her face. "Amazing."

———

So, of course, it wasn't true that he had changed. Sam hadn't doubted that, and now that she'd seen it with her face, she loathed to leave the woman and child in his grip. For her though, it still hurt to walk and even speaking sent spikes of pain through her jaw. This wasn't the time for her to attack him.

At least, that was what she told herself before the rage subsumed her thought processes and replaced everything inside of her with white heat. She launched herself through the doorway and clawed at his face.

Jackson hadn't been expecting it, which was clear by the way her fingernails quickly and effortlessly gouged his left eye partly out of its socket. But she didn't stop there, because to stop meant to give him time to think, and that would have let him come recover enough to put her on the back foot.

Sam wasn't a fighter when she'd run. She had only been an "escort" model, only trained in the art of seduction. But that was before she'd joined SNO, and before she'd helped liberate hundreds of models just like her while working with them. And that was before she'd been strong enough to even talk back to this man. Now, with deftness and accuracy, she plunged a knee into his ribcage, knocking him over at the waist. Then she pulled the same knee back up and reveled in the satisfying crunch of his nose breaking.

Deirdre did nothing.

Sam hadn't expected her to. She knew the position the woman was in and wouldn't have asked her to help, either. Nor did she need the help because right at that moment, Jackson wasn't just Jackson. Jackson was the men who'd cornered her and stolen her agency away with their actions. Jackson was the man who'd screwed the lid down on the vat as the fluids inside licked pain against her skin. Jackson was the entire world that shoved and wedged her into the tiny, helpless soul she'd become.

He fell to the ground and she fell atop him, swinging wildly like a tornado of hands and nails. He tried to defend himself and for one moment, managed to get a hand around her throat. That was when Deirdre finally acted, and planted a kick, a rather indecisive and short kick, into his ribs that Sam had thought she'd probably broken. He pulled back into himself, and Sam engaged again, this time with knees and elbows, and finally, with her fists. Again and again, she hit him, seeing nothing but red, until four fingers slid over her shoulder. Then she got the message.

Enough.

It surprised Sam to realize she'd been crying this entire time. She wiped her face clean of tears and gazed up into the stoic brown eyes of someone who'd been as abused as she had. She lowered her fists to her side and pulled herself off of him. Sam planted a weak kick into his side to prompt him up onto his feet as her mind raced through what she might say to fix the situation. A model attacking her owner for the first time was unheard of. Twice would get her killed. But she could convince him not to talk, somehow.

He didn't move.

She kicked him again.

Still nothing. A tiny squeak came from Deirdre.

"Did you kill him?"

The evidence was in that probably she had. Sam hadn't necessarily been trying to kill, only to hurt and to pour all of her own pain into him so that maybe, if there was anything in there to reach, he could hurt too and finally understand. But Deirdre was right. He wasn't moving.

"I guess I did," she said, then quickly, "Sorry."

Deirdre motioned to him.

"Check," she said.

Reluctantly, Sam knelt down, feeling her pain again as her leg bent awkwardly. She pressed two fingers to his neck and watched for breath. No pulse, no breathing. Dead as burnt coffee. She looked up at Deirdre. "Does he still have the basement?"

Deirdre said nothing. Sam recognized herself in this, too. In a former life, she'd freaked out internally when she'd thought she'd killed him. Not anymore, and never again. The only way to shake Deirdre out of it was to possibly scare her a little. Sam narrowed her eyebrows, feeling a knot in the pit of her stomach as she did what she had to do.

"Now, Deirdre. Tell me how to get there. Is it in the same place? Do you have the key? Or do you want to be found responsible for this mess?"

"Biometric," she said, nodding toward the kitchen.

"Good," Sam said. "Good. Now, I'll take care of this. You two need to run. Take his volantrae and go to Fourth Avenue. There should be an SNO branch there, and they can protect you. But you have to go, now."

Deirdre got her child and fled. It was probably best, as she was just going to get in the way. Sam dragged the body across the kitchen floor until she neared the refrigerator. There was a panel that looked like a pantry door, yet when she tried to pull it open, it held fast. She pulled the body the rest of the way toward the door and then tried. It clicked open.

Sam listened first. She heard a shuffling sound from below, and she thought whimpering perhaps. She shoved the body through the door and watched it tumble down the flight of stairs with grim satisfaction. Then, arching her back just once to stretch, she made her way into the darkness. As she approached the bottom, the light came on.

No, he hadn't stopped.

In cages beside where the body had come to a stop were three women, all models, and two of whom were immobile. The horrific stench of decay told her that at least one had been dead a while. In the other cage, no larger than a dog's kennel, was another, cowering in the back. She opened the kennel and extended a hand.

The woman staring back at her had wild eyes and wilder hair, and cuts on her face. It took five minutes for her to convince the woman to come forward, and another ten to convince her to run. The SNO branch wasn't far, and Sam still had work to do. Once the woman was safely out of the house, Sam surveyed the room.

Then it hit her: let the police deal with it. He fell down the stairs one day and didn't get up again, leaving the door to the torture dungeon open for all to see. All she had to do was get rid of any evidence that she was here. She walked slowly around the room and didn't see any cameras. With the same deliberate, slow, exploration, she covered the inside and outside of the building. No cameras, probably because cameras would not have been good for his extracurricular activities. It was good enough.

Sam took a quick shower, borrowed an outfit from Deirdre's closet, and left as quietly as she'd come. She wasted no time in distancing herself, catching the evening loop back to Seattle. It wasn't until she passed the city limits sign that Sam let out a deep, lengthy exhale and then, unexpectedly, dropped into a parade of sobs. Nobody on the bus bothered to tell her it was okay because, after all, she was only a model.

RESENTMENT AND HOPELESSNESS

I SHOULD LEAVE.

The thought came upon Dandelion without warning. Sam had run off over eight hours ago. Both Stephen and Larken had searched for most of that time, but wherever Sam was, she hadn't gone to any of her usual sulking spots. While they were gone, Dandelion found herself alone in the hotel room with Clayton, who only paced around like Sam's abandoned puppy and made things even weirder between them.

Yet Dandelion stood there, circuits connecting and disconnecting inside of her, neural networks labeling her emotions according to the standard model she'd developed from observing human behavior. She found two new ones. The first of which flared up whenever she looked at Clayton pacing in small circles, hand on his chin. This emotion carried with it a touch of fear at the sure knowledge that Clayton would never be hers. Longing, fear, and anger all wove tightly together into a little ball of a new sensation she decided must have been jealousy.

That realization, along with the way Clayton sometimes

stole glances toward her, his eyes falling just below the hem of her short dress and then away, made her feel something else. This emotion was sadness coupled with anxiety. This one she knew because she'd felt it before, but not in a very long time.

Shame.

Dandelion cleared her throat to say something to Clayton, and his head swiveled toward her as soon as she did. She found she had nothing to say. The words that she'd thought might smooth the situation didn't seem enough. Sam was her patient, and not her enemy, in love or any other way. Clayton was her former coworker. And, as she had been for most of her life, Dandelion was still alone.

I should leave.

What was she doing there anyway? Her "patient" had gone and would very likely get herself killed. Larken and Stephen were gone and Clayton couldn't look her in the eye. What was even the point?

Every time she thought of leaving, Dandelion's thoughts floated in another direction. The idea of leaving Clayton here pacing alone wasn't something she could make okay in her mind. He was almost frantic with worry. His usual chipper conversation and endless musings about justice and hope had all come to an end, making the silence that occupied the space between them even more salient.

"She'll be okay, Clayton," Dandelion said, not sure why. She then realized that she was pacing as well and stopped herself just short of another passage through the kitchen. Clayton stopped too and turned his wide, glassy eyes in her direction.

"You think so?"

"She's strong. I've known her a lot longer than you have. She's stronger than you know."

She watched him to see if her words made an impact. Nothing at first, not at the superficial level at which most humans examine other humans. But his pulse did drop, as she could tell by close monitoring of the fluctuation of the heat in his extremities. It wasn't much, but enough that she knew that her words still mattered to him, which was more than she'd hoped for. This time, his eyes kept hers instead of calling to the outfit—for a second. Then they dropped again and for the first time in hours, she saw a thin start of a smile on his lips.

"What's with the outfit, anyway? You never dress that way."

Shame. Embarrassment. She labeled the emotions as they came. The next was fear, and finally when all of those slammed against the immovable rock of desire, determination. She returned the wavering smile.

"You don't like it?"

He shook his head. "I didn't say that. I've just never seen you dressed like that," he said. To her surprise, he moved in closer to her. "Never before that I can remember."

His eyes took one more trip over the length of her body before he was too close to do another body scan. Clayton leaned his head in close, and for one unreasonable microsecond, Dandelion thought that he might be expecting a kiss. Expectation. Hope. Then disappointment as she turned away from him. Whether he wanted a kiss or not, it wouldn't be her that he was kissing in his mind. But it turned out she was wrong.

"Is it that Stephen guy? Do you like him? I mean, he's

kind of skinny, but everyone's got a type. If you want, I think he's okay with me. I could talk to him for you."

Dandelion was still looking away, mulling her response, and forcing herself out of her emotional spiral.

Self-loathing. Guilt.

Loneliness.

She knew these emotions well.

"No," she said, her voice less than a whisper. "No. I just had been wearing the same clothes for too long. Larken had these extras, so I borrowed some. Not my usual style because it's not my style. I feel a little..."

Exposed. Vulnerable. Hopeless.

"Underdressed?" Clayton chimed in, nearly getting it exactly right.

She turned slowly, correcting her face by tightening different nano-servos in her cheeks and around her eyes until the signs of worry faded. Then, she plastered on a fake smile that she, unlike humans, she could force all the way up to her eyes.

"Yeah," she replied, followed by a slight chuckle. "Yeah, definitely that."

To emphasize, she pulled down the bottom of the shirt-dress only to expose about an inch more cleavage.

The door burst open, pulling both her eyes and Clayton's toward it, still within inches of each other. As Dandelion realized how close the pair were, and the possible message that might send, Sam breached the doorway. Her eyes went first to Clayton, then to Dandelion whose hands had frozen mid-pull at the shirt-dress hem, and then to Dandelion's cleavage in a scan that was almost too quick for even Dandelion to see. Dandelion let the shirt hem go and regretted it instantly as the hem snapped up and revealed much more than she'd intended to, almost rising over her waist. Dandelion grabbed the hem once again and pulled it taut. Better to show too much cleavage than everything under her shirt.

Sam didn't act as though she thought anything untoward was going on. Dandelion could see it in her eyes, though. Vindication hid waiting to be meted out.

"He hasn't changed," Sam said, her voice echoing through the room with the tenor of her voice.

"Who?" Clayton said as he inched away from Dandelion.

"Jackson Grayson," Sam said. The authority in her statement and voice brought the next question from Dandelion.

"You talked to him?"

Sam nodded.

"Are you okay?"

Sam nodded again.

"I met the wife. Not through holovid or ansible, but in real life. He abuses her. I'm sure of it. He's not a good person in the least. This whole thing he's doing is marketing. Trying to get ahead of public sentiment. He's..."

The narrow gap of space between Dandelion and Clayton seemed to catch Sam's attention as she stopped midsentence.

"Where's everyone?"

"They're out looking for you, Sam," Dandelion said. Sam's cheeks took on a soft pink tone. She pulled her hands to her elbows, crossing her arms before her. The door clicked into place behind her.

"And you both have been here alone this entire time?"

"Well...," began Dandelion.

Sam's face scrunched up into something resembling a

glare. "This entire time, while everyone else was out looking, you—"

Sam stopped speaking. She closed her eyes for a fraction of a second, and Dandelion knew that whatever came out of her mouth next was going to be suspicion and fear talking. She could have overpowered Sam's voice with her own interjections. That's not what friends did, though. Not at all, and she still wanted Sam as a friend—or she thought she did. Sam stared directly at Dandelion.

"What's wrong with you? Are your circuits blown? What makes you think what you're doing is okay?"

"My circuits...," Dandelion began but couldn't think of what to say next. She looked at Clayton, seeking a sign that he had interpreted the question as a figure of speech but got nothing from his hopeless stare.

"For an AI, you make dumb mistakes sometimes. Most men aren't into robots, Dandelion. It's a fact. Clayton doesn't like you."

Unnecessary cruelty.

Thirty million people across the planet own companion droids, and more than that lease. Seventy million people lease models for evenings of debauchery, some on long-time contractual basis similar to the geishas of history's past.

The thoughts flowed into Dandelion's mind, preparing her to win an argument that would be useless to have. Clayton's eyes widened as Sam's unmistakable accusation landed. His irises swiveled toward Dandelion.

"You're a..."

"Person. I'm a person, Clayton," Dandelion insisted and reached toward him with one hand. Clayton recoiled and covered two feet in about a second of backing away from her. Dandelion searched Sam's face just in time to see the anger fade. Those hard eyebrows softened, and Sam's hand came up to her lips, and back down again.

"Dandelion," she started.

Dandelion didn't listen. Sometimes it was good to be a robot, as Sam had called her. Dandelion didn't have to listen as humans did. She sped toward Clayton who tried to back away more only to collide with the kitchen counter and stop. Dandelion didn't stop. She shoved past him and, watching the evolving emotions across Sam's face, didn't bother to process what any of them might mean.

Shame. Embarrassment.

Betrayal.

Dandelion pushed past Sam too and ejected herself into the hallway. No tears. Not a single damn one. In another life, or maybe in this one, she would gift herself tears and the catharsis of a good, deep cry. For now, she rode the wave of emotions toward the elevator and past a couple of men in long coats with priest collars.

She almost didn't register the meaning of that. Her mind, working on its own, time-traveled back to the bus. The whistle brought her back. As the elevator doors closed, she heard it. They were the bounty hunters, but the doors had shut by that point. She slammed the buttons for the next floor above and below. She didn't care which, she just needed to get out of the elevator.

The elevator chose up, and the door to the elevator opened slowly after only a short lift ride. Dandelion sprinted out, ignoring the looks of a family of five who seemed to be on their way for a swim. She accidentally elbowed the father of the group hard enough to send him face-first into the wall. Issuing a quick apology, she didn't slow down until she got to the stairs at the end of a hall that seemed entirely too long.

Dandelion took the stairs two at a time as she descended down the vandalized hallway, only wondering for half a second what sort of good time could be had by calling Becca's ansible number before the crude drawing beneath illustrated at least one thing Becca must have been good at—in far too much detail. Dandelion reached her floor in less than five seconds and burst out into the hallway. Staring the length of fifteen rooms down the hallway, she saw light on the floor before the open door to Larken and Sam's room. Half a second later, she heard a high-pitched scream—Sam's scream, followed by the thud of something heavy falling to the floor. Dandelion sprinted toward the open doorway and peered in through the opening.

Clayton was crumbled on the floor in a mound. He didn't move or shake, and a deep gash above his left eye told her why. The two men held Sam by the arms and were in the process of dragging her over Clayton's body and toward the door, blocked by Dandelion. One of the men noticed her and stopped in his tracks.

"Move," the man said. "This has nothing to do with you, whoever you are. Go away and you won't get hurt."

Sam's wide eyes caught on Dandelion's. Dandelion gave her best reassuring look and examined both of the men closely. Neither held a weapon on Sam, so that was good. A baton hung from the belt of one of them, swinging loosely as though it had just been placed. A red droplet suspended from the end that Dandelion suspected to be blood. The man on Sam's right had no baton. Through the bulk of his jacket, Dandelion made out a shape statistically likely to be a proton rifle. He would be first.

Without another word, she ducked behind the couch arm, crouched down low and sprung over the couch in one smooth motion. She crossed the room in less than a second and connected one hand with the neck of the man with the hidden proton rifle. The stiffness of her fingers crushed into his Adam's apple and the man crumbled atop of Clayton. With a spin, Dandelion lifted her left leg into the air and curled it back as she twisted. Her calf and thigh wrapped around Sam while her heel connected with the other man's face. A second later, and he too was down, and Dandelion was as motionless as a statue.

Dandelion lowered her leg and twisted back around in one single motion before she knelt down and peeled the men off of Clayton. Using the palm of her hand for a more accurate reading than she could get with thermal imaging, she clocked Clayton's pulse was slow enough that he was likely unconscious but didn't seem anywhere close to being in danger. She ripped one of the man's brown coats to create a makeshift bandage strip and dressed Clayton's head with it. Then she lifted Clayton in her arms and glided toward the couch, placing him gently atop the pillows that had been dislodged by her initial leap. Dandelion felt a gentle touch across the back of one of her elbows as she rose.

"Thank you," Sam said, her voice wavering but not breaking. "Thank you, Dandelion. You've saved me again."

"I'm programmed to," Dandelion shot back. "No thanks necessary. We robots do what we're told."

The words tumbled out, to Dandelion's dismay, and she wanted them back. It was too late, though, and as much as she didn't want to have said them, she wasn't confused about the truth they conveyed. Sam, a model and outcast herself, had maligned Dandelion and betrayed her. Dandelion couldn't conceive what words might make that okay.

"No, you're not," Sam said. "I'm sorry. I shouldn't have said what I did. I...I shouldn't have."

Dandelion ignored her.

"Clayton will be fine," she said. "Clayton will be fine, and you both will be happy. I'm certain of it."

Words gone and lacking more, Dandelion guided Sam's hand to Clayton's forehead.

"Keep a little pressure there. I don't think he'll need stitches."

As soon as Sam's hand was firmly in place, Dandelion rose and turned, ignoring the fact that her hair jutted out in precarious angles from her head or that her shirt-dress revealed much more than she'd wanted. What did it matter anyway? To anyone who knew her, all the shirt dress revealed were servos and nano-servos and fake skin. Dandelion made no effort to hide herself as she crossed the room for yet another time, heading toward the door.

"Don't open it until you confirm it's Larken or Stephen," she called back over her shoulder. "Be safe."

"Dandelion, come back. I'm sorry. I'm so, so sorry."

"No," Dandelion replied. "I don't think you are. I think you and Larken both come to me when you need me, but neither of you give much thought to who I am. I'm a useful robot who happens to always say yes. But you're right, you know."

"Right about what?"

Dandelion slowed by the entryway. "I don't have to help you. I don't have to help either of you. I was stupid enough to think that we could be friends."

She passed through the door into the hallway and, at first, headed toward the elevator. But then the thought occurred to her that if Larken and Stephen came back, they would likely use the elevator, so she passed it by in favor of the stairs. And, checking for the first time that day, she only had about half a charge left.

Half a charge and no hope left.

Resentment. Abandonment.

Hopelessness.

One step after another. Slow. Steady. Aimless.

CHAPTER 29
TURNING TABLES

"THAT MAN," Larken said, pointing with her head as Stephen and she played the part of romantic partners on a date. It was uncomfortable and awkward to occasionally grab Stephen's perpetually clammy hands, but romantic partners made for good camouflage.

"I see him," Stephen replied. "He's not going in."

Larken checked again. The man stopped outside of the door and fiddled with what looked to be a communicator. Larken stared at the man's lips moving.

"He's talking to someone," she said. Just as she did, the man's hand went for the door handle, and he yanked hard on it once. It swung open, and he shook his head in disapproval. Then he punched something into a number pad beside the door that Larken hadn't noticed before. One more good yank (and this time, it didn't open), and the man was off down the street.

"He could just be the landlord," Stephen said. Larken was about to agree when the man pursed his lips up and began whistling that same tune she'd heard so many times before she had to fight the urge to whistle along.

"It's him," she said. He looked different—maybe it was the clothes—but she was certain it was the same man.

Following him shouldn't have worked. Larken scooted slowly with her cane in front of her and her back throbbing behind her, struggling to keep up with Stephen, who managed to temper his brisk pace to just faster than she could hobble. The man didn't seem overly concerned that anyone might be following him, which helped. And the man kept the whistling up for most of the time they stumbled down the alleys and across streets in pursuit. While they were in the city proper, Larken could see how the walk could have invigorated someone like Stephen, whose back probably didn't torture him with every step.

Several escalators delivered them down to Strata o. Larken immediately became more cautious, examining every nook and cranny for the odd hidden criminal ready to lurch forward. But none did, and save the man before them, no other people graced the empty alleyways. The city had already begun to fall asleep. Larken felt the weight of suggestion drain her momentarily.

The buildings thinned out, and the streets grew even quieter. Larken became self-conscious of the scraping sound her cane made sliding over the pebbles spread over the road. The pavement showed cracks the farther they went along, ducking behind foliage whenever the tan-coated man ahead ducked seemed to slow or stopped suddenly.

Something about the trail sparked something in Larken's memory. It might have been the stars that suddenly peeked out as they passed into a clearing, or the sound of nearby water trickling through rocks. She wasn't certain as she clipped along in the dirt. Larken stumbled and her cane went wide out from under her. Biting her lip as she fell, Larken braced for the inevitable collision with the ground. When it never came, she opened her eyes. Stephen lowered her the rest of the way to the ground and ducked beside her.

"Stay down," he said, then motioned ahead. Look, his head movement said, Look at where we are.

Larken sucked in her breath as her eyes riveted to the gray iron walls climbing up into the sky. Behind this building, she knew, lay sewage pipe dumping fluids into a brackish pond, if it was operational again.

"Bremerton," she said in a low sigh.

"Yeah," Stephen agreed. "And look over there."

Up ahead, free of the confines of the forest trail, the man walked to the front gate. The doors slid open wide enough for Larken to see the lines of models awaiting their fates. It had to be operational again—somehow. Thin, emaciated bodies formed chains, many of whom didn't seem like humans with only the leathery covering wrapping their bones, yet somehow they stood. The door slid shut, slowly, pulling two giant sections of wall to meet together.

Larken remembered the blows to her neck and chest. She remembered the evening that she'd fallen and thought for a second that she would finally feel the sweet mercy of death only to be caught in the clutches of the pale android with the partially-completed face and a smile that widened with each blow. The muscles in her back tightened as the pair approached the building, careful to stay in the brush. Larken shuddered as the thought ran through her mind. The android who had given her, her limp was not so very much different than Dandelion.

She cast a glance to Stephen, whose wide eyes told her

what she needed to know. If Sam was here, then she had likely gotten captured and was in one of those lines. It would take an army to get her back out again.

Tall and ancient dying trees stretched out of the uncut brush that concealed Larken and Stephen, reaching toward the sky.

"How do we find out?" asked Stephen.

Larken didn't answer. She had an answer but didn't like it. Even SNO would be wary of trying to break into what had become a military complex more than a reclamation center with its obvious fortifications and newly added guard towers. She tumbled through responses in her mind only to run out of ideas that instilled hope. If Sam was in the building before them, then Sam was lost to them.

The sound of tin bees rattling against each other reminded her that her communicator was still on. She fumbled it out of her pocket to turn it off and sighed in relief when she saw who it was. Larken switched the receiver to private mode and answered.

"Dandelion's gone," came Sam's voice over the ansible connection.

"Where are you, Sam? You had us so worried."

Sam paused momentarily as though she hadn't expected the question even though she'd been gone for over eight hours.

"I'm at the hotel. Where are you?"

"Looking for you. We followed your attacker to the Bremerton Reclamation Plant. Stephen and I were sitting here trying to figure out how to get inside and rescue you."

The tail end of Sam's sigh whispered through the receiver. Larken thought the sigh was about their wasted time investigating the plant.

"Stephen's there?"

"Uh...yeah. Why?"

"Am I on private mode?"

"Yeeessss."

"You and I have to talk. Are you coming back?"

"We'll be there shortly."

"No. You. Larken, I don't want Stephen back here. I know he means well, but he's too much. And he's got work to do anyway. His owners are kind and very generous, but he does have responsibilities, like that coffee stand. How long can he keep that coffee stand closed? Do you know how hard it is for models to get paying jobs? Tell him to go back to work. You and I need to talk. It's about Dandelion."

"I'm not doing that."

"But..."

"If you don't want him there, then you tell him. I'm not coming between you two."

"There isn't a we two, Larken. That's the problem."

A mosquito landed on Larken's arm, and she swiped at it, tucking the communicator between her shoulder and ear and glancing toward Stephen as he talked, evidently having over-heard more than she thought he could.

"She doesn't want me there. I'm fine with not being there, Larken. I'm not going to force myself back into her life."

"No to you too. Nobody's talking through me."

She pointed with her right hand, and the communicator slid forward. She swiveled on her cane and pulled her hand back to catch the communicator against her clavicle. With a grunt, she flipped the switch on the side into projection mode, sending Sam's image into a shaded enclave behind them against some short rhododendron bushes. That was the only way the camera worked on her cheap junk communicator. Larken aimed the camera end toward the building and heard Sam inhale deeply. Her projection didn't have anything flat to hit, so bits of Sam spread across the leaves and trees in front of them.

"What the hell did they do to it?"

"Fortified after the fight, I guess."

"Hold on," Sam said then muttered something off-camera that Larken couldn't make out. Sam continued. "Clayton did some searching. He says that this plant was sold off recently. Emergent Biotechnology sold it to Liberty Group last year at a loss. There are four other sales by Emergent-owned facilities on this coast. Prescient sold five of theirs on the East Coast to the same people."

"So there are nine strongholds like this in the nation?"

"Probably more. Larken," Sam said, "Clayton and I are packing up the hotel. Is there anything you don't want to leave behind?"

"W...why?"

"HPM followed me back from Jackson's. It's what we have to talk about."

"Followed you back—"

"Long story, Larken. No time now. Come back. We'll wait for you but hurry, okay?"

"Don't hang up, Sam," Stephen said. For half a second, Larken awaited the telltale click of disconnection, but to her surprise, Sam kept the communication open. "I just wanted —I mean—"

"Stephen, whatever it is, it can wait. You guys are going to get caught over there."

"It can't, Sam," he protested. "I'm sorry about the way I've been acting. You make your own decisions, and I should respect them. I understand why you didn't want me around, and I'm sorry I've been acting like a jerk."

"Fine," Sam said, but her tone said anything but. Then the connection went dead. Stephen looked at Larken, and she noticed the exhaustion in his eyes. Like her, he'd been there the entire time, even if he had been difficult and stubborn for most of it. She flashed a smile and turned to leave the facility.

"Got to go," she said as she pushed her cane forward onto the leaf-covered animal trail they'd followed through the trees to come to this concealed clearing. Over her shoulder, Larken said, "Come or don't. Up to you."

"Fine," he retorted in a low growl that seemed just as convincing as Sam's curt response.

The laughing face of the android woman who had hospitalized Larken flashed through her mind, morphed into Dandelion, and then was gone. All that remained was the unsettling feeling that something had broken in Dandelion—something she should have seen, and something she could have prevented. Stephen pushed through the underbrush with his boots. At first, Larken glared at him in the darkness, willing him to silence. Then she realized that they'd been in the woods for so long that there was no way anyone could hear them now. The brush cleared, and they emerged on Strata 0, at the foot of an escalator that stretched into the sky.

"After you," Stephen said, his voice gruff and curt.

Larken didn't acknowledge. She'd insisted that he come, but his attitude and the cold ambivalence he pulled on for protection grated against her nature. He wasn't a soldier, yet lacked the initiative to be a leader. She wondered if having him with them was worse than not having him.

Beggars can't be choosers, she reminded herself. He had to do until something better came along.

Most of the walk back passed in silence. Larken shifted her weight on the escalator platform, trying unsuccessfully to quell the perpetual ache in her back; she couldn't maintain the illusion. She knew what she was up against, and she couldn't shuck it onto someone else's back. Her role was larger than even Lancaster's hulking frame, whether she wanted it or not.

CHAPTER 30
A MOMENT OF INSECURITY

SEVENTEEN MISSED CALLS.

Clayton didn't even know seventeen people. As he flicked through the numbers one at a time on his communicator, shaped like a fat palm-sized envelope, he didn't recognize a single one.

"Are you going to give me your number?" Sam asked without lifting her legs from his lap. He smiled and slid his fingers over her calf muscles.

"What makes you think I want you to call me?"

"One would usually expect—"

Her face seemed to scrunch up when she stopped as though she'd just peeled a lemon, sliced it into bits, and crammed the entire thing into her mouth at once. She sealed her mouth shut and turned, then seemed to exhale slowly. Clayton immediately jerked forward to find himself pushed backward by her legs as she also came forward at the same time.

One second, maybe two, she spent biting on her lower lip with her eyes scrunched shut. The couch, despite its plushness, suddenly felt hard and uncomfortable. Clayton only stared as her cheeks went pale white and then billowed outward in slow motion. Half a second later, as if she'd made her decision, Sam twisted to the side and unloaded the contents of her stomach onto the floor in front of him.

Clayton gritted his teeth as tightly as he could and use all of his willpower to keep the bile down. Triggered by the smell, he worked his stomach and chest muscles to keep from contributing to the mess dripping down the couch cushions.

It didn't help.

As soon as Sam had recovered, Clayton's stomach clenched together all at once, and vomit flew from between his teeth. Worse than anything Sam had done, he caught the table and Sam's lower legs with green and fuchsia chunks. Somewhere in there was the doughnut, freshly made with actual real ingredients that they'd purchased earlier at the doughnut shop a block up from the hotel.

Sam giggled.

Finding nothing funny about his most recent humiliation, Clayton did not giggle.

"Are you a sympathetic regurgitator?" Sam asked. He met her green eyes and saw her raised eyebrows that hovered over a grin stretching ear-to-ear. At first, he fought the urge, but finally he cracked his lips apart and let a tiny harumph escape. Then he zipped his mouth again, but he let the corners of his lips stay where they were.

"I'm glad you think that's funny. It got all over you," he replied.

"I know. So much worse than I could have done. You definitely win the prize."

"There's a prize for this?"

The heat of embarrassment disappeared as the humor of the situation finally penetrated Clayton's shame.

"What happened?" he asked, carefully pivoting her legs off of him to examine the damage to his pants. He was certain he saw the smile disappear from her face. Then it reappeared so quickly he thought he might have imagined it.

"What do you mean?" she asked. "I don't think anything happened. I mean, I feel a little nauseous is all. After all that's happened though, I don't think it's such a big deal."

"Have you been nauseous this entire time?"

This time it was clear. The smile left Sam's face completely. It didn't come back. He heard the door open, and Sam switched from looking at him to looking over his shoulder.

"Larken, you're back."

"Of course, I'm back. What about the—"

That also wasn't his imagination. As soon as Larken's eyes landed on Clayton, she stopped talking.

"About the...," he asked, encouraging her to finish.

"Nothing," Larken said, her eyes drifting to the mess on the floor. "Just be careful Sam, okay?"

"I'm fine, Larken," Sam retorted. "Just feeling a bit nauseous. That's all."

There was something there. Clayton was typically good at figuring out when he was being lied to, which was one of the reasons he didn't have very many friends. Once in high school he'd broken up with a girl who told him he looked great when he didn't. Only a little white lie, but if she saw fit to lie about that, what else would she lie about? There was definitely something up, but he didn't have time to parse out what it was. He had Sam's and his vomit-covered legs to worry about.

"Here." He heard Stephen's voice but didn't see him yet. It took Clayton a moment to figure out that the voice had come from behind Larken, who from his angle, blocked everything to the door. A cloth sailed over Larken's head and landed on Clayton's lap. He dutifully took the cloth and wiped fluids from his legs as Sam's feet lowered to the carpet.

"Sorry, Sam," Clayton muttered.

"There's nothing to be sorry for."

"I threw up on your legs, so maybe that is something."

"I did it first. You're okay," she assured him. Another cloth sailed at them. This time it was from the kitchen. Stephen had moved quickly, as Larken still stood hunched over her cane by the door.

"Take it easy, please," Larken said to her. Then, in a voice so low that he almost didn't hear, he heard: "At least until you decide."

"Decide what?" Clayton asked as he saturated the next towel with the remainder of his lap-vomit. He turned one eye toward Sam, who seemed to be edging herself away from him.

"Any word on Dandelion?" Sam asked, directing her question toward Larken and notably not responding to Clayton. He felt the heat rise in the back of his neck.

"Decide what?"

Sam made to rub her eyes, but her hands were still slick-shiny from vomit cleaning. She stopped her arm midway from her side to her face. Sam's green eyes swiveled from Larken to Stephen and back to Clayton. Gritting her teeth again, this time without any vomit-induced pre-actions, she nodded to Clayton as though she'd decided to tell him something important. He gulped.

"The baby," she told him. Then she seemed to notice that

her hand was on her belly, and he noticed at the same time. She lowered her hand down to her side. "Whether to keep the baby."

"They...," he began and then stopped, his lower lip quivering beyond his control. "They did that to you?"

Sam didn't nod. She didn't even acknowledge the question. Instead, she only gazed at him, her soft green eyes going glassy but unwaveringly connected to his own.

"I thought models couldn't get pregnant."

That was a stupid thing to say. He gritted his teeth after the words escaped his lips. A tear escaped Sam's emerald eyes and fled down her lightly-freckled cheek. And, as she turned away from him, he lifted his arm to try to stop her. He touched her on the shoulder only to get a shrug in response. His face felt flush and damp as his stomach roiled. It was impossible to tell the cause of the tightening of his gut. Clayton tried to pull in the air and use a breathing technique —long, slow breaths—to unroll the panic in his gut. He felt starved for oxygen as he tried, leading him to faster and faster breaths, one after the other. It was Larken who finally responded to him.

"One in a thousand can," Larken said while Sam busied herself doing something in the small kitchen area. Clayton's eyes followed Sam's walk around the island. Larken's voice dropped. "But whether the child will make it to term is impossible to know. And just so you know, your reaction to this isn't working for you."

"Reaction?" He knew exactly what she was talking about. The blood pounded between his ears, and he felt like a frayed wire sparking, ready to ignite something nearby— anything. They had done this to her, and they would suffer for it. But he didn't know how. Clayton was good at protesting and playing the occasional video game. Even in nursing, courtesy of his wide-ranging interests acquiring him a psychiatric nursing certificate to complement his masters of social work, Clayton was only mediocre at best. He'd come to terms with that years ago. No one had ever called him good at relationships.

But as quickly as he'd become the focal point, the focus shifted. Sam moved away from him and onto the story about the people who'd invaded the small apartment, which Clayton had spent most of the time unconscious, except when he awoke in time to help Sam drag the bodies into a nearby stairwell. From Sam's telling, it was Dandelion who leaped over the couch and side-kicked a man, then demolished the other assailant, in less than about five seconds.

His coworker was a secret ninja, and the woman he'd been talking to—bonding with— for over a week now was pregnant and hadn't bothered to tell him.

They hadn't known each other that long. And, his mind tried to rationalize, it wasn't like they were married or anything. So he had no right to feel one way or the other about her pregnancy, and yet still he did. Or...as he thought it through...maybe it wasn't the pregnancy that bothered him as much as the fact that she hadn't told him. They'd spent every waking moment together since they met because it seemed natural and like they'd been together forever and would be on into the future. Yet, here a significant, life-altering, thing existed that she'd not bothered to tell him. And maybe, she'd never intended to, which meant...what?

Clayton's lips cracked into a smile, though there was nothing to smile about. His vision blurred and little floats hovered before his eyes, distorting the background beyond. A vise squeezed his mind, smashing it flat inside his brain.

Larken spoke to him, saying something else, but he couldn't make it out over the incessant and annoying sound of hummingbirds amplified by a thousand in his head. Then he thought the hovering spots were a hummingbird army, arriving to take him away from the absurdity of his life.

His eyesight slowly returned, and instead of hummingbirds all around, he saw only Sam with her eyes fixated on him. Clayton tilted his head sideways to see Larken also staring too, and Stephen standing on the far side of Larken from where Sam was in the kitchen, gaze fixed in Clayton's direction. But no, Stephen wasn't staring at Clayton, but past Clayton. From Stephen's perspective, Clayton was also between him and Sam.

"I'm the one with the child," said Sam. "You don't get to freak out about it. There's a parasite inside of me, and I have to decide whether to keep it or not."

"Why would you keep it?" asked Clayton, ignoring Larken's wide eyes and raised eyebrows, and the red flashing light in his mind that told him not to ask. Was it too fast? Why was Clayton even still in this apartment with a bunch of people he barely knew? His heart sank in his chest as he realized the answer was that he simply hadn't left. Basically, he had wandered into Sam's life and thought he belonged there, but suddenly he wasn't so sure.

"One in a thousand," Sam said. "One in a thousand chance." She lowered her eyes to the counter. "I know how it sounds. I've always wanted to know what it would be like to have a child and to raise her. I've always wanted that, but it's something that they deny to us, didn't they? Just like our freedom."

"So you're going to keep it?" Clayton asked, taking a step toward Sam at the counter. He could finally fill his lungs with air, but Sam looked different. He acknowledged that she was someone he didn't know, however much bonding they had done and however close he felt to her. He didn't know her, and the person he thought he knew was too strong to allow herself to carry a rapist's baby.

But it wasn't his baby, any more than it was his business what she did with it. He knew this in his heart. His emotions ricocheted off of each other and against his insides, drowning out the noise.

Clayton wanted to look at her. He wanted to see her the way he had before, with those huge green eyes even staring out from among the bruises, most of which had faded now. He longed to go back in time five minutes and leave the fucking room that he'd never been invited into.

He stumbled at first, when his feet tried to take him toward the door but he refused to take his eyes off of Sam. She'd only cried a single tear. A lump formed in Clayton's throat. He opened his mouth to speak.

"I can..."

He closed it as the words didn't come out. Clayton didn't know what he would say, but he opened his mouth to try again. He licked his chapped lips.

"I can't..."

The words still wouldn't come, but his legs had finally decided to work. They took him backward. His eyes refused to leave Sam. Had he imagined her beauty? he wondered. Did he imagine the tragically elegant woman he thought he had seen? The bags under her eyes, had those been there the entire time? He couldn't tell. Whatever the attraction had been, and whatever had pulled him so tightly into her orbit, he couldn't see it anymore.

In a way, it was a relief.

"I can't," he said. "I just..."

Sam wasn't looking at him anymore. She didn't cry and didn't seem to care that he was leaving. That was also good because it meant she would let him leave. As he neared the door, Stephen crept into his periphery and passed, staring with a sneer plastered across his lips. Clayton almost stopped to try to explain. Instead, he only motioned toward Sam, on whom Clayton could now see that the bruises weren't as healed as he'd thought. Her red-brown hair that he'd tucked his chin into only half an hour earlier was almost shaggy to the point of matting. Why hadn't he seen that before?

The door opened behind him. It took Clayton a second to notice his hand had turned the handle without him. Then, with no sound from anyone else in the room, he passed through and let it slam shut behind him.

"I can't."

The sound of his failure, as quiet a mutter as it had been, bounced off of the walls around him and ricocheted back to him like a proton rifle blast, knocking him backward. Then a flash of light caught his attention. Followed by another. And another.

"Clayton Wilson, the police are still looking for you. Do you have anything you'd like our audience to know? They say you are almost singlehandedly responsible for destroying a downtown city block. Is that true? How did you do it?"

The barrage of questions came from a cluster of reporters standing between Clayton and the elevators.

"I can't," was all Clayton could say. He turned to run from the reporters, but as fast as he was, the drones they used were faster. He could imagine the national news headlines: "Model Protestor Found in a Hotel Room with a Pregnant Model. Who is the Father?"

Too much. There was just too much. He sprinted toward the stairwell and punched through the exit doors. The one advantage he had over drones was that they didn't have hands. The unlocked doors were enough to keep them at bay. He sprinted down the stairs, two at a time. One thing that he knew about the H Hotel was that the stairs he was on took him all the way down to Strata o. As he thought about it, he neared the arm rail and peered over, still sprinting. The door above him burst open, and three drones slid through the opening. Clayton ran faster, staying ahead of them as he flew down the steps. One big leap allowed him to clear three steps and land on a platform. He tried another to cover the stairs in half the time.

As he came down, his foot teetered on the edge of a stair. For a half a second, he thought he'd gained purchase. Only when he tried to flatten his foot and plant himself back on the stairs firmly did he realize that he'd not only missed the step but made a crucial mistake in his attempt to recover. The shoes that he wore lacked enough grip to hold him in place. Instead, he collapsed, knees buckling beneath him and one foot flying forward while the other flew back.

The first collision slammed one knee into a stair, and the next toppled him forward to slide head-first toward the landing. His head connected to the hard cement, and the world flashed bright. When he could see again, he was upside down, legs sprawled beneath him, and his head twisted sideways so that he stared down to the next landing. Clayton tried to move his body only to find that it didn't respond to his commands. A drone hovered down in front of his face as the warm taste of blood filled his mouth. He spit it out and bloody mucus dripped down his chin. The drone crackled its audio.

"Can you tell us what you're doing in the H Hotel? Are you hiding from the police here? Who are the people you're with?"

"Urnngghh," he replied, unable to form the words. "Nggath."

Another drone came down behind that one and then another. A completely unnecessary clicking noise chattered from all the drones at once as they captured still shots of Clayton Wilson, laying helpless in the stairwell.

CHAPTER 31

LIFE AND WEAK TEA

SAM'S HAND shook as she contemplated leaving. Agitation wore her body like a cloak and there was little she could do about it. Her eyes had fixed themselves wide and her teeth chattered in her head. Whatever came next, Sam recognized that she couldn't do it until she'd gotten herself under more control. With clenched teeth, she punched in the code for her stress-reducing tea into the replicator, trying not to think about the fact that she'd had to step over two saucer-sized blood stains to do it. The replicator buzzed for a minute, then she retrieved her cup from the machine.

With a trembling hand, Sam lifted the weak tea to her lips. She allowed her hand to rest on her belly now. There wasn't a reason to keep the secret any longer. Sam wanted to hate Larken for spilling her secret, but she couldn't. Clayton would have known sooner or later. In truth, it was better for him to act the way he did now and excise himself from her life than when she was actually counting on him to be there for her. She could handle it, she told herself. It was her problem anyway, and he'd been here helping for longer than she could have expected anyone to.

The tea was chamomile and jasmine. She'd wanted lavender but couldn't remember the code for it, not their antiquated replicator that didn't actually have a menu option or voice controls. It was archaic and used up, kind of like she felt. Her belly hand crossed over to gently stroke the little white box on the counter that had delivered her tea. Kindred spirits, both without futures.

"Are you okay, Sam?"

That was Larken. She asked because she cared, or at least Sam thought she cared. Sam nodded, and sipped, letting the warmth take away what little of the pain it could.

"You don't seem okay."

That was Stephen. He probably thought that if she had the baby, she might keep it, and she'd need a partner to help her raise it. Stephen probably thought that she couldn't do it by herself. Or, even if Stephen didn't think that, she did. She had so far felt only the queasiness in her belly. Would she even be able to breastfeed? How much damage had Emergent Biotechnology done to her genes?

"Sam?"

Sam snapped back to the present.

"We can go in tonight," Larken said. "They won't expect us. We can sneak in through the sewage drain."

That was Larken. Clayton walking out on them had no effect on her. Lately, nothing seemed to have an impact. She was doing schoolwork most days, and in the evenings following up on her vendetta.

"I can't," Sam said.

"What?" Larken said, desperation leaking into her voice.

"Three of us, Larken. Do you have any idea how stupid that is?"

"Do you have a better idea?"

"Canada."

"It's my turn to say I can't, Sam," Larken said. Larken tapped her cane into the carpet hard enough to make a dull thudding sound and then pulled herself toward Sam. "I can't not try. If we don't stop it now, then when will we?"

"Me with just two other people? He's got an army. No."

Sam waited for Larken to take her meaning. The realization fell over Larken's face like a stocking mask. Sam was out. She wasn't partially out, or a little out, but out-out. Larken's eyes shifted toward Stephen, who nodded and clenched his teeth. Stephen was still very much in, as Sam knew he would be. Who cared what Sam thought?

"If that's what it takes," Larken said. Larken straightened her back, using her cane to push herself up straight. In a strange hobbling walk, she left Sam standing there at the counter. Stephen's hand went to the back of his neck and he looked first at Sam and then after Larken, who steadily gained on the door. No planning, no backup. They were going to get themselves killed. But if that's what they wanted, Sam would have to let them. She had something else to worry about. Her hand again rested across her belly, where there wasn't even the slightest bump yet to prove her pregnancy was real. Now that she was seeing things more clearly, she could see a future playing with a little girl. Canada could provide that future for them, free of HPM, and free of all of the chaos that had monopolized her life for as long as Sam could remember.

When the door opened, Sam hadn't expected anything except for the progression of the last two friends out of her life. She would not have predicted the influx of drones and the mob of reporters. Larken staggered backward and, without the support of her cane, fell to the ground as reporters spilled into the tiny apartment.

"What's your relationship to Clayton Wilson?"

"No comment," Sam said as she bolted around the kitchen island to help Larken to her feet. Stephen was there when Sam got there, already lifting. The three of them pushed forward toward the door. The mob—which Sam saw was only five reporters, however intrusive they'd seemed— backed up as the three of them advanced.

"Get out of my apartment," Larken said, scowling at them. Suddenly, the entire group seemed very interested in Larken alone.

"How long have you had this apartment? Madeline-Beckett Enterprises, the owners of this hotel, don't normally let people use this hotel as an apartment. What relationship do you have with the owners that makes you special?"

"Out," Stephen repeated as he stood and punched at a nearby drone that hovered out of reach. His knuckles connected, and he pulled his hand back, curling his fingers into his other but still using his body as a battering ram against the press members flowing through the door.

"He's a model!" someone shouted from the back. "She is too. They're both models."

Larken muttered, wobbling on her cane, "This is my home. Get out, all of you...before I call security."

At first, it didn't seem as though they were listening. But when Larken righted herself finally and the wobbling stopped, Sam felt the force against her slacken, and the man who had until that moment been self-righteously waving a press badge in her face donned a scowl and backed away.

Others followed suit until finally the room was quiet-ish again, except for the damaged drone which buzzed against the wall. Stephen retrieved it and launched through the open door before slamming it shut.

"Is that what it takes?" asked Larken, whose demeanor crumbled as the door closed. "Just two of us?"

"What are you going to do, Larken? One fewer won't make a difference against that building. You saw how many men with guns were inside. Guard towers, too. Don't do it. We can find another way."

"By the time we find another way, every model who was lined up inside will be dead, Sam."

It was the truth, but hearing it from Stephen sparked the rage that she felt in her blood. Her hands trembled so much she clutched them to her elbows.

"Do you remember what happened the last time we were in that building?"

Larken nodded, and her mind went to the dull throbbing that never left her back.

"We had to then, too."

"We didn't, did we? We could have left and gone to Canada. It's three hours. Three hours and we could have been free. I'm tired of watching my friends die around me." Sam fixed her gaze on Larken first, whose dark brownish-black eyes seemed immovable. None of her words had landed, and Larken clearly didn't care. However much pain she was in—and Sam knew Larken was always in pain— Larken hadn't changed. At least, her stubborn streak hadn't gone anywhere, and now it was going to get Larken killed. "Larken, you have to listen."

"To what? I thought you cared, but I guess I was wrong. You think I want to do this?"

Sam's heart dropped listening to the words. It fell even farther when Larken hobbled her way toward the door, and Stephen, after one last glance backward, followed. The door swung open wide as drones snapped photographs. The hallway buzzed with activity as reporters shouted a litany of questions. Stephen cut in front of Larken and used his body to force some of the reporters away from the door. Through the shrinking gap, Sam saw Larken straighten herself, swipe a hand down her clothes, and lift her head to face them. The last thing she saw as Larken raising an arm. To Sam's amazement, the chatter went silent after the door clicked shut and only Larken's voice and the occasional clicking of the drones came through.

"I don't know any Clayton Wilson," Larken said. "But I do know that there's a problem here in America and world-wide—and it's called the Human Pride Movement."

"How long has Clayton Wilson been hiding with you? Are those his clones?"

"Questions about HPM only, please."

Silence. Not a single journalist seemed interested from what Sam could hear through the wall. They were there for one thing: Clayton Wilson. Then Sam heard a faint voice that she guessed was far from the door.

"What do the HPM have to do with Clayton Wilson?"

"That's a great question," Larken said without a single waver in her voice. "Nothing. At least, nothing directly as far as I know. HPM have been buying up old reclamation centers that had been abandoned after the model uprising. Money from their operation go into funding the organization, I think. And if you think it through, those reclamation centers effectively make enemies disappear."

Larken's distinct voice cut briefly.

"If I had to guess," she continued, "I'd say that Clayton Wilson would very likely be protesting HPM due to their treatment of clones if rumors I've heard about him are true."

"The architect of the Massacre of Downtown? Didn't he kill almost everyone in that protest a few weeks ago?"

"I've heard differently from people who were there," Larken said. "What I heard was that the massacre was a Human Pride Movement operation. If you think about it, it makes sense. Where would one person get those mechs from?"

"Are you saying that what most of the news organizations are saying is incorrect? Did Clayton Wilson prep you to say that?"

"Again, I don't know Clayton Wilson personally. I do know some people who were there. That's all. Any more questions about the Human Pride Movement?"

Again none. Sam listened for the door to determine whether Larken would return to the room. It turned out, she didn't have to.

"Clear a path then," Larken said. "I've got errands to run and you're getting in my way."

A shuffling sound drifted through the door, followed by the click-slide of Larken's cane as she left. Sam stared at the packed bags on the couch and her eyes welled with tears. Her bag and Clayton's, side by side, were a testament to a future that she thought she would have. The gaggle of press outside and Larken's public claim made that room the safest place for her to be—protecting her from HPM attack as well as any possibility that Clayton might burst through the door, heartbroken and apologetic. She pressed her hand to her belly, feeling for whatever was growing in there, but she found nothing. Only the vague feeling of nausea that never really went away told her that anything was happening.

A single tear trickled down her cheek and fell onto the suitcase that she'd loaned to Clayton. She popped the lid and saw Clayton's old clothes that he'd changed out of days before and a blanket she'd given him just in case. Atop all of these items sat a statuette of Gulmen, the demon god, that had been a gift from Jocelyn. He must have found it when packing. Sam wrapped her hand around the demon god and held it up where she could see it better.

Another tear dropped. This one splashed over Gulmen's face and traced a trail down Gulmen's belly. As the tear rounded over the top of the demon god's basketball-shaped abdomen, Sam sank her hand into the thin layer of fat atop her abs. Her body shook, and another tear fell and splashed against her hand to die a quick death of absorption into the mattress of the couch below. Five minutes passed with her in convulsive silence. When the time ended, she wiped her eyes, closed her luggage, and went to the door.

HPM still knew where she lived, and despite whatever grandiose ideas Larken might have had, Sam had no intention of being around when the HPM decided to show up again.

CHAPTER 32

LESSONS UNLEARNED

THE HAIRS on the back of Larken's neck prickled even though the evening air was unusually warm for Seattle so late in the evening. Ten o'clock had come and gone as Larken trudged through the undergrowth, an effort complicated by her cane and a bad back. Earlier in the evening, she had been fueled by the urgency of Sam's safe return. Now, she found herself plagued by doubts, which hampered every single step she took through the thick foliage. Twice Stephen helped her to her feet after her cane no longer supported her.

Foolish. That was what Larken would have told anyone else who intended to rescue a hundred models or more while dislodging a clearly disciplined and better-armed militant group entrenched inside of a fortified compound. Suicide, perhaps. She could have gone on and on, but it didn't matter. She wasn't going to stop. From the determined frown on Stephen's face, he had no intention of stopping, either. Neither had said more than a couple of words before leaving Sam alone in her room.

Sam.

Larken's stomach twisted thinking about the woman and the fact that Larken had told the secret that Sam had asked her to keep. At the time, the words just kind of fell out. Okay, they'd been aided by Sam's constant waffling on whether or not to support Larken's cause, almost to the point of sending Stephen away when they'd already lost Clayton. It wasn't lost on Larken that the wedge she'd inserted between Sam and Stephen was the same wedge she'd accidentally used to pry Clayton away. If there were any signs of Larken being the great leader equal to the task of defeating the HPM then Larken definitely didn't know what they might be.

"There," Stephen said as he hunkered beneath a rhododendron bush. "I see three, maybe four, guard towers. But I don't see any guards in them. Do you?"

Larken craned her neck to see over the tops of the trees that still separated them from their concealment bushes and the complex.

"I can't tell," she said. "They may not need people up there. The entire system might be automated. You saw the gun barrels, right?"

"Yeah," he confirmed. "I saw. So what's the plan?"

He turned to her, still crouched down sitting on his heels.

"I don't know," she said. "I hadn't thought that far."

Another stellar move for a great leader. Larken shook her head to clear the nagging feeling that kept her eyes scanning the bushes at every shaking leaf or trembling branch. The darkness and the towering building behind the walls brought her back towhen she'd been younger and braver bordering on foolhardy. Not that she had improved much in that regard. The only difference between now and when she had battled the deceptively gorgeous—and lethal—android was that now she had wisdom to be terrified.

Something about that terror tickled her mind. Some possibility hid within that she poked at with her thoughts. The memories came flooding back. The woman had stood thigh-deep in the reclamation pond and handled Larken with so much ease that had her friends not intervened, she wouldn't be standing there even with a cane.

"The reclamation pond," she said, milking her fears for inspiration. "Around the back."

"Back where you nearly died?"

"Unless you have a better idea. There's an outflow pipe there that we can hopefully use to get into the building, remember?"

"The outflow pipe that's also filled with the body parts of dead models and whatever chemical soup they put in the vats to decompose bodies? That outflow pipe?"

The thought of the pipe brought with it a vision from the past: a gush of fluid erupted through the opening and dumped a pinkish-grayish-green fluid into the pond. Experience taught her that the pond was inert. Whatever mixture they'd used in the vats was diluted and used up before it was dumped. That same experience made her chest tighten. Larken pulled in a quick succession of rapid breaths to try to catch more air. It didn't seem to work as her lungs complained and her heart beat out its unsteady rhythm on her ribcage.

"That's the one," Larken replied when she finally caught her breath again. She ran her hand over her mouth and down her chin. "Do you remember how to get there?"

Stephen shook his head. His face seemed tired, she thought, a major difference between now and then. Her mind tugged at the thread of her memory and more came out. Stephen had been less serious, more engaged, more human. Larken hadn't wondered at the time why Stephen had gone with them, or why any of them had gone with her. Especially now, when his tired brown eyes lingered on hers and stubble coated his boyish face. He wiped his hand across those eyes and blinked.

"What?"

"Nothing," Larken replied, turning her eyes downward. "Are you ready to try it?"

"Now's as good a time as any," he said, sounding only vaguely like a cowboy in a revamped spaghetti western. For half a second, his sense of humor broke her out of her funk and she felt the smallest smile play at her lips.

"Do you remember all those nights we spent trudging through the woods?"

He smiled back.

"Yeah. You and your brother were heading to Canada. Only you got lost or something. And that android started tracking us."

"And the mech."

"The mech, yeah. That nearly killed you."

In response, she thrust her cane toward the woods beside them and took the first step. It would be a wide circle, as far back as they were from the gate and to avoid detection. Stephen crunched through the brush behind her.

"Did you know that Dandelion's an android, too?" Larken asked in a quiet voice.

Stephen nodded. "She told me," he said. "She was a lot less guarded back then. I don't even know who she is now."

"I don't think she does, either," said Larken, stepping over a log. "I think that she's evolving. Growing or something. I think she's hung up on Clayton."

The foliage was thick enough to force Stephen behind

Larken in single file. He walked close enough to her that occasionally she felt his breath on the back of her neck, which was still sensitive from her flitting mind's insistence that the android woman would appear from nowhere. Stephen stopped.

"Can androids be hung up on someone?"

Larken shrugged off Stephen's question and continued her relentless march through the tall conifers. In the distance she could still make out the tall walls surrounding the building, stretching up into the sky. Stephen crashed through the brush behind her a second later.

"It should be somewhere in here," she said, pointing ahead. The wall was still beyond the trees. If Larken had to estimate, she'd have guessed they were within only about fifty feet of it. The top edge was all they could see through the trees, and that seemed to drop off thirty feet from the corner which they had just circled. Larken couldn't tell if the wall had stopped or if it just was shorter through the dense foliage.

"Closer?" Stephen asked from behind.

Larken looked up toward the top of the wall, the part that she could see. No more gun turrets. No towers on this side. She clenched her hand so tightly around the knob of her cane that her knuckles went white. Her pulse still felt as though her heart might jump free of her chest and leave her dead carcass to bloat in the woods. She forced a breath in.

There's no android here. No mech. It's only us—only us and about a hundred militants beyond those walls.

It was insane, and her mind sought out an escape. She wanted to call it off, but all she could think about was that line of emaciated models. Every few minutes, she imagined one dropping into the vat, and the lid pulling to a close over the top of them. For some reason, she imagined the sound that the vat made to be that of an electric mixer, and she felt the vibration of popping joints in her imagination.

There were five rows. Each row was at least ten deep, if she had to guess. That meant fifty people would die if nobody did anything, and the only people there to do the doing were her and Stephen. She swallowed hard and took another step.

The pond had snuck up on her. When she reached out to place her cane again in the soft forest floor, she met no resistance until she tried to reposition it. The pond mud sucked her cane down the harder she pulled until finally, it came free in one quick movement.

"We're here," she announced in a croaking whisper.

"I don't see an out valve," Stephen said, pointing out the obvious lack of any fixture jutting out from the side of the building. The wall ended and joined with the back of the building, but there wasn't an outlet. Stretching her memory back, Larken couldn't recall whether or not there had been one.

A cloud passed before the moon, soaking them in darkness. When the cloud moved on, Larken found herself staring into the pool. The water still had that pinkish tint to it. She didn't doubt for a second that beneath the surface she would find half-digested limbs, hair, and other body parts. And such things had to have come from...

"Oh," she said, as a breeze sent fuchsia ripples across the water's shimmery satin surface. Closer to the building, she saw a cluster of bubbles rise up into gleaming opalescent domes and then explode.

"You see it?"

Larken nodded.

"And I guess you want me to go find it?"

Larken nodded again. Somewhere under the surface was a pipe large enough, from her memory, to at least jettison a leg out into a swirling cesspool.

"And you don't want to turn back?"

This time Larken swung her head side to side, thinking of what it must be like in one of those vats. She glanced at Stephen's face behind her. His face had scrunched up into a frown, eyebrows drawn together in disgust.

"In there?"

Larken rolled her eyes and tossed her cane at Stephen. Larken stepped into the soup, watching from the corner of her eye as Stephen's eyes widened and his hands flew up to snatch the cane out of the air. She took one breath, then another, and finally ducked down into the fluid, careful to blow out through her nose and keep her eyes closed while she felt around. The liquid pushed her up and supported her body weight, taking pressure from her back and providing the first pain relief she'd experienced in days. Larken executed three strokes in quick succession, pulling her down through the fluid toward the bottom where she felt around for the entrance to the tunnel that she remembered from last time.

Her mind fought her fingers for explanations of what they came into contact with on the bottom of the pond. Her fingers insisted they were shards bones and pieces of undigested flesh, but her mind, at her insistence, visualized coal-black shards of volcanic rocks and okrani fruit, fresh from Mars and scattered across the bottom with its blue and green and red bulbs in various stages of ripeness.

She kept this image with her until she realized that she hadn't found the pipe, and her lungs were screaming for air.

Larken was about to push back up to the surface when her foot kicked against something hard and immobile. Clenching her teeth, she ducked back down and her hands found purchase on the lip of an opening that was almost as big around as she was. Larken tested the entrance and found that she could fit inside, but by then her lungs were thrashing about inside of her, and she had to shove upward out of the tunnel into the air.

The water was deeper where she was than where she went in by the edge. When she breached the surface, her feet didn't even touch the top of the pipe. With one hand and her right leg, she trod water. She tried out her left leg too, but there wasn't much she could do with that one, so her treading was noticeably lopsided. Larken still jerked one hand out of the water to wipe the soup from her eyes before opening them.

"Did you find it?" Stephen asked.

Before she could say anything, she felt a hand close around her hand and lock into place, as hard as a vise. She tugged at her leg, but it only brought her lower into the water. Larken cut her lip on her teeth as she clenched her them and put all of her effort into kicking with her one good leg and pulling upward with her hands. She sucked in air and screamed into the night sky, only for a half a second, before her entire body sank below the surface.

Larken's mouth came open on its own as she struggled for air and despite her efforts to force it back closed, the sticky, slimy fluid that surrounded her invaded. The taste was foul and abrasive and pricked at her tongue like a pablano pepper—threatening to inflame, but not strong enough to follow through. The smell of sulfur transformed into the sensation that crossed over her lips and gagged her with unidentifiable chunks of material.

Okrani fruit, she reminded herself. That's all. Okrani.

As hard as she clung to the concept in her mind, the oblong shards of what must have been bone that wedged themselves into her hair were difficult to ignore. A shudder worked its way from her lower back through her shoulders, twisting her even more sideways until she was unsure which way was up and down. She forced her eyelids up in the vain hope that she might be able to see through the murk, only to be presented with a wall of black. The last few bubbles pushed out through her lips and she saw them as a slight discoloration of the black background before they disappeared above her head.

Up. That was up.

But she had no energy left. Her left hand shot up toward the surface only to find more fluid, and the force of this last effort shoved her body down even faster. Seconds passed. Her lungs filled with more of the fluid as her diaphragm worked against her wishes to defiantly save her, yet condemning her at the same time.

Hands. Strong. Metal? One closed around her leg and yanked. At the same time, another closed around her hand and pulled upward. For a terrifying beat, Larken felt herself motionless, suspended between the darkness above and the darkness below before the hand on her ankle gave way. Rather, it stayed latched on but whoever it was pulling pried them both out of the murk.

Half a second later she broke the surface, her stomach, throat, and mouth full of the cast off from the reclamation plant. Her illusion that there were only okrani in the water burst the minute a clump of hair swung down in front of her face holding something that looked like a human ear. Larken coughed and sputtered and tried to swim. Convulsions rocked her stomach as she flopped through the water, helpless. Whoever it was that had grabbed her swam in strong, sure strokes toward the shore and tossed her onto the grass before rolling over beside her.

"Thought you were a goner," Stephen's voice cut through the fluid draining from her ears.

"I—" she began and then stopped as another convulsion rocked her body. Something came up in her mouth that she hastily discarded onto the grass—and didn't examine.

"I'm okay," she assured him. Then, remembering the hand clasping her foot, she glanced down. There was no hand. Instead, a thin, water-soaked reed had wrapped around her ankle and brought with it a clump of earth. Her glance turned into a stare. There had been fingers, she thought. Had she imagined the first time?

"What happened out there? You said you found it, then..."

"I...I can't, Stephen. I can't go. I keep seeing her," Larken said.

"After all this, you can't? Can't what?"

"I don't think I can rescue those people," Larken admitted, her face feeling hot even under the cool film of liquid. "There's a tunnel down there. Over there, where those bubbles are. It should lead inside. But I keep..."

Just then, she saw the face. It looked human but too perfect, too flawless. And that wicked smile that the android had presented, mocking almost. But it was on Stephen's body now, and Larken knew that wasn't real. Or at least, thought it wasn't real.

Unless the android could shape-shift somehow.

Even Larken knew that the idea was completely unreasonable. A fraction of a second later, the face was gone and Stephen's had replaced it again. Larken dropped her head, letting her soaked hair hang down and hide her face. The mission had failed, and it was time to admit it. She crawled her still shuddering body back away from the water's edge and toward the cover of the forest. With a shaking hand she reached for the cane that lay where Stephen must have dropped it before he came in to rescue her.

"What now?" he asked.

"Nothing," she said, "nothing. Fucking nothing."

She put her wobbling cane into the dirt and slowly shuffled back toward the hidden path they'd taken to get to the Bremerton Plant. HPM didn't even know they were there, yet Larken couldn't save anyone. Faces in the darkness threatened to come forward and underline how unstable she'd become.

"We can't now," Stephen protested, though Larken noted that he did traipse along right behind her anyway. "We came here to rescue people."

"I can't even take care of myself, Stephen. Rescue them if you want. I'll only get us both killed."

"Do you want to talk about it?" he asked, his tone soft as the few stars visible in the night sky this close to the city.

"No," she said, shaking her head. "There'll be plenty of time to talk when we get back to the hotel. Let's go."

"Okay," he said, then not another word as they disappeared into the trees.

CHAPTER 33
AN INATTENTIVE PRESS

EVEN AFTER THEY determined that the press corps had wandered off somewhere and lost interest in their hotel room, Larken didn't explain anything to Stephen. She had nothing to say to him. He was there. He'd seen her dive down, he saw her nearly drown, and he saw her freaking out about the android woman. He witnessed her in all her weaknesses.

Perhaps that was why when he insisted on leaving the empty apartment to go seek out Sam, who had left during their absence with a full container of luggage, Larken only sank into the couch with no response.

"Say something," Stephen commanded, his voice breaking at the edges and leaking frustration.

"What's there to say, Stephen?" she asked with an even keel. "I'm no match for HPM. I'm just one person, and nobody believes me."

"I believe you."

"They have armies." She paused for a second. "And it wouldn't matter anyway," she whispered. "The damage is done. I can barely focus without that woman's face jumping at me from the darkness."

"But you and I are it, Larken. Like Sam said..."

"A booby prize? No thanks."

"I'll get her then. You," he started then furrowed his eyes into a glare, "You just relax there I guess."

That's the last thing he said before he crossed the shag carpeting and slammed the door behind him, leaving Larken alone dripping pink fluid onto the light-gray cushions. It would probably stain, especially behind her head where her brown hair was still clumped together into damp tangles. A shower and then clean the couch. Then...

Larken planted her left foot on the floor, leaning her weight onto it to squish out from under her boot what was left of the offal from the pond. Then she did the same with her right. Her back screamed at her to get her cane, and the muscles between her shoulder blades felt so taut that Larken thought they might snap away from her bones and curl into tiny balls of pain. Still, she leaned forward without her cane, resisting her old crutch, and centered her weight on her feet. Then she clenched the muscles in her atrophied thighs to swing her torso over her legs.

Shower. That's what she was after. Pinkish slime that had settled into the folds of her clothes dripped down her stomach and legs.

One step. Then another. Her back stabbed at her, and the room swam as her headache intensified. Larken didn't stop. Everything in her life was falling apart, and she would be damned if she couldn't have one full shower without that crutch and without help, even if it killed her.

One step, then another. That's all it would take. She imagined the twenty or so steps from the couch to the bedroom, and then another ten from the door to her bedroom into her private shower. Swallowing once, Larken cringed as some of the slime that had made its way in worked its way down her throat. The shower might also be accompanied by a bath.

She took another step. As she placed her right foot on the floor, the sound of thunder shook the room. Larken gave an involuntary shake before she put that foot all the way down. It didn't land well. Almost ten degrees slanted from what she wanted. Without hesitation, Larken switched over to moving the other foot. Only, when she lifted it into the air, her right foot slipped to the side and out from under her. She collided with the table and heard a crack, but she knew from the familiar feeling what that crack was. A spinal disk out of place. Her head hit the table next and a flash of darkness replaced the room for a second before it returned. Larken lay on the floor, staring at the clawed-feet of the couch.

She hadn't known they were clawed feet. As the thoughts wove through her mind, she realized that she should have been more focused on the fact that she couldn't move. Probably the slipped disk had pinched a nerve or something.

Larken flexed her back muscles, twisting her torso to the side. At least she could do that, even if when she next tried to move her arm, the arm seized up. She bit her lip to keep her tears at bay and twisted one more time. A knot in her back protested. It wanted to come out, but the more she did the only thing she could do—writhe around on the floor like a snake—the more the knot eluded her. Sweat beaded on her forehead as she twisted herself almost in two.

One more try. She swore to herself silently that if it worked, she would graciously retrieve her cane and never do anything without it again. Lesson learned. At least that lesson.

With a pop, whatever was wrong in Larken's back righted itself. and Larken could feel her legs and move them again. She propped herself on her hands and then pulled her legs beneath herself, this time mindful of the pain of each movement and stopping in starts when the pain became too much. On her hands and knees, Larken shimmied across the floor beside the coffee table that doubled as a holovid. Hips wobbling as she crawled, the sideways motion slammed her left hip into the corner. Wincing, Larken covered the remaining foot or so to retrieve her cane with one hand massaging her bottom. Then, slowly and using the couch as back support, Larken regained her footing.

Half an hour later, Larken hid in her shower, steam rising from her back and tears intermingling with the residue of shampoo and whatever other things she'd picked up in the water at the reclamation plant. The burn on her skin told her that she would come out of this one pink, but she needed it. Larken could still feel the unnamed pieces of discarded flesh and bones bumping against her. Her entire body shook so violently that she lost her grip on the shower support and landed on the bottom of the shower, seated, with water splashing down over her head.

"Three minutes of shower time remaining," a helpful automated voice reminded her. Water rationing would kick in soon, and Larken had used nearly all of the available shower water for the entire apartment. She still didn't feel clean. The shower ended with her seated beneath the faucet, dripping water into the basin under her.

Larken was able to reach the shower support with her weaker left hand, but she still managed to pull herself back up to standing. The shower faucet dripped behind her as if to tease her that there really was more water, just not for her. She stood unmoving for a second, just long enough for the last of the tears collected in her lower eyelids to expunge themselves. Then, with a sniffle and rickety movements, Larken worked her way over the ledge of the tub—at one point sitting full onto the somehow still cold lip.

Half of the people she loved were still at risk. The other half weren't speaking to her.

Banner friend.

Hobbling out of her bathroom, Larken plodded her bare feet across the carpeting, all synthetic. She pulled sparkling pants out of her closet, covered in silver sequins from the waist to the end of her feet. She'd worn things like that when she was at Brighton only occasionally, when she really needed a pick-up. Larken hadn't worn them in almost the entire five years, yet had been too attached to get rid of them. The pants and a black halter top that looked like a short corset that laced in the center.

It took another half-hour to don the pants and lace the halter correctly after two failed attempts. When she examined herself in the full-length mirror by her bed, she could see bits of her younger self peering through. In her chest, she felt lighter, and for a second, the clothes were all that mattered. The cane didn't exactly match the outfit, and kind of ruined the immersion, but if she stood just right with the cane tucked behind her back leg, she saw herself staring back. The eyes were the same, dark and deep with heavy eyebrows and an almost smile that lingered around their edges. Somewhere along the way she'd lost herself. But now, here, she was there again.

She could keep herself.

All she had to do was walk away.

With a heavy sigh, and decision somewhat made, Larken pulled her suitcase from her closet and folded it open on the ground. Panting with the speed, she pulled every item of clothing she thought she could still fit into—most still fit, since she'd been basically wasting away—and tossed them into the container. A handful of minutes later, she did the same at the dresser with underwear, socks, and then into the bathroom with toiletries where she had to make some trade-offs. There wasn't room for her instant hair-dryer and the ball gown she'd worn the only year she'd attended a school dance. Larken held the gown up to her chest and squeezed it, smelling the remnants of the fragrance she'd overindulged in to attend the high-school prom. She'd been one of only a few freshman girls who'd been invited that year.

No time for memories.

Larken used her cane and the rolling luggage for support as she pushed it over the carpet. Standing at the door, she took one last glance over the room, her eyes resting for a second on the trail of pink slime that traced her original route to the bathroom. Larken would have to explain that to Torrent who had convinced Gallatin Hamilton, hotel owner and owner of Madeline-Beckett Enterprises, to allow Larken and her friend Sam to stay. He'd understand.

Aayushi wouldn't.

But Aayushi wasn't real, was she? Larken had first seen Aayushi when her body had been so damaged that she spent eight months in recovery. Aayushi had spent most of that time with her, tumbling through her mind and following from memory to memory. Aayushi had reminded her of her destiny, and Aayushi had helped to set her on it.

Unlike everyone else in her life, Aayushi could not be outrun.

But Larken could try.

She bit her lower lip and settled her mind on the idea that if she hadn't been here, and if she hadn't brought all of these troubled people together, they might have solved their problems some other way. All of them might be living better lives without her. And now, without her, they might actually get a chance.

From now on, it would only be her. And if she could help it, there would be no more vendetta. She took one look back at the empty room, pulled her luggage behind her, and stepped through the doorway.

CHAPTER 34

A NOT-SO-GENTLE REMINDER

LARKEN STALLED JUST beyond the door.

She didn't know where to go.

Deciding to leave was one thing, but actually having a plan was another. She could go up to Bellingham and try to catch a ride into Vancouver, British Columbia, Canada. That was only about an hour by road, if there were still any roads now that the skyway connecting the two had been completed for nearly a decade. Larken might be able to find a way across, especially in Bellingham where it seemed like people looked for an excuse to flaunt their freedoms over the law.

To do that, she'd have to get to Bellingham. Larken had cash coins enough for the trip.

In fact, Larken could easily catch the Fifty-Nine northbound to the edge of the city, then get the high-speed light rail to Bellingham. From there, a couple of cash coins or even just a smile might get the right person to help her into Canada. There, she wouldn't have to worry about whether or not the police would show up looking for her. A blood test could easily prove she was a model, and she could take advantage of the relocation program that Canada offered: job and housing placement.

Larken could be herself again. And, Gulmen willing—not that she believed—she could convince Molly and Oliver to make the same trip. As far as she knew, HPM didn't have the success in Canada at recruiting that they apparently had in the United States. They might be there, she guessed, but they weren't nearly as prominent. Even if they were, she could still stay invisible, a nobody. Once enough time passed with her being a nobody, and once she could trust herself to steer clear of danger instead of running toward it, then she could reach out to Molly and Oliver. She could convince them that Canada was a better place to raise their child. Larken could convince them that they could be family again.

All she had to do was leave. Like Clayton. Like Sam. Like Dandelion. And finally, like Stephen.

And in Canada, she thought, I could get the medical treatment to fix my back all the way. Dandelion had managed to keep her alive at the free clinic, for which Larken was thankful. But without actual papers to support Larken's new identity, she wasn't able to get the treatment that could seriously repair the damage. In Canada, where they didn't check if someone was a model before offering treatment, Larken could get her back fixed. Her eyes watered at the prospect of being able to walk without a cane and without the pain that never seemed to leave her lower back and head.

That alone almost pushed her through the door.

But she found herself turning around. Inside, she stood with her back to the door, letting it close behind her. She plopped her suitcase on its side. Then, lowering herself slowly, sat atop it. Larken dropped her cane to the floor where it sank into the plush and lowered her exhausted head into her hands.

And what of the millions who will die?

Aayushi had told her that. Millions would die. Empires would fall. And it all hinged on her ability to stop it. The fact that she was thinking about that made her question her mental acuity. It had been an addiction for a hot minute.

"You're wrong," Larken shouted through her hands. "It's not me. I can't do it."

"Maybe you're right," came the familiar voice that often haunted her dreams. Larken lifted her head to see Aayushi standing before her. She had black hair, and those hazel eyes that seemed focused on something far off in the distance. The most compelling thing was the sadness that filled the room every time Aayushi appeared to her.

She really was losing it again.

"Maybe you're right," the woman repeated, her lips not moving but it was definitely her voice. "Maybe we need someone else to do it. Maybe someone else can save these people."

"Exactly. Why not Lancaster? He's already got an entire organization. SNO can help you."

"Me? I'm dead, Larken. I don't need any help. That's not why I'm here."

"You're not dead. You're in my head, and I can't get rid of you."

Psychotherapy in Canada. The best she could afford. Then no more Aayushi. But for now, Larken had to deal with the very real-seeming woman before her.

"It's fine, Larken," Aayushi said in a tone that indicated otherwise. "Maybe there's someone else, someone stronger. There's already someone that I think might be able to help."

"Good. Then we're agreed."

"You tell me. Are we?"

Larken retrieved her cane then lifted herself off of her suitcase with it.

"We are," she said, without hesitation. Larken lifted her bag onto its wheels, then pushed forward. Aayushi didn't move from her spot between Larken and the door, even as Larken got closer. Larken kept going and the bag went through Aayushi first. The woman began to fade, and by the time Larken's body came to where Aayushi's had been, the woman was gone.

Larken clutched her cane in one hand and pulled the door open with the other. A second later, she stepped back through, shoving the bag in front like a protective shield.

WITH NO OTHER destination to lead her, Larken followed her memories through the streets of the still-sleeping city. A different city, Seattle still had a Strata 6 somewhere, just like Portland. Instead of endless layers of bridges over the Willamette River, the city canopy of Seattle challenged Mt. Rainier for height, but only because of the forced perspective of the mountain in the distance against the city skyline. Still, the canopy and escalators were so similar to Portland that following the empty walkways sparked the memories of that night when she'd wandered into Portland, a young girl unaware of a future that would consume her life.

Larken had no concept of what time it was except that it was late night, possibly early morning. The trees of the emerald city had become more visible, even in the absence of streetlights. The occasional volantrae zipped by overhead, and she swore she even heard the chatter of voices drifting up from below.

The thing about not having a destination meant that Larken was free to poke her curious nose into any sound she heard. Rejuvenated by the shower and kept awake by the emotional pain that accompanied the physical in wracking her body, Larken turned her attention to the only distraction available and lugged her bag onto a down escalator and leaned into the side. While she coasted down, she thought of where she might go, humoring only a moment's thought of arriving on Molly and Oliver's doorstep, luggage in hand.

It had to be Canada. As Larken, she was persona non-grata to her friends and family, and Seattle wasn't big enough to avoid screwing up their lives. Nobody knew her in Canada.

And she would go.

She thought that leaving the city she'd called home for almost six years would break her heart more than it already was. Larken simply couldn't leave yet. And even if she had been emotionally ready to make that trip, the buses didn't begin to run for—judging by the glacial lightening of the sky —another hour or two at least.

Plenty of time to distract herself with the sound of human voices below. As the escalator crept along, bringing her closer to the utterances, her ears picked a voice out of the buzz.

"Now when they show up—and they will—you want to become a sack of potatoes. It takes two to three others working together to move a hundred-and thirty-pound person. By being dead weight, we prolong the protest."

"But what if they shoot at us? Or attack us with mechs, like what happened to you?"

"Run. You can't beat them, Cali. Metal beats bone every time. Be aware, and plan your escape route in advance. Are you ready?"

When she arrived at the bottom of the escalator, ten

heads all turned at once. One of those heads floated in a sea of brown puffy hair-halo.

"Clayton," she said, forgetting to step off of the bottom of the escalator until the teeth chewed at the wheels of her luggage. Larken stepped forward onto cement and pulled the luggage behind her.

"Larken? What are you doing here? Are you here to join the protest?"

"Are you insane, Clayton? That's going to put you on national news. Again. They're going to arrest you."

He shook his mane and shot her a half-smile. The sky had gained color in the last handful of minutes so that Larken could see darkness tinged with blue.

"Well, maybe. But I figured that's free press, isn't it? Every protest I'm in now until the time I get caught will get national coverage. I've got a handful already planned—not just here in the city, but down in Olympia, Federal Way, Auburn. Even Kirkland."

Keeping busy. Larken had a guess as to why. His eyes held a sadness that had little to do with models being freed. Clayton turned to the group.

"Practice your potato sacks," he told them, flashing them a wide, toothy grin. "Me and this one have to catch up." Then he turned back to Larken as several of the group seemed to listen and plopped down onto the ground.

"Larken, have you seen Sam? I called her, and she's not answering. Is she okay?"

Heartbroken. That was the look, with eyes glistening and holding back the tears that would explode out if he focused for too long on his loneliness. Larken had done that to him. If she'd waited and let Sam tell Clayton in her own time about her predicament...

"No," she almost whispered. "Clayton, I'm sorry."

"For what?"

Larken could feel the sincerity in his question. He didn't know—couldn't know—how he'd been manipulated. And she wasn't going to admit to him that she'd guessed his reaction ahead of time.

She wasn't going to confess that she knew there was a good fifty/fifty shot that he would leave them and that she'd intentionally gotten him to leave so that Sam would help Larken locate the bounty hunters who'd attacked her and maybe lead them back to their headquarters. Larken couldn't divulge that while helping Sam was important, fighting HPM had always felt more important, and she'd willingly sacrificed their relationship on the altar of future justice. Hindsight.

"Nothing," she said.

"Good," Clayton replied. "I know what you did, and I know why you did it. But it wasn't you who made the decision to leave, was it?"

She hadn't thought of it that way. All Larken could do was shake her head in agreement.

"Was it the pregnancy, Clayton? Is that why you left?"

"Yes," he said at first then shook his head. "Well, no. No, not really. I mean, I was furious that nobody had told me, and everyone seemed to know but me. It took me a while to get over that. But that's not why I left. If she's pregnant and wants to keep the child, that's fine. If she doesn't, that's also fine. That's not it."

"Then what, Clayton?"

He licked his lips. His deep brown eyes shifted toward where one of his acolytes did something resembling a downward-dog.

"Not like that," he said. "It's easy. Just flop down and go limp."

Then he turned back to Larken, setting his eyes on hers.

"We'd spent so much time together, and things were moving so fast. I realized when she didn't even trust me enough to tell me about something as serious as...that, then the relationship I'd thought we were building was in my head. And it was predicated on such violence, Larken. Such violence done to her, and violence done to me...It was like at that moment I realized that we were both crippled and holding onto each other as we limped through each day. I couldn't do that to her. And I definitely couldn't do it to myself."

"I'm not buying that. You stormed out of there in a hurry. You were pissed."

"Oh, I was furious...until I got to the elevator. Then I stood for a good five minutes thinking it through."

Larken slid forward toward Clayton and away from the escalator in case anyone else happened down it.

"In a way, I should thank you. Without saying what you said, I wouldn't have left and I'd still be there and she still wouldn't trust me."

The crowd behind him seemed to be finished with their flop exercises and milled about, chattering to each other.

"Why this, Clayton? Why when you don't even have a home to go to?"

"Oh, I'm staying with Karl," Clayton said, motioning to a slim boyish man in the back of the crowd with coarse red hair. "But you're right. I don't have anything except for what I carried from your place. They're still watching my home if you can believe that."

"Well, they won't have to soon, will they? When does the protest start?"

"Two hours. Yeah, they won't, will they?"

He sidled up to her and the two walked. Clayton quickly addressed the group.

"We've got a couple of hours. Get breakfast, coffee, whatever, and then come back. We'll start here and work our way down Fifth. I think if we block the ramps at Sixth and Seventh, we'll get attention pretty fast."

As the crowd dispersed, Clayton shoved Larken's bag in front of them as he pushed forward, taking a slow enough pace that Larken kept up with her cane giving a slow eighty-beat-per-minute tap against the cement as they walked side by side.

"Coffee?" Clayton asked. "We can talk on the way."

"Sure."

"I hated you for a few minutes," Clayton said. "Only I realized something. I realized that you were doing what you can, while I was running and hiding. I also realized something about you."

Larken swallowed. The moment she'd been waiting for had arrived. Clayton was no doubt about to lay into her, and she definitely deserved it. A second passed. Then another.

"What, Clayton?"

"Wh...oh. You're trying to save everyone. Like, not just the people you care about, and not just the models, but everyone. And the more you try, the more you fail, right? Because it's a lie. You can't save everyone. Nobody can."

"But you have to try, Clayton," Larken said, feeling the hairs on the back of her neck stand up as she prepared for a fight. But that was the old her. This her needed to listen. "I'm sorry. Please go on."

"You can't. I learned that watching you fail at it," he said, his mouth curled back into that infectious, goofy grin he sometimes donned.

"But what—"

"You do what you can, Larken. Maybe you can't rescue those models. You can listen to your friends, and you can get Sam the help that she needs. She's nowhere close to finished processing what happened to her, Larken. You're her best friend, as sad as that is. You can do that, you know?"

———

The walkway became more familiar looking to Larken, as though she'd been there before. She looked at the sides of the buildings, and she thought she recognized where she was going, but she couldn't be sure. A lot of areas downtown had people sleeping in bags on the ground and boarded up building fronts, especially at ground level. Only when they turned a corner did Larken understand where they were going for coffee. There, before them, stood the coffee stand that Stephen was supposed to run.

"Perfect cup of coffee, every time," Clayton bragged, his grin widening. "Stephen, you back there?"

Rattling sounds came from behind the shuttered coffee shop. The barrier slid up slowly to reveal Stephen rubbing the sleep out of his eyes.

"What do you want?"

"Coffee, man."

"Seen Sam yet?"

"Not yet. She'll come around when she's ready. Look who I did find, though."

When Stephen's eyes settled on Larken, the barrier lowered again.

"No thanks. Not opening today," Stephen said through the closing gap.

"Is he living in there?"

"I think so," Clayton responded after the barrier settled. "Got nowhere else to go, kind of like me. I've been coming by here to check if Sam has shown up, but she hasn't so far." Then Clayton banged his fist against the metal barrier. "Stephen, I still need some coffee."

"Go somewhere else."

"Just talk to us, Stephen. Look. Larken has her bags. She's leaving and wants to say goodbye."

Larken shot a look at Clayton, who only shrugged in response.

"You are leaving, aren't you?"

"Yes," she said. "Before I do any more damage."

The barrier rose again.

"What about Sam?" Stephen asked through the waxing gap. "If you leave, how do we find her?"

"She doesn't want me to find her, Stephen. This time, I'm going to respect what she wants. If she wants isolation, then I'm going to let her have it."

"What about HPM?"

"If her best friends can't find her, then they won't, either. She's just got to take care of herself for a while."

"Bullshit," Stephen said, his words dripping with pain. "HPM have been following her, remember? She's not safe. Not in this city."

"Then where..."

"I don't know. That's why I'm sleeping in the back of a coffee shop, isn't it? Just in case she comes by."

"You don't think she'd come by your home?"

Larken chanced a glance at Stephen. She knew the answer as well as he did. There wasn't a chance at all that Sam would make the trip to Stephen's home alone, the way it ended with the two of them. Stephen swallowed but didn't answer. The meaning was plain.

"Okay then, she doesn't want to be found. And I think we should respect that," Clayton said. But even as he said it, his words slowed and his eyes darted to the left. He was still looking for her, and when he did Larken couldn't help gazing in the same direction, as though their collective willpower was enough to force Sam to materialize from the continually-brightening sky.

Larken couldn't help thinking back to when she'd exposed Sam's secret in front of Stephen, and the reaction that she'd gotten from Sam then. The shock, and the betrayal. Larken's second betrayal in the same twenty-four hours.

"I'm sorry," she said, the words forming from her lips though she wasn't sure to whom she apologized. Stephen didn't make any move to indicate that he'd thought the apology was for him. Larken wasn't sure it was, either. The one person upon whose feet she needed to throw herself at to plead for forgiveness wasn't even there. The idea of leaving suddenly felt like fleeing, like abandoning her post during wartime.

"Sam's out there," she whispered at first, catching Clayton in her side-eye. "Do you...think we need to rescue her? I know she might need some time, but still."

"I don't know," Clayton replied. "I don't. She wanted space like I did. I think maybe we should just wait."

Save Sam.

The thought spiked into Larken's consciousness and grabbed her by the back of her brain. Sam needed rescuing, and nobody could do it but her.

Only, she didn't, did she? Larken turned felt a tingling behind her right ear and turned in that direction to see Stephen staring back at her, his tired eyes searching her face for...something. Probably he was waiting for her to do something, like they always seemed to do.

"I've got to go, guys," Clayton said then turned once more to Stephen. "Any chance you've got coffee made up back there somewhere?"

Stephen's face went hard at that ask, only to soften a second later.

"Yeah. Yeah, okay. I could use some, too. Hold on."

When he left to go to the back of the shop, which wasn't very large so the room couldn't have been much more than a broom closet, Larken found herself pushing her luggage forward and backward, clicking the wheels over a seam in the cement.

"You going to do it?"

Larken cocked her head. "Do what?"

"Go running off after Sam and try to find her?"

Now named, the tooth-clenching feeling of pressing anxiety came on full force. She stopped rolling the suitcase back and forth, and switched her cane over into her other hand. Automatically that hand began tapping on the knob on the top of the cane, fingers interpolating rapidly.

"I didn't say I would do that."

"But you're thinking about it? Listen, I know you are because I am, too. I wouldn't if I were you. I mean, you probably know Sam better than me, sure. But if you do find her, and nothing at all is wrong, she's not going to be happy you showed up uninvited."

"I have to find her sooner or later," Larken rationalized poorly. "Got to send her stuff somewhere if she doesn't come back."

The idea of Sam not returning made Larken's back tighten. The pain in her head made her pull her hand up to her temple. The apartment, or hotel, or whatever situation they were supposed to be living in, seemed empty in her mind, but not the kind of empty of someone stepping out for a day or even a week.

This emptiness was perpetual, like what she'd learned in school about the beginning of Equilibrium, when people in the midwestern United States caravanned out of the region as the nascent desert bloomed there, supplanting the fields of grass and crops over only a couple of years. The abandoned homes in the holovid images had looked as though they'd died. Not the people, but the homes. Even when there were such signs of life as a wilted flower or something on a table, there was an unmistakable quality to those visuals that drove home the climate change event. Homes that would never see life again. And now, in her mind, her own home made the list.

If she let it. But if she didn't, then what would become of her former roommate?

Not her problem. She couldn't solve everyone's problems. Larken couldn't even walk without a cane. And what problem did she have anymore? Sam couldn't have made it clearer that she wanted to be left alone.

"I think you're right," she finally said to Clayton, realizing that a full minute had passed since he'd said anything to her.

The wafting odor of fresh coffee drifted before Stephen as he arrived. He carried three cups—one for each of them—and Larken accepted hers without complaint. Coffee to her was a practical necessity. She envied Clayton, who held his cup between his palms and waved it in slow motion just beneath his nose, inhaling the bitter fragrance.

"So what do you say, Larken? Want to come to another protest?" Clayton asked.

"Not on your life," she replied.

CHAPTER 36

MEA CULPA, I'M SORRY

LARKEN LET out a deep sigh that began in the bottom of her belly and worked its way up her insides like a pressure valve slowly coming undone. The weight behind her eyes tugged on her eyelids.

The blue suitcase with a black rubberized seal rolled in front of her over the cement, surprising her as it went in the direction of Clayton's protest. She stepped backward toward where she'd swiveled it around her body, pushing it along, and she clicked a few times with her cane. Her eyes lingered on Stephen's for only a second before she turned her body as well to follow the case. Nothing was left to say here.

"Larken, you can't just..."

"I can, Stephen. And you can, too. Sometimes you just need to take the hint."

Clayton plodded behind her. Unlike Larken, he still had his coffee cup, and she could hear the coffee sloshing around in it as he fast-paced to catch up to her. Stephen's footsteps pounded after them.

The sun had risen to above the building tops and flooded

the ground with light. Clayton and Larken walked side by side as they arrived at the clearing where Clayton had been talking to his fellow protestors. The group had grown to about thirty, many already projecting their posters before them. One read "Models Are People," and another read "Humans Are Humans." The latter was roughly the size of the front window of a construction truck.

The idea crystalized in Larken's mind even though she didn't ask for it. Even though she didn't want it and could barely muster the energy to consider it.

"What if," she began and then stopped when she realized that the entire group had focused on her the moment, she opened her mouth. "Never mind."

"What?"

"Just thinking. HPM can't be everywhere at once. We can create a pretty good distraction by protesting by Bremerton instead of...where were you all going?"

"Emergent Biotechnology downtown," Clayton replied. "Taking the fight to them."

"They're not the enemy though," Larken insisted. "HPM are."

"They're the ones who've been selling the reclamation plants to HPM, Larken," Stephen said, his low voice trying to hide in the din.

"But it's HPM. Emergent gets boycotted six times a year at least and protested fifty. They're used to it. You know who's not used to it?"

The idea was growing into something she thought just might be workable. But it couldn't be her alone. She began to understand her mistake more deeply. It hadn't been her goals that had scared everyone away, but her treatment of them.

And this she intended to alter, starting with a smile, something she only rarely did.

"What about protesting there?"

"Where?" Clayton asked, then a second later the color drained from his cheeks—or most of it did. He still maintained his impossible-to-remove dark tan complexion, only a few shades lighter. "You want to go—"

"Bremerton," Larken said, careful to shield her own apprehension in a faux half-smile. "Go there, and HPM will be too busy dealing with us to do anything with Sam. Bonus if we save some lives."

Maybe she'd leave tomorrow instead.

CHAPTER 37
CURIOSITIES

UNTIL ONLY THREE WEEKS BEFORE, Dandelion had never had a crush on anyone. How could she? She might have had the right body parts, but they were all superficial. No hormones coursed through her, ratcheting up her emotions until she couldn't think, or steering her to intrinsic and predictable outcomes. No synapses fired and provided feedback loops that worked with her sensory and olfactory organs to overcome her thoughts. She wasn't human that way.

And yet, Clayton was all she could think of. His angular jawline, easy smile, and thick curls that stretched up and away from his head like a fuzzy halo all settled something inside of her. She'd become too complex to figure out what had changed. Her quantum neural networks had expanded over the years as she'd learned to deal with emotions and respond in kind. Even the last time she'd saved Larken's life in the emergency room, she could have identified the particular node or value that caused a specific response. The retirement community—and endless conversations with her wards—had forced her to reallocate more resources to the task of mimicking human behavior. Now, at over a trillion parameters and countless hidden levels, it would take an equally complicated machine purely dedicated to the task to tease out the cause and effect of anything she did. So her obsession with Clayton was as impossible for her to change as her tempered yet growing aggression toward Sam.

Infatuation. Jealousy.

The labels helped but didn't make the feelings go away if that's what they were. And the labels had been hard won. After leaving Sam and Clayton, she'd dismissed the idea of her infatuation, chalking her obsession with a programming glitch somewhere. Leaving Clayton behind, she thought, could change that and free her of the chains of her emotions.

The feeling didn't change, though—not even after she returned to her own home for a recharge. There, in her bed— a contactless recharging station of her own design—she tossed and turned but the image of Clayton wouldn't leave her memory banks.

It confused her. Dandelion had worked with Clayton for years and barely given him a thought. Now, after them both nearly dying together, and after her treating Sam, her patient, something had clicked in her and she couldn't free her mind.

Is this what humans have to deal with? she wondered as she tried again to push her thoughts away and powered down slowly into an uneasy recharge. It was already an hour past midnight, and sometimes low batteries got her in a funk. But her mind hadn't slept while charging this time. Her mind had scoured the Labyrinth network for mentions of Clayton to see what he'd been up to. Her mind stalked him, which she only discovered when a flashing alert broke her out of charging mode.

Protest. Downtown. Led by Clayton Wilson.

Which was impossible because he was currently in recovery and being helped by his one true love, Sam. The thought made her teeth clench together and grate, an act she'd seen humans do so much she'd internalized it. But he couldn't be leading a protest, unless...

Her internal clock told her she'd been charging for an entire day. Full batteries, at least, but wasting the day had been completely unnecessary. If it hadn't been for the alert, would she ever have awakened? That question was followed by another. Would she have wanted to awaken?

They were questions for another day, though, because another alert followed behind that one. Massive power draw from the abandoned USPS building in SODO. She immediately recognized the signature of an android draining power from the grid. That may have been why she'd taken so long to charge. Her personal charging station had been designed to avoid detection. When spikes impacted the power grid, it would have lowered the draw to help her avoid detection and blend in with the background more. Hence, a whole day. But how many androids would it take to spike for that long?

Load monitoring and analysis detected spikes in third and fifth harmonics typical of the standard charging apparatus for androids based on power draw. By itself, Dandelion would have found the spike interesting and worthy of inspection, but at the same time as a new Clayton Wilson protest? Dandelion wondered about that coincidence, partially because she was still obsessed and a little because now she saw Clayton as another patient. His "patient" status was a half-step toward waning her off of her problematic obsession in that it gave her some distance, but it was all she could convince herself of. To get all the way to friend, she thought, would take more time.

Sam hadn't crossed her mind until she realized that Sam hadn't crossed her mind. Then, Sam was all Dandelion could think about. Rather, why had her first patient, who had been the focus of her attention for so long now, suddenly become irrelevant to her? Try as she might, Dandelion couldn't quite make herself curious about Sam. The irritation that Dandelion had felt from earlier seemed to have overpowered her patient loyalty so that now, she didn't want to see Sam again.

Emotions were shitty things to have because she definitely felt bad about that fact and her sense of obligation was in full effect, so Dandelion knew that she would check in on Sam eventually. Dandelion would most likely just be irritated while she did it.

But first, she had to vent her irritation to Clayton about putting his stupid name out into the Labyrinth, coupled with a protest no less. Human Pride Movement, Siblings of the Natural Order, possibly even Humanity in Crisis Council, would all find that very interesting after the news coverage that Clayton had been getting. There was zero chance that the protest would go on without incident. Maybe that's what Clayton was going for? Dandelion didn't know. But she did know it was stupid.

With a heavy and completely unnecessary sigh, Dandelion rolled out of bed. She took the time to throw on some overalls with a T-shirt beneath and some heavy work boots before she left the darkness of her bedchambers and entered into the early morning streets of Seattle.

CHAPTER 38
THE DO-OVER

THE SUN WAS WELL OVERHEAD by the time the group arrived back at the Bremerton Plant. Stephen emerged first, leading the group. Clayton was behind him, followed by Larken, struggling to keep up, but stubbornly insistent that she wouldn't be left behind.

Behind her were twenty protestors. There was nothing subtle about their advance through the underbrush. When they breached the trees that formed the final perimeter before the clearing in the front of the building, Larken could make out bodies in the tiny turret windows almost three strata up. The weapons, predictably, were trained on the group. A loudspeaker blared in the distance.

"Go home," bleated a raspy voice that cut through the trees and sent a flock of birds scattering into the sky. The protestors gathered set up their signs and began marching again, this time in small circles before the plant. "There's nothing for you here."

Larken shot a quick look to her left, where Clayton stood. He smiled a mischievous grin and lifted a sign-handle that looked like an oversized communicator up above his head. As he clicked the button to shoot his projected sign into a four-by-four-foot square, a humming sound caught Larken's attention. She followed the sound with her head until it swiveled away from the guards to the tops of the trees. There, a solitary news drone hovered in the distance. She could almost make out the camera zooming in and out as the drone rose and fell with the wind.

When the sign was fully projected, the drone swooped closer and hovered about a foot above it, scanning the words that Larken had to read in reverse and upside down: Reclamation is murder. Whatever other protest Clayton had had planned, the sign worked perfectly. A second and a half later, another drone joined the first, and then another and then another until there were so many that Larken lost count.

Good.

It wasn't part of the plan necessarily, but all of these witnesses meant that the HPM would have a difficult time using those fancy guns up on the turrets against them. Even the really, really bad guys must be mindful of public relations. That was covered in her class the Politics of Community Organizing. Her major was finally starting to pay off.

"Now," she said, in barely more than a whisper. The protestors behind her funneled past, forming a large marching oval before her, moving counterclockwise around the oval's perimeter. The guns moved. At first, one of the cannons quickly spun around toward the protestors. But when a flock of drones broke off from the cluster in the direction of the weapon, Larken noticed one of the other turrets which had just begun to move stop dead still. A break formed in the protestor line as a van crept through.

Channel Six news, nationwide.

"Why are there so many news people here?"

Clayton's grin widened. "I figured we could use a witness and called in for support," he told her. "Those news crews will be happy enough to find me here. I wonder if they'll be as curious as we are about why HPM are secretly buying up the reclamation plants."

More news vans. A volantrae or three overhead, following closely behind the drones.

"This air space is private," came a voice over the speaker, the same raspy voice that had already told them ineffectually to leave. "There is no designated roadway over the building. You are in violation of regulation three dash nine dash four of the air safety code."

Nobody was listening. Everyone's attention, even Larken's, was focused on the skyline clutter.

"Ready?" Stephen asked, calling up from behind her.

"As ready as I'm going to be," she said. "Let's go."

The crowd began to chant loudly, "Reclamation is... murder." This caught the attention of at least one more of the turret weapons and the majority of the drones. Clayton handed off his sign to someone who looked about college age and then backed toward where Larken stood motionless by the tree line. Stephen, who for some reason was wearing heavy black boots that she'd never seen on him before, crushed through the vegetation behind Clayton. They both stopped at the same time.

"Coming?" Stephen asked.

"Yeah," Larken said, stilling her beating heart as much as she could—which amounted to the equivalent of slowing a speeding volantrae from two-hundred miles-per-hour down to about one-ninety. A deep breath, and she followed, testing the ground with her cane before every step.

She could have walked the path with her eyes closed and from memory. Of course, she didn't dare to close her eyes because the android might have been lurking somewhere, despite her fake confidence. And the foliage was actively trying to kill her. Larken tripped as she became entrapped in a cluster of leaves and branches that had a vaguely human-esque quality to them. Her cane jabbed hard into the earth to keep her upright As Larken recovered. She looked ahead. Clayton and Stephen both had already turned the corner. Raising her eyes to the wall, Larken saw that the turrets were still there and still aimed directly at the protestors—the brave protestors, from the looks of the size of those weapons. A little closer and she could now see that the barrels of the guns were as large around as a lofting ball. But she guessed that whatever ammunition came out of them would likely do more than bounce off of whatever it hit.

The smell hit her. The pool was nearby. Air floated in over the top of the offal, and the stench made her eyes water. She didn't recall it smelling quite so bad before and wondered casually if they had made a recent dump of chemi-cals and whether or not that would change anything.

No, it wouldn't. The fluid in the pond was diluted enough with water that it had to be being mixed in some-where inside of the building, probably for safety reasons. The worst that she thought might happen to them is if someone swallowed an eyeball.

But she'd never recover from that experience.

Suddenly, there was silence.

That drew her attention back to the present and away from any speculation she might have been doing. The sound of crunching through the underbrush had diminished into nothing as Clayton and Stephen widened the gap between them and her. Calling out would have alerted the preoccupied guards to what they were doing, straying far from the protest site. A lone cricket called out somewhere, and then went silent as a twig broke behind her. Swinging around knocked Larken off balance, and she almost tumbled to the ground. When she didn't, she wished she had.

There, silhouetted against the light, was another person. This person, tall and thin, had dark brown hair and a face that was too perfect. A perfect face that she had seen before.

"Miss me, Larken?" the woman sneered.

Larken closed her eyes and shook her head, but when she opened her eyes a second time, the woman was still there. Her mind went through all of the possible ways she could be seeing the woman, who she was certain had been destroyed. It all came back to her losing her mind. It was finally done. She'd cracked under the strain.

"Get away from her," Clayton called. He'd come back around the corner, and, apparently, he could see Larken's hallucination, too. Larken stared at the gratuitously crimson lips and purple-topaz eyes. The placid look of the woman's features seemed contrary to Larken's memories: the punches that seemed so hard that they might push all the way through her chest and out her back, the strangling grip the woman had once had around Larken's throat, crushing the breath out of her, and the immoveable arm that had once held her beneath the water's pink sludgy surface. Larken backed up a step. The android advanced. Almost too fast for her to think, the cane was gone and Larken found herself on the hard surface of the earth.

"Did you really think that you could sneak in here?"

"What do you care?"

She thought for a moment. This woman was an android,

kind of like Dandelion, in a strange way. Perhaps talking to her might do something.

"What's your name?" she asked, working her way back to her knees. "And who do you work for?"

The question took the woman by almost as much surprise as it took Larken. The woman staggered backward into a bush and stopped unnaturally fast.

"I...I don't know," she said at first. Then her eyes met Larken's and for a quick second Larken thought she saw them glistening—an impossibility. "I don't have a name. I don't have..."

The woman's lips curled into a wry smile as she belted out laughter.

"I can't, really," she said, staring unblinking at Larken. "I mean, I've got quite a lot to do right now. I've got to kill you, for starters. Then everyone you love. And then everyone they love. It'll be a busy couple of weeks, all said and done. And you're asking me what my name is?"

She let out a deep, long laugh.

"Felicity," she called out, when she finished. "There. Now how useful is that to a dead woman?"

Larken rose for the second time in twenty-four hours without her cane for support. Wobbly, but not falling, Larken faced her opponent. Terror sucked her breath away.

"Might as well get started," Larken said, motioning behind her back to Stephen and Clayton to enter the facility and hoping they wouldn't protest. Once again, she was the bait. Figured.

"I don't suppose HPM hired you for this? Have you been in that soup the entire time?"

The last question seemed to wear on the woman and

slowed her hands that until that moment had been making their way up from her sides.

Then, faster than all her memories told her, the woman had the front of Larken's blouse clutched in her unbreakable grip. Larken dangled in the air, her feet at least six inches from the ground. Larken couldn't see Clayton or Stephen. All she saw was the woman's placid face, a killing face that betrayed no emotion. Did Dandelion start out like this? she wondered, as the woman lifted her opposing hand and clenched it into a fist. With any luck, Larken thought, it would take more than one punch and buy enough time for Clayton and Stephen to make it through the filth and into the tunnel. Larken knew she could take a punch, though she wasn't certain how many.

Larken clenched her teeth together. The terror that had accompanied her imaginings from earlier had been replaced with the cold, calculating will to survive. She considered working on the woman's fingers, but she knew there was only metal beneath that skin, and no amount of clawing would cut through titanium or whatever it was that built the woman's artificial skeleton. She considered the blouse she wore, buttoned up safari-type suit. This may have been her opportunity. The woman had clutched the fabric together below the third button.

Larken widened her eyes as though she'd seen something behind the woman's head. Felicity turned to look at the same time that Larken's right hand shot up to rip apart her own blouse at the top button. She lifted her arms above her shoulders and fell through the top into a crumpled heap on the ground. Then, a second later, felt a thud into her side as the woman's foot connected with her ribs. Larken thought she imagined a crack, but the pain was no worse than the pain that she always carried with her. And as a bonus, the robot-woman had kicked her in the direction of the pink water, which was far too murky for human eyes to penetrate as Larken knew from experience. It might offer some protection from android eyes as well. Or it might not. But it was better than nothing.

Using the momentum given to her by the android, Larken rolled, her shoulders and back wincing with every revolution. The slight gradient of the ground toward the pond sped her up until she felt nausea growing in her stomach. At least if she reached the pond, her vomit would be unnoticed as the least-disgusting thing in there. She didn't even bother trying to imagine anything other than what she knew to be a soupy tribute to hundreds if not thousands of violent deaths.

Footsteps. Too fast, and gaining. If she didn't figure out how to move quicker, she wouldn't reach the water's edge. Larken tried to use the muscles in her back and her arms to speed up and clenched her teeth against the increasing sting of bile in the back of her throat.

The footsteps stopped.

A second later, her body collided with something that felt like an iron lamppost right in her gut. She wheezed out and sucked in air through gritted teeth.

Too late.

She listened for some sign of whether Clayton and Stephen had made any progress and heard nothing but the sound of fluid dripping slowly into the pool. They were gone, somewhere, and she could only hope that they'd made the entrance and that the entrance led somewhere that had actual air inside. Her friends could just as easily drown before finding a way out of the sewage pipes.

Long shots. All she ever had.

Larken felt herself being raised into the air. She felt the tension in the woman as she wound up for the punch.

A second passed. Then another. No punch.

And as suddenly as if Felicity had been stopped, Larken found herself falling to the earth. She landed flat-faced on the edge of the pond and rolled again. A couple of revolutions and she fell into the foul-smelling liquid. With renewed vigor, Larken forced her way beneath the surface, seeking out with her hands anything that might stick her to the bottom. A large rock—or something that felt like a large rock—that had just enough ridges for her to lock her fingers around and hold herself in place.

A shockwave nearly broke her grip as it pulsed through the water toward her. She resisted, yet her fingers slipped as another wave and another undulated over her. Something was happening in the pond, something violent and involving so much force that the rock itself, a boulder bigger than her torso, slid inch by inch deeper into the fluid.

Larken pushed herself with all of her might back toward the surface. Her only thought was that some of the protestors might have come to see how they were doing and now were getting beaten into large bags of pulp by the android woman. But as she broke the surface and wiped clear the chunky fluid from her face, she made out the outline of the android woman and only one other who she couldn't make out beyond.

If her imagination wasn't playing tricks, Larken saw the other person's fists hanging by their sides, visible on either side of the android woman's back that blocked the view. Each fist was surrounded by a ball of what looked like bright bluish-white light. The woman stepped to the side as she dodged what seemed to be a projectile that went just over Larken's head. Then, Larken caught a glimpse of the face.

There, features wrenched up into a scowl that Larken had never seen before, and dwarfed in size easily by over a foot of height, stood Dandelion. Her eyes glowed with the same energy as her fists. Faster than she could see, one of those hands connected with the android-woman's torso. The woman didn't move an inch, but the force bent the ground near her feet up into a hill that made the dirt move like water until the energy wave slid into the pond. This time, Larken braced for impact, but still the wave threw her back at least five feet from where the rock lay beneath the surface. Larken watched as Dandelion pulled her fist back.

CHAPTER 39
CLASH OF THE ANDROIDS

"RUN IF YOU CAN," Dandelion said when she saw that Larken staring up at her. Then she let her fist go and collide against the woman face. What little of her processing wasn't focused on running predictive algorithms, attempting to block the android's onslaught was entirely planted on Larken, who seemed to think that the correct thing to do when Dandelion bought her a little time was to sit there dripping and gawking. "Go!"

She should have used all of her focus on prediction. A metal hand connected with her chin and drove her head backward. Unlike a human, who would have probably died from a broken neck at the force of that blow, Dandelion worked the servos in her neck to bring her head back forward, suffering only a slightly-misshapen lump near where an Adam's apple could have gone. Then, she let loose her own flurry of punches and kicks, each one blocked by the woman almost as effortlessly as Dandelion had. Only two of twenty connected, and of those, one was a glancing blow.

Dandelion would have loved a weapon. Anything would

have helped—a stick, a knife, or even a rock. But when she and Sam had arrived, there was no time to think of such things. Larken had been a punch or two away from death.

"You fight well," said the android, who then dodged another strike at her head while simultaneously strafing out of Dandelion's reach. "What model?"

"Mark 34 Foxtrot," Dandelion told her, guessing the woman had never heard of it, being a United African model. Dandelion had to guess, she would have suggested the woman was a Prescient Model 1, best in class military special-ops five years ago before when they'd made quick work of her while rescuing Larken the first time. Dandelion hadn't been there for the event. "You're slower than I thought you'd be."

The woman leaped forward, ready to throw more punches. Dandelion had been working on her personality for literal years and still had problems sometimes. This woman— evil as she was—didn't seem to have Dandelion's problems. She got angry quickly enough anyway, as Dandelion inter- preted from her hasty and poorly planned response.

Dandelion easily dodged the woman's attack, but in doing so ended up with her back to the woman, which she soon discovered was a mistake. Only when another punch landed solidly in the center of Dandelion's back did she realize that the attack, and the attitude, might have feints.

"Felicity," the woman said. "That's my name. Felicity Weir. You seem familiar."

"You wouldn't know me," Dandelion said, sidestepping another blow and twisting her body so she could finally see the woman. "But I know you."

Unlike Dandelion, tiny fissures creased down Felicity's face. They were joints that held her face together. Whoever put her back together, it didn't look like they'd quite finished sealing the seams.

Dandelion steeled herself as another punch connected to her midsection, taking this punch instead of parrying so that she could use the opportunity to get at that face. Sacrificing power for speed, Dandelion connected three fingers directly on one of the seams. Felicity screamed and raised her hands to cover the quarter-inch gap that showed hints of wiring beneath.

It was a better strategy, Dandelion realized, and something she could do instead of trade body and head blows. She skirted the edge of the pond and moved herself just out of Felicity's reach.

"Are you going to tell me your name?" Felicity asked, hand still to her cracked face. A bluish-green fluid leaked between Dandelion's fingers.

"Dandelion Lemaire," said Dandelion, letting the words sit in the air as she moved around them and the pond to a position farther from Felicity's reach. Then, in a single jump, she covered half the distance to Felicity.

Dandelion had intended to cover the full distance. Instead, she felt Felicity's hand around her neck, squeezing as though Dandelion had a larynx instead of a voice box. Dandelion screamed and forced two fingers of her right hand deeper into the cracked face.

Felicity tried to pull away, but she couldn't pull too hard without risking her features. Dandelion used the few milliseconds Felicity thought through her options to wedge fingers of her left hand into the crack and pull as hard as she could. Felicity shrieked and dropped Dandelion to the ground. Dandelion only stayed down for half a second, and then sprung back to Felicity.

A movement out of the corner of her eye distracted Dandelion from her attack. It was Sam, Sam and Larken both completely soaked with pink goo and wading out of the pond.

A punch connected with Dandelion's head and brought her back into the fight. Her strategy had been decoded because she spent too long watching Sam. Now she had to rethink. Landing lightly on her feet, Dandelion wasted no time in moving backward toward the tree line. The woman's faceplate to the left of the seam where Dandelion had ripped showed exposed wires. Dandelion could see nanites working quickly to repair the skin in real-time. She didn't have long to get back at it, so she crouched and jumped once more.

Dandelion could have attacked and parried more. She could have done a lot of things to end the fighting quicker, but what she wanted was to not be alone. Seeing Sam again brought Dandelion back to thoughts of Clayton and spurred emotional routines she didn't have time to process. She shook her head and dove instead of attacking.

Dandelion slid under the lip of the water and hid among the slime. Dandelion's entire body was submerged, and Felicity had come looking for her. A second after Dandelion entered and smiled to herself when she heard Felicity break the surface. Rage was guiding Felicity or some rudimentary form of it. More dangerous, but less controllable. That was her assessment of the difference between Felicity and her. It might have only been the time that Dandelion had to refine her personal skills working in the free clinic, then in the retirement community, but Dandelion didn't get lit up the way Felicity seemed to. Even now, as she switched to sonic sensors instead of her normal visuals so that she could actually see Felicity's hands coming for her, she didn't feel the grip of hostility that she thought Felicity must be experiencing.

That was good for Dandelion. As soon as those hands were close enough, she helped them along with a good yank forward, one of her hands on each. That might not have been enough to topple Felicity had it not been for the force of a powerful thrust as something large, possibly an explosion, sent more shockwaves through the water. Dandelion's pull turned into a freefall as her weight combined with Felicity's, and they both tumbled beneath the water's surface.

Sparks. It worked better than Dandelion had expected, with one small complication. As fluid filled the cavity in Felicity's head, circuits became connected by the fluid that weren't supposed to be connected, and hence the sparks. She heard the sparks with her vision, and as she slipped down what turned out to be a steep underwater embankment, she saw Felicity's face betray something that seemed like surprise with wide eyes and her mouth agape. They tumbled downward together, head over heel, entangled among their own limbs and other pieces of human bodies that had made it past the reclamation plant filters, to come to a sliding halt in the soot and remains in the bottom of the pool.

Felicity stopped moving.

It was the worst possible time for Felicity to come to a complete stop because she was still very much on top of Dandelion. Another difference between Felicity and Dandelion, composite materials. Dandelion had been one of a kind. Her carbon-alloy skeletal structure and combination of nanites with servos for mobility were designed to be a normal "human-like" weight. This human likeness had come in extremely useful for her pre-nursing career as flight security on transports. Now it worked against her, as the weight limitations also limited her physical strength, and Felicity didn't have a single carbon-alloy anything in her body. She was a tank of an android, and currently the tank lay over Dandelion, pressing her into the mud.

Dandelion made a few breathing sounds and expanded and contracted her chest. Of course, no air entered her body. She did this to see if perhaps that gave her the space to wiggle from beneath, but as her chest tightened, Felicity only sank them both farther into the mud—still not moving. There, deep in the sediment, Dandelion found herself without distraction, save the unidentified objects floating past.

At least the threat had been neutralized. Her core glowed with that knowledge, she guessed since she'd fulfilled her security duties for the first time in years. Satisfaction. A job well done. And, she'd solved the problem of her Clayton obsession for the final time. Down in the muck, she was trapped by Felicity's body, possibly forever or at least until her body lost the last of its power. Sam wouldn't have to worry about her any more.

Fifteen percent, her body told her. The fight had drained most of her reserves and with only fifteen percent, those earth-shaking blows she'd been trading with Felicity were all but impossible now.

Fourteen percent.

Thirteen percent.

Too fast. Her power was draining too quickly. Something had broken inside of her. She didn't know what, and worse, she didn't know who, if anyone, could possibly fix her anyway.

Ten percent.

Shut down auxiliary power. Basic functions only. The

feeling of fluid against her skin faded away as power to her detection functions dried up. Then the slosh of the water from drain pipes disappeared. Finally, the faint glow of light that lined the inside of her eyelids. There was nothing but blackness.

Nine percent.

But it didn't matter. Nine percent wasn't enough and eventually it would work its way down to zero. Dandelion wondered if she would still have enough energy to witness that final moment when her android body shut down or if she would just cease to be. And what happened to androids after they died, anyway?

Before she could answer that question, the body pinning her in place moved. The woman didn't wake up, rather something shoved her off of Dandelion. Then a hand reached toward her through the muck, and lacking better options, Dandelion reached for it and closed her fingers around a forearm. Together, she and the mysterious person pulled, yanking her inch-by-inch from her trapped position.

THE FIRST SHOCKWAVE sent Clayton careening forward through the tunnel. His back slammed into the side with enough force to knock the wind out of him. The gust of breath that he found himself powerless to hold in his chest pushed past his lips to form a bubble around the seal of his mouth.

Involuntary breathing kicked in, and he sucked the bubble in as well as surrounding fluid, which he could tell from the alkaline-slick feeling of heavy fluid that slid between his gums and cheek. No chunks, so at least he was spared having to fumble around with his tongue and remove someone else's body parts. But his coughing fit wasn't quite over, and with his eyes squeezed shut, he had no idea how close they were to anything that resembled an exit.

Worse still, even as he gagged when his lungs filled with fluid while coughing through clenched teeth, another shock-wave shoved Stephen into his back, tumbling the two of them farther into the pipe and defying him to try to find his way back before drowning in the muck. Clayton imagined a room full of people in suits discussing why the outflow into the pool had gotten backed up. He imagined them sending a diver down to investigate and discovering his rotting corpse wedged into the pipe somehow.

Clayton's hands brushed against one side of the tunnel. Hazarding a guess as to which way was up, Clayton shoved off with his fingertips in a direction that may have been correct while he willed his coughing to stop to little effect. His head broke through the surface of the fluid. For a second, he felt air chilling the slick film over his eyes and mouth. With a gurgle, Clayton was able to expel some fluid from his lungs, but soon discovered that it wasn't enough. The breath of air he tried to suck in next wouldn't fill his chest completely and only brought on another ill-timed coughing fit as another shockwave forced him forward and down under the surface again.

I'm going to die here.

Facing his own death wasn't as scary this time. The first time, being pursued through the streets of the city with HPM mechs firing rockets at them, he'd envisioned his death as a painful affair. His overactive imagination had killed him fifteen ways before he'd somehow been saved by a "terrorist" organization SNO.

Giving up the fight for survival in this pipe was easier. He already had lungs full of the milky fluid and who knew what kind of damage that was doing. After all, he'd known before diving in that this fluid was the cast-off from melting tanks capable of fully digesting a human body in a little less than half an hour. Or, by the random body parts he'd experienced, at least mostly digesting them. It wasn't as though all of the corrosive stuff could have been completely filtered out of the cast-off. Some of it was likely working on his lungs so that even if he did somehow manage to find air, whether he would be able to breathe again was still an unanswered question.

So he let himself float. He stopped struggling, and as he did, the coughing stopped as though his body now understood there was no point. He floated in the fluid, occasionally colliding with the walls, but not in an unpleasant way. He thought about Dandelion, and how she'd saved his life there in the hotel room, moving impossibly fast. The memory of her navigating her way through the tunnels when she'd come to get him from SNO, which only now seemed strange enough to be concerning.

An android.

He'd been avoiding thinking about since he'd heard it because it seemed impossible. But the memories he'd just gone through made it obvious how true it was. Especially the kick. One second, she was standing upright, and the next she was standing next to him with the HPM member on the ground. Nobody moved as fast as that. As strange as it seemed, his memories seemed segmented. Before that moment, she was a human nurse, caring for the elderly in the retirement village. Sweet, docile, and perhaps a little bit strange in affect, but definitely very human. Afterward, she was a killing machine.

He ran out of thoughts. Had his eyes not been squeezed shut, he might have noticed the fade to black as oxygen deprivation settled over him like the mist from a fog machine. Had he not been so preoccupied with teasing out the exact moment that Dandelion ceased being Dandelion and had changed instead into a menace and threat to anyone nearby, he would have noticed the increasing tingling in his limbs had faded, and he couldn't even feel them any longer. The moment of death was upon him, and he hadn't even noticed its arrival.

———

It was an opening. Stephen was certain of it as the first shockwave hit. He'd opened his eyes and steered himself upright so that his head poked just above the water just in time to see Clayton shoot into the side wall. Stephen tilted his head backward to take advantage of the little air he'd found, and his eyes skimmed across the surface before him until they came to rest on a pink glow. His being able to see at all meant there was some sort of light creeping into the tunnel from somewhere. He couldn't see a thing moments earlier. The tunnel had to be the one they'd been searching for. How many tunnels could the place have, anyway?

The second shockwave catapulted him forward toward the light and past where he'd seen Clayton go under. Stephen made a futile effort to grab for Clayton where he thought the man might be. A small whispering voice chided him for his efforts. This voice told him that the man who'd come between him and Sam wasn't worth saving and that he should be thankful instead. Stephen scowled at himself, his eyes darting across the top of the water as another shockwave pushed him farther still away from where Clayton had gone under, and there was no longer a choice in the matter. He floated down the stream as the ceiling rose and rose and the tunnel expanded until he found himself in a pod-like chamber with a walkway around it.

And a ladder leading up from the soup onto that walkway.

But he had to time it right. The shockwaves of whatever

was happening outside them had reversed the flow of the liquid through the tunnel, but even now he felt the viscous liquid slowing its movement and preparing to reverse course again. Stephen scanned again for any sign of Clayton one last time before he diverted his attention back to the ladder.

He approached the ladder, able to get a head and shoulders above the mix and still floating along with the impulse from the shockwave. He wanted to turn back and head out into the open air. The smell was making him sick, not that he had enough air in his nostrils to smell anything. His muscles ached with each stroke that he issued forth to stay aloft in the murky fluid.

The first attempt failed. Going too fast, Stephen had miscalculated the speed and grabbed nothing but air when he approached. Then, he had to swim against the current, pulling himself as quickly as he could, pounding the water with each stroke. Every inch forward cost him four strokes, but he made them. Closer and closer he came until at last, with one final effort, his fingers found purchase on the bottom rung. They slipped away first, but he was able to grab hold.

Whether it was good or bad luck, Stephen wasn't certain. But just as he grabbed on, he felt something soft and heavy thud into his leg. His first thought was Clayton. Before he could talk himself out of it, he had already let go of the rung he'd fought so hard to get and dove beneath the surface. Stephen shot back up through the water with strength that he didn't know he had, towing what he hoped was Clayton along behind him.

Checking back, he saw that he'd lost about a foot from the ladder in the process. Cursing under his breath, and spitting out what he could of sludge from his mouth, Stephen found that he had to work nearly twice as hard to move toward the ladder with one arm as it had with two. His muscles throbbed and pulsated with pain as they burned past their tolerance, but he swam on.

After a second or two, he noticed that the ladder seemed to be going the opposite way. The current in the fluid seemed to be picking up speed in the wrong direction, and he didn't have the energy to beat it. It was so close that he thought, just on chance, he might be able to lunge and grab it. Stephen swung his arm down through the fluid and felt a slight impulse in the right direction. He broke the water's surface and hurled his body at the side of the pit, stretching his fingers out before him...only to come up short. In dismay, he watched his fingers grasping at air.

Then another shockwave surged behind him, reversing the fluid again. Stephen's free hand closed on the ladder and with what was left of his effort, he dragged himself and his prize up the ladder and onto the walkway. It was Clayton he had grabbed, but there was something wrong with him. The man had been underwater too long and had to have lungs full of fluid. Stephen's mind raced through possibilities of what he might do. It was the re-emergence of SNO training that brought him a solution. Clayton had minutes at the most if he was going to survive, and step one was to get oxygen into his lungs.

Stephen flipped Clayton onto his back. The man looked strange without that annoying grin that Stephen had always interpreted as a challenge. "I've got your woman." That was what Stephen thought the first time he'd seen Clayton, hand intertwined with Sam's, fingers locked together so tightly that he would have had to cut them off to separate them. Yes, he could still walk away. He could leave Clayton on the walkway and speak of his selfless bravery and all the blather that people did about people who died doing something heroic.

No. Even here, even with plausible deniability, it still didn't sit right with Stephen, even if he could come out of it as the masculine shoulder that Sam would cry on and the man who she would learn to love. No. Not that way. He felt the heat behind his eyes as he lowered his mouth to Clayton's and blew with whatever energy he had left. Then he pounded on the man's chest, hearing the words of the SNO instructor, "You're battling death, so you don't pussyfoot around." Stephen felt a crack when he pushed. "If something breaks, you're doing it right."

It didn't sound like a break, more like a popping neck. Stephen counted to five and then breathed again for Clayton, pushing down he urge to vomit as he inhaled the foul stench again and blew.

Still nothing.

And that scared him. A quick glance around told Stephen nothing about where he was or what he should do next. By himself, what could he do except swim back toward the exit where, if those shockwaves indicated anything, the android was probably working its way through the pulp that used to be Larken. It had been a stupid idea. The thought that they'd come all this way, and nothing would change for it, formed a lump in his throat, sadness. Then anger.

He swung both hands down into Clayton's chest, and finally the body responded. Clayton lurched over sideways and expelled what looked like a gallon of fluid along with possibly half a finger. Then Clayton gagged and vomited more, letting a nearly endless supply of fluid from his mouth down to the floor.

"It—" Clayton began, then dry heaved before continuing. "It's dry."

"Yeah, I think this is a maintenance tank or something," Stephen said, the pressure behind his eyes lifting and the bulge in his throat working its way back down. Clayton's black hair fanned out around him when he lay back down before Stephen on the deck.

"Thanks," he said, not looking at Stephen, but there wasn't anyone else for him to be talking to.

"Don't mention it," Stephen said, finally ready to let his body give in to the lack of strength. He collapsed beside Clayton, staring up at the overhead light, a flickering bulb wrapped in a protective wire shield. "Seriously don't mention it."

"I want to tell you something," Clayton told him, still not looking directly at him. "Sam told me about your history together."

It was all Stephen could do not to laugh. Of course, she had. Figured.

"Now? This is the time for this conversation?"

"We might die in here," Clayton replied, "But before we do, I just wanted you to know that she doesn't hate you. She understands where you're coming from. You two just aren't the same people anymore."

No, Stephen thought, of course not. And then he once again mentally cursed himself—this time for saving Clayton's life—and the fact that now that he'd had time alone with the guy, he actually kind of liked him. This annoyed Stephen even more since that mean that he would be a dick if he still pined for Sam. But if he was honest with himself—and nearly dying does something to aid honesty along—Sam had already very clearly indicated what she wanted, and however much Stephen hated the fact, it wasn't him.

"Don't bother," Stephen said. "It doesn't matter anyway, does it? Do you actually think that we'll get out of here alive?"

Clayton shrugged. "Don't know. Maybe?" Then he grinned. "Uh, actually, yeah, I think we will."

"What makes you so certain?"

"That," Clayton said, pointing to a blue and green box near the platform.

"And that is...?"

"That is a motion sensor, which means that over there is a hatch." Clayton seemed so certain that Stephen believed him about the hatch. He didn't feel so confident about whatever was on the other side of the hatch, though. For all they knew, there could be a thousand bad guys with guns. Still, after sucking in the stale air for a minute longer, Stephen figured whatever it was had to be better than staying in the tunnel with the disgusting fluids and the never-ending stench.

CHAPTER 41
VICTORY?

LARKEN COULDN'T TELL whose hands grasped at her and pulled at her and yanked her with little respect for her bodily autonomy, but she was thankful all the same when she found herself gasping on the shoreline—and decidedly not dead.

"Mrmthhm," she mumbled, hearing the not-words tumble from her mouth out into the world.

"Relax," Sam's voice said, soothing in its lower tenor. "Relax. You're okay. No need to talk."

Flames went off in Larken's mind as she mentally relived the last few minutes. Somewhere in the darkness through which Larken could not see was the face of the friend she'd betrayed. A friend who saw fit to come out to the middle of the woods and rescue her. She would have wept if she could have, but it hurt far too much to move.

"The android," she managed to mutter.

"Is right here," came another familiar voice. Dandelion had come, too. That made Larken seriously question whether or not she had actually died and this was something like an afterlife.

"No," she finally said. "The other android."

"Deactivated," said Dandelion. "Deactivated and somewhere down in the muck."

"Got to make sure," Larken followed up. "Can't do this again."

She opened her eyes to the welcome sight of Sam smiling which was something Sam hadn't done—not really—since the incident. Over her shoulder, Dandelion had something that might have been a cross between a smile and a sardonic grin.

"I'm sorry, Dandelion. I shouldn't have told," said Larken as Dandelion only grinned in response. Her words came out slow as though they were floating without gravity or propulsion, lingering above anything else.

"Shut up, Larken," Dandelion told her. "Sam and I are fine. Now. You're the one who decided to take on HPM's reclamation center with a bunch of protestors. What were you thinking?"

"Nobody else was going to do it," Larken said and then turned toward Sam. "We had to save you somehow."

"I didn't need saving," Sam said. "I was at SNO headquarters."

Siblings of the Natural Order wasn't exactly a safety net. They kidnapped people, tortured people when they needed information, and made people disappear that they thought needed disappearing. The self-righteousness of the organization was exactly the thing that called to Stephen and pushed Sam away. Sam had outgrown them, and Stephen hadn't. It was as simple as that from Larken's perspective as she'd watched their relationship deteriorate.

"We need to get inside," Larken told them, pivoting quickly to get focus back where it needed to be, on their friends and the lines of models waiting to be rescued. "Stephen and Clayton are in there."

She motioned to the building, tilting her head toward it and letting her eyes follow. Her heart skipped as she saw plumes of smoke rising from beyond the wall. The guard towers had been desiccated into empty husks and from the look of the plume of gray-blue rising into the sky, something large had exploded. It could have been a good sign, or a bad one. There was no way to know from her vantage point. With her muscles screaming that they were too weary, and once again she asked too much of them, she pushed herself to her knees. Her trusty cane fell to the ground by her hand, and without help of anything but that, she raised up to her feet. Breathing hurt her chest and her head spun as she got there, but she did manage to get there.

"Let's go," she said.

"I can't," Dandelion immediately replied. She stood almost motionless. Her bright eyes seemed dim and faded. For a second, Larken thought it was because of the smoke blotting out the sun. "Those hits took too much energy. If I go in there, I won't be able to fight off a chipmunk."

Dandelion swayed slightly as a gentle breeze blew and chilled Larken's neck and arms, making her hairs prick up and stand at attention.

"I'm not going," Sam said. "Leave that to the others. They'll sort it out soon enough."

"They're protestors," Larken refuted. "They were only here to create a distraction. Every single one of us has more combat experience than all of them combined."

"Not those others, Larken. We didn't come alone."

———

When the hatch swung open, Clayton recognized the room immediately as the one that they'd seen through the open gate when they'd followed the HPM bounty hunter as a group half a week earlier. It had seemed so long ago now that he could scarcely believe less than a week had passed. Instead of looking at lines of models waiting to be murdered, Clayton saw a room rife with chaos. Models ran forward and backward between the tanks, putting out fires. Some had fire extinguishers, others used the discarded clothing of those unlucky ones who had been in line before them to beat back the flames. Half of the reclamation pods had blue-white flames, licking like the tongue of a child trying for a lollipop just out of reach.

"Move over. I'm right behind you."

Clayton pushed himself the rest of the way through the hatch and rolled sideways. He tried to make it to his feet in a single motion, but his slicked boots had other ideas so he went up and down quickly. Just as well since when he fell a tendril of flame swiped the air where he just stood.

"You again," came a husky voice from behind him. Wincing, Clayton lifted his eyes to see the bottoms of two crutches first, and he knew that he hadn't been mistaken about the voice's origin. "It had to be you, didn't it? Stay away from the fire. Even diluted, there's no telling how flammable that stuff is."

"Lancaster?" Clayton's jaw dropped. From his position on the ground, Phineas Lancaster's nearly useless legs supported his massive torso. For just a second, Clayton mistook him for Larken, but the only thing they had in common was the way their supports made them walk. He shook off the impression and rose again this time more slowly and deliberately.

"Still am," Lancaster suggested in a gruff voice. "Mr. Wilson, glad to see you're still alive. Didn't think you'd last this long after we saved your ass in that massacre."

Clayton sensed movement behind him.

"Stephen," Lancaster said and pushed past Clayton knocking him wobbly. While Clayton tried to ensure that his feet supported him without again slipping from beneath, he saw Lancaster and Stephen grasp hands and shake.

An explosion sounded behind him, followed by a yelp. Clayton's face swiveled toward the sound, and he witnessed one of the HPM fall into one of the flaming tanks and then a splash of flame shot skyward. He felt his eyes go wide as the heat flashed across the skin on his face, drying his eyes immediately even from a distance of about forty feet. Stephen and Lancaster both seemed unfazed.

"Are you and Sam still together?" Lancaster asked, as explosions rocked the background. Clayton watched in amazement as the two had a casual conversation in the midst of—

He ducked as a projectile flew over his head. When he lifted his head back up, he found Stephen's gaze locked onto his. Stephen replied to Lancaster almost as though he were talking to Clayton instead.

"Not a couple. Just friends. It turns out Sam and I just aren't all that compatible."

———

After a good forty minutes, the burning was contained. Not a single fire truck showed up to the building site, something that concerned Larken and nobody else. Why hadn't any fire trucks or police shown up when there were very clearly still tens of news drones overhead that had to be broadcasting real time? When she mentioned it to Sam, Larken didn't like the answer.

HPM were bigger than Larken had thought, Sam guessed. Lancaster had told her he had the same suspicions that HPM had people in the police and fire departments. Sam thought that once it was clear that the HPM were losing, they wanted the fire to destroy everything in the building from the vats where the fires had started, sparked by the SNO's initial attack when they had to lob explosives over the walls and then blow the doors in.

"That was their plan? Explosives?"

"They didn't intend to hit anything critical. The old plans for the reclamation facility that they had were outdated and so, yeah, mistakes were made."

Models had been killed. Too many models. Even as they tried to rescue them, some of those who had already been in the tanks had to be put down like rabid animals. Sam's eyes had welled when she told Larken about that part of it as they stood outside the front gate, having decided not to go in and instead let the SNO do what they did best and rescue models.

Their conversation was interrupted as two man-sized silhouettes materialized against the backdrop of the plant. One limped slightly, and the other seemed to be constantly wiping his face to get the goop away. Sam was midsentence when she stopped and stared, her eyes glistening in the firelight.

"Clayton," she murmured, and then rushed toward the pair. Stephen saw Sam first, and Larken saw him tap Clayton on the elbow and nod her direction. Clayton then extended a hand to Stephen, who pushed it aside and slapped Clayton into what must have been a disgusting, slimy hug that made Larken cringe the longer it lasted.

Finally, the hug broke and Clayton pulled free and ran toward Sam, who picked up her speed to a slow trot at first, then gave up all appearances of impartiality as she ran toward Clayton. The two embraced in what must have been a sticky mess, but even the disgusting pink goop didn't stop them from kissing in the longest, deepest, and most vomit-inducing display of affection Larken had seen in ages. About thirty seconds later, Stephen passed them, and another fifteen seconds after that, Larken had her own disgusting hug to deal with without any kissing involved.

TWO MONTHS OF RECOVERY—SIGNIFICANTLY less than the last time Larken had battled a killer android—and Larken's life had settled back into some a sort of routine. Only now, part of her routine involved news interviews, or would soon, if her buzzing communicator was any indication. She shifted her weight so from her right to her left side, leaning into the chaise in her hotel room.

"Yes," Larken said, answering her communicator buzz as soon as she saw the KIRO logo in her communicator's display.

"My name is Janet Austin with KIRO news, and we'd like to do a live interview with you about the recent events at Bremerton."

"I said yes," Larken repeated. "Send me a time and I'll be there."

She thought for a moment.

"I don't mind KIRO hosting the conversation, but I need widespread coverage. Do you understand, Janet? There's something festering here, and it must be rooted out."

The woman didn't answer. Larken couldn't tell if she'd decided that Larken was a crazy person. To her surprise, the woman agreed.

"You're so fucking right," she said. "Listen. I can get national coverage if you give me a week. Two weeks, and we'll get nearly ninety percent of the university presses, too. Trust me to cover you, and you'll get to speak your piece."

"It's not my piece, Janet," Larken said. "I've been attacked by HPM multiple times now. My friend was nearly killed by two of their attackers, still at large. It took everything we had to stop a killer android from destroying us all. Once is a mistake. Twice is intentional. HPM don't think the law applies to them. That's a problem for every single one of us."

The news anchor's silence lasted for five seconds.

"Can I tell you something, Larken?"

"You may as well."

"My cousin joined HPM. I tried to stop her, but she's buying into their talking points. In central Texas, there's a strange stronghold for HPM, just north of League City. She bought in hook, line, and sinker. I'm hoping that your story can reach her. I'm hoping that you can save my family. And I'm not the only one. So many people have latched onto the hate."

"My best friend's ex-boyfriend was HPM. It's easy to get sucked in if you're not paying attention. But it's gone too far, Janet. It's time that we do something about it, right?"

"You won't regret talking to me. I'm on your side, and we'll do what we can to widen your audience."

"Good. Because after what happened here in Bremerton, I don't even think SNO have the resources to fight them, and the federal government seems to be asleep at the wheel. If anyone's going to do anything, it's going to be us. It has to be, but it can't just be us. All of us, all over a billion United States citizens, have got to protect our nation and our loved ones. We're all in this together."

More chatter about times and dates, and eventually Janet of KIRO disconnected to go chat with "her people" and figure out the details.

———

Larken wore a teal sari with an elaborate diamond lacing pattern across the back. She didn't wear it well because she didn't know how to properly wrap it, but it was a tribute to her delusion. Aayushi had told her that she was destined to fight HPM, and however much she'd have preferred not to, Larken had landed in exactly the position Aayushi had said. The teal sari was what Aayushi had worn in her hallucinations, although the black undershirt that Larken wore beneath to stay modest in case the bunching unraveled was all her own doing. Jocelyn dabbed powdered foundation over her cheeks and the bridge of Larken's nose, hiding the minuscule barely noticeable scars that feathered there.

"You don't want to do a pantsuit or something a bit more professional?" Jocelyn asked, as she finished up the foundation and moved on to bright-red lipstick.

Larken patiently waited for her to finish dabbing the stuff on before she smacked her lips together.

"This gives me confidence," she said. It reminded her of Aayushi, who always seemed to wear a teal sari in her visions. Aayushi, who had told her the future she would see, couldn't explain it in a way that made sense—until now. Jocelyn tilted her head and smiled.

"You look beautiful," she said.

Larken knew that wasn't true. The pain that limited her mobility also atrophied her arms and legs into practical sticks. Where two years ago, perhaps she would have looked thin but attractive and appropriate to the role of a nascent college student, now she looked almost skeletal. Jocelyn's makeup skills helped a lot on her face, but there wasn't anything she could do about the rest.

"Are you ready to go?" Jocelyn asked.

"Where's Dandelion?"

"Here," Dandelion said from the living room area. Larken had to get used to Dandelion's abilities. Hearing her voice made Larken feel safe, like she was at home and protected. She shuffled through the open doorway and couldn't help grinning at what she saw. Following her style choices, Dandelion had opted for a bright magenta dress with an embroidered shawl draped across one shoulder. It was an inspired look. Not quite a sari, and not quite a suit, and definitely not standard fashion. Larken could tell from the proud look on Jocelyn's face that she'd played a not-so-insignificant role in the outfit coming together.

"I like it," Larken said as Dandelion approached her from across the room.

Dandelion glanced toward Jocelyn, and Larken did the same, catching on then that collusion was happening. Then she recalled the advice and help she'd given Dandelion earlier, when Dandelion was in the maddening and insanity-inducing throes of obsession. Larken's eyes went wide as she turned back to Dandelion, who now looked up at her with those massive blue wells.

"I'm not sure how to say this," Dandelion said. She pulled her free hand through her hair. "I don't want to be here for crises, Larken. I don't want to be someone you call when things are going wrong. I deserve better than that."

"You do," Larken admitted. There was no argument to make there. Larken glanced up at Jocelyn, who only shrugged. Larken let out a deep sigh. This was going in a weird direction.

"I want to be more to you than someone who patches you up," Dandelion told her. "I want to be part of your life. I want to be there with you every day."

"Where did all this come from?" Larken asked. The words couldn't have meant what she thought, what she hoped. Her cheeks warmed as her heart pounded in her chest.

"Just what I've been thinking about," Dandelion replied. Dandelion didn't blush, and she didn't back away. She held tightly to Larken's hand and when Larken tried to sneak another look toward Jocelyn, Dandelion tugged her hand gently and wove her fingers through Larken's. "You're the best friend I've ever had."

Friend. Okay. Larken's mind twisted in circles as she tried to reconcile what was happening.

Anyone could see that and Dandelion wasn't particularly good at hiding her emotions when they cropped up. But the endearing look in Dandelion's eyes...somewhere in there were circuit boards and nanites and...

The kiss caught her by surprise, as deep in thought as Larken was. The lips connected with her own, soft and pliant and perfect. Dandelion tasted of roses and limewater, and to Larken's surprise, she didn't pull away. She leaned in, and every part of her that came into contact with Dandelion screamed in excitement.

Only the kiss didn't actually happen. Instead, Dandelion gave Larken's hand a quick squeeze, as friends sometimes do, and let go, leaving Larken's heart banging like a timpani drum.

"Oh," she said, her lips and cheeks flushed and her forehead tingling.

"Larken," squealed Jocelyn in glee, her voice triggering House.

"You're blushing," remarked House, unhelpfully.

"Shut up, House," Larken said. The four of them laughed. In the process, Larken nearly fell down again as her cane slipped away from her grip. Dandelion caught her effortlessly as breathing and held her up.

"Are you ready?"

Larken's smile crept up to her eyes and tingled down her spine into her legs and toes. She nodded as Dandelion extended her arm, and then she took the offered arm without hesitation. It wasn't exactly what Larken wanted, but it still felt good to be appreciated by her apparent new best friend.

"Let's go then," she said. Jocelyn let out another squeal and they left the hotel room. Next stop: KIRO headquarters.

———

Larken wasn't as ready as she'd thought to embrace the national spotlight. A flotilla of drone-supported cameras hovered before her. Dandelion stood in the back of the room, more terrified of newscasters than Larken was. Jocelyn stood just to Larken's left, on the edge of the small stage where a stagehand was struggling with her efforts to find a place to attach the small camera. Finally, camera secured, the stage hand exited, leaving Jocelyn, who seemed like she'd rather be nowhere else at all, grinning wide.

"Ms. Marche," said Janet, the first reporter and the woman who'd roped Larken into the conference-style interview, "welcome to KIRO headquarters."

A brown mop of hair told Larken that Hari Newman was in the audience. For some reason, it seemed important to have him there.

"Janet, we have a problem here in our city and in our nation," Larken began. "You know who I am. I think if you're from this area, you probably know about my recent troubles with the Human Pride Movement. They tortured my friends, and I don't mean this in exaggeration. Tortured. And they threatened my life and the lives of my loved ones. See this cane?"

Larken held it up for all to see, clutching the podium to keep from falling.

"It was a gift from a friend," she said, smiling and glancing at Jocelyn before continuing. "But it shouldn't be necessary. HPM stole from me my ability to walk and to be normal. Look at this."

Larken nodded, and Jocelyn rustled with something to project a holograph of Larken's image two and a half years earlier, scoring the winning goal at a lofting match.

"That was me, and I was the youngest on my lofting team. Think about that. I was on track to a career, all planned out. I was going to go to play with the Angels, even if they didn't know it yet."

A handful of chuckles sprang up. Dandelion never broke her gaze.

"This is what I lost because of HPM. And you know

what? They said they were sorry. They thought I was a model sympathizer. And let me tell you, even if I was, would this be okay? Eight months I found myself medicated and in and out of hallucinations, strung out on painkillers because the types of pain I now have, there is no cure for. I'm in pain all the time because I might have been a model sympathizer.

"Is that enough of an excuse?"

Murmurs and heads shaking. Her message seemed to be resonating, and the more she spoke, the angrier she became at what she'd endured. Her eyes burned as she blinked back tears.

"This could be you. I could be your daughter. I could be your son. I could be your lover, or your child, or your mother. It doesn't matter to them. There can be no place for them in our homes.

"I...I want you to know that I...no, that's not right," she said, turning to meet Jocelyn's gaze and then back to the room to stare into those beautiful orbs of adoration from across the room. "I want you to know that we are putting a stop to it. Not just us here. But all of us. You, me, and everyone you know. It's time to stop them. It's time to stop all of them, and make them pay for what they've done. Walsh and Moody will be helping us to sue HPM for damages that will make them pay attention. We're giving them the very certain message that hate isn't an option. Not anymore. If you, too, have found yourself a victim of HPM's dangerous vigilantism, come forward. You'll see our ansible number in your holovid shortly. Just let us know, and together we'll end this scourge."

The press corps mumbled, and Larken raised her hand, pointing to Janet.

"Questions?"

"How do you plan to beat an organization with resources as deep as HPM has proven to have?"

"Jocelyn Reed has already scheduled meetings with many of HPM's benefactors. Once they realize the extent of the damage that HPM has caused in our society, I'm sure that they will rethink their collaborations."

"And if they don't?"

"That's up to us, isn't it?" Larken asked. She winked at Janet and pointed to someone else. Confidence flared under her skin as she realized she was in control.

"Rumors are you have ties to Beckett-Madeline Enterprises. They pay for your room at the H Hotel, right? Don't they torment models with their Immortality Program? Where do you stand on that?"

"Beckett-Madeline Enterprises didn't send a military mech to destroy a sixteen-year-old girl and her brother. Nor did they repair a killer android to try to kill me...again. On the level of bad to worse, we all have choices to make. How long will we let the worst happen under the guise that the bad exists? I don't see a conflict here."

An absolute lie. There was a serious conflict there, but Larken was already working on fixing that. Bremerton would be her new home eventually, with modifications and a fair amount of trust money. Larken planned to make sure that the former reclamation facility could never be used to murder models again. In the meantime, Dandelion had offered her home.

There were several other questions that passed in a blur. The entire time, Dandelion's unbroken gaze gave Larken strength. The time came for one last question, and Larken pointed out into the audience toward a gaggle of reporters all waving wildly. Someday, Larken knew, she would finish her college career. But the time was now to act, and in lieu of college, for now, her education would come from the world into which she immersed herself. College could wait, but HPM wouldn't.

CHAPTER 43

THE RESISTANCE IS FORMED

MONTHS PASSED in a whirlwind of activity. Every day it seemed hundreds more donors or volunteers or activists offered their support. Through donations Larken had gained the funds to buy the Bremerton Plant outright, and she'd spent a good deal already transforming it.

Larken watched as Clayton's knuckles turned white with the intensity of the grip that Sam had on them. She counted the seconds he would tolerate it, and to her surprise got upward of thirty before he discretely slipped his hand out of hers and massaged the muscle between his forefinger and his thumb, only to return it to her clutches moments later. Larken turned to Dandelion beside her and squeezed her hand, motioning to the pair with her eyes.

Sam smiled real, true, authentic smiles. Her green eyes smiled too, even if there was a tinge of sadness left in them that never really seemed to dissipate. She reminded Larken of Aayushi in that way. Her eyes mirrored Aayushi's hazel ones from Larken's dreams, and like the woman who still occasionally haunted Larken's nights with predictions of pending doom, Sam didn't focus those eyes on Larken. Sam looked at her, but through her at the same time as though there were something perhaps inside of Larken, or inside of each of them, that only Sam could see.

As Larken shifted her gaze from Sam to Clayton, she wondered how she could ever have thought to come between them whatever her ambition. Clayton stuck to Sam like a forward keeping a lofting ball within range. Larken could make out cracks of concern that had formed at the edges of his eyelids. The fact of his tumultuous and dramatic departure and reunification with Sam didn't seem to faze him aside from those giveaway ridges. In all other ways, he seemed indomitable, and not for the first time, just a little bit too unimpacted. Larken smiled at him regardless. He seemed to detect the warmth of her projected (if not completely heartfelt) approval, as manifest in a quick glance and probably the truest, widest, and whitest grin of which any of them were capable. From his brown-hair halo, he lit the room.

No, Larken wasn't concerned for either of them. They would be fine, whatever Sam decided to do with the child. Larken's eyes slid down to Sam's belly only after Clayton broke their gaze to return it to his star. One hand rested there. Soon it would be too late to back out, and something about the way Sam protected the bump made Larken believe that the baby would be welcomed into this world.

She knew in her heart that Sam would make an excellent, if not crude, mother. Either way, they would figure it out. Larken couldn't have been more certain of that fact had a hand come from the sky and scribed it into a wall before her.

Stephen still loved Sam though, even if he tried to hide it and knew, knew, that Sam simply didn't love him back. Even there at dinner—the first dinner they'd had out in a month as a group—Larken still caught him stealing occasional glances. Little micro-expressions flitted across his face when his eyes darted for just a millisecond over to Sam and back. Larken didn't know that they could all ever really be friends again.

Larken spared a glance toward the other end of the table to her SNO counterpart, Phineas Lancaster, who somehow in all of the violence and destruction that followed him through his life, still managed a smile almost as bright as Clayton's. When their eyes met, Lancaster nodded and took a swig from the large mug before him. She didn't have to guess to know that there was real beer in that mug, probably something he'd brewed himself instead of "replicated swill." She nodded back and, garnering what she could of stability by clutching the table with her left hand, opened her mouth to speak.

"We asked everyone here," Larken said, motioning to the cloth-covered cityscape before her on the center of the table, "to show you something we've been needing for a long time."

Molly didn't smile. She hadn't wanted to come to the Bremerton Plant, even if it had been several months and truckloads of money had been spent to clean out everything that had made it a reclamation plant in the first place. There were no more vats, and the cesspool outside had been drained and filled with soil, converting it into an introspection garden with a dedication plaque on of gold and ivory that read "For those murdered before their time. May we always remember." The walls still were cratered and half destroyed, but the violence had never touched the room they'd seated everyone in.

It had only seemed fitting to do the reveal here, where they had wrested loose HPM's clutches on Bremerton.

Whatever happened in the rest of the world, the United States was in the midst of a self-purge. When Larken's eyes met Molly's, all of the memories of a lifetime flooded back, and she felt her eyes growing heavy with tears. One escaped but only one. She wiped it quickly away with her right hand.

What the cloth revealed was nothing short of a compound. The compound showed revived turrets but more of them, and more disguised. There were no ostentatious guns mounted in them. In fact, from the outside, they looked like glass buildings atop a glass wall. It wasn't glass, at least wouldn't be. Rather it was polished, reinforced, armoring that lined the entire complex. That wasn't all. Beyond the walls, there was a playground that extended for the equivalent of what would be four city blocks. And farther still inward would yield housing units and something that resembled a miniature downtown.

"We've contracted the work already. We'll have the world's first planned community for displaced models in just over a year. This complex will hold more than a thousand models. Educational opportunities for the young ones here." She pointed to a tiny building near a playground with red walls and a steeple pointing to the sky. "There will be deprogramming over here, too. With this in place, models can live a life free of outside interference. They...we," she looked at Oliver first, then Molly three seats away from him. Molly didn't seem convinced, but Oliver nodded along. Larken guessed from their seating arrangement that the fallout from the infidelity was still underway and made a mental note to catch Oliver before they left.

"Then we move in. Community quarters are here and here." She pointed to what looked like two separate residential neighborhoods far inside the fortified walls. A sidelong glance caught Lancaster's glowing grin as he wiped beer foam from his lips yet ignored his saturated beard.

"There's more," Larken said. She wobbled a bit, and Dandelion caught her before she could fall. Once she reasserted her footing, she continued. "Barracks here and here," she pointed to two long buildings near the complex's front gate. "This is where our security volunteers will train. SNO trainers have committed to teach us, so we will not be unprepared next time."

Several smiles. Applause. And then dinner, during which she finally managed to summon her brother to her side. Now that people were mingling, she offered him the recently unoccupied seat beside her. Molly remained at her table farther away, stealing glances at them both.

"You've been busy," Oliver said.

"Not so busy," Larken said. "What's up with you two?"

"Nothing's up," he answered. "Nothing at all. She needs some space, and I'm giving it to her. It's kind of hard still living in the same house, but we manage."

"You're giving Molly space? After she cheated on you?"

He nodded, seemingly completely oblivious to the fact that it should have been the other way around. And the fact that they were still living together probably meant that he would never leave her. Larken could already see their future in her mind: Molly doing whatever she wanted, as she'd always sort of done, and Oliver following her around like a lapdog. She rubbed her eyes.

"We all make mistakes," Oliver said.

Larken felt her teeth grinding together before she knew she was doing it. She bit her lower lip to stop herself from screaming at him.

"And Declan?"

"It's just for a few days. He's staying with a sitter. It's better that way, while Molly and I work some things out."

It took every ounce of energy Larken had to keep that scream inside. She inhaled through her nose and closed her eyes. When she opened them again, she had enough control to ask, without stuttering, "Are you happy, Oliver?"

He blinked.

"I'm serious," she continued, steadying her gaze on his eyes. "You wanted school and a career, remember? Maybe it's time to stop focusing on Molly and get your life together."

Oliver didn't reply to that with words, but the way he looked at Molly, Larken knew from a lifetime of interaction that he wasn't actually listening to her. Oliver was hung up on Molly, and Larken was pretty sure that he always would be. When Molly glanced their way and flashed a patented demure smile at him, it was all Larken could do not to confront her then and there. She contemplated launching her salad across the impromptu dinner/conference table.

But at that moment, when Oliver was stumbling through whatever explanation he was building about how what Molly did wasn't really all that bad, the buzzing chatter seeped into her ears. She heard a mixture of excitement over the new complex and questions about the various details that Jocelyn, her confidant, and newly minted legal advisor, answered with a fair amount of legalese and hedging.

The conversation broke into groups, and people ate together for almost an hour as the night wound down. Finally, an exhausted Larken allowed Dandelion to escort her to Dandelion's single-family home, which Larken had moved into ever since Sam had moved out of the H to live with Clayton.

"We survived, Dandelion," Larken told her with a thin smile. Dandelion smiled the way she always used when she didn't want to engage in conversation because she was too deep in thought about something else. "What is it?"

"You. For so long, struggling. How do you handle being alone all the time?"

Larken sucked in her breath. Until that very moment, she hadn't considered that she had been the epicenter of relationships and bonds and yet was very much isolated. Dandelion absently rubbed Larken's shoulders with the gentle touch of a well-practiced masseuse. She reached up and lay her fingers on the back of Dandelion's hand while swallowing down the lump in her throat.

"I'm not alone," she said, catching a glimpse of Dandelion's eyes in one of the few photos that lined her mantle. Dandelion seemed to sense her looking—because Dandelion always knew—and stared back, her green eyes with gold flecks meeting Larken's brown ones. Larken smiled and squeezed Dandelion's hand.

"I've got you," she insisted. It was very definitely her imagination that showed her a sheen in Dandelion's eyes as she lifted them back to hers in the reflective surface. Dandelion's hands stopped moving on Larken's shoulders, and they stared until Larken's weariness told her it was later than she'd thought and time to go to bed. She'd once again have to leave the partying to those with energy.

"It's time," she said. "I'll see you in the morning, Dandelion."

Dandelion escorted Larken to the guest bedroom and helped her prepare for the night, another thing that Larken could have done alone but went oh-so-much-faster with Dandelion's help. Dandelion handed Larken two large pills, which Larken swallowed down quickly. Moments later, she drifted slept a deep, dreamless sleep.

No Aayushi.

No explosions.

No armies.

Yet by the time she awoke, a city had fallen overseas. This one in Portugal. Liberti Custodi, like a foreign version of Human Pride Movement, moved more quickly than anyone had thought possible. Larken turned off the holovid almost as soon as she'd turned it on.

Deep down, her back muscles twitched, and some secret part of her whispered what Larken knew to be the truth even if she refused to admit it. Of all of the people on the Earth, Larken was the one with the ability to make a difference. She twisted to pop her back, but it wasn't enough to do the deed. The throbbing persisted. Five words materialized as feelings in her gut. Empires will crumble before you. Only when Dandelion finally emerged from her bedroom with her hair a tussled mess did the discomfort fade away. Larken inadvertently mirrored the infectious smile that Dandelion wore at the start of every day. Dandelion looked down and then busied herself making coffee.

"I had a dream," Dandelion said softly. She punched numbers into the replicator that Larken didn't even try to remember. "It was about Clayton."

"I'm sorry," Larken said.

"I'm not," Dandelion replied, turning toward Larken as the replicator buzzed and whistled. "I was, but they seem so happy together. They seem perfect."

Then Dandelion did something unexpected: she ran her

hand down to the throbbing muscles in Larken's back and worked her fingers into a knot there. Larken felt warmth spread through the area, relaxing her muscles and the pain finally stopped. She closed her eyes and rolled her head back in reveille. She had to remind herself that the touch didn't necessarily mean affection with Dandelion. And so far, what she'd learned of Dandelion's type was that it involved poofy hair, easy grins, and a strong jaw line. Larken had exactly one of the three. She let out an almost imperceptible sigh as Dandelion finished and pulled her hand away again.

"What next?" Dandelion asked.

Larken switched her mug from one hand to two and cocked her head to the side.

"I have no idea, Dandelion. More news interviews, I guess. All I know right now is that it's time to stop hiding. The Human Pride Movement has done enough damage. It's time to show people who they really are."

Larken sipped the coffee and screwed up her nose at the bitter taste.

"Clayton would never have approved of this," she said.

"I dodged a proton blast there, didn't I?" Dandelion shot back. She let out a slight giggle that didn't seem mechanical in the least. Larken responded with a laugh of her own as the warmth spread down into her belly. There was a lot of work to do, but Larken felt that finally, she had a purpose, and that was something.

- THE END -

DEAR WONDERFUL READER, you've made it to the end! But this is only the beginning of Larken's saga. I have a dire word of warning for you: things are about to get dark! In the next novel, you'll see some things you can't un-see. The world will change in a critical and visceral way that will astound and perhaps even intimidate the faint of heart. But have courage. If you've made it this far, then you've already felt the pain of betrayal, the heartbreak of unrequited love, and the crushing blows of a killer android rain across your face. You've been made stronger, and braver, and no doubt can bring these skills to bear on the next title.

You are my hero.

Now, there's something I need you to do. As you've taken this journey with me into an uncharted future through a dystopian universe, then I trust you implicitly with this task:

follow the link below and add a comment or review for this novel. If you do, then others can find it and suffer (ahem, be entertained by) my words as you've been. If you loved it, let people know and share the love you felt. If you hated it, let people know and share the pain. Really, either way works, just get out there and do it!

Virtual Wars Series

And without further ado, there's only one last thing to add: be well and have fun. Life is hard. This is a true fact we all share knowledge of, even if we disagree on the minutiae. Your life and mine are both trials at times, and it is through these written words that we escape and find solace. I truly hope that I've provided that escape for you, and I truly wish for you to share this gift with others.

You have my humble appreciation,
Andrew Sweet
(your servant of words)

LARKEN MARCHE

DOB: 1/31/2185, **Age:** 17.5

Hot-headed Larken is always quick to defend a friend in need —and she always seems to find one. Samantha Caldwell is not just a friend, but an ally. She and the so-called terrorist group to which she belongs have helped Larken on more than one occasion. Even though Larken's body is constantly in pain, and her mobility is impaired by her run-in with a killer android, she still can't help but get involved when people around her are suffering. That's who Larken is, and why she's the protagonist of Virtual Wars.

FELICITY

DOB: UNKNOWN ,**Age:** UNKNOWN

Felicity means happy. No, that doesn't mean that *she's* happy. That's only a literal translation of her name. Felicity is a killer android. She's only happy when hunting down her latest victim, at the behest of the extremist Human Pride Movement. She goes where they send her, and she kills who they want her to kill...usually. No questions, with complete obedience to orders. A company girl through-and-through, if HPM need a dirty job done, they turn to Felicity.

––––––––

DANDELION LEMAIRE

DOB: 4/21/2123, **Age:** 79

Dandelion is a the most well-traveled naive person in existence. Or...it's quite possible that she's only acting inexperienced. But whether it's make-up or men, Dandelion's hopeless. Featured more prominently in this novel and the rest of the series, Dandelion is the most open, caring being in her found-family, down to the unsettling crush she develops on Clayton, her former co-worker, part-time revolutionary, and bumbling ineffectual, but endearing, activist.

———

For more characters, chapters, and generally anything else in this AI universe, come join my Patreon community! Whether you want to just browse, or become a Serial Killer (get it? get's you access to my serial fiction), or Accomplice (get's you access to pre-release novels and chapters, as well as other goodies).

Join our Patreon community! Come be part of the creative process!

https://patreon.com/user?u=104217131&utm_medium=
clipboard_copy&utm_source=copyLink&utm_campaign=
creatorshare_creator&utm_content=join_link

THE GENERAL
CHAPTER 1, FROM VIRTUAL WARS BOOK 3: INERTIA AND MOMENTUM

LARKEN MARCHE WALKED the perimeter of her office, clipping her cane rapidly against the floor with each step. Too many red pinpricks of light speckled the globe suspended in the air before her, each representing a country where different anti-modeling groups gained territory. The enemy, *their* enemy, had made great strides over the last year.

"You need to stop pacing, Lark," Dandelion LeMaire said, staring at her from behind a desk in their shared office. "You'll blow out that repair work on your back."

The burn above her tailbone told Larken that Dandelion was probably correct, as she so often was. But Dandelion should have known by now that *telling* Larken to stop would have little effect. The cool touch of Dandelion's fingers on her shoulders moments later did stall Larken's frenetic tapping—for the moment.

"It's too fast, Dandelion," Larken said. "The United States is holding strong, now almost completely solid green. But almost everywhere else in the *world* is flipping red. And look at this here."

She pointed to the middle of the United States and then toward the east coast, a sprinkling of red lights spread across the country. These were townships, cities, and states where the extremist organization Human Pride Movement—the United States home-grown anti-clone extremists, similar to the Liberti Custodi on the rise in Europe, still had a presence. As Larken looked on, a blue light flickered, blue meaning significantly split support for HPM and against, and then changed to red. This last one was within thirty miles of the cosmopolitan city of Caldwell, Texas, home to nearly three million people. Caldwell itself shone bright green, immune to HPM's false promises of freedom for polli on the backs of re-subverted models.

Strong fingers dug into Larken's shoulder muscles and steered her toward her seat. For a handful of seconds, Larken resisted. Larken finally resigned herself to allow the guidance and caned her way to the ergonomic chair that was *supposed* to help her back heal—if she ever sat in it for longer than fifteen or twenty minutes at a time. The fingers kneaded her stiff muscles into compliance. Larken lifted her hand to her shoulder and patted Dandelion's hand.

The office was of modest size, so the two desks—both composite faux-eik since luxuries like real wood were a waste in her fledgling organization. Larken's was styled like a white writing desk from almost a thousand years before, down to the broken drawers that had to be jiggled open and stuck incessantly. Dandelion's was more of a utilitarian design, with one single drawer that slid out effortlessly—for Dandelion. For Larken, it took both hands and bracing. Dandelion's super-human strength only made it *look* easy, super-human strength that extended all the way to the tips of the super-human fingers that channeled ease into Larken's tense and throbbing back.

"Look at what's happening in France," Dandelion said. Larken's eyes involuntarily swiveled to Paris, one massive green circle weighted by almost a hundred million people. But that was all. One massive spot of green in an ocean of red. The red had begun to bleed into Germany, too, working its way from the French border eastward and covering nearly half of the state. Larken let out a sigh that lingered in the air. "The United States would look like that without you."

Dandelion wasn't wrong, even if it didn't feel like enough. In the last year, the support Larken had found on the west coast had spread through most of the nation. Everyone knew who she was, bringing with it stalkers and a cadre of death threats from armchair HPM enthusiasts. However, the official HPM hadn't tried to attack her directly since Dandelion had completely destroyed their expensive military android. It helped that Larken had taken over one of their facilities on the west coast.

The rest of the world was a mess.

The Iberian peninsula was beginning to turn, despite the multitude of political parties in the state having coalesced into one giant counterweight to Liberti influence. They'd waited too long, and it was obvious to Larken at least that if Spain fell, as she expected Paris to any day now, France and Spain would unite to overpower Germany, Italy, and Portugal. And all Larken could do was watch and continue to help contain their US version of fascists. She slumped into her ergonomic chair in a way that wouldn't at all help her back. Made of aluminum alloy and powered by a minuscule fusion reactor, the chair was boasted by the manufacturers in Nigeria to be the same chairs that adorned the United

African Induna Council grand hall and would last for a thousand years or more. Larken wouldn't be alive to see that. She'd settle for fifty, though some days, she questioned if she would make it that long.

The globe spun as it revealed United Africa. At least there, the lights were all green, from top to bottom of the glowing continent. She closed her eyes and honed her focus in on the fingertips pressed into the knots in her upper back.

"Think they'll listen?" she asked of Dandelion.

"Even the Induna and the forces of United Africa can't stand against the rest of the world. How long until the Liberti trashes trade agreements that have been in place for centuries? They *have* to listen."

"But can Oliver convince them?"

"Why wouldn't he be able to?"

Larken's brother had become her formidable diplomat in the last year. She thought he mainly traveled to get out of his farce of a relationship: being overseas meant he didn't have to deal with his girlfriend or wife or whatever's latest infidelity. LarkenBut he'd surprised Larken by securing a meeting with the Induna of Africa. At that very moment, he might have been addressing their grand assembly, explaining to them how Larken's campaign had been effective in the United States and how what Larken's foundation had learned about the Human Pride Movement could help them keep Liberti out. And, no less important, Oliver had told Larken he planned to understand how they'd managed to do the same so far. Finally, Oliver wanted to find allies in a war, which, as Dandelion had alluded to earlier, they weren't technically fighting.

"Okay. But what about Mexico?"

"You can't do that. It's not fair to you; frankly, it scares me. You're *looking* for a problem to solve. Can't you be happy for a little while that the United States, at least, is weathering the storm so well?"

Dandelion's even tone didn't betray fear, but her fingers did. When Dandelion became scared, one sure way to know was to be in her grasp at the time. Her fear *hurt* because she ignored her own strength when she was afraid. Dandelion seemed to realize this, stopped her massage, and then worked her way around Larken's levitating chair to her front. Larken slowly opened her eyes and took her in.

Larken used to think of Dandelion as *the android*. The idea that the slight woman with freckles and freshly dyed green and purple hair who now blocked her view of the globe was anything other than human had evaporated the longer she knew her. The skin-clad synthetic wasn't Caldwell-beautiful. Caldwell, Texas, had grown to three million people because of the escort modeling industry that thrived there. Those models were so perfect that Emergent Biotechnology, the corporation that made them, had begun introducing tiny physical flaws to make them more approachable. Dandelion wasn't like that, even with the smokey-eye make-up and base that tried and failed to hide her freckles. She looked more normal than the Caldwells did. Still, Larken knew that beneath Dandelion's smooth synthetic skin tissue lay a spike of insecurity from which Dandelion never seemed free.

Dandelion stared her sky-blue eyes like daggers into Larken's brown ones with an intensity that told Larken it was time to stop sulking. "You've united the west coast, and HPM, for the most part, are defunct in the States. That should be enough. You're going to have to let some things go."

Larken wasn't good at letting things go. She hadn't let

HPM go when they kidnapped her brother, so she limped today. Nor had she let things go when her friend Sam had been captured and tortured by HPM. Too many people were suffering in too many places for Larken to slow down or stop. One day, Dandelion might understand Larken's bull-headed march forward. Until then, Larken sometimes pretended to let things go for a while, and Dandelion pretended to believe her. Larken willed the tension to ease from her facial muscles and forced them up into a smile. Only then did Dandelion's mascara-thick eyelashes waver from their obstinate openness.

"Good. Besides," Dandelion told her, "today's lunch with Molly, remember?"

Larken had forgotten, as she so often did. Round number nine-hundred something in trying to convince her former best friend Molly to stop sleeping around.

"Are you sure it's today?"

"Every month," Dandelion responded with her usual endless patience allowing not even a hint of derision in her voice.

"What time is it?"

"Nine-oh-eight"

"Shit. What are we doing here, then? We need to go back home."

"Exactly."

Dandelion shoved the chair forward with one hand and didn't give Larken her cane back. Larken had no choice but to let Dandelion guide her through the automatically-opening doors and out onto the volantrae landing where a streamlined bird-shaped Falcon awaited them. Larken took a breath as she looked out over what used to be the Bremerton Reclamation facility. From the fourth floor of her building, she could see over much of the compound. *Her* compound.

Was she really only twenty-two? Larken wondered. It seemed like yesterday that Molly Kostic had first announced her interest in Larken's brother at their high school, Brighton Academy, in Portland, Oregon. Dandelion gently lifted Larken from the chair and into the back of the volantrae, which was something Larken could easily have managed herself, but Dandelion was like that. Fastening Larken in was a quick task, and then Dandelion returned the chair back to the intentionally-accessible office while Larken watched the other volantrae zip by.

Dandelion slid into the seat next to Larken almost before Larken knew she was back. Larken pondered what mood Molly would be in without Oliver there for balance as the volantrae lifted off into the sky. Then her thoughts turned to Dandelion, who seemed to be watching the trees go by in fascination beyond the opposite window.

"Why do you do this?" Larken asked.

"Do what?" Dandelion turned to face her.

"Take such good care of me."

"Who else is going to?"